THE CAPTIVE QUEEN OF SCOTS

As a child Jean Plaidy developed a passion for the past together with a desire to write. During her teens she experimented with short stories and eventually began her series of novels.

Inspiration for her books is drawn from a variety of sources – a picture gallery, a line from a book, Shakespeare's inconsistencies. She lives in London and loves music, secondhand book shops and ancient buildings. Jean Plaidy also writes under the pseudonyms of Victoria Holt and Philippa Carr.

THE CAPTIVE
QUEEN OF SCOTS

Jean Plaidy

Pan Books

First published 1963 by Robert Hale & Co.
This edition first published 1967 by Pan Books Ltd

This new edition published 1989 by Pan Books
an imprint of Macmillan Publishers Ltd
25 Eccleston Place, London SW1W 9NF
and Basingstoke

Associated companies throughout the world

ISBN 0 330 37018 9

1 3 5 7 9 10 8 6 4 2

A CIP catalogue record for this book is available from
the British Library.

Printed and bound in Great Britain by
Mackays of Chatham PLC, Chatham, Kent

CONTENTS

CHAPTER ONE

THE PRELUDE

'Burn the murderess!'

The words were still echoing in Mary's ears as she rode through the night. Her hair had escaped from beneath her hood; the wind tore at it, tossing it this way and that with as little respect as she herself had been treated so recently in her capital city of Edinburgh. Beneath her cloak her gown was in shreds; she herself had torn it from her shoulders in a frenzy of despair as she had stood at the window of the Provost's house while the mob shouted below. She could still see their cruel faces, the red glow from the torches reflected in their eyes, while they shouted: 'Burn the adulteress!'

Not one friend among them, she had thought. Is there no one in this cruel and barbarous land to help me?

Maitland of Lethington had walked shamefacedly on the other side of the road. He was the husband of her dear Mary Fleming who, with Mary Beaton, Mary Livingstone and Mary Seton had been one of her four devoted Marys, those who had shared their childhood with her. She had cried for help to Maitland but even he had passed by.

So there was no one. Bothwell had fled. She dared not think of Bothwell, for that would reawaken more turbulent emotions. Where was he now, the man who had taken her by force, the man who had arrogantly linked his life with hers, to her degradation and destruction? Yet would she have cared about that if he were with her now?

But if he were with her now her enemies would not have dared to treat her thus. She would not be riding through the darkness, their prisoner.

Surely Moray, her half-brother, would come to her rescue. Where was Moray? Where there was no trouble! Could it be accidental that always where there was trouble Moray was not. He is after all my brother, she thought; whatever happens he must always remember that.

But she was too tired for thought; she was exhausted by fear and rage, by despair . . . yes and even hunger; she had forgotten when she had last eaten; she had not thought of

7

food since before Carberry Hill, that decisive battle which had brought her to this state. She had been exultant before the battle, believing that she must be victorious because Bothwell was at her side. But even he, magnificently virile as he was, could not fight an army when his own followers—and hers—had deserted to the enemy. There had been nothing but disaster since Darnley's death and, because it was generally believed that she had played a part in his murder, it was easy enough to turn her army against her. Yet she had been confident because Bothwell had been with her; brave, defiant, cruel, he was ruthless and unfaithful; all knew it, and she herself had reluctantly and most bitterly learned it, but there was not a braver man on either side of the Border, not a braver man on Earth.

He obsessed her as he had ever since, with his Borderer's audacity, he had forced his way into her apartment and committed rape – 'the rape of the Queen'.

'Leave him,' they had said. 'He shall go free if you will return with us to Edinburgh.'

And like a fool she had believed them, although he had not.

She would remember that last fierce embrace as long as she lived, for there would never be another like him.

'Fool!' he had cried. He had treated her as a Queen only on State occasions; in private she was a foolish woman completely under his domination. 'Don't you see they want only to separate us so that they may more easily destroy you. Leap on to your horse. We'll escape them yet. We'll go to Dunbar . . . together.'

'No!' she had cried, although she had longed to ride with him. They would have killed him. They longed to kill them both. They had offered her his life if she would deliver herself into their hands that they might inflict that which was more bitter than death: the humiliation, the degradation which they were forcing her to suffer now.

So she had parted from him. He had escaped to . . . she knew not where; and for her there had been the terrible journey to the Provost's house, the night of horror there, in the room which looked on the street; and placed outside her window was that hideous banner on which was depicted the murdered Darnley and her little son James—hers and Darnley's—kneeling as he prayed 'Judge and revenge my cause, O Lord!' And all through the night the mob roared for her destruction like wild beasts roaring for their prey.

In the morning had followed the fearful walk to Holyrood House, the banner held before her, the mob pressing close.

That was the very depth of despair. There could be nothing more horrifying than that which she had already suffered. But perhaps there could be.

On she rode, the prisoner of those grim and silent men . . . to what destination?

CHAPTER TWO

LOCHLEVEN

IN THE CASTLE of Lochleven which was built on an island in the middle of the loch an exciting expectancy prevailed.

All through the day, the serving men and maids had been aware that they must prepare for an important visitor, and rumour had seeped through to them that this was none other than the captive Queen. Ears were strained for the sounds of arrival; eyes continually turned to the strip of water which separated the island from the mainland on which could be seen the roofs of the houses of Kinross. She would embark there and the boat was ready, waiting for her.

The castellan of the castle, Sir William Douglas, was uneasy; he did not relish the responsibility which had been given him; he foresaw trouble. Yet it was a commission which he dared not refuse; he should, he supposed, have been grateful because his half-brother, James Stuart, Earl of Moray, would wish him to be the Queen's jailor. Yet he knew that a tense and stormy period lay before him. Wherever Mary Stuart was, there was trouble; it was hardly likely that Lochleven would escape it.

Now he was waiting for her arrival which surely could not long be delayed; and he decided that once more he must impress upon his mother the importance of the task which had been given them; and for this reason he made his way to her apartments.

He found her seated at a window; like most people in the castle she was gazing out across the lake, and with her was William's younger brother George.

Margaret Douglas looked eagerly at her elder son as he

entered. He noticed with a twinge of jealousy that she looked younger than she had before they had received the news. He knew the reason; it was because, by keeping the Queen a prisoner at Lochleven, she would be serving Moray. Why had he felt the need to warn her of the importance of this duty when all that she did for Moray she would do well?

'Is there news?' she asked, and the animation on her beautiful, though ageing face, was startling.

William shook his head.

'I trust all will be well. Jamie will expect us to do our duty.'

'We shall do it, have no fear of that,' William replied. He might have reminded her that Moray—now that the Queen was a captive—was the most influential man in Scotland, that before long he would be the ruler of Scotland, which was what he had always intended to be. If one hoped to live in peace in Scotland, one must obey Moray; he, William Douglas, castellan of Lochleven since the death of his father, Sir Robert Douglas, would have been prepared to do that even if Moray had not been his half-brother, and his mother's bastard.

'Jamie will expect us to do this duty well,' went on Margaret Douglas complacently.

Young George clenched his hand in disgust; he was eighteen, romantic and chivalrous, and could not bear to contemplate his mother's dishonour.

As for Margaret she was unaware of any dishonour, for in her opinion there was nothing but honour in bearing the bastard of a King. Often she delighted in Jamie's resemblance to his father. She had not been the only woman to catch the roving eye of James V of Scotland and to offer the world living proof of what had passed between them. To her he had been faithful for a while and she would never forget that. She had been jealous of the others. How she had hated Euphemia Elphinstone when she had borne the King her son Robert; not that Robert was the only one. James was a King who could be gay and melancholy, and when he was gay he was very gay; there had been numerous known bastards, and even James did not know how many unknown ones. Yet, she thought wistfully, all the Stuart charm was his and to have known it was to have drunk deep of pleasure. There were no regrets. And when she looked at her Jamie—James Stuart who had been Earl of Mar and was now Earl of Moray—how could she refrain from thinking what a cruel fate it was that had made him the bastard, and that giddy girl, Mary Stuart, the King's only legitimate heir? Jamie resented it–oh how bitterly. But perhaps now the bitterness was less acute.

She smiled. It was ironical that Mary should now be in the hands of one who had been her father's mistress and who would do everything in her power to further the aims of her own son. It was rough justice of a sort. Sometimes she believed that her clever fox of a Jamie had all along intended that something like this should happen.

'And the silly giddy girl deserves her fate,' she said aloud. 'Something like this was bound to happen sooner or later.'

'She is a brave woman. She was not afraid to venture on to the battlefield with her army at Carberry Hill.' That was young George, and as he spoke his face flushed. He wondered why he had spoken; he should have known better and kept his thoughts to himself. He did not share the opinions of the others. The Queen was a beautiful woman in distress. His half-brother, the bastard, who should surely shame his mother every time she thought of him, was a ruthless man. George knew whose side he himself was on. But it was foolish of course to say so before his brother and mother.

Fortunately they did not appear to have heard him. I am too young for my opinions to be of any importance to them, thought George resentfully.

His mother was speaking to his brother William. 'I hope you have increased the guard about the castle.'

'Naturally,' replied Sir William.

'Is it wise to keep her on the ground floor? Escape would be easier from there.'

'She will be well guarded there for the time being. Perhaps later I shall make other plans.'

Sir William was suddenly alert. He had thought he had seen movement on the mainland. But it was not that band of riders who were escorting the captured Queen.

Margaret said: 'She will not be here for some time. They would not set out from Holyrood until nightfall. It would be too dangerous. The mob would tear her into pieces.'

William did not answer, but George could not restrain himself. 'Might that not be what they wish?'

'No, no, Geordie,' said his mother soothingly. 'You are too vehement. The last thing Jamie wishes is for any harm to befall his half-sister. Don't forget that she is his own flesh and blood.'

'Bearing a similar relationship as that between him and my-

11

self,' murmured George with a hint of cynicism in his voice which was lost on his mother. If she could only know, thought George, how I hate these casual relationships which can bring about such havoc in families.

'Perhaps,' William put in, 'we should go to sup. It is foolish to wait, when she may not be here until morning.'

'Then let us go,' said Margaret.

In the dining hall the company had eagerly been awaiting the appearance of the castellan and his mother and, as they came in, the tension relaxed. The daughters of the family, who were seated near the dais, whispered together that this could only mean that the Queen was not expected that night.

As Sir William took his place on the dais with his mother, there came to stand behind his chair a boy of about fourteen who was wearing a jerkin which had once belonged to George. He was a bold-eyed boy, with hair of a carroty tinge, and a freckled face; and the position he held in the household was unique, because he was not quite a servant nor yet a member of the family. George could not remember exactly when this boy had come to the castle; he had heard it said that as a baby the boy was left at the castle gates, and that one of the servants had found him there, but George had never received confirmation of this, as his elders were evasive on the matter. He was cheeky, that boy, sensing his specially privileged position; one of his duties was to wait on Sir William at table. No one asked questions as to who he was and why he should be different from the rest of the servants. Perhaps it was because there was a look of a Douglas about him; he was in fact always known as Willie Douglas.

George had had an affection for the boy which dated from the days when he was about ten and Willie six. That was before George had discovered how much he hated the casual relationships of grown-up people which led to unorthodox results. He suspected now that Willie was the result of one of his brother William's indiscretions; but that could not change his affection for the boy once it had been firmly founded.

As he seated himself at table Willie whispered to him: 'Great days in store for Lochleven, eh, Geordie?' And gave George a wink that made his pert, freckled face slightly more comical than it had been before, so that George could not help smiling.

The meal progressed; and when the night had fallen there came with it a return of that brooding tension.

*   *   *

Dismounting, Mary could scarcely stand. The noise of those raucous voices was still echoing in her ears. Lord Lindsay who was at her side, said in a tone which had an edge of roughness in it and was devoid of the respect due to a Queen: 'The boat is waiting.'

'Boat! Then where are you taking me?'

'You will know in time.'

How dared they! She turned to Lindsay, and goaded out of her exhaustion, cried: 'I'll have your head for this, my lord.'

Lindsay did not reply.

Lord Ruthven who had come to stand beside her said gently: 'It is only a short distance across the lake, Your Majesty.'

Mary turned to him eagerly for she fancied she heard a note of compassion in his voice. So desperately alone did she feel that any sign of friendship lifted her spirits.

Ruthven did not meet her eye; he was ashamed of his mission. She thought: He is so young. He is not yet grown cruel like so many of my Scottish lords.

'Thank you, my lord,' she said.

Young Ruthven looked uncomfortable, fearing, Mary suspected, that Lindsay would have heard his remark and accuse him of softness towards their victim.

It was young Ruthven who helped her into the boat, where she sat listening to the rhythmic suck of the water as the oars displaced it.

'My lord Ruthven,' she whispered at length, 'where are they taking me?'

'To Lochleven, Your Majesty.'

'Lochleven! To the Douglases! Ah, I see. To Sir William-the half-brother of my half-brother, Moray. He will doubtless make a good sailor. And conducted there by Lindsay – his brother-in-law.'

'Your Majesty . . .' The young man did not continue; he was turning his face away that she might not see his emotion.

She said softly: 'Do not be ashamed, my lord Ruthven, to show pity for a poor woman who is surrounded by her enemies. She will not forget that you alone showed her compassion on this fearful night.'

Ruthven did not answer, perhaps because Lindsay, hearing the murmur of voices, had edged nearer to them.

There was a silence now, broken only by the dipping of the oars.

Mary, dazed and exhausted, felt the years slipping away from her; the only way in which she could endure the present was to return to the past. Once before, long long ago, she had been in flight from her enemies; and then, as now, she had sat in a boat and been rowed to an island in a lake.

'Inchmahome!' she whispered; and found comfort in the name. Inchmahome . . . where she had lived for a short period of her childhood when it had been necessary to find a refuge from her enemies; and how pleasantly she had lived in that monastic community. Inchmahome . . . Lochleven. Oh, but there was a difference. Then her enemies had been the English, who had crossed the Border and inflicted defeats on the Scots, culminating in the disaster of Pinkie Cleugh. How much more tragic when there was strife among Scotsmen; when she was a prisoner of her own subjects!

'Inchmahome . . .' she whispered. 'If I could but go once more to Inchmahome!'

The monks she had known would be long since dead. But there would be others, gentle monks, who tended their gardens, who worked together in peace, away from the world of intrigue and ambition.

Ruthven whispered: 'We are there, Your Majesty.'

She saw the dark shapes of people, and in the light of torches the grey shape of the castle loomed up before her. A fortress! she thought; my prison.

Sir William had come forward. He was bowing over her hand. So there were some who remembered that she was their Queen.

'I and my household will do our best to make Your Majesty's stay at Lochleven comfortable,' he told her.

And there was she who had been Margaret Erskine, who was now Margaret Douglas–the beauty who had been her father's mistress and was her brother James's mother.

Margaret curtseyed.

'Welcome to Lochleven, Your Majesty.'

Mary answered: 'I am so tired. Take me to my bed.'

'Your Majesty would like to rest before taking a little food?'

'The thought of food sickens me. I want only to rest.'

'Then come this way.'

So Mary entered the castle of Lochleven, knowing that she entered a prison. But she was too weary to care. There was only one thing she craved now. Rest. Quiet, that she might shut out the memory of those cruel faces which had leered at her, that she could for a while forget the words which had been shouted at her. Oblivion. That was what at this moment she needed more than anything in the world. She was aware of faces as she passed on her way through the quadrangle to the south-east tower. They looked almost ghostly in the lights of the cressets on the castle walls.

There was one which held her attention for a few seconds; it was the face of a young man with a gentle mouth and eyes which betrayed his sympathy as he looked at her. Perhaps she half smiled at him; she was not sure. But that face did have the power – exhausted as she was – to hold her attention for that short moment.

There was one other, she noticed–a young boy with a mischievous expression; his alert eyes were fixed on her and she could not read what thoughts were going on behind them.

These faces became mingled with the hazy impressions of that grim and fearful night.

She had entered the room which had been made ready for her and, without waiting for her servants to prepare her, she threw herself upon the bed and in a few seconds had lost all consciousness of where she was.

The Queen was sleeping the sleep of complete exhaustion.

*   *   *

When she awoke it was daylight and for some moments she could not remember where she was. As she looked at the lofty yet gloomy chamber, she was aware of a certain odour; it was not unpleasant and she wondered where she had smelt it before. It was faint yet haunting; and it was when she realized what it was, that memory came flooding back. It was the dank smell of lake water which could take her back in time to that period of her childhood which she had spent at Inchmahome. She remembered then that she was a prisoner in Lochleven.

She raised herself on her elbow and looking about her, saw that the room was sparsely furnished in the Scottish manner. She would never grow accustomed to it. Yet in this castle, in this very tower were those rooms which she herself had furnished, for in the past she had lodged here when on hawking or hunting expeditions, and because her visits were so frequent she had hung her own tapestries on the walls and had her own bed installed. Why then was she brought to this dismal room? It must be to impress on her that she was no longer an honoured Queen, but a prisoner.

15

The sound of tramping feet was audible, and glancing through the window she saw the sentinel pacing up and down. So they had determined to guard her well. She could trust Lindsay for that. At the thought of that dark bearded face her anger began to rise; and the hideous memories came back. If she did not restrain her thoughts she would be living it all again – the absolute hell of that night in the Provost's House, that walk to Holyrood House and the ride through the darkness to Lochleven. Nothing could be worse, and she hoped never to be called upon to live through the like again.

She thought of Bothwell then and she was sick with longing for him. It was a wild sensual yearning, a mad desire for the man who had first awakened sexual knowledge in her and taught her that she was a voluptuous woman. He would come for her surely. But she must be reasonable. Bothwell had never loved her as she had loved him. It was her crown he had wanted; many of his mistresses had beautiful bodies to offer him; but she was the only one who had a crown. He had not denied this when she had taunted him with it; he was too sure of himself to lie. Yet at the end he had been tender.

He will come for me, she told herself. He must come. Then he will take that black Lindsay by the beard and throw him into the lake.

A woman rose from a chair not far from the bed. Mary had not noticed her until that moment.

This was Jane Kennedy, one of her maids of honour.

'So they have allowed you to remain with me,' she said.

'Yes, Your Majesty. And Marie Courcelles is with us. We shall do our best to serve you. Your French apothecary is here also. So if there is anything you need. . . .'

'There is only one thing I need, Jane: my freedom. And that is something they have determined to take from me.'

'It will not always be so. Shall I see about food for Your Majesty?'

'I am not hungry and the thought of food nauseates me. What hour is it?'

'It is well after noon.'

'Then I have slept long.'

'Your Majesty was quite exhausted. And still is, I'll swear.'

Mary put her hands to her face. 'Oh, Jane, how do I look? I am filthy. There is the grime of Carberry Hill on me . . . and the Provost's house. . . .'

'I will fetch water.'

'Help me up first.'

Jane did so but when Mary stood she felt sick and dizzy.

'You should rest, Your Majesty. I pray you, lie still while I bring the water.'

Mary lay back obediently; but when Jane returned she found her mistress had become listless.

'Your Majesty, when you have washed and eaten you might be allowed to explore the castle. I do not see how they can prevent your doing that. This state of affairs will not last. Your faithful subjects will soon come to rescue you from your enemies.'

Mary said quietly: 'My faithful subjects? Those who deserted from my army? Those who called out that I should be burned as a murderess . . . as an adulteress?'

'Come, allow me to wash your face. Then I will comb your hair and bring a mirror that you may see the result. It is all that is needed to make you the most beautiful woman in Scotland.'

But Mary could not rouse herself from her melancholy.

Marie Courcelles came in and when she saw that the Queen was awake she expressed her pleasure.

'Your Majesty will soon be well again. You will make a Little France in this dreary old Lochleven.'

But Mary turned her face away and began to weep silently.

'It will pass,' whispered Jane to Marie. 'She has yet to recover from the shock.'

'If only my lord Bothwell were here all would be well. He would make her gay again.'

Mary turned and looked at them. Her voice seemed devoid of all hope as she said: 'Bothwell has fled. I have a feeling that I shall never again see his face. And what is happening to my son? How will my little Jamie fare without me to care for him?'

'All will be well, Your Majesty. Do you think Lord Bothwell would leave you to your enemies! I have heard it said that he has gone North to take refuge with Huntley. They will come to release you.'

She shook her head. How she wished she could have believed that! And why could she not? Why was she so certain that she could never see Bothwell again?

And if I do not, she asked herself, what reason have I for living? *He was* my life. At times I hated him; he was harsh to me – always cruel, determined to dominate me, to go on as he

17

had begun when in Buchanan's House, he stole in on me unawares and took his will of me. I tried to resist him then and yet I knew – as he did it – from that moment I was in his power.

It is not because I have lost Scotland that I mourn. It is because I have lost the two I love more than any in the world – my lover Bothwell, and James my baby son.

She lay down and listened to the sound of her women whispering anxiously together; she heard the tramp of the sentinel outside her window. That was like the tramp of doom. They were determined that she should never escape from Lochleven. And in that moment, so deep was her despair, she believed she never would.

She was sunk in melancholy and would do nothing to rouse herself.

Now the nights and days began to merge one into another and she lost count of them. Her French apothecary came to her bedside with potions for her to drink, but she would not touch them.

'Madame,' he declared, 'you will die if you will not try to save yourself from death.'

'Let me die,' she answered. 'I should be happier dead than a prisoner in Lochleven Castle.'

She lay in a haze of memories; she was happiest when she could not remember where she was, and that was often the case. She thought she was in France, the petted idol of the Court there, beloved of Henri Deux and his mistress the dazzling Diane de Poitiers; the adored wife of young François Deux; the hope of all her Guise relations. Through that dream the figure of Catherine de' Medici moved like a menacing ghost, sending her back to Scotland when those who loved her were dead, sending her to unhappy marriage with Darnley, to the nightmare of his death – but to Bothwell. She must always remember that when she came back to Scotland she came to Bothwell. And then to Carberry Hill and Lochleven.

Lady Douglas came to her bed and tried to coax her to eat. But she had no desire to speak with Lady Douglas. Sir William came in the company of Lindsay and Ruthven; she turned her head away and would not even look at them.

Once a young man, whose looks proclaimed him to be a Douglas, came to her bedside and stood looking down at her.

He whispered: 'Your Majesty, if there is some commission with which you would entrust me, gladly would I perform it.

18

But she could not answer him because the expression on his face brought a lump to her throat; so she had closed her eyes, and when she opened them he had gone.

On another occasion a boy had stood at the end of her bed watching her . . . a strange boy, with a pert, freckled face. He had said with a broad accent: 'Hello, Queen.' And she believed he must have been part of a dream, for suddenly he winked at her and was gone.

So the days passed in a melancholy haze.

Jane remonstrated with her. 'Your Majesty, it is fourteen days since we came to Lochleven and you have scarcely eaten or drunk in all that time. You must rouse yourself. What if my lord Bothwell were to come for you? How could you escape with him, weak as you are?'

'I could not stand, could I, Jane,' she said. 'There is no strength left in my limbs.'

'Your Majesty,' implored Jane, 'before it is too late save yourself . . . for Scotland. Think of your son who needs you.'

Those words kept repeating themselves in Mary's mind. Save yourself. . . . Save yourself for Scotland and your son who needs you.

The next day she ate a little; and the following day a little more.

Word went through the castle: 'The Queen is beginning to take an interest in her surroundings. After all, she has decided to live.'

*   *   *

George Douglas lay on the grass, his eyes never straying long from those windows which were hers. He had thought of her continually ever since he had heard that they were bringing her to his home. He had pictured her as he had so often heard her described – beautiful beyond imagining; gowned in rich cloth of gold, velvet and silver, a crown on her head. He had remembered all he had heard about her romantic life; her early flight to France where she had become Queen; her three marriages, all ending in tragedy. He had heard the scandals which had been whispered about her when Darnley had been murdered. They called her adulteress, murderess, but he did not believe them. He had always believed her to be a deeply wronged woman, and since she was also beautiful she had become the centre of his dreams of chivalry.

He was misunderstood in this rough country where men such as Bothwell were looked up to, where cold passionless men like his half-brother Moray were those whom others were ready to call their leaders.

When he had seen the Queen dishevelled after her ordeal, almost demented, her gown tattered, her lovely features spattered with mud, his feelings had been more intense than he had imagined they ever could be. He loved the sick and lonely woman more than he ever could the Queen in her crown and royal robes. He was excited almost beyond endurance, because she was here in his brother's castle, within his reach, and because she was a friendless prisoner and it might be in his power to help her.

During the last weeks he had sought excuses to go into her apartment. She had been unaware of him, lying listless in her bed, her eyes closed; and he had been afraid that, since she clearly no longer wished to live, she would die.

Once she had opened her eyes and seen him and he had looked at her with such yearning that he believed he aroused some response in her. He had been begging her not to die, for if she died he wished to die also. He was young and of little account in the castle where his mother and brother ruled, and where Moray was considered to be the most important person in Scotland, but he was fierce in his desire to help her; he wanted to give his life for her. Willingly would he do so and count himself blessed. That was what he had tried to tell her.

Did she understand? Was it coincidence that a few days later he heard that the Queen was taking a little nourishment?

'Hi, watchdog!'

George turned quickly and glared at young Willie who had crept up silently and flung himself down on the grass beside him.

'Where did you come from?' demanded George, embarrassed to have been caught by this alert boy gazing at the Queen's windows. 'And your doublet is filthy.'

Willie grimaced, and wriggled his bare toes as though in ecstasy.

'*She* does not notice my filthy doublet, Geordie watchdog. Why should she look at me when handsome Geordie's near?'

George leaped up to cuff the boy but Willie was even quicker on his feet. He stood some little distance away and, placing his hands as though he held a lute, rolled his eyes like a lovesick troubadour in the direction of the Queen's windows.

'You go to the kitchens. There'll be work for you there, Willie Douglas.'

'Doubtless, doubtless,' cried Willie. 'But there's other than scullion's work for me in the castle when we've a Queen living with us.'

George did not answer; he lay down on the grass once more and leaning on his elbows propped his face in his hands, this time making sure that he was looking, not towards the castle, but over the lake.

Willie watched him for a while; then he said: 'There's always fishing boats on the lake, Geordie.'

'And what if there are?'

'Nobody takes much notice of 'em, Geordie. They come and go between the island and the mainland.'

'Be silent,' said George fearfully and he rose to his feet again.

Willie hopped back a few paces, assuming the posture of a troubadour.

George went after him, and Willie sped away, laughing over his shoulder. Down the slope he went to the shores of the lake, George in pursuit; but before George could catch him Willie was running into the lake where George, for fear of spoiling his sturtop boots, could not follow.

Willie stood, the water about his knees, still playing the troubadour.

Watching him in exasperation George's eye was caught by a boat which was setting out from the mainland. As his keen eyes picked out the figures in the boat, he saw that they were not fishermen nor ferrymen, but strangers – grand personages with a look of the Court about them.

'Visitors for the Queen,' he said; and Willie turned to look.

Willie came out of the water to stand beside George; and forgetful of all else they stood side by side watching the approaching boat.

*   *   *

Sir Robert Melville, Scottish ambassador to the Court of Elizabeth of England, stepped ashore and looked at the castle of Lochleven.

A strong fortress, he thought. As impregnable as could be found in Scotland. She would not find it easy to break out of this place.

Melville's feelings were mixed. He would have been far more sorry for the Queen if she had not acted so foolishly over Bothwell. It was natural that a suave diplomatist should hate the fellow – rough, vulgar Borderer that he was; and the fact that Mary could have become so besotted about him lowered her in her ambassador's estimation. From the moment he had heard of the marriage, Melville had been ready to ally himself with her enemies.

She had been good to him, he was ready enough to admit. Because he had strongly opposed her marriage to Darnley it had been necessary at one time to take refuge in England; but Mary was not a woman to bear grudges; she had pardoned him and, because of his knowledge of the English had agreed that he should become her ambassador to Elizabeth.

He had been revolted by the murder of Darnley and had planned then to retire from politics, but Mary had insisted that he return to the English Court in the role of her ambassador; and as an escape from Scotland, Melville had done so.

Now he came to her with a mission – a most unpleasant one which he did not relish but which he was reluctantly obliged to admit was a just one.

Sir William Douglas was waiting to greet him as he alighted. With him were Lindsay and Ruthven; Lady Douglas came forward and her son George whom Melville had seen on the bank as the boat ran ashore, hovered in the background.

'Welcome to Lochleven,' said Lady Douglas. 'I have had apartments made ready for you.'

'My lady is gracious,' murmured Melville.

As they walked towards the castle, Sir William said: 'I believe you will agree that it would be well for us, with my lords Lindsay and Ruthven, to talk in private for a while before you visit the Queen's apartments.'

Melville said he thought this would be desirable. So Sir William turned to his mother and asked that wine should be sent to his small private chamber, and there he would confer with the visitor.

While Lady Douglas summoned one of her daughters and bade her give orders in the kitchen, Sir William went into the castle with Lindsay, Ruthven and Melville.

Left there in the sunshine, George felt shut out. Something important was about to happen and he knew that it threatened the Queen.

He felt angry with his powerlessness, with his youth and lack of experience. Why could he not enter the castle in the company of those men? Why could he not know what was said between them?

22

Someone was tugging his coat, and he turned to find Willie beside him.

'Do ye think they're planning to murder her in her bed?' he whispered.

'Be off with you.'

'There's murder in their minds, depend upon it,' whispered Willie. 'What are you going to do about that, eh, Geordie Douglas?'

George was silent. What could he do? There must be something.

* * *

The Queen was lying on her bed when Melville entered. Jane was seated by the bed reading to her mistress while Marie sat at the window looking over the lake. She had seen the arrival of Melville, so the Queen was not surprised when he came in.

'Your Majesty.' Melville knelt by the bed and kissed the delicate hand.

'You see me indisposed,' Mary told him.

'Which grieves me sorely.'

'It is comforting that someone is moved by my plight. You have been in the castle for more than an hour, my lord. Did it take you so long to find me.'

Melville spread his hands. 'I had to make sure that you were well enough to receive me.'

'And confer with your friends. I fear they *are* your friends, Melville. In which case you can be no friend to me.'

'Your Majesty, forgive me, but that is not so. Your welfare is my greatest concern.'

'You should tell me why you have come. I have been through such miseries that I tire easily.'

Melville looked at Jane and Marie significantly.

'What you have to say is for my ears alone?' said Mary quickly. 'Very well. Jane and Marie, you may leave us.'

When they had gone, Melville said: 'I would have Your Majesty know that I merely bring you a message from the Confederate Lords. That which I have to say to you is none of my doing. I am merely the messenger.'

'I see that you bring me evil tidings, and I pray you do not keep me in suspense. I have suffered so much that I can doubtless endure a little more.'

'Your Majesty, it is the wish of the Confederate Lords that you sign a formal abdication in favour of your son James.'

23

'Abdicate!' She had visualized so much that was evil, but not this. 'James,' she whispered. 'He is but a baby, being little more than a year old.'

'Your Majesty, the Confederate Lords would acclaim him King of Scotland.'

'And appoint a Regency!' she said bitterly. 'A baby could do little to stand in their way, could he?'

'Your Majesty . . .'

She turned her head away wearily. 'I am too ill for such matters,' she said. 'How cruel of them to confront me with this . . . now. Could they not let me live in peace for a few more weeks that I might recover my strength?'

Melville was silent. He was moved by her plight. It was difficult for any man not to be touched by Mary. Her beauty was indestructible, but it was not merely her beauty which was so appealing; it was a certain helplessness; a certain fragility; she was completely feminine, possessed of all that was most appealing to men.

He had to steel himself not to turn from his principles and offer her his help. He might have told her that certain of the nobles were planning to liberate her. That Huntley, the Cock o' the North, and the leading Catholic, was ready to bring his Highlanders to her support. That Fleming, Argyle, Herries and others were with him. But to do so would merely serve to stiffen her resistance and he had not been sent to Lochleven to do that.

Mary said mournfully: 'Sir Robert Melville, have I not always dealt fairly with you? Why do you place yourself beside my enemies?'

'Your Majesty, if it were in my power to help you . . .'

She turned back to him and stretched out a white hand, perfectly shaped but very fragile.

'You can help me,' she said. 'You can take a message to my friends. Surely I have some friends. The Flemings . . . the Setons. I can always rely on them. Mary Fleming and Mary Seton were as my sisters. Where is my brother? Why cannot I see him? I do not believe he would act against me.'

'I can take no message from you to anyone outside Lochleven,' Melville told her. 'I came here but to advise you to take this course which is the only one left to you.'

'Abdication!' she repeated.

Melville took a step closer to the bed and looked furtively over his shoulder.

'Your Majesty, if you signed a formal Abdication now, and later escaped from this place . . . you could always repudiate that signature with the plea that you had signed under compulsion.'

She looked at him sharply. 'And that is your advice?'

He did not answer, but lowered his eyes.

'How can I know whom to trust?' she demanded.

Melville seemed to come to a sudden decision. 'Your Majesty, may I speak frankly?'

'I should be pleased if you would.'

'I believe Scotland would be happy to see you on the throne if you would but repudiate Bothwell.'

'Repudiate my husband!'

'Scotland will never accept him, Madam . . . nor you while you remain his wife.'

'I *am* his wife. Nothing can alter that.'

'That unholy marriage must be repudiated. Only if you are ready to mount the throne without him at your side will you be allowed to do so.'

Mary was silent. To speak of him was to make his image rise vividly before her eyes; she could almost hear his rough laugh, feel his rough hands on her. Bothwell, she thought, where are you now? And she was sick with longing for the touch of his flesh against hers.

'It is the only way, Madam. I implore you to realize this before it is too late.'

'Where is Bothwell?' she asked, and she sounded breathless.

'I heard that he is in the North with Huntley.'

'Then he is collecting troops. He will come to rescue me from my enemies. Then it will be their turn to despair.'

Melville shook his head. 'The whole country is against him. Scotland finished with him on the night Darnley was murdered.'

'There is much you do not understand.'

'Come, Your Majesty, give me your promise that you will sign the deed of Abdication. Give me your promise that you will repudiate Bothwell.'

Mary crossed her hands over her breasts and suddenly cried: 'You are asking me to repudiate the father of the child I am carrying. I will never do that.'

'So . . . you are carrying a child?'

Mary lowered her head. 'I long for its birth,' she said. 'I long to have a living being to remind me of him.'

Melville looked at her sadly.

Was there ever such an unfortunate woman? Turned from the throne! Loyal to a murderer whose child she now carried!

Indeed she must be persuaded to sign her Abdication.

'Please leave me,' said Mary. 'I am too weak as yet to deal with State matters.'

Sorrowfully Melville left her apartments.

He would have to report his failure to Lindsay and Ruthven.

*　　*　　*

That night Mary awoke in pain. She called in alarm for Jane Kennedy who came hurrying to her bedside.

'Bring me my apothecary,' she cried. 'I feel sick unto death.'

The apothecary came with Marie Courcelles in his wake.

The man took one look at his royal mistress and, turning to the two women, he wrung his hands and cried: 'The Queen is grievously sick.'

Then he recovered himself and began to give orders. He wanted to call a physician but Mary heard this and forbade him to do so.

'You three are the only ones in this castle whom I have reason to trust. Do what you can for me and we will leave the rest to God.'

The apothecary mixed a hot brew for her and when Mary had taken it, he whispered to Jane: 'What can be expected! She has suffered so much. It is bound to affect the child she carried.'

'She is in danger?' whispered Marie Courcelles.

'Birth is always dangerous; but an unnatural birth doubly so.'

Tossing on her bed Mary was calling for Bothwell and little James, then murmuring in French, her mind obviously wandering, while Jane and Marie knelt and prayed that their mistress might emerge from this new trial as she had from all others. Their prayers were answered, for before morning Mary had been delivered of still-born twins. 'With care she will recover,' the apothecary assured them.

Marie and Jane exchanged glances. Bothwell's twins! they were thinking. And they hoped, for the sake of the Queen, that the loss of his children would be the end of his connexion with Mary.

*　　*　　*

Mary had not left her bed since her miscarriage. She felt physically weak, but strangely enough she could contemplate the future in a different light.

She mourned the loss of her twins and thought of them continually. His twins. She could not help wondering how like him they would have been. It had been too early to determine their sex, and she was almost glad of this; she had enough sorrow, and it seemed easy to forget them if she did not know them as belonging to either sex.

She shuddered to contemplate what their future would have been.

But her listlessness was less defined. Pregnancy had had its effect on her mentally as well as physically; and now that she was no longer pregnant, her thoughts turned more and more to the prospects of escape; and the desire to win back her crown was stronger than it had been since she had turned her back on Carberry Hill.

She lay in bed watching the wild geese flying across the lake, listening to the tramp of the sentinel outside her window, wondering now and then whether that fresh-faced boy, who had given her looks which long experience, both in the French and Scottish Courts, had taught her to interpret, was still in the castle.

As she lay there Jane Kennedy came into the room to tell her that Melville was back at Lochleven and that he, with Lindsay and Ruthven, were now demanding to be brought to the Queen without delay.

'I will receive them,' said Mary; and within a few minutes they were at her bedside.

Melville began by expressing his sorrow to find her still indisposed, and his hopes that she would soon recover.

She nodded in acknowledgement of his good wishes, but her eyes went to the scroll he carried and which she guessed to be the documents relative to the Abdication. Her hazel eyes hardened as she looked up to find Lindsay's baleful black ones fixed upon her.

'I think I know to what I owe the honour of your coming, my lords,' she said with a trace of sarcasm in her voice.

'Sir Robert Melville has acquainted you already with the wishes of the Confederate Lords,' began Lindsay.

'They are not my wishes,' retorted the Queen.

'You will realize, Madam, that on account of your present position, your wishes are of no great moment.'

The man was insolent; and this depressed her. Lindsay must believe that her hopes of escape were poor, since he treated her with such a lack of respect. How she hated him!

She addressed herself to Melville. 'I gave you my answer when you visited me on a previous occasion. Need you inflict this on me again?'

'I fear so, Your Majesty,' replied Melville soothingly. 'I would like to advise you that I believe it to be in your interest to sign this deed of Abdication.'

'To sign away my throne? I cannot see how that would benefit me.'

'Your son would take the throne, as you would expect him to do one day.'

'That day is far distant,' she retorted hotly and was surprised at her vehemence, when but a short time ago she had been longing for death.

Melville came closer to her; it was as though he wished to tell her something which was not for the ears of the others.

'Madam,' he said, 'it would be to your advantage to sign. This is the view of your friends.'

'Who are my friends?' she asked bitterly. 'Where are they?'

Melville drew his sword and laid it on her bed. Then from the scabbard he took a letter. He held it out to her and whispered: 'It is from Sir Nicholas Throckmorton who Your Majesty knows is the ambassador of the Queen of England. He is now in Edinburgh and tells me that his mistress is deeply shocked at the insult offered to royalty by your imprisonment in this fortalice.'

'I rejoice to hear it,' answered Mary. 'It is what I expect.'

'Sir Nicholas Throckmorton his written this on behalf of your royal cousin. I pray you read it.'

Mary read the document which warned her that she would be in danger if she did not sign the deed of Abdication. She must ensure her personal safety, and the Queen of England doubted not that ere long she would be free of her enemies. Then she could justly repudiate what she had been forced to sign in prison.

She raised her eyes to Melville who was watching her expectantly.

'You think that the Queen of England is my friend?' she asked.

28

'I think that the Queen of England is deeply disturbed by any insult to royalty.'

'Then she must be deeply disturbed at this moment,' retorted Mary bitterly.

'Her advice is sound, Your Majesty. I can assure you that, if you will repudiate Bothwell, there are many nobles in this land who will be ready to fight at your side until all that you have lost is restored to you. Atholl gave me this turquoise. He says you once gave it to him and he has treasured it. He sends it to you now as a sign of his devotion to you.'

She took the turquoise and looked at it. 'Such a gesture could have little meaning,' she murmured.

'Maitland of Lethington once received an ornament from you. He also sends it as a like token.'

Melville laid in her hand an oval piece of gold enamel. Engraved on it was Æsop's mouse liberating the lion.

She smiled, remembering the occasion when she had given the trinket to Maitland. He had recently married her dear Mary Fleming, and she had been delighted to see Mary's happiness.

Now she thought of Maitland who, such a short time ago, had passed by on the other side of the road.

'I am not impressed by these gestures,' she said. 'They could mean nothing.'

Lindsay had come over to the bed, arrogant and impatient.

'Come,' he said, 'it is time that your signature was put to this document.'

'I have not agreed to sign it,' Mary reminded him.

'Read the document!' Lindsay commanded.

'I refuse to look at it,' retorted Mary.

Lindsay's eyes blazed in his dark face. 'Madam,' he said quietly, but in tones which indicated that he meant every word, 'you will rise from your bed without delay. You will be seated at yon table. There you will sign the deed of Abdication in favour of your son.'

'And if I refuse?'

Lindsay unsheathed his sword. The gesture was significant.

'You would murder me in cold blood!' demanded Mary.

'Madam, my blood grows hot with this delay. Come, rise from your bed.'

His sword was close to her throat and she saw the purpose in his eyes. She looked at Melville and Ruthven, but they would not return her gaze.

He means it! she thought. He has come here to say: Sign or die.

She looked about her helplessly; she was here on an island, far from any friends she might have had. The cry of wild fowl suddenly came to her ears. They would murder her as many had been murdered before. Perhaps they would bury her body under some stone slab in the courtyard, or under a stair that was little used.

Now that death was so near she longed to live; a greater desire than she had felt for Bothwell was with her now; she wanted to escape, to regain her throne, to punish these men who had dared degrade her royalty.

She reached for a robe. They had expelled Jane Kennedy and Marie Courcelles from the room, so there was no one to help her. Ruthven took the robe and put it round her shoulders; as he did so she detected a burning gleam in his eyes; he was sending her a message of some sort; she was not entirely sure what. Perhaps it was merely desire for her body. But somehow it gave her a small comfort.

She was out of bed and, because she was still weak, Melville gave her his arm. She felt his fingers on her wrist and she believed there was something reassuring in the touch.

It was Lindsay who was her enemy, Lindsay with his black flashing eyes and his ready sword.

The quill was put into her hand; she sat down and read the document. Once she had put her name to it she would no longer be the reigning Queen. Scotland would have a King – James Stuart, son of Mary Stuart and Darnley.

She wanted to shout her refusal but Lindsay was standing over her, his sword still drawn.

She signed the Abdication and threw down the pen. Then she was on her feet, facing Lindsay who with a slow smile of triumph was putting away his sword.

She felt hysteria overcoming her. She shouted: 'I was forced to it. You held a sword at my throat and forced me to sign. Is that justice? Rest assured, my lord, that when I am free the first pleasure I shall allow myself will be to see your head severed from your body. And I tell you this: These documents to which, under duress, I have put my name, have no meaning. I signed under compulsion, and I do not consider my signature valid. Do not think that I am entirely friendless. I shall not always be your prisoner. And then . . . my lord . . . beware.'

30

Lindsay continued to smile as he murmured: 'So you do not think you will long remain our prisoner? Lest there should be some meaning behind those words we must make sure that your jailors double their precautions. As one of those jailors, Madam, you may rest assured that I shall do my duty to Scotland.'

Ruthven said: 'The Queen is ill. I will help her to her bed.'

He put an arm about Mary and held her firmly. His face was close to hers. He was undoubtedly trying to convey some message to her. Had she not felt so ill she would have understood, she was sure. Was he telling her that he was her friend?

She stumbled on to the bed; she felt sick and dizzy.

Vaguely she heard voices from afar – Ruthven's and Melville's.

'The Queen is fainting. Her maids should be sent to her.' And when she opened her eyes again she found that Lindsay, Ruthven and Melville had gone, and that Jane and Marie were at her bedside with her French apothecary.

* * *

Mary quickly recovered with the help of her maids and her apothecary. Her anger against those lords who had forced her to sign away her rights was so intense that it was like a crutch to her weakness.

'The impudence!' she raved. 'How dared they! Jane, Marie . . . Lindsay held the sword át my throat. Let him be sure that he shall not escape my fury.'

The maids exchanged glances. They were delighted to see their mistress's animation. Anything was better than the listlessness she had displayed since her arrival at Lochleven, no matter what was the cause of it.

'I shall not be here for ever,' Mary continued. 'I have friends. . . .'

'Your Majesty must keep up your strength,' Jane warned her. 'When the time comes to leave this dismal place you will have to be well.'

'You are right, Jane,' answered the Queen. 'This is an end of my lethargy.'

They brought her food and she ate it. She called for a mirror and studied her face with more attention than she had bestowed on it since the beginning of her incarceration. She had lost her pallor and her delicately tinted complexion was regaining its beauty; her lovely mouth was no longer melancholy; slightly parted it disclosed her perfect white teeth, there was a sparkle, left by recent anger mingling with new-born hope, in the long, deeply-set hazel eyes; her chestnut hair, hanging over her shoulders, was regaining its lustre.

She rose from her bed and walked a little, leaning on Jane's arm. Then she stood at the window looking out over the lake. She could see the mainland, and caught glimpses of distant mountains and forests. It was such a small stretch of water which separated her from freedom that she wondered why she had felt so hopeless.

'Somewhere on that mainland,' she mused, 'are friends who will help me.'

* * *

Dusk had fallen. Outside her window the sentinels patrolled. With the coming of night two others would take their places. Lindsay was determined that she should not escape.

She was feeling so much better. She believed she would soon be free. All her life she had recovered quickly from adversity because her optimism had been one of her strongest qualities and, she guessed, always would be. Rarely – and the days and nights which followed Carberry Hill was one of these periods – had she been completely bereft of hope. But to lose a kingdom, a lover and a beloved baby son at one stroke had been too much even for her resilient nature.

Now she could look back on her despair and say: There is always hope. There always must be hope. All through her life – except that gay and romantic period at the Court of France – there had been trouble. And even in France the insidiously powerful Catherine de' Medici had been her enemy from the moment they had set eyes on each other.

So hope came now. Somewhere in Scotland there were friends waiting to help her. She believed she would find them.

Jane had been right when she had said she must build up her strength. Lying in bed and refusing food was folly. Once she felt quite well again her natural gaiety would return. And when she had recovered her high spirits, her belief in her destiny, she would be happy again. Scotland would be hers once more. And Bothwell?

Now that she was calmer she could look back with a clearer vision at that turbulent period of her life. With him she had reached an emotional climax which she had never attained before. Through him she had known a savage joy and a savage despair. There would never be another like him, and

32

she knew that if he came back tomorrow she would be entirely his slave. Should she say the slave of her own body's desires? With him she had experienced sensations which she had not known existed: Erotic bliss which never seemed to be without its companions – humiliation and despair.

She had experienced enough of these two to wonder whether anything was worth the price.

Since she had made herself realize that she was a Queen with a Kingdom to fight for, Bothwell's image had faded a little. Let that suffice. And in due course, if and when he came back to her, it might be that he would find a different woman, a clever woman, a woman of some judgement who, while she welcomed him as her husband, would ask him to remember that she was his Queen.

But Bothwell was far away – she knew not where. And she was a prisoner in Lochleven. Her first duty was to escape, and if she were to break out of this fortalice she would need all her wits to do so. She would not achieve that end by dreaming sensual dreams of Bothwell.

She rose from her bed and wrapped her robe about her. She was growing stronger and now able to walk about the room without the aid of Jane's or Marie's arm.

While she was wondering whether they would increase her guards now that she was able to leave her bed, she realized with a little shock that the door of her room was being slowly and cautiously opened.

Startled, she drew her robes more tightly about her and, seeing who the intruder was, she cried: 'Ruthven!'

Ruthven came into the room hesitantly. He stood before her and dropped to his knees.

'Your attitude has changed, my lord, since you came here with those fellow-traitors.'

He lifted his eyes to her face and now she understood the expression in them. It angered her, yet at the same time she felt exultant. In the extremity of her grief she had forgotten the power she had always possessed to make men her slaves.

Ruthven rose to his feet.

'Your Majesty,' he said, 'if you could but know how I have suffered for my part in this!'

Mary turned from him and took a seat by the window.

Ruthven said: 'Your Majesty, do not show yourself to the guards. It would be well if we were not seen . . . together.'

'You have something to tell me?' she asked, rising and

moving away to a part of the room which could not be seen from outside. Ruthven brought a stool and she sat down.

'I can go back and forth between the mainland and the castle, Your Majesty,' he said.

She wanted to laugh aloud. Had she not known that some way of escape would be offered her?

'And I have friends on the mainland . . .' she murmured.

'Seton, Fleming, Herries . . .' he said.

'Huntley,' she added. 'Bothwell.'

'They are in the North, Your Majesty. There are others nearer . . . not far from this island, on the mainland across the water.'

'And you have a plan for helping me to escape from this prison?'

'Not . . . yet, Your Majesty. I wished to talk to you of such a plan.'

'Tell me one thing first. Why have you changed sides?'

Ruthven was silent. He was a connexion of Darnley's and had joined those nobles who had determined to avenge the murder. He had been against the Queen at Carberry Hill. Her adversaries had considered him sufficiently her enemy to put him in charge of her – with Lindsay – on the ride from Edinburgh to Lochleven. And now he was ready to be a traitor to his friends for her sake.

She must be cautious. But because there had been so many men ready to serve her she asked the question of Ruthven merely that he might confirm what she believed she knew.

'It has caused me much pain to see Your Majesty treated in this way.'

'You gave no sign when Lindsay had his sword at my throat.'

'Had he attempted to harm you I should have killed him. I stifled my anger because I thought I could serve you better in secret.'

'And how do you plan to serve me?'

'By obeying your orders.'

'How can I trust you?'

Ruthven took a step towards her. She was amazed when he lifted her from her stool and, putting his lips against hers, kissed her violently.

She tried to draw away in anger, but she was so weak that she found herself powerless in his arms.

'You . . . are insolent,' she panted.

34

'I love you,' said Ruthven. 'I have fought against this without avail. I will bring you out of this prison. I will set you on the throne. They speak true when they say you are the most desirable woman in Scotland. I would say in the whole world. . . .'

'I command you to release me,' she cried.

But he laughed at her. He had heard rumours of the manner in which Bothwell had swept away her protests. She was a Queen, it was true; but she was completely feminine. It was her submission to Bothwell which had brought her to her present state. She was not meant to be a lonely monarch like Elizabeth beyond the Border. She was meant to be a woman first. It was merely by chance that she was also a Queen.

Bothwell had conquered; so would he.

His impatient hands were on her robe, and she cried in panic: 'Jane! Marie! Where are you?'

But now his hand was over her mouth. It was meant to be like that scene in Buchanan's House, when Bothwell had come to her unannounced and torn her garments from her quivering body. But it was so different. The memory of Bothwell was vivid; and this was no Bothwell.

'Mary,' he cried breathlessly, 'do not bring them here. That would spoil our plans. If it were known that you and I were lovers. . . .'

With a great effort she held him off and, although he still kept his arms about her, their faces were no longer close. 'You insolent fool!' she said. 'Do you think that I would take *you* for my lover? Do you think you merely have to break into my room and insult me, to have me begging for your favours? You must be mad, Lord Ruthven. And if you do not take your arms from about me I shall shout for help. I shall tell Master Lindsay what you have done . . . what you have said to me.'

He would not release her; he had caught her against him once more, and she felt his face hard against hers. She tried to catch at his hair but he only laughed wildly.

'Is it too much to ask?' he whispered. 'I will make you free. All I ask is a little affection.'

'My affection would never be yours, Lord Ruthven.'

She tore herself from his arms and ran to the door. He was there before her, barring her way.

'You act like a coy virgin,' he complained. 'All Scotland knows you are not that.'

Her face was very pale and she was shaking with anger.

'I have loved men,' she said quietly, 'and men have loved me. I never offered myself for profit, my lord Ruthven. You are mistaken. You have invaded the privacy of your Queen, not any man's harlot. Go now. It would be well if I never saw your face again. Then I might find it easier to forget your conduct on this night. It would go hard with you if I, escaping from this prison, remembered it.'

She looked so regal standing there that Ruthven was overcome by dismay at what he had done.

He stammered: 'Forgive me, Your Majesty. I fear my love for you was greater than my good sense.'

'Go,' she said. 'And if you would please me, keep from my sight.'

He bowed and went out, and she leaned against the door; her heart was beating madly and she was still trembling. She stumbled over to her bed and lay there.

She was thinking: At any time he could come in to me. So could others. I have subdued him on this occasion, but will there be others?

Jane and Marie must in future sleep in her apartments. Otherwise she would never feel safe from the lechery of those who were supposed to be guarding her.

I must escape, she told herself. There must be some who would help me . . . without conditions such as Ruthven's.

*　　*　　*

Mary lay dozing in her bed. Jane slept at the foot of it and Marie on a pallet on the floor. She had not told them the reason why she had insisted on this arrangement, but they guessed that she had been disturbed by the attentions of some male member of the household, for they looked upon this as inevitable now that she was regaining her health and with it her beauty.

A sudden explosion split the silence. Jane and Marie were on their feet exclaiming with surprise because there was a reddish glow in the room.

The Queen sat up in her bed, shaking back her luxuriant hair.

'The Highlanders have come to rescue Your Majesty!' cried Jane.

'Is it so?' said Mary excitedly; and as she rose from her bed and Jane ran to help her on with her robe another explosion was heard.

Mary was at the window. In the sky was a glow and there was a smell of smoke in the air. Near the lake a great bonfire was blazing and she could see men about it – soldiers with pikes and halberds.

Then again came a shattering explosion.

'They are firing the ordnance of the castle,' she said. 'What does this mean?'

'It would seem, Your Majesty,' suggested Marie, 'that they are celebrating some great event.'

'I must know what,' insisted Mary.

She went to the door of her chamber; a guard, who was standing outside her door, immediately turned to her and she asked: 'It would seem some great event is being celebrated. I would know what.'

The man let his eyes wander from her head to her feet in their velvet slippers which showed beneath her loose robe. There was insolence in his manner which he scarcely troubled to hide.

'The coronation of the King of Scotland,' he answered her.

He was resentful because he was not outside, taking his part in the celebrations; he had to remain at this door and guard the prisoner. And who was she? he asked himself. Nothing but a whore if rumour was true – a whore and a murderess. And there was he, denied the pleasure his fellows were enjoying – because of her.

It was true that he had drunk rather freely of the wine which had been brought to him by one of his comrades; and since drinking it he had felt a fine fellow, which made it all the more irritating that he should have been left to guard the woman.

'Coronation of the King of Scotland!' repeated Mary aghast.

'That's what I said,' the soldier gruffly answered.

Mary did not hear the step on the stair; and when a voice said: 'You forget you address the Queen!' she was startled. And looking up she saw the young Douglas – the one with the earnest eyes and frank, open face.

The soldier's attitude changed slightly and the young Douglas went on: 'Stand to attention when the Queen addresses you.'

The soldier obeyed.

The young man came forward and bowed. 'Your Majesty, I trust you have not been subjected to a lack of respect.'

37

'It is something to which I have become accustomed since entering this place,' she answered.

'Then I ask forgiveness for all who have failed to treat Your Majesty with the homage due to you.'

She smiled, and the young man said to the soldier: 'You may join your friends outside. I will take your place.'

'Sir,' began the soldier, 'my orders were. . . .'

'I give you orders now. Go and join the revels.'

'If you'll take responsibility. . . .'

'I will.'

The soldier saluted and went away.

Mary looked at the young man and again she smiled. He did not step nearer to her; he stood looking at her as though he were not quite sure whether he was dreaming. The authoritative manner which he had used towards the soldier had disappeared. He now looked extremely young.

'Thank you,' said Mary. 'I feel less like a prisoner now.'

'Oh . . . my most gracious Queen . . . if I could only do something to help!'

'You have already done something.'

He lifted his shoulders in a gesture of frustration. 'I would I could show Your Majesty. . . .'

'Please tell me what is happening.'

'They are celebrating the coronation of your son at Stirling. They are calling him James VI of Scotland.'

'It is to be expected. I signed my Abdication . . . with a sword at my throat.'

'How dared they!' he whispered.

'They dare much when they believe they have little to fear. I am friendless, alone and in their power.'

'Not friendless, Your Majesty.'

'Who are you?'

'George Douglas . . . at your service now . . . and for as long as I shall live.'

'Thank you, George Douglas. I shall sleep happier tonight knowing that I have such a friend within these walls.'

He came to her then and, kneeling before her, lifted the hem of her robe and kissed it.

'You had better rise, George Douglas,' she said. 'If any knew that you were my friend they would be watchful. They do not wish me to have friends.'

'In me you have a friend who is ready to die in your cause.'

'It is strange that I can believe you on such a short acquaint-

38

ance. I have lived my life among flatterers and sycophants. Men have said they would die in my cause but when my fortunes changed they have proved themselves to be anything but my friends. How old are you?'

'I am eighteen, Your Majesty.'

'I feel it is not very old. I am not yet twenty-five but I feel that to be very old indeed. It is experience which makes us old, and I have already passed through a lifetime of experience.'

'Your Majesty, ever since you were brought to the castle I have longed to serve you. If there is any commission. . . .'

'There is one thing I desire above all others: To leave this place.'

'I would willingly give my life to satisfy that desire.'

'Thank you.' And she repeated softly: 'I believe you.' There was a brief silence while they looked at each other and, because of that recent scene with Ruthven, she felt more drawn towards this young man than she would otherwise have been. There had been so many to cast languishing glances in her direction, and admiration was something she had grown to take for granted. For as long as she could remember she had been eluding the passionate entreaties of men who desired her. She had learned how to assess the advances of men; and the look in this young man's eyes reminded her of her first husband, young François, King of France, who had been her humble and adoring slave from the day when they had met and had both been about six years old. She felt a great desire then to be back in those happy days when she had been the darling of the French Court, when all – except the terrifying Catherine de' Medici – had petted and done their best to spoil her.

Because he seemed in a daze of delight she went on: 'You have put new hope in me. When I heard the revelry and learned its cause I felt a deep despair, because I knew that ambitious men had put a baby on the throne that they might rule. But you will help me. We will devise a plan . . . together. . . .'

'Together . . .' he murmured ecstatically.

'Listen,' she said.

She had heard the sound of angry voices and hurrying footsteps.

Sir William was saying: 'You fool! How dared you leave your post?'

Mary whispered: 'It would be better if we were not seen talking together . . . my friend.'

She went quickly into her room, shutting her door behind her.

Sir William, his face purple with anger in which fear mingled, confronted his brother. Behind him the soldier sheepishly followed.

'What is the meaning of this?' cried Sir William.

'The fellow was eager to join the revellers. I thought to give him a little respite,' answered George.

'You young idiot!' cried Sir William. 'You talk as though it is some drunken soldier we are guarding for the night. Don't you realize who our prisoner is? Why . . . at such a time she might attempt to escape. And you send the guard out to enjoy himself!'

'While I took his place.'

'So you are the young philanthropist!' muttered Sir William. He opened the door of the Queen's chamber and looking in saw the prisoner with her two women gazing through the barred window.

Mary said: 'Good day to you, Sir William.'

Sir William returned her greeting and shut the door.

'Sentinels who desert their posts pay with their lives,' he warned the soldier. 'It is well that I am in a lenient mood this night.'

The soldier did not speak but stood at attention.

'Come with me,' said William to his brother.

He took him up the stairs to a small room on the next floor. There he spoke to him very severely, reminding him of the importance of guarding the Queen, of the attempts which would very likely be made to help her escape. What George had done was folly. What did he think their half-brother Moray would do if they were so foolish as to let Mary escape? In such an event their lives might not be worth very much.

George was not really listening. He could think of nothing but the Queen as she had stood there smiling at him, her long chestnut hair rippling over her shoulders; her deep-set eyes, which were a little darker than her hair, so melancholy and sad when he had seen her talking to the soldier, and sparkling with something like pleasure when he had told her of his devotion. He thought of that exquisite face which was a perfect oval, that straight nose, the mobile mouth and the white teeth which showed when she laughed.

He was in love. A thought which made him shudder with delight. To be in love did not mean the same to him as it did to Ruthven. He longed to prove his chivalry; he wanted to lay down his life for her. She was his first love and he was certain that she would be his last.

'For the love of God do not act so foolishly again,' Sir William was saying.

'No, brother,' he answered, but he was not thinking of what he said – only of her.

'Then go away and remember it,' retorted Sir William.

George came from his brother's room and went to his own. He threw himself down on his bed and began to go through everything that had happened. He remembered every word she had said.

For a while – a very short while – he would give himself up to this delightful reverie and then he would begin to work out a plan.

The door of his room opened very slightly; Willie came in and stood at the end of his bed.

'Your Majesty,' he mimicked, 'I would willingly give my life to satisfy your desire.'

George started up to stare in dismay at the mischievous urchin. 'Where were you?'

'That's telling.' Willie made a deep bow. 'Ever since they brought you to the castle I have longed to serve you.'

George was out of bed, but Willie was nimble. He was out of the room and George heard his mocking laughter floating back to him.

It was no use pursuing him. One could never be sure where Willie got to. But how much had he heard? And what would he do about it?

George went back to his bed and threw himself on it. He did not believe he had anything to fear from Willie. There had always been a bond between them. They were friends. Often he had helped Willie to escape a whipping. They never mentioned this bond – but it was there, and they both knew it.

Willie's object was solely to tease. He would tell no one else of what he had seen and heard pass between George Douglas and the Queen.

The door opened again and Willie's grinning face looked round it.

'Willie!' cried George without rising.

Willie was alert, ready to run. 'Yes, Geordie Douglas?'

41

'You'll not tell a soul what you heard?'

Willie put his finger to his lips and looked very profound.

'It's important. I mean it.'

Willie gave one of his winks and drawled: 'Ay, but she's a bonny lass. Geordie Douglas, you're not the only one who thinks so.'

Then he was off, whistling.

Willie was trustworthy. George went back to his dream of delight.

*　　*　　*

It had been one of the happiest days for Mary since her incarceration had begun. That morning a large box had arrived, which had been sent on the instructions of Sir Robert Melville.

Lady Douglas and Sir William came to her chamber to see it while it was unpacked, being suspicious as to what such a box might contain.

Mary's spirits rose as she read the letter from Sir Robert Melville which accompanied the box, and which stated that, being sure she missed the comforts to which she was accustomed, he was therefore having a few things sent to her from Holyrood.

Smiling with pleasure, Mary called Jane Kennedy and Marie Courcelles.

'This can only mean that Melville regrets his treatment of me,' she explained. 'He is anxious to let me know that he dissociates himself from that brute Lindsay. It's a good sign.'

It was then that Lady Douglas entered; she was a bright-eyed woman in spite of her advancing years, and could not hide her curiosity as to the contents of the box. If it were not for the fact that she knew Mary's incarceration to be of such importance to her beloved son Moray, she would have been entirely sympathetic towards the Queen.

'I pray you be seated, Lady Douglas,' said Mary. 'I can see you are as curious as I am to know what the box contains.'

'I crave Your Majesty's pardon for intruding,' whispered Lady Douglas. 'But. . . .'

'I understand,' said Mary. 'You, like everyone in the castle, must obey the orders of those who now govern us.'

Lady Douglas lifted her shoulders resignedly. She had enjoyed her life, and the most exciting period was when she had been mistress to Mary's father. When after his death she had married Douglas of Lochleven life had continued to be good.

She had a large family on whom she doted; she would never be lonely and life would never lose its zest for her because there would always be some son or daughter on whom her affectionate hopes would be fixed. She had borne thirteen children – six to James V and seven to Douglas. Her favourite was James Stuart, Earl of Moray, the man of destiny; but the others, like her dear Geordie, were more comfortable to live with.

As for Mary there was a resemblance to her father in her face, which warmed Lady Douglas's heart every time she looked at her, and brought back memories that made her feel young again.

Jane Kennedy was bending over the box, drawing out a pair of black velvet boots trimmed with marten.

Mary gave a cry of delight: 'Oh, how glad I am to see them again.'

Marie Courcelles held up a cloak of red satin also trimmed with marten.

Mary snatched it up and wrapped it round herself. 'Now I am beginning to feel alive again!' she declared.

Sir William who had joined his mother looked on and his expression was sardonic. He would have liked to depart, but how could he know what might be hidden among all the fripperies!

Lady Douglas had gone over to the women. She looked into the box and cried: 'Sir Robert Melville has made a goodly choice.'

Mary took up a grey velvet robe and held it against her. 'It is long since I wore this!' she said laughing. 'But I shall enjoy wearing it more than I ever did before. What else, Jane?'

Jane and Marie were plunging into the chest and there were cries of pleasure as they held up a pair of crimson sleeves edged with gold fringe.

Jane said excitedly: 'They can be attached to this silk camlet . . . oh look! It is the one decorated with aglets. How grand we shall be!'

'Let me see, Marie.' Mary took the sleeves and put them on. She clapped her hands. 'How can I thank Melville for his thoughtfulness?' she asked, and there were tears in her eyes.

Sir William looked on with exasperation. It was well, he believed, that a Queen who could be so moved by fripperies should be compelled to abdicate.

Lady Douglas had brought out a black velvet coat.

43

'Magnificent!' she cried, and slipped it round the Queen's shoulders.

'And he does not intend us to be idle,' said Jane, her head in the trunk. 'Look what I have here.' She brought up a packet of coloured silks.

'We shall be able to embroider,' cried Marie.

'And here are canvases to work on and some Spanish chenille,' exclaimed Jane. 'Look at the colours!'

'Oh, good Master Melville!' murmured Mary gaily.

The chest was emptied and the clothes were strewn about the floor. Sir William shrugged his shoulders and signed to his mother to remain in the apartment to keep watch and examine the clothes more closely.

Lady Douglas nodded. Mary, of course, knew why she remained, but the woman was only obeying instructions so she did not hold that against her.

'I will help your maids put the garments away, Your Majesty,' said Lady Douglas, as her deft fingers were feeling in the black velvet boots to discover whether a note was concealed there.

Mary smiled at her. 'Please do,' she said. 'Ah, what a difference it makes to have one's own things about one.'

'Your Majesty finds life restricting here?'

'Inevitably, I fear.'

'I wish we might make life easier for Your Majesty.'

'You do your best, Lady Douglas, but I am a prisoner and nothing can alter that.'

'I will ask that you be allowed the freedom of the castle and the island. Now that you are so much better you must find confinement to one set of apartments tiresome.'

'All captivity is tiresome to me, Lady Douglas, but I thank you for your kindness. It is pleasant, in such circumstances, to find some who try to make my stay here more comfortable. Your son is already my friend.'

'William regrets that he must be your custodian.'

'I was not thinking of William, but your younger son.'

'My son George, Your Majesty. So you have noticed him!'

'I did, for I liked well his manners.'

Lady Douglas smiled happily. It was pleasant to hear compliments about her children. George *was* a handsome boy. Who knew, the Queen might not always be a prisoner. If she were ever back in power she would remember those who had pleased her during her captivity, and George might profit from

44

the fact that he had found favour with the Queen. That would be wonderful. But alas, if the Queen were returned to power that would mean a loss of power for her dear son Moray, and that was something which must never happen.

Lady Douglas sighed, and turned her attentions to the new clothes which Melville had kindly – perhaps cunningly – sent for the Queen's pleasure.

* * *

That same evening at seven o'clock Mary was seated at supper in her apartments when a boat came to the island and a most illustrious person disembarked.

Mary did not see his arrival but Jane Kennedy came in to tell her.

'Your brother is at the castle.'

'Jamie!' cried the Queen and her face lit up with pleasure. No matter what hard things she heard about James, she had always found it difficult to believe that he was anything but her friend.

'He is coming to see you,' whispered Marie.

Mary laughed. 'I'm glad some of my clothes have arrived. I should have hated to greet Jamie in my rags. How does this silk camlet look?'

'Very beautiful with the aglets sparkling.'

'So I look a little more like a Queen?'

'You would always look like a Queen, Your Majesty, no matter what you wore.'

'And I still have subjects to flatter me! I can scarcely wait to see Jamie. He will come straight to me. Jane, I have a feeling that he will not allow me to remain here.'

'He is coming. I can hear him now,' said Jane.

The door opened and James Stuart, Earl of Moray, bastard brother of the Queen, stood on the threshold.

'Jamie!' cried Mary; and was about to go forward to embrace him when she saw that he was not alone. With him were the Earls of Morton and Atholl, and by the demeanour of them all she understood that this was not merely a visit of brother to sister; it was the would-be Regent calling on the dethroned Queen.

James's face was expressionless. She had always teased him, told him that he was as cold as a fish. He took such a delight in never betraying his feelings. Now he stood, holding himself

45

at his full height – which was not great – his tawny colouring the only real resemblance he bore to his royal father.

James Douglas, Earl of Morton, was yet another connexion of the Douglas family and one of Moray's closest friends and supporters. Mary did not like the man. She believed he had arranged the murder of Rizzio; it was between him and Atholl that she had entered Edinburgh after the débâcle at Carberry Hill. It was thoughtless of James to come and see her in the company of two men who must bring with them such bitter memories.

'I heard you had come, James,' she said restrainedly. 'It is a pleasure to see you.'

'I was near Lochleven and could not pass without a visit.'

'I am only a prisoner now, James.'

James looked uncomfortable. He was longing for this visit to be over but had felt it necessary to make it. He had determined not to see Mary alone, and it was for this reason that he had insisted that Morton and Atholl accompany him although they were as uneasy as he was. Neither of the three men would meet the Queen's eye. She well understood their shame. She felt her anger rising against Morton and Atholl, but she remembered how James had played with her – in his solemn way it was true – when she was a child and had later told her that if she needed counsel she must come to him. He had often reminded her that he was her brother and that must mean that the ties between them were strong.

Others might warn her against him; she had never believed them; it had always been a fault of hers that she endowed others with the warm generosity which was her own.

'I trust you are comfortable here?' he murmured now.

'Comfortable! In prison? Do you think that possible, James?'

'You are safe here from your enemies . . . who are numerous.'

'I thought I was in the hands of my enemies,' she said a little sternly, and her eyes were scornful as she glanced from Morton to Atholl.

'William and my mother are treating you well, I trust?'

She shrugged her shoulders. 'They do not starve me, nor illtreat me physically. But, as I said, I am their prisoner. James, I wish to talk to you . . . alone.'

James hesitated. It was the very thing he was trying to avoid

46

and yet he saw that he could not escape it without seeming churlish and he was anxious not to appear that.

'Oh . . .' he said awkwardly, 'very well.' He turned to his friends. 'You hear my sister's request. Perhaps you should leave us.'

Morton and Atholl bowed slightly and retired. When the door had shut on them Mary sighed with relief.

'I rejoice in their absence. They are no friends of mine.' She went to her brother and laid her hands on his shoulders giving him her most dazzling smile; but he was one of the few people who were not affected by it. When he looked at Mary, ambitious James did not see an attractive woman in distress; he saw the crown which had been taken from her and which – although he could not wear it – would be as good as his until her son reached his majority.

All the humiliation he had suffered could be appeased if he were ruler of Scotland. He could never be James VI, but he could be King in all but name . . . while his sister remained in captivity. He would exchange the term Bastard for Regent. It was the only balm for the wounded vanity of years. Mary was a fool to plead to him for help. She should have known that he was the last person to help her to freedom which must necessarily mean his own fall from power.

But Mary was a foolish woman – a beautiful and fascinating one, it was true, but a sentimental fool.

He had come here for one purpose – to make her implore him to take the Regency. He believed he could do this, for she had always thought him to be her friend.

He laid his hands almost gingerly on hers; his were cold, as she remembered they always had been.

'Ah, Mary,' he said, 'you are in a dire state . . . a dire state.'

'But I feel happier today for two reasons, Jamie. Today Melville had a box of my clothes sent to me. . . .'

Frivolous woman! thought James. Her crown lost, and she can take pleasure in clothes!

'And,' she went on, 'as though that were not enough, my dear brother comes to see me.'

'Your food grows cold,' he said, because he found it embarrassing to look into her radiant face which betrayed her love for him. She made him feel mean and shifty, which he did not believe himself to be. He was a man with a stern sense of duty. He believed that there was one man who could make Scotland strong and deliver the country from the state into which Mary,

47

with her two disastrous marriages, had plunged it; that man
would be the Regent Moray. He had never betrayed his
emotions, so she did not expect him to be demonstrative now,
which was a mercy, for he would have found it difficult to
feign love for her at this time, when he was planning to rob
her of her kingdom.

He led her to the table and sat down with her.

'You must eat with me, Jamie.'

'I am not hungry. But you should continue with your
supper.'

He sat down and stared broodingly before him.

'In the old days,' she said sadly, 'you thought it an honour
to give me my napkin.'

He did not offer to do this service and she went on: 'It is
difficult serving a Queen in the fortalice of Lochleven from
doing so in the Castle of Edinburgh or Holyrood House.'

He was moodily silent and she cried: 'Why, I embarrass
you, Jamie. Never mind. It warms my heart to see you.'

'Pray finish your supper.'

'It seems inhospitable to eat alone. I do not think I am in
the mood for food. Tell me, Jamie, what news do you bring
me?'

'John Knox preaches against you in Edinburgh.'

'That does not surprise me. He was ever my enemy.'

'In the streets the fishwives speak against you.'

'I heard them shouting below my window. I saw their
vacuous faces alive only with evil.'

'I could not answer for your safety if you went back to
Edinburgh.'

'So I must remain here, a prisoner?'

'For your own safety.'

'But I have heard that there are some lords who would be
ready to rally to my side. The Flemings and the Setons were
always my loyal friends.'

'Who told you this?' ne asked sharply.

'I do not remember. Perhaps no one told me. Perhaps I
merely know it to be true.'

Moray's mood was thoughtful. He was going to tell his
brother William that they must be more vigilant; he was not
pleased with the measures of security which were being taken.
He fancied he had seen a change in Ruthven. There was a
certain witchery about his half-sister which – and this was be-

yond his understanding – seemed to have a devastating effect on men, so that they were ready to jeopardise their careers.

Mary threw aside her napkin. 'No,' she said, 'I shall not eat alone. Let us go for a walk in the open air. I shall be considered safe if you are my companion.'

He took a velvet robe – which had come in Melville's box – and put it about her shoulders.

'Come then,' he said, and they left the apartments and went into the grounds.

'They allow you to walk out here, I suppose.'

'They are most vigilant. I have taken a few little walks but always surrounded by guards.'

'I do not see why you should not walk when you wish and go where you wish in the castle.' He was looking at the boats moored at the lakeside. He pondered: I shall tell William to have her more closely watched. But at the same time he wanted her to go on believing that he was her friend and that he had come to assure himself of her comfort and to give her as much freedom as he could, at the same time ensuring her safety.

'Oh, Jamie,' she cried, 'I knew you would help me.'

'My dear sister, ever since the murder of Rizzio there have been murmurs against you. Your marriage with Darnley was undesirable. You know how I warned you against that.'

'Because, dear brother, you are such a stern Protestant, and you would rather have seen me make a Protestant marriage.'

'And his mysterious death. . . .' Moray shook his head. 'And then, before he was cold, the marriage with Bothwell. My dear sister, how could you have allowed yourself to be led into such folly?'

'Darnley's death was none of my doing.'

Moray's lips were hidden by his tawny moustache but they were tight and stern.

'Rizzio murdered; Darnley murdered . . . and then that hasty and unseemly marriage!'

'What news of Bothwell, James?'

'None that is good.'

'Good for me, James, or for those who wish to destroy him?'

James said: 'He fled North. He is said to be there with Huntley.'

He will come for me, she thought triumphantly, and when he comes this nightmare will be over.

Moray was thinking: My first act will be to send a squadron North to capture that traitor. There is little the people of Edinburgh would rather see than his head on a pike.

'Mary,' said James, 'you must be patient during the next months. You must resign yourself to your confinement here. Willingly would I free you, were it in my power to do so, but it would not be for your good.'

'How long will it last?'

'Who knows? Until the affairs of this country are in order.'

'They have made my little baby King of Scotland. Poor innocent child, he knows nothing of this. What will he think, I wonder, when he is old enough to know that they made a prisoner of his mother in order to rule through him?'

'It is a dangerous situation.'

'So many of them struggling for power,' she agreed.

'What Scotland needs – until the people are prepared to receive you back on the throne – is a strong man who can rule.'

'If Bothwell were here . . .'

'Bothwell is far away in the North. The people would tear him to pieces if they could lay their hands on him. They want someone who is not afraid of them to restore order. Someone who will give his life if need be . . . for our troubled country.'

'Yourself, James?' she asked gently.

He frowned and pretended to be reluctant.

'I? Our father's bastard!'

'The people do not hold that against you.'

''Twas truly no fault of mine. Had I been consulted I should have asked to be born in wedlock!'

'You are the man, James. Our father's son. Sober and religious in a manner acceptable to the people, strong, firm, destined to rule.'

'You are asking me to take over the Regency until that time when you are allowed to assume the crown?'

'Why yes, James, I suppose I am . . . if I have any say in the matter.'

'You ask a great deal,' he said, and there was no hint in his voice or manner of the exultation which was his. The purpose of his visit was achieved, and he saw no reason why he should dally longer with his sister. It was true she had no power to bestow the Regency, but being the man he was he preferred to have her approval.

They were silent for a while, looking over the lake. It would soon be dark and Mary gazed longingly at the mainland. The biggest of the boats, which brought household articles from the mainland, creaked on its chains. Suppose he were to take me away in that boat, she thought; who would be waiting on the mainland to help me? Some of my friends, surely.

Moray was thinking how gullible she was. How fortunate for him that she had committed folly after folly which had brought her to Lochleven. Here must she remain. There was so much he might have told her. Many of her cherished possessions had been given away as bribes by the Protestant lords; he had helped himself to horses from her stables. He might have told her a very interesting piece of news which could have caused her serious alarm. But not yet. He and Morton had not yet decided what use they would make of the silver casket which was in Morton's possession. Morton declared that George Dalgleish, a servant of Bothwell's, had discovered this after Bothwell had fled; and in this casket were letters and. poems which left no doubt of Mary's guilt as murderess and adulteress.

No, as yet that little matter was a secret to be brought to light when it could be most useful.

Mary had turned to him questioningly. In the dusk she seemed to see him more clearly than she ever had before.

James, who was never on the spot when there was trouble. Was it accident or design? What calculation went on behind those cold passionless eyes?

Standing there by the lakeside Mary was suddenly aware that Moray's purpose in coming to Lochleven had not been to soothe her, not to assure himself of her comfort, but to persuade her to persuade him to accept the Regency.

The Regency.! It was what he had always set his heart on.

She wanted to laugh loudly and bitterly. But James was saying: 'The air grows chill. Let me conduct you to your chamber. Then I must say farewell.'

'Ah yes, James, there is no longer need for you to stay, is there?'

He appeared not to have heard as silently he conducted her into the castle which struck her as chill and forbidding; it seemed to her now as much a prison as it had in those first days.

He is no friend to me, she thought. Once I am free the Regency would pass from his hands.

How alone she felt! How deserted!

As she went towards her apartments escorted by James she saw George Douglas. His eyes went to her at once and became alight with the longing to serve her.

Not entirely alone! she thought as she went into her apartment. Not entirely deserted.

*　　*　　*

Sir William visited Mary the next day and said: 'My lord Moray is disturbed on your behalf, for he is eager that you should have as much freedom as is possible in the circumstances. He says your apartments are dark and possibly damp. He thinks that you should be given the apartment you occupied on previous visits to Lochleven.'

Mary was delighted for since she had furnished those apartments herself they were the most elegant in the castle.

'I shall be delighted to move into them immediately,' she told Sir William; and smiling he conducted her to them.

They were in a more modern part of the castle which was known as the New House, and situated in the south-eastern tower. Mary gave a cry of pleasure as she saw the presence chamber which was a circular room with a low ceiling; and from the windows she had a magnificent view of the surrounding country. First she went to a window and looked out across the loch to the mountains.

From the presence room she went into the bedroom and it was comforting to notice that the beautiful pieces of tapestry with their hawking and hunting scenes were still hanging there. There was the bed which she had had brought here; it was shaped like a chapel and made of green velvet; the counterpane was of green taffety. There was the regal canopy and her sofa and chairs of crimson satin fringed with gold.

As she looked from her bedroom window, she could see the other three islets of the loch; and she could almost imagine that she was staying here after a hawking expedition, as she gazed at the ruins of the priory on that islet known as St. Serf's Inch.

Then she saw the town of Kinross on the mainland and immediately began to wonder how many of her friends were nearby, in the hope that they might come to her aid.

Lady Douglas came into the apartments and Mary expressed to her the pleasure she felt.

'And,' went on Lady Douglas, 'my lord Moray fancies you did not look as healthy as he would have wished you to look.'

52

'Was he surprised?' Mary asked with faint sarcasm.

'He was indeed,' replied Lady Douglas; 'and he has said that you should take more exercise. He does not see why you should not ride about the island if you wish.'

'He is most thoughtful,' murmured Mary.

Lady Douglas bore the look of a proud mother; she knew that very shortly she would be hearing that her son was the ruler of Scotland. It was something to make a mother proud. Ruler he would remain for as long as this woman was in captivity. She would see that there were no means of escape.

Sir William was thinking of his half-brother's words: 'Give her more freedom within the limits of the island, but double the guard, particularly at night, and make sure that the boats are securely moored when not in use.'

So under the semblance of greater freedom Mary's imprisonment was in fact to become more rigorous.

Moray had added: 'Watch Ruthven. I fancied I saw a certain fondness in his eyes when they rested on my sister.'

Sir William was therefore far from easy in his mind.

* * *

In her new apartments, Mary set to work on her tapestry, using the canvases, wools and silks which Melville had provided. It was a great pleasure and relaxation to be doing such delicate work again, and both Jane and Marie Courcelles shared her enthusiasm. Mary could forget her irritation with her imprisonment as she planned the design, which was a series of pictures of ladies and gentlemen richly dressed in brightly coloured costumes and jewels. With the glazed flax thread which Melville had had the foresight to send she worked the jewels in satin stitch using white dots for the pearls. So as she worked out her schemes with these elaborately dressed men and women in their backgrounds of castles, bowers, terraces and country scenes, she was able to imagine herself free of her prison.

Melville could not realize how he had served her; he had in fact, on receiving her thanks, sent her another box containing more of her clothes and her working materials.

There was yet another joy. Now that he had achieved his end Moray, anxious to appear her friend and to make her believe he had no wish that her term of confinement should be one of rigorous imprisonment, ordered that she should have more servants. She should have her own cook in her suite of

53

rooms and two domestic servants whose duties should be to wait on her alone.

The greatest delight of all was when Jane arrived in Mary's apartments, to tell her that a visitor had called at the castle to see her and was asking permission to present herself.

'Herself!' cried Mary. 'Then it is a woman!'

'See for yourself, Your Majesty!' said Jane; and the newcomer was ushered into the apartment.

Mary gave a cry of great joy when she recognized her dearest friend, Mary Seton, the only unmarried one of the four Marys who had shared their childhood with her, and the one who had been most dear to her.

For some moments they could do nothing but cling to each other. Mary was laughing and crying at the same time and Mary Seton, who had always been the most restrained of the four Marys, was near to tears.

'Oh how happy I am to see you, dear Seton!' cried Mary, using the name by which she had called this friend of her childhood, for as there had been four Marys as well as herself it had been impracticable to call them all by their common Christian name. 'I can bear my trials so much more easily with you as my companion.'

'I have been imploring the Confederate Lords to let me come, ever since they brought you here.'

'My dear, dear Seton!'

'They were very suspicious of my intentions. I had to assure them that I was quite incapable of arranging your escape. They would not believe that I only wished to share your imprisonment.'

'They would never understand friendship such as ours,' murmured Mary.

So there was the joy of showing Seton the castle, of hearing news of the other Marys, of Seton's family's devotion to their Queen, of recalling other days when they had been together.

The happiest thing which had happened to the Queen since she had come to Lochleven was reunion with Mary Seton.

*　　*　　*

There were times when Mary longed to escape from watching eyes; she knew she never did. Although she was allowed to wander at her will about the island, she was aware that, from the windows and turrets of the castle, vigilant eyes were fixed upon her. There was no escape.

One day as she sat alone by the lake she saw a boat being rowed across from the mainland, and as it came nearer she realized that its occupant was George Douglas.

He saw her and to her astonishment gave no sign of recognition and as he brought the boat near to that spot where she was he shipped his oars and said in a voice which was scarcely audible: 'Your Majesty, please forgive my remaining seated. It is the best way. If I come ashore it will be seen that we are speaking together. I shall pretend to be occupied with the boat while I talk to you.'

'Yes, George,' she answered.

'I have sought an opportunity to speak to Your Majesty for some days. It has not been possible. I have met Lord Seton who is not far away from Lochleven. He is trying to find a means of releasing you. He is enlisting the help of the Hamiltons. John Beaton is with him. They hope to bring in Huntley and Argyle.'

'Your words fill me with hope.'

'Your Majesty, you may entrust me with any message you wish to be sent to them. It will give me the utmost pleasure if you will look upon me as your messenger to take your orders to your subjects and to bring their plans to your notice.'

'This is the best news I have heard for a long time,' she told him.

'I must pass on now. It must not be noticed that we converse together.'

'Thank you. Thank you, George.'

She sat watching the boat skim lightly over the water. She felt elated by the adoration of this earnest young man. Ruthven's burning gaze met hers from time to time. He was contrite, and was trying to convey that he was deeply ashamed of his outburst and was now ready to serve her . . . and hope.

She began to feel that her situation was not without advantages.

* * *

The summer was passing and the damp of autumn was in the air. Each day the memories of that terrible June seemed a little fainter. Mary was glad of the passing time but she was saddened by the arrival of autumn; summer was the time for escape. Mist rose from the lake and penetrated the castle; the cry of wild fowl sounded melancholy during the dull days, which all seemed so much alike. The Queen walked a little, dined, supped, prayed for her deliverance, sat at her tapestry, gazed longingly across to the mainland and wondered when her friends would come to deliver her.

She invited members of the Douglas family to her apartments sometimes to supper sometimes after the meal. Lindsay was not staying on the island although he paid periodical visits to the castle; Ruthven was often present at the gatherings, when his smouldering gaze would fix itself upon her and he would seek to converse with her. She avoided him; he might appear more docile but she was aware of the burning passion behind his eyes. He would be ready to help her but he would expect to be paid for his services. He might be curbing his tongue, but his motives were the same as they had been on that night when he had come unbidden to her apartment.

What a pleasure it was to turn to George Douglas. Dear George, being so young and earnest, was quite unable to hide his devotion, which was a pity; and yet she was moved by it, knowing that there was no motive behind George's actions but to serve her.

So she would single George out for her attention, and he often sat beside her while his mother watched them, as did others present.

Ought she to warn George? wondered Lady Douglas. Ought she to tell Moray that George was so much in love with the Queen that he was clearly prepared to do something foolish for her?

Lady Douglas studied her young son. He was such a charming boy. Not like his half-brother Moray of course – not even like William. George was gentle; he would need someone to help him if he were to make his way in the world.

She would ask Moray to take him into his service . . . not yet . . . later. Lady Douglas liked to keep the members of her family about her as long as possible. But suppose the crown was restored to the Queen; dear Moray would perhaps not be so influential then. And the Queen would not forget George, her devoted admirer in adversity.

How an ambitious mother's thoughts would run on! Mary was an impetuous woman. She had married Bothwell, who was no royal Prince. As she had married Bothwell, why should she not marry a Douglas?

So dreams ran on, sweeping aside all obstacles. Bothwell could either be killed or divorced from the Queen to make way for Lady Douglas's handsome son.

Therefore if those two did talk dangerously, Lady Douglas could look on blithely. Mary could not escape from Lochleven until Moray was ready to let her go, but that was no reason why she should not enjoy her pleasant game of make-believe with Lady Douglas's bonny son Geordie.

Mary Seton played the lute and there was dancing. Trust the Queen, thought Lady Douglas, to bring gaiety even into her prison. There she was, her chestnut hair escaping most becomingly from her coif, dressed in a gown of blue velvet trimmed with miniver, which Melville had sent to her, looking at young George as they danced together. She is making a Little France in Lochleven, thought Lady Douglas. And in the Little France of Holyrood House Mary had taken Rizzio as her favourite, had married Darnley, had loved Bothwell. Why should she not love George Douglas in the keep of Lochleven?

Mary was saying to George: 'You must not look at me so devotedly, George. Others will notice.'

'They should not be surprised,' he said vehemently. 'All the world must be devoted to you.'

'You should have seen your brother-in-law, Lindsay, with his sword at my throat.'

'He is a monster.'

'I agree, George. I feel my anger rising when I think of him. I tell myself that I will have his head . . . when I escape. When, George, when?'

'It shall be soon, Your Majesty.'

'If all men loved me as you do, George, I should have nothing to fear.'

'My plan is almost complete, Your Majesty.'

She moved nearer to him in the dance. 'Can you tell me . . . without seeming to? Speak low; your mother watches us.'

'Your Majesty, when you are free, you will not hold it against my mother and brother that you were held in their fortalice?'

'Nay, George. It seems that I shall be so grateful to one Douglas that I shall love the whole family.'

'When you say such things I am filled with such happiness that I forget aught else.'

'Oh George, you must not love me so devotedly that you cannot help me to escape. There is one thing I long for beyond all others. Only when one has lost freedom does one realize how precious it is. I shall never forget you, George. For if I never leave Lochleven I shall remember that in my darkest hour you gave me hope.'

'Then I have not lived in vain. If they discovered that I had tried to help you, doubtless they would kill me. If that should come to pass, do not grieve for me. Remember that I should be the happiest man on Earth on the day I died for you.'

'Do not speak of dying for me. Rather live for me.'

George looked melancholy. 'I am aware, Your Majesty, of the gulf that lies between us. You are a Queen. My only hope is to serve you.'

'You are too modest, George. I shall never forget that you are my very dear friend.'

Her long eyes were soft and full of affection. She wanted to take his head in her hands and kiss him. She was young and passionate; she was also very lonely, and the image of Bothwell was growing dimmer each day. Perhaps she had had enough of brutality; what she craved now was gentleness; this adoration, this loving homage which the charming boy was laying at her feet.

'My very dear friend,' she repeated.

Had he been more calculating he might have read an invitation in her words. Any other might have given her a passionate look of understanding and, when the castle was sleeping, she would have opened her eyes to find him beside her. But not George. He had no thought beyond service; he did not think, as Ruthven did: I will help the Queen escape and in exchange she may take me for her lover. George only asked to serve.

It would have been easy to divert to George Douglas that passionate desire which had once overwhelmed her for a different kind of man.

He was too young to understand. He did not know how he might so easily have become her lover.

He was whispering: 'Have you noticed the large boat moored at the lakeside? It is not securely moored. Be ready when I give the warning. It may be very soon.'

'You would take me to the mainland in this boat?' she asked. 'How should we elude the guards?'

'You have many supporters on the mainland. I have suggested to them that they come in force to attack and force their way into the castle. While you and I take the boat and go to the mainland, they will engage the guards until we have made our escape.'

'It sounds simple,' she said. 'But are there enough men to prevent our being caught before we reach the mainland?'

'I will arrange it,' said George.

She smiled; but she thought: Is it possible?

George had no doubt; she could see by the happy smile on his lips.

Seton had stopped playing the lute and the dance was over. Lady Douglas watched benignly while George escorted the Queen to her chair.

*   *   *

It was dusk and George bent over the chains by which the boat was fastened.

A simple matter, he thought. He wished they could have a rehearsal. He would make his way straight to the keep, where she would be waiting in her cloak. Then they would hurry out of the castle while the invaders held off the guards. On the mainland Lord Seton and others would be waiting for them with fast horses.

'Is aught wrong with the boat, sir?'

George started on seeing Will Drysdale, the garrison commander, looking down at him. George flushed, annoyed because he could never cover his embarrassment. 'Oh . . . no . . . It seems secure enough.'

Drysdale bent over the chains to examine them. 'H'm,' was all he said. Then he straightened himself and stared beyond George to the mainland. 'I believe this boat causes you some anxiety, sir. I saw you examining it the other day.'

'I think it's secure enough,' said George turning away.

Drysdale looked after him and scratched the side of his face. He watched George until he was out of sight; then he went to find Sir William.

Sir William was in his apartments and Drysdale asked: 'Could I have a word with you alone, sir?'

'Anything wrong?' asked Sir William when they were alone.

'The big boat is not very securely moored, Sir William. It would not be difficult for anyone to release it. I suggest that we make it very secure. If we do not —'

'You have discovered something, Drysdale?'

'Well, Sir William, I hardly know. It was just that I wanted to make sure.'

Sir William eyed him quizzically. 'You'd better tell me, Drysdale.'

'It may be conjecture on my part, Sir William, but Master George seemed uncommonly interested in that boat, and anyone can see with half an eye that. . . .'

'The Queen is a very desirable woman,' sighed Sir William, 'and my brother is a chivalrous young man. . . . That's what you mean, is it?'

Drysdale nodded.

'I should not like the young fool to run into trouble,' said Sir William.

'Where the Queen is, trouble will soon follow, Sir William. What shall I do?'

'Make the boat doubly secure, strengthen the guard, and keep your eye on my young brother. And so will I. For the time being let that suffice. And . . . say nothing. He is young and inexperienced. I would not like this to reach the ears of my lord Moray. He would not understand the emotions of a young boy in love. My lord Moray could never have been that. Such as we are, Drysdale, are more lenient, eh. This could cost the boy his life.'

'Very well, Sir William.'

'But remember, we have been warned.'

*   *   *

George lay stretched out on the grass moodily staring up at the keep. She was seated in her window, her tapestry in her hand.

He had failed! George was telling himself what an ineffectual fool she would think him. The plan had had a chance of success but he had had to raise their suspicions by his too careful examinations of the boat. Now that they suspected him, he would have to think of something very ingenious if he were going to give her her freedom.

But he would succeed; he was determined to. In his imagination he saw himself at her side, defending her for the rest of their lives, his sword drawn ready for all who came against her. All that he asked was to be her slave. When she rode away from Lochleven he would go with her, no matter in what guise; he would not care. He would be her page, her scullion . . . anything – all he asked was that he might be with her.

A low chuckle at his side brought him out of his dream of chivalry. He frowned; he was in no mood for young Willie so he ignored the boy stretched out beside him until Willie began

60

to whistle untunefully. Then George cried: 'For the love of God, be silent!'

Willie, resting his elbows on the grass, propped his face in his hands. 'You were a daftie, Geordie Douglas,' he said. 'It was a poor plan, did ye know?'

'What do you mean?'

'To think to go off in the boat and then let old Drysdale know it by looking over the old vessel every few hours to make sure it was worthy to carry your Queen.'

'So you knew —'

'Hey, Geordie Douglas, what have I got this pair of peepers for, did ye think? Now if I was going to rescue *my* Queen I'd go a different way about it, that I would!'

'You rescue the Queen!'

'And why not, Geordie Douglas? I may wear your cast-off breeks but I am a man for all that . . . and she's a bonny lass though a Queen.'

George sprang to his feet but Willie was quicker. George lifted his arm to cuff the boy but Willie dodged away; he stood some distance off, poised to run, grinning insolently.

I have indeed been a fool, thought George. Even Willie would have done better.

*　　*　　*

December had come and as Mary sat with Seton over their tapestry she said: 'I shall have to wait for the spring before I can hope to escape from this place. How long that seems.'

'The next three months will pass quickly,' Seton comforted her.

'It is the monotony of the days which is so hard to bear; to look out from my window every hour of the day and see the same stretch of lake. Oh, I am happy that you are with me. I am fond of George, and Lady Douglas seems to be a good friend as far as her fondness for our Regent will allow her. But there are times when I feel very melancholy.'

She did not mention Bothwell, but she was thinking of him. During the last weeks she had had a premonition that she would never see him again. Through George news was brought to her from the mainland; no one had been able to stop that, and she knew that Moray had sent Kirkcaldy of Grange to capture her husband.

Bothwell, learning of the plan to capture him, had left Huntley and taken temporary refuge at Spynie with his great-uncle and old tutor and guardian, Patrick Hepburn the Bishop of Moray. He had attempted a feat which was typical of him when he had tried to enlist the help of pirates in order to raise a naval force with himself as its commander. Indeed, it seemed that he had not hesitated to turn pirate himself. He would have brought many an uneasy moment to Moray and his friends, for Bothwell was the man they feared more than any in Scotland. How often had Mary wept for the strength he could have given her as well as that erotic satisfaction which, having tasted, she often craved for. But there was no substitute for Bothwell; there never would be. She was aware of this and that was why the fear that she would never see him again was as acute as a physical pain.

But even Bothwell had not been sufficiently prepared to make a stand against Moray's might, and he had gone to the Orkneys and Shetlands where he had narrowly escaped capture; but Kirkcaldy in hot pursuit had been wrecked on the rocks, while Bothwell escaped across the North Sea to be captured off the Norwegian coast by a Danish commander and taken to Bergen. There he was allowed to take up residence, but a certain Anna Thorssen was, to Bothwell's misfortune, residing in Bergen, and when she heard that he was in that town, determined to settle an old score. The buccaneering Bothwell had gone through a form of marriage with her some years before, taken possession of her considerable fortune and then deserted her. His sins were catching up with him. She brought a suit against him and, only by promising her an annuity when he returned to Scotland, did he manage to elude the law. He had been expelled from Bergen and was now in Copenhagen.

While he was free there was hope, and yet with the passing of each day the bold Borderer seemed to become more like a figure in a dream than in reality. There were times when she could not bear to think of him, when looking back on her life she knew that it would have been different if she had never surrendered to Bothwell, if she had never allowed him to make herself the slave of her senses.

That had brought her to Lochleven . . . here in the castle surrounded by the lake, where only the companionship of her women, the unswerving devotion of a chivalrous young man could in some measure compensate her for all she had lost.

'Before this,' she told Seton, 'I never had the time to look back on my life, and consequently never learned the art of contemplation. Life passed too quickly; it was like playing a part in one pageant after another. It is different now.'

'Very different, Your Majesty.'

'I begin to see events in the right perspective. I see people for what they are. Do you know, Seton, before this I believed Moray was my friend. What a stupid woman I must have been! Moray could free me tomorrow if he wished. Of course he does not wish to do so because once I am free he loses his power. All his life brother Jamie has longed for the power which his illegitimacy denied him; always he has been saying to himself: "Where Mary is, there might I have been had I been born in wedlock." '

'He is a very ambitious man.'

Mary laughed. 'For the first time I see my brother Jamie clearly, and I know that almost everything he has ever done has been a step towards the Regency. It is the most he can attain. How he would love to be James VI; but my little son bears that title. Still, Regent Moray has all the power that would have been his even if he had been James VI. My half-brother was always shrewd, Seton. What does a name matter? That is what he will be asking himself now.'

'Shall I bring out the tapestry, Your Majesty?'

'Ah, yes, Seton. Working those beautiful scenes soothes me, as you know. I can almost feel I am there . . . with our ladies and gentlemen. But perhaps it is not wise to be so soothed. Perhaps I should be making plans.'

'Plans are being made, Your Majesty. When, the spring comes. . . .'

'Meanwhile there is the whole of the winter before us, Seton. How shall we endure it in this gloomy prison?'

'We shall endure it, Your Majesty.'

Yes, thought Mary with a grim smile, because we may have our tapestry and our music, because we have our hopes, because of the devotion of young George Douglas.

*   *   *

The winds of late December swept across the island when Moray came again to visit his half-sister.

This time he came with the Earl of Morton and Sir James Balfour – two men whose actions had certainly not endeared them to Mary, and when they entered her room she found it difficult to restrain her anger.

The wind, howling about the castle made it at times almost impossible to hear each other speak. She looked straight at Sir James Balfour and immediately remembered that it was he who had provided that house in Kirk o' Field which had been destined to be the scene of Darnley's murder. He had been the lawyer who had arranged Bothwell's divorce from his wife in order that he might marry Mary; and in exchange for these services had been made governor of Edinburgh Castle. But there was not a more vile traitor in Scotland; Balfour's lawyer's mind was alert for disaster and he was determined not to be on the losing side. So, as soon as he knew that the defeat of Mary and Bothwell was imminent he had surrendered the castle to their enemies, asking, as his reward, for the priory of Pittenweem, an annuity for his son and, should there be a trial of those involved in Darnley's murder, a free pardon for himself.

And this was one traitor whom Moray brought with him to Lochleven.

As for Morton, in his treacherous hands was a certain casket of which Mary had heard rumours. It was said to contain letters and poems written by her to Bothwell, and to be one of the most important pieces of evidence in the Darnley case.

And James himself – her half-brother, Jamie, as she used to call him in the days of her childhood – what of him? There he stood, his cold fish-like eyes upon her. He may be Regent, she thought, but I am the Queen.

'How the wind howls,' she said coolly. 'Such a noise must of necessity be for some arch-traitor.'

Her scornful gaze rested on Balfour who had the grace not to meet her eyes.

Moray went forward and would have taken her hands, but she drew away from him.

'Pray do not tell me of your concern for my wellbeing,' she cried. 'I know your concern to be non-existent. My health has improved since we last met and I am sure that is a matter of deep regret to you.'

'Your Majesty!' began Moray who had stepped ahead of Morton and Balfour, but she cut him short.

'I will not listen to your soft words. I think of your actions. If you are my friend, my lord Moray, how can I remain your prisoner? Do you know how long I have been in this place? Six months! You have achieved your purpose. You have forced me to abdicate. You have set a baby on the throne. And you are Regent.'

'My dear sister,' Moray replied coldly, 'what has happened to change you? When we last met you were loving and prepared to trust me.'

'Because I did not know you then, my lord Moray. While I have been in captivity my eyes have been opened. I have been thinking of the past . . . and the present . . . and the future. James Stuart, how many times have I given you my sisterly affection? How many times have you been disloyal to me, and have I accepted your excuses? When I had power I did not forget you. You were my bastard brother, but I could not have given you more honours if you had been a brother without the stain of bastardy upon him.'

'My dear, dear Mary, my sister, my Queen,' said Moray, 'you have been listening to idle gossip. I am your friend now as I always have been. I come to discuss with you the possibility of your freedom. I come to lay certain conditions before you.'

'Conditions!' she cried. 'You would offer me conditions! Let me tell you this: I would rather remain in this prison for the rest of my life than accept any conditions *you* might lay before me, for I know full well that those conditions could only be for the good of Bastard James and not for Queen Mary. I know that you have hunted Bothwell from this land because you feared him. I know that all those who are friends of mine are no friends of yours. Do not imagine that, because I am your prisoner, because you hate me and seek my destruction, all are of your mind. I have friends, James Stuart, and one day they will free me from this castle and then . . . there will be no conditions. . . .'

She walked past them to her own private apartments.

James Balfour, his colour heightened, his lips tight, spoke the thoughts which were in all their minds: 'It is clear that she has a friend within the castle . . . someone who is in touch with her friends outside and brings her news.'

Moray and Morton looked at each other.

'Have no fear,' said Moray angrily, 'we shall soon discover the traitor.'

* * *

Moray, alone with Sir William, expressed his displeasure. 'Not everyone in this castle is with us,' he snapped. 'Someone here brings information to the Queen.' Sir William flinched. 'Why brother,' he said, 'it is the wish of us all to please you.'

'Yet the Queen has information which could only have been given to her by traitors in our midst. Someone is talking too freely, and, it would seem, is more eager to serve her than me.'

'I have noticed that Ruthven is casting languishing glances in her direction,' said Sir William.

'I too was aware of that. Ruthven is to leave at once for Edinburgh.'

Sir William did not mention the matter of the boat. He had no wish to incense Moray against George, particularly as he himself was inclined to shrug aside George's devotion to the Queen. Calf love, he thought. It happens in the very young and George often seems to be young for his years.

Later when they were at supper – the Queen supped in her own room and refused to join the family and their visitors – Moray was aware of the expression in his young half-brother's face when Mary was mentioned.

Lady Douglas, alert where her sons were concerned, realizing that the very manner in which George spoke the Queen's name betrayed his feelings, was very uneasy. Moray was the son of whom she was most proud of course – son of a King, Regent of Scotland – what more could a mother ask! But she loved wee Geordie too, and fervently hoped the lad was not going to fall into trouble.

Her hopes were vain. Moray left the supper table quickly and summoned his young brother George, with his mother and Sir William to a private chamber.

He came straight to the point and, looking into George's face, he accused: 'I believe you are concocting some foolish plot to rescue the Queen.'

'There is no such plot,' answered George; which was true, for try as he would he had found nothing satisfactory.

'But if you saw your opportunity you would be ready to serve the woman?'

'Do not speak of the Queen so disrespectfully in my hearing,' retorted George.

An oath escaped Moray, which was rare with him. He was really shaken.

'You lovesick fool!' he muttered. 'So it is you, is it? It is because of you that I find her so changed. You have fed her with news and promises of help. You fool! And you call yourself a half-brother of mine!'

Lady Douglas, distressed to witness conflict between her loved ones, said: 'Geordie meant no harm, Jamie.'

'No harm!' cried Moray, turning on his mother. 'This is not a boy's game. Remember that. This Geordie of yours could plunge Scotland into civil war.'

''Twas nothing but a little flirtation, Jamie. What can you expect of young people?'

'Young people! That woman is old in sin, Madam.'

'Geordie would never go against your interest any more than I or William would.'

Moray was impervious to her distress. He glared at his half-brother through narrowed eyes. 'You will get out of Lochleven,' he said. 'When next I call here I shall expect to find .you gone.'

'This is my home,' insisted George.

'It was. It is no longer.'

'Mother . . .' said George, turning to Lady Douglas; but what could she do? Moray had spoken.

George strode out of the room and Moray, who disliked scenes of this sort, signed to his mother and brother that he wished no further reference to the matter.

That night Moray left the castle.

* * *

Lady Douglas watching him go was sad. Where would Geordie go? she was asking herself. It had been a favourite dream of hers that Moray would find some place of honour for George. Families should stand together. And now they had quarrelled. Oh, how distressing!

Sir William understood her feelings; he laid his hand on her arm. 'James is right,' he said. 'Young George is playing with fire.'

'He has been so happy since she came. Oh, William, he has become a man through his devotion to her. He is different from the rest of you. He was always so gentle and affectionate. And where will he go? We cannot drive him from his home.'

'You heard what James said.'

She sighed. 'But James will not be back for some time. Let George stay awhile . . . until he has made plans. I'm sure James did not mean him to go away at once . . . just like that. It is monstrous.'

Sir William gave her a look of affection. It was so like her to try to please all her sons. How distressing for her when they ranged themselves on opposite sides! As for Sir William himself, he did not see what harm George could do. It was hard on the boy to be banished from his home merely because he had done the most natural thing in the world – fallen in love with a beautiful woman.

James had gone. So there was no hurry for George to leave.

* * *

George went to his own chamber and began to pace up and down there. He was angry. How dared James order him from his home! He was shocked to realize how much he hated James. All his life he had been taught to admire his half-brother. James Stuart had been as a god to the Douglases. Lady Douglas had made sure of that; and George had never been envious of his mother's preference for her bastard son, because it was not in George's nature to be envious. He had no great opinion of himself, and it was only since he had become obsessed by his love for the Queen that he had rebelled. Now his pride made him long to leave the castle; but any personal feelings would be swamped by his desire to do what was best for the Queen.

If he could stay in Lochleven for a week . . . two weeks . . . he might be able to perfect some plan of escape. What a pity that the weather was so bad. If he were exiled from the island, how could he keep in touch with the Queen?

His door opened slowly and a mischievous face appeared to grin at him.

'Oh, Willie, go away.'

Willie's response was to come into the room.

'I heard you get your marching orders,' he said.

'You hear too much.'

'Dinna be a daftie, Geordie. No one can hear too much.'

'I don't want to talk to you now, Willie.'

'Which shows how soft you are, Geordie. For if you're out there . . .' he pointed through the window '. . . and if you mustna' set foot on the island, how'll she know when you're ready for her to leave . . . without Willie Douglas tells her?'

George stared at Willie who grinned almost bashfully.

'Ye'll be over there, Geordie Douglas,' he said, 'but Willie'll be here . . . and he can do all ye did . . . and better.'

George strode across the room and gripped the boy's shoulder. 'You'd be in this, Willie? You'd help?'

'Oh ay . . . I'd do it.' He grinned. 'She's a bonnie lassie!'

George was excited. He made his way to the Queen's apartments, which was rash, but for all he knew there might be little time to lose.

Seton was with the Queen who received him at once and asked Seton to leave them.

George's heart beat fast when he found himself alone with the Queen. He could scarcely speak, so deep was his emotion. Then the words came tumbling out. Moray had discovered his devotion to her and as a result he was to be exiled from the castle.

The Queen turned pale and put one of her exquisite hands to her throat. 'Oh no . . . George,' she whispered, 'that would be more than I could bear.'

He stared at her as though he could not believe his ears.

'It's true,' she went on. 'Nothing has given me so much courage to live through these dreary months as your presence.'

'Your Majesty. . . .'

'Oh George, how I hate Moray. This is his doing.'

'It seems, Your Majesty, that he discovered my love for you.'

'When you are older, George, you will more easily hide your emotions.'

'I could never hide an emotion so great that it is my whole being.'

'I have had sonnets written to me, George, but nothing has ever pleased me quite as much as those words of yours. Have you come to say goodbye?'

'I trust not. Moray has gone and I may have a few days left to me. I would like to see some of your friends on the mainland and tell them what has happened, and myself tell you what they plan to do.'

'We shall have to wait for the spring for my rescue, George.'

'It will give us three months in which to perfect our plans, Your Majesty.'

'And this may mean that any day . . . perhaps tomorrow, I shall look for you in vain and be told that you have gone away.'

'That could well be.'

She took a pearl drop earring from her ear.

'Take this, George,' she said. 'You shall have one and I the other. If you send a messenger to me with that earring I shall know that the messenger truly comes from you.'

He took the earring and held it reverently in the palm of his

69

hand. For some seconds he seemed bemused; then he said: 'Your Majesty, I believe that young Willie Douglas yearns to be made use of in your service.'

'The little freckled-faced boy? I often find him watching me.'

'He is a strange.boy, Your Majesty, but is a friend of mine . : . and of yours.'

'I need all the friends I can muster . . . and more so when the most trustworthy of them all is taken from me. Then I could send Willie Douglas with a message to you . . . if the need should arise?'

'I know he would bring it to me, Your Majesty.'

'Oh, George,' she cried, 'I am going to miss you so much.'

He knelt and kissed her right hand while she laid her left on his head; stooping suddenly she kissed it, and when he raised his wondering face to hers impulsively she bent and kissed his lips.

He looked dazed, and then his face was illuminated. 'I never thought . . .' he began. 'I never hoped. . . .' And then he went on hurriedly: 'Your Majesty, have I your leave to retire?'

For one moment she thought to detain him, then she nodded and turned her head so that she could not see his perplexed face.

It was the moment for him to go. If he had stayed she might have been tempted to change the relationship between them. It must not be so. A short while ago she might have kept him with her; but she had changed since Carberry Hill. She was a wiser woman; never again would she allow her emotions to lead her to disaster. At least she would make some attempt to curb her sensual longings that they might never again control her destiny.

Perhaps, she thought when she was alone, I was never loved before, as George Douglas loves me.

She would remember that through the dreary months which lay ahead.

*   *   *

Willie Douglas had always freely roamed about the castle and its grounds; when the boats went from the castle to the mainland he often went with them. He performed his duties now and then and if he were missing for several hours no one took much notice. Willie had always been in a specially privileged position and, although Sir William appeared not to notice the boy, instinctively the servants knew that he would not welcome complaints against the urchin.

So Willie went his own way. When the Queen took her walks in the castle grounds he was often seen with her. She seemed to be amused by his mischievous ways. As for Willie he showed no awe of her and behaved as though there was little difference between queens and scullions in his opinion.

George had left Lochleven, for even Lady Douglas could not arrange that he should stay. Moray might descend upon them any day and, moreover, there were always tradesmen and suchlike coming and going between the island and the mainland so that the news would soon have spread that George had remained at Lochleven.

Both Lady Douglas and Sir William knew that George was not far off; they knew also that somewhere in the Kinross area many of Mary's supporters were lodging in the houses of loyal townsfolk, waiting for the day when an attempt would be made to free the Queen from captivity. That must not happen of course, for Sir William would be blamed if she escaped; he did not believe any attempt would be made until the coming of spring, but then he would have to be more vigilant, if that were possible. He believed – and so did Lady Douglas – that George had joined forces with Lord Seton and his friends, and they were not many miles away.

Young Willie Douglas's shrill whistle could be heard through the courtyards; he swaggered a little, which seemed all part of the business of growing up. Now and then he enticed the guards into a gambling game, for Willie had a coin or two to jingle in his pockets. Nobody asked where he procured the money. Willie would have had his answer ready if they had. He had been given it for some service rendered to some merchant on the mainland. Willie was never at a loss.

While he played with the guards he watched the arrival of the boats and the supplies for the castle being unloaded.

'Keeping a sharp watch-out, laddie,' said one of the guards. 'They might make you do a bit of work for a change and you wouldna like that at all.'

'Oh ay,' said Willie absently staring at the laundresses, who were going into the castle to collect the soiled linen which they would take away and bring back clean.

March had come and the first signs of spring were on the countryside. The winds were still strong but now and again

71

they would drop, and when the sun shone there was real warmth in the air.

One day Willie was helping to unload food from a boat which was moored on the shore, and his industry pleased those he was helping. When the unloading was done he leaped into the boat and sat there waiting.

'Coming back with us, young Willie?' asked one of the boatmen.

'Oh ay . . .' answered Willie nonchalantly.

'Come on then, lads, back to Kinross.'

Willie whistled as the boat carried him across the water. When it touched ground he jumped out, saluted the boatmen and ran off.

He skirted the town, now and then breaking into a run, sometimes leaping in a rush of high spirits. When he came to a small hillock he stood for a few moments and looked about him. He could see the roofs of the Kinross houses and a quarter of a mile or so away the woods. Assuring himself that no one was following him he made quickly for these woods and was soon on the narrow path which led through them.

He began to whistle, and after a few minutes his whistle was answered.

He stood still waiting, listening. Then he heard the rustle of twigs; George was coming through the trees.

'I thought you were never coming,' said George.

'It took so long to unload the boat.'

'Are you sure no one followed you?'

Willie looked exasperated. 'Who d'ye think I am, Geordie Douglas?'

George smiled. Willie was a first-class agent, because not only was he alert and nimble but it was scarcely likely that anyone would suspect him.

'Let's sit down . . . away from the path . . . here where the trees are thickest. Then we shall hear anyone approaching. And speak low. Voices carry.'

'Ye dinna need to tell *me* that!'

'No, Willie, but we have to be very careful. If the plan fails how can we say what they might do to her?'

'Oh ay,' Willie agreed.

When they were seated, George said: 'Listen carefully; we are going to send a large box to the Queen, purporting to come from Melville. We will load it with some heavy substances – perhaps stones – and we shall say it contains articles

72

and documents for the Queen. You must tell her that this box is to arrive shortly, and when it comes she is to take out the contents and hide them, and after a few days we must ask for the box to be returned to Melville. When the box is taken out of the castle, she will be in it.'

Willie stared at George and his light eyes suddenly crinkled with amusement. Willie held his sides and began to shake, giving a display of uncontrollable mirth.

'What is it?' said George impatiently.

'It's just that *you* make me laugh, Geordie Douglas.'

'This is no laughing matter.'

'That's were you're wrong. It was one laughing matter when you planned escape by boat and then go sniffing around till Drysdale says: "Now why would wee Georgie be taking such interest in the boat?" And this box is another.'

'It is not for you to laugh at your elders . . . and betters, Willie.'

'Oh ay,' said Willie mockingly disconsolate.

'All you have to do is to tell the Queen our intentions. I cannot say when the box will arrive, but you must come and tell me when it is to be sent back. Then I shall be ready for her . . . and I shall not be alone. We shall have horses waiting for her.'

Willie sat silently nodding. 'You understand?' said George impatiently.

'Oh ay,' repeated Willie. 'I understand. The box goes in . . . and Lady Douglas and Sir William watch it unloaded. "What lovely stones!" cries my lady. "What is the Queen's new pastime to be? Throwing stones from the keep windows on the sentinels?" '

'We have to arrange that the box arrives when Sir William is not there.'

'If Sir William is not there, someone else will be. Hoch, man, dinna ye know that our Queen is a prisoner and that everything that goes into her apartments is watched and ferreted over. Talk sense, Geordie Douglas. You wouldna get farther than the castle courtyard before they'd see through your game with boxes. Nay, Geordie Douglas, think again.'

George was silent. It was true that he had put forward one or two grandiose schemes which Lords Seton and Semphill had thought impracticable. The trouble with George was that he saw himself as a knight who was ready to die for his Queen; he would have preferred to go boldly to the castle and fight his way through to her. Lord Seton had said that it was subterfuge which was needed. Those who could best help the Queen would be crafty spies rather than bold knights.

And now even Willie was scorning his latest plan, and George had to admit that there was a great deal in what the boy said.

'I thought of something,' said Willie. ''Tis a better plan than yours, because it could work. It was when I watched the laundresses bringing out the dirty linen that I thought of it. You know the shawls they wear . . . some of them . . . over the head and gripped round the shoulders . . . and they carry the bundles of linen on one shoulder. Well, I thought to myself, Who counts them that goes in? Is it four or five? Who'd know if six came out?'

'What's this?' cried George.

'Your Queen would have to wear a laundress's shawl; she'd have to carry her bundle. I reckon Geordie Douglas would think that was summat a Queen shouldna' do . . . even if it meant she got her freedom by doing it.'

George's eyes began to sparkle. Willie's scheme was so simple. And yet Lord Seton had said that they needed a plan that was too simple to be suspected.

He gripped Willie's arm. 'There may be something in this.'

'May be, George Douglas? I tell you there is summat in it all right.'

'When do the laundresses come?' George asked.

'This day week.'

'We'll arrange that two whom we can trust shall be with them. Willie, you're a bright boy.'

'Thank ye, George Douglas.'

'I am going to make plans to carry out your idea. You go back and, at the first opportunity, tell the Queen what we hope to do. Be here the day after tomorrow and I will give you instructions. The Queen shall walk out of the castle with the laundresses. Now Willie . . . go. And for the love of God take care.'

'Oh ay,' said Willie; and whistling shrilly he went to the shores of the lake where he waited for a boat that was going to the castle to carry him back.

* * *

'Oh, Seton,' whispered the Queen. 'This could be successful. If I escape I shall send for you as soon as possible.'

'Do not think of that now,' said Seton; 'think only of the

part you must play. Do not speak, whatever happens. It must succeed, for it will all be over in fifteen minutes. Out of the castle . . . into the boat . . . and then across to the mainland. There your friends will be waiting for you with horses. You will always be grateful to these Douglas boys.'

'Give me the shawl. There! Is that right? How do I look?'

'So tall, so regal. Could you stoop a little? The bundle you carry will help. Let me pull the shawl forward so that your face is hidden. Like that . . . no one would guess.'

The two laundresses came to the door of the apartment then.

'The bundles are ready,' said Seton.

The two women came in. They were not the usual laundresses but two who had taken the place of those whose custom it was to come to the castle. They looked at the tall shawled figure with some apprehension.

'She will walk between you when you go out,' said Seton. 'Go straight down through the courtyard to the boat, and do not speak to her, yet try not to give the impression that she is any different from the rest of you.'

The women nodded and the Queen watched the way in which they carried their bundles and tried to imitate them.

The moment had come. She followed them down the stairs, and out through the courtyard. At the castle gate young Willie Douglas stood idly watching the boat and the oarsmen.

He began to whistle; then he turned and went into the castle.

*　　*　　*

The two oarsmen were talking together. They were young, and while they had waited they had been on the look out for any comely serving girl who might appear. There were usually one or two who made some excuse to come out of the castle when they were about.

They were telling each other of their latest conquests trying to cap each other's stories to prove their virility.

'These laundresses are a poor lot,' one bewailed. 'I remember one pretty laundress I used to row over. . . . Ah, she was a beauty.'

They exchanged stories about the saucy laundress until one of them said: 'Here they come. You're right . . . a poor lot.'

'Their ankles get thick through too much standing at the washtub,' agreed the other. 'And their hands are rougher than an ordinary serving girl's.'

'That's true.'

75

The women were preparing to step into the boat, while the connoisseurs of women watched them without much interest. It was true, they were thinking, that standing at the washtub thickened the ankles.

One of them caught his breath as a laundress stepped into the boat; then he saw that his companion had noticed too. What a pair of ankles! As neat and slim as any Court lady's. It was not true then that all ankles were thickened at the washtub.

Two pairs of eyes travelled up that slim body which, although enveloped in its shawl, they saw was comely. This woman was taller than the rest and the shawl was wrapped so closely about her head that it was impossible to see her face. She almost dropped her bundle as she stepped into the boat, and one of the other women put out a hand to steady her and there she was, throwing down her bundle and pulling the shawl even more tightly across her face as though she suffered from a toothache.

'I wonder if her face is as pretty as her ankles?'

'I'd like to find out.'

'I mean to ... before we put them ashore.'

They had put only a short distance between them and the island, when the bolder of the two men called: 'Hey, my beauty.'

The tall woman did not look in their direction, but kept her eyes steadily fixed on the mainland.

The man leaned forward to seize her shawl and when, as he jerked it, with a little cry of protest she put out a hand to prevent his snatching it, the hand attracted even more attention than the ankles; it was very white; the fingers were long, the nails the shape of a perfect filbert nut. It was the hand of one who had never done a day's washing in her life.

The two men stared in amazement at the hand before it was hastily hidden within the folds of the shawl; then one of them grasped the shawl in both his hands and sought to pull it away; now two white hands were visible – equally perfect, as in grim desperation they gripped the shawl, holding it up to her face.

But she was of course no match for the oarsman; in a few seconds he had ripped off the shawl and was looking into the flushed face of the Queen.

There was an immediate silence. The laundresses looked on open-mouthed; the oarsmen were speechless.

Then Mary spoke. 'Continue to row,' she ordered. 'Take the boat to the mainland. You will not regret it if you do.'

One oarsman scratched his head and regarded the other.

'That is a command,' Mary continued imperiously. 'If you do not obey me your lives are in peril. I am the Queen.'

The second oarsman said: 'I'm sorry, Madam, but it would be more than our lives are worth to take you to the mainland now.'

'It will be more than your lives are worth to take me back to the castle!'

'We canna do it, Madam.'

'Why not?'

'Our orders are to carry the laundresses . . . and only they.'

'But I have given you orders, and I am the Queen.'

The men were still perplexed.

'Come,' persisted Mary, 'I am in a hurry.'

But the oarsmen continued to look at each other. 'They'd take us prisoner,' whispered one. 'They'd cut us into collops—'

'I would reward you,' Mary began, but even so she saw the futility of pleading with them, for what were the promised rewards of a captive Queen worth?

'We'd like to do it, Madam,' said the first oarsman.

'But daren't,' added the second. 'Turn the boat, lad. We must row her back to the castle.'

As the two men applied themselves to their oars, Mary cried in desperation: 'I beg of you, have pity on me.'

But they would not look at her. There was that about her which could make them weaken, and they had their lives to think of.

'We've got to take you back, Madam,' one of them said, 'but we'll say nothing to Sir William. If no one's missed you . . . there'll be no one to know —'

Mary was almost weeping with frustration. The plan had so nearly succeeded. And when would there be another chance?

She could not bear to look at the island. Is there no hope? she was asking herself. Does everything I attempt have to end in failure?

It seemed so. For at the landing stage Sir William, who had seen the boat returning, was waiting to know the reason why.

There was a grim purpose in his eyes as he helped her ashore.

*　　*　　*

77

When the Queen was safely in her apartments Sir William went to his mother and told her what had happened.

Lady Douglas was shocked. 'And what would Jamie have said if this had succeeded?' she asked.

'He would have *said* little, as is his custom,' replied Sir William grimly, 'but his actions would have been far from insignificant. This must never be allowed to happen again. It points to one thing. There is a traitor in the castle and I am going to find out who it is. I have a shrewd idea.'

'You cannot blame George now.'

'But indeed I do blame George. George is involved in this. You may be sure of that. George is on the mainland with Seton and Semphill . . . and certain others. They were waiting there to receive her. Don't you see the importance of this? By God, there might have been civil war – and George . . . your son George would have been responsible.'

'He is your brother,' Lady Douglas reminded him.

'I'm afraid young Willie has also had a hand in this. He goes to and from the mainland at will. He gambles with the soldiers. Where does he get the money with which to gamble?'

'Oh, Willie's a sharp one. There are several ways in which he could get money, I dare swear.'

'I intend to find out.'

Sir William strode to the door and called to a servant. 'Find Willie and bring him to me without delay,' he ordered.

Lady Douglas left him. There would be trouble, Willie would doubtless be beaten, and she did not want to witness such a scene.

Willie came boldly into Sir William's presence. Willie was not perturbed. He had believed that Sir William was his father and that he must have had a special fondness for his mother to allow him to be brought up in the castle.

'Come here, boy,' said Sir William blandly.

Willie approached lightheartedly, and as he did so Sir William shot out an arm and gripped his shoulder.

'What do you know of this attempt of the Queen's to escape?'

'Oh,' said Willie, 'I know a lot. I saw her go out. She looked like the others . . . only taller. I saw her get into the boat and them row her away.'

'I mean how much did you know *before* it happened?'

Willie looked puzzled. 'What should I have known before it happened, Sir William?'

'You knew there was a plot for her escape, did you not?'

'I reckon there's been lots of plots.'

Sir William went on: 'You gamble with the soldiers. Where do you find the money?'

'An odd job here and there brings its reward,' said Willie, slightly less truculent than usual.

Sir William took the boy by the shoulders and shook him until his freckled face was scarlet. 'George Douglas gave you the money, did he not? You have been to see George Douglas on the mainland. You keep him informed of what is happening in the castle, do you not?'

Willie was silent. Sir William, who was not a violent man, was now a frightened one, and Willie's stubborn silence alarmed him further.

He threw the boy across the room. Willie fell, knocking his head against a table. He felt the warm blood on his face, and as he picked himself up he was looking for the door. But Sir William was not prepared to let him go. He strode towards him and said in a quiet voice: 'If you do not tell me all you know, I will give you the severest whipping you have ever had in your life.'

'It's that I don't know much, Sir William,' Willie began, but Sir William struck him again and this was no light blow. Willie felt as though the floor was coming up to meet him. He clenched his teeth together, and unfortunately Sir William noticed this and knew it meant that Willie was determined to let no secrets escape him.

'You've been seeing George Douglas,' he said. 'You've been acting as a spy in the castle. The reward of spying is death. Did you know?'

Willie did not answer.

'What other plans are there?' Sir William demanded.

Willie whispered: 'I don't know, Sir William.'

'You've been seeing George though. George gave you the money?'

Willie thought quickly. What harm could he do by admitting that? They knew that George was on the mainland. It was obvious that they would have met. He could not do harm by admitting that he had seen George and that it was George who had given him money. All he must do was deny his part in the laundress plan, for Sir William would say that if he had helped once, he would do so again, and then, when the time came to put another plan into action, he would be a suspected person.

'I did see George,' he said.

'And he gave you money. Why?'

'Because he likes me,' answered Willie promptly.

'And you convey messages from him to the Queen?'

'Messages . . .?' began Willie and clenched his teeth again.

Sir William's anger was dying. There was something appealing about the boy; but he knew that he had been acting as a spy; he knew that he was as dangerous as George had been. He could not afford to have Willie in the castle.

He liked the boy's boldness; his refusal to betray his part in this was admirable – or would have been if he had been on the right side. But this was too important a matter to allow sentiment to get in the way of common sense.

Sir William put his hand into his pocket, and brought out a gold coin. He held this out to Willie who looked at it in amazement.

'Take it,' said Sir William. 'You may need it.'

Willie took it in his grubby hand.

'And now,' said Sir William, 'you will get out. This castle is no longer your home.'

Willie stared at Sir William disbelievingly, but the man would not meet his eye.

'Get out,' continued Sir William. 'Get out while you're still alive, you imp of Satan. Get out of my castle. Get off my island. We don't harbour those who spy against us.'

Willie went to the door, clutching the gold coin; an impulse came to him to turn and plead with Sir William, to ask him to remember that this was his home. But he would not do it. He held his head high and walked out of the room and out of the castle to the shores of the lake.

He called to the old boatman who worked the ferry.

'Row me over to the mainland,' he said.

'I don't know as I will,' was the answer.

'You should, you know,' retorted Willie. 'It's Sir William's order. You're to row me across and leave me on the other side.'

Then he stepped into the boat, and not once did he turn to look back at the castle; his eyes were fixed on the mainland, on the woods. Not far away, he was thinking, was George.

*　　*　　*

The Queen was in despair. Not only had she lost George but Willie also.

There were new restrictions, and Sir William had ordered that one or two of the female members of his household must share the Queen's room, so that she had no chance of making plots with her women. This meant that one or more of his sisters were in constant attendance; they were beautiful and naturally amiable women but they had been warned that they must act as spies.

They would come into the apartment and sit with the Queen, Seton, Jane Kennedy and Marie Courcelles while they all worked on the tapestry. It meant that conversation must be guarded for any remarks likely to arouse suspicion were reported to Sir William.

Mary had not felt so hopeless since those early days of her incarceration and she thought longingly of that period when she had been able to see George Douglas and be assured of his devotion; she thought sadly of Willie who amused her with his quaint ways but who had inspired her with hope as much as had the romantic George.

One day another member of the Douglas family came to her room presumably, thought Mary, for the purpose of spying on her. This was a young woman who had married Lady Douglas's son Robert and was therefore a Douglas only through marriage; Mary was inclined to like her the better for that. She was modest and a little apologetic.

'Your Majesty, I am Christian, wife of Robert Douglas. My father was the Master of Buchanan.'

'But of course,' said Mary pleasantly, 'I could not forget the Countess of Buchanan who was once betrothed to my half-brother.'

As the Countess flushed slightly Mary remembered that Christian had no reason to love Moray.

'Welcome to my apartments,' went on Mary. 'I trust you will not find them as dreary as I do.'

'Your Majesty is a prisoner and that is why you hate your prison. It grieves me that I should be a member of that family who are your jailors.'

'Thank you for those words. Come, sit down. Are you fond of needlework?'

'Yes, Your Majesty.'

'Then take a look at our work. I think we shall make it into a screen.'

'It is very beautiful,' murmured Christian.

'It is our great pleasure to work on it,' Mary told her. 'There is something so satisfying about tapestry. It lives on after us . . . and consider, in years to come people will say: "That is what Mary Queen of Scots did while she was a prisoner in Lochleven." '

'Let us hope, Your Majesty, that they will say: "The Queen started it in her prison of Lochleven but completed it in the royal apartments at Edinburgh Castle or Holyrood House." '

Certainly Christian was more sympathetic than Lady Douglas's daughters, thought Mary; and she was not wrong when she surmised that she might be an ally.

Very often Mary was alone with her, and on one of these occasions Christian said: 'I shall never forget the time when Sir William was in disgrace with Your Majesty. The Earl of Moray was in England and you sent word to Lochleven that Sir William and his family were to surrender the castle and leave Scotland within six hours.'

Mary nodded, remembering the occasion well. They had tried to prevent her marriage with Darnley, and at that time she had been very eager for the marriage. Moray had taken up arms against her, and of course the Douglases were, as ever, firmly beside him in all he did.

'It was a terrible day when we heard the news,' went on Christian. 'I was in labour with my first child, and the thought of leaving the castle was alarming. Sir William had had to take to his bed with sickness.'

'I remember,' said Mary. She had been sceptical of Sir William's illness but there had been no doubt that the Countess of Buchanan was in childbed.

'And you gave orders that we might remain,' went on Christian. 'All you asked was that the surety of the castle should be at your command. I shall never forget the relief. And I shall never forget my gratitude to Your Majesty.'

'Naturally,' said Mary quickly, 'I should not have thought of turning you out at such a time. But Sir William does not feel equally grateful, I am sure. He has little pity for my plight and thinks only to serve my ambitious brother.'

'Your Majesty . . .' Christian looked over her shoulder . . . 'you may know something of my story. If that is so, you will understand that I feel no great desire to serve your ambitious brother.'

'I know,' Mary told her, 'that you were once betrothed to

82

him and that he forsook you for Agnes Keith, the daughter of the Earl Marischal.'

'A match more to his liking!' retorted Christian meaningfully. 'But that was of no moment. Matches which are made for us in our youth often come to nothing. But I was also his ward, and I was an heiress. He was not eager for marriage with me, seeing a more advantageous one elsewhere, but at the same time he did not mean to lose my fortune. I think he was rather sorry that there was no convent into which he could force me. So he sent me here to his family, and in this castle of Lochleven, Your Majesty, I was as much a prisoner as you are now.'

'My poor Christian! I fear I have thought so constantly of my own woes that I have given little thought to those of others.'

'Your Majesty is well known for your generous heart. And my plight was made less hard by the sympathy of Lady Douglas, who, although she would serve her bastard son, is always ready to be kind to those in distress, providing of course that in doing so she does not go too much against the wishes of Moray. Even so, she is ready to risk a little . . . as in my case. When Robert and I fell in love she helped us to marry . . . and she did not let Moray know what had happened until we had gone through the ceremony.'

'So then there was nothing he could do about it!'

'Oh yes, Your Majesty, he is always resourceful. That is why he has reached his present position. He still kept me a prisoner at Lochleven and he has taken my fortune from me. So here I remain – no longer an heiress – dependent on the bounty of the Douglases because I am Robert's wife.'

Mary was silent. Then she said thoughtfully: 'It is a marvel to me that I always believed so firmly in the goodness of my half-brother. It is only now that I have time for reflection that I see him in his true light. Again and again he has stood against me; then when he was in my presence, his calmness and his appearance of stern devotion to duty deceived me. It will do so no longer; one of my greatest enemies in Scotland today is my own half-brother, Regent Moray.'

'But Your Majesty has good friends. The Setons, and the Flemings are with you. And the Huntleys in the North.'

'The Setons and Flemings have always been my good friends. Mary Seton and Mary Fleming were brought up as my sisters. Then there is Lord Semphill who married Mary

Livingstone, another of my Marys, and he is also on my side.'

'And I understand, Your Majesty, that Lord Semphill, with Lord Seton, is not far off at this moment. I do not doubt that they often look towards your prison from the mainland.'

'It's a comforting thought.'

'Then you have friends abroad.'

'The King of France greatly desired to marry me,' mused Mary. 'I am certain that he would help if he could; but he is ruled by his mother, Catherine de' Medici, and she never liked me.'

'Yet no Queen is happy to see another in captivity. It is an insult to royalty, which they must needs resent.'

'If I could but write to them . . . if I could but make them see my humiliation and the indignity of my position. . . .'

'I am sure Your Majesty's eloquence would move them to pity.'

'I have no means of writing. No writing materials. They have been taken from me. I have no means of conveying letters to my friends.'

Christian was silent, and Mary picked up her tapestry and began to work with a desperate concentration.

But the next day when Christian came to see her she brought writing materials.

'Your Majesty must have a care that you are not seen with these,' she said. 'But if you wrote your letters I could see that they are delivered to a reliable messenger. They do not watch me, you see. They do not fear that I shall escape. Here I have my home and my family . . . and my fortune is already Moray's.'

How quickly hope was ready to spring up. The Queen sat at her window looking out over the lake. She had lost George and Willie, and now Fate had offered her Christian.

Charles of France would help her. She knew he would because he had loved her with all the force of his strange, twisted nature; although he was much younger than she was his jealous rage, when she had married his brother François, had been alarming to behold.

But he was entirely ruled by the mother whom he feared, and Mary knew that any letter she sent to Charles would first pass through his mother's hands. So there was only one thing to do. She must write to Catherine de' Medici and try to arouse in her the indignation all queens must feel for insulted royalty. She must hope that the Queen would show her letter to her

son; and then the King of France would long to come to her
aid.

There were few moments when it was safe to bring out
those writing materials, and she had to wait her chance.
But it came at last, and Seton and Jane kept watch while she
sat at her table and wrote.

Her appeal was pathetic.

'. . . I am so closely guarded that I have no leisure but
when they are at dinner or sleeping, when I rise stealthily,
for their girls lie with me. This bearer will tell you all. I entreat you to give him credit and reward him as you love me.
I implore you both to have pity upon me for unless you take
me hence by force, I shall never come out, I am certain.
But if you will send troops all Scotland would revolt from
Moray and Morton on perceiving you took the matter in
earnest . . .'

She sealed the letter. And when Christian came to her apartments next day she took it and assured the Queen that it
should be dispatched to France at the earliest possible moment.

*   *   *

How long the waiting seemed! How long before she realized
how foolish she had been! To have written to Catherine de'
Medici, to expect help from her, surely showed how blind she
had become. The woman had hated her from the moment they
had first met when Mary was a child and she, the neglected
wife of Henri Deux, was taking second place to the dazzling
Diane de Poitiers.

Why should Mary expect help now when she was alone and
helpless? But it was in her nature to dream of the impossible
and, if it were pleasant enough, imagine it would come true.

She could picture the slow smile on that flat, expressionless
face as Catherine de' Medici read her appeal. She could hear
the sudden loud laughter which she had always found so
unattractive.

Young Charles would never see the letter.

How foolish to have hoped for succour from that direction!
But for what else could she hope? She was only in her twenties. Was she to spend the rest of her life in the dreary island
fortress of Lochleven?

The waters of the lake had begun to have a great fascination
for her. They were dappled now with April sunshine. Spring

was here but it brought her little hope. George was lost to her. She had not realized until she had lost him how much he had done to make her life tolerable.

When she sat at her window looking down on the lake, she began to picture herself walking there and letting the water lap about her ankles (those ankles which had betrayed she was no laundress to the observant and lecherous boatmen) and not pausing but walking on and on until the whole of her body was submerged in the water of the lake.

She would not struggle for life, for what had life to offer her? She would eagerly embrace death because she was weary and hope had fled.

But that was folly; it was sinful. Whatever happened she must go on living; hope would return to comfort her; it had never deserted her for long.

*   *   *

Sir William and Lady Douglas were alone in the latter's apartment and on a table before them lay a letter which they had both perused with some concern.

It was from George, who wrote that he realized there was nothing for him in Scotland, since he had ruined his hopes of advancement, and he planned to leave for France where he hoped to make his fortune. Before he left, however, he wished to see his family. Would Sir William be prepared to receive him at Lochleven? He merely wished to say goodbye and would be gone within an hour. But he had a great desire to see his mother as he did not know when they would meet again.

'Of course he must come!' cried Lady Douglas. 'I cannot agree, William, that he should be allowed to go to France without saying goodbye to his mother.'

'All this time,' Sir William murmured, 'he has been in the Kinross area. He will have been with Seton, Fleming, Semphill and the rest. How do we know that this is not yet another plot?'

'Nonsense!' snapped Lady Douglas. 'He is going to France. How could he plot from there? He says he will not remain more than an hour. I insist on his coming. He is my son, William, as much as you are.'

'And have you thought what your other son might have to say if he knew George had come back after he had banished him?'

'Jamie need never know,' retorted Lady Douglas compla-

86

cently. 'Or if he does, it will then be too late for him to protest, for George will be in France by that time. It is a sad
thing when a mother must plead to be allowed to say goodbye
to her son.'

At length William gave way and replied to George's letter
that they would see him at the castle.

George arrived half an hour before supper and was received
with tearful embraces by his mother, and even William was
not unmoved. There had always been deep family feeling
among the Douglases; and William, being really fond of his
young brother, sincerely deplored the fact that he had made
what he called a fool of himself over a woman – not that
William could not understand that.

'Come along in, my dear son,' cried Lady Douglas. 'Come
to my own private chamber. I have much to say to you. You
come also, William.'

When they were alone, Lady Douglas looked in consternation at her younger son. He was thin, she declared. How had
he been living since he left the castle? She had suffered many
a sleepless night on his account.

George told her she was not to worry. He was well able to
take care of himself, for he was not a boy any longer.

'I suppose,' said William, 'you have been with Seton and
Semphill on the mainland?'

George nodded.

'And you've been within a stone's throw of the island, I'll
swear.'

'Where else did you expect me to be?'

'And you were in that plot to smuggle her out as a laundress, I'm certain.'

'You should not feel so disgruntled about it, brother. It
failed.'

'And might so easily have succeeded,' growled William.

'Don't you see,' said George, 'the matter is hopeless. That is
why I want to get away to France.'

Sir William was pensive. He was thinking: Out of sight, out
of mind. He is no longer so enamoured of his Queen. He is
weary of the plots and subterfuge. Well, he was but a boy
suffering from the pangs of calf-love.

'Look here,' he said, 'your mother does not wish you to
leave Scotland.'

'Oh, George,' cried Lady Douglas, 'stay in Scotland. I am
sure that Jamie would give you some position with him . . . if

87

you could only assure him that you would serve him faithfully.'

'He is, after all, your brother,' added Sir William.

'I do not think Moray will ever be my friend again,' said George. 'No, it is better for me to get right away. Perhaps in a year or so I shall return and by that time Moray may have forgiven me. But I think it best now that I go to France.'

Lady Douglas continued to persuade and Sir William joined with her; but George shook his head and at length they realized that he had made up his mind.

As it was supper time, Lady Douglas said that George must take the meal with them. George said he would be delighted to join them, and so once more he took his place at the supper table.

He noticed the keys beside William's plate, and William followed his gaze.

'We have been doubly careful since the attempted escape,' he told his brother, 'As all the guards are off duty during mealtimes, when they come to table I lock the castle gates and the Queen's apartments, and during that time the keys are never out of my sight.'

'Ah,' said George, 'you had a good warning, brother. You were nearly caught once. I'll warrant you will not be so easily caught again.'

Sir William drank freely of the wine which the page had poured into his goblet. He was feeling sad, partly because he was wearying of his commission to guard the Queen, and partly because he was saying goodbye to his young brother.

'No,' he said firmly, 'it shall not happen again. We're determined on that. We watch her night and day. She would not now be able to slip out of the castle in the guise of a laundress. Everyone who leaves is closely scrutinized.'

'William,' said George, 'there is one request I would make to you before I go. I trust you will grant it.'

'I will if it is in my power to do so.'

'It concerns young Willie.'

'That young rogue!'

'Oh, not such a rogue, William. I admit he worked with me. I gave him money . . . and he was always my friend, as you know. We were like brothers.'

Sir William nodded.

'You cannot blame him for doing what I asked him to '

'So you admit you asked him to help you.'

'I do. You should blame me for what happened . . . not Willie.'

'You might have caused God knows what damage between you. You weren't rescuing a lady in distress, brother. You were freeing a Queen and preparing to start a civil war.'

'I know. I know. I was young . . . so was Willie. It was my fault. But I ask you not to blame Willie. He has been with me since he left the castle. What will happen to him, think you, when I go to France?'

'You're taking him with you?'

'That was not my plan. I am going to ask you to take him back into the castle. He can do no harm; I shall be in France, so there'll be no temptation to. He's sharp but he's too young to roam the country by himself. He'd starve to death or fall in with robbers. William, will you take young Willie back?'

Sir William hesitated. He would not have admitted it, but he had often thought of the engaging lad, and he was secretly pleased to have an opportunity of bringing him back.

He pulled at his beard. 'Well . . .' he began, and tried to make excuses for his leniency. ''Tis true the fellow who now serves me at table is a clumsy loon.'

'So you will? I thank you, William. Now I can go with an easy mind.'

George did justice to the food on the table. Not at all, as Lady Douglas said afterwards to Sir William, like a lovesick young man.

Afterwards they conducted him to the boat, for in spite of his seeming indifference Sir William could not run the risk of his seeing the Queen.

No harm had been done. He had been with George all the time he had been in the castle, and even Moray could not take exception to that.

He stood with Lady Douglas beside him watching until the boat reached the mainland.

'Did you notice,' he said to his mother, 'that George did not once look up to the keep?'

'I did. Jamie was right to banish him for a while for the trick has worked. But how I wish that he could now come back to Lochleven.'

*   *   *

The soldiers whose duty it was to guard the Queen found the days somewhat monotonous. The importance of their task was continually being pointed out to them, but that did not alter the dullness of their duties which consisted of standing in one spot for a number of hours, or pacing back and forth a few paces each way.

They were continually thinking of ways to pass the time. Gambling was a favourite occupation; another was rough horseplay; and one of the favourite games was what they called 'liberating the Queen'. In order to play this they divided themselves into two sides and had a mock battle, using lumps of turf, for ammunition, with which they pelted each other.

This game caused great amusement, not only to themselves but to watchers in the castle. Serving men and maids would call from the windows urging on this side or that, and sometimes they would even take part in the mock battle.

Even Will Drysdale, the commander of the garrison, found the game irresistible, and one day to make the battle more realistic he fired a hackbut, which mistakenly he believed to be loaded with powder only, into a group of the 'enemy'.

The result was that two of the men were wounded in their thighs, so what had begun as a game turned out to be a serious matter.

Mary, who had been watching from her window, immediately sent her French apothecary down to see what he could do to help.

The two wounded men were carried into the castle and their wounds dressed; but when the apothecary returned to his mistress he was thoughtful.

'A sorry end to their play,' the Queen remarked.

The apothecary grunted.

'It would seem you do not agree with me?' went on the Queen, astonished.

'Your Majesty,' answered the apothecary, 'I noticed that one of these men is he who is in charge of the boats.'

'He is badly wounded?'

The man lifted his shoulders. 'His wound will incapacitate him for some time, Your Majesty.'

Mary understood his meaning and she sighed. It might have been important when George and Willie had been in the castle. They might have devised some plan. But now, who was there to help her? Sir William had redoubled his precautions. There were always soldiers on guard except at meal times when she was locked in her apartments and the castle gates were also kept locked; and Sir William never let the keys out of his sight.

That accident to the boatman might have been significant and advantageous when George and Willie were in the castle.

A few days later Willie returned to Lochleven.

* * *

It was the first of May. This should be a joyous time of the year. In the past Mary had ridden out with her courtiers dressed in green to go a-maying. Such occasions only served to bring home more bitterly the plight to which she had been reduced.

The sun shone into her room and, rising from her bed, slipping on her robe, Mary went to her prie-Dieu and there knelt, with her hair streaming about her shoulders while she prayed for what now would seem like a miracle.

When she rose she felt exhilarated and, as those members of the Douglas family who shared her bedchamber were still sleeping, she went into the small ante-room and, cautiously taking out her writing materials from where she had hidden them, began to write.

This letter was addressed to Elizabeth of England, and she was making an appeal for help.

'From Lochleven this first of May, [she wrote] Madame, my good sister, the length of my weary imprisonment and the wrongs I have received from those on whom I conferred so many benefits are less annoying to me than not having it in my power to acquaint you with the reality of my calamities and the injuries which have been done to me in various ways. Therefore, I have found means to send you a line by a faithful servant. . . .'

She paused and listened. There was no sound from the adjoining chamber. She thought of those days at the Court of France when she had heard that Mary of England was dead and when her uncles, the Guises, and her father-in-law Henri Deux had insisted that she claim the title of Queen of England. Elizabeth would not be very pleased about that. Yet she could not hold it against her now. She must understand that it had been no wish of Mary's to claim a title which was not hers.

'. . . I implore you, on receiving this letter, to have compassion on your good sister and cousin, and believe that you have not a more affectionate relative in the world. . . .'

91

When she had finished the letter she signed it 'Your obliged and affectionate good sister and cousin, Mary R.'

She sealed it and, carefully putting away her writing materials, went quietly back to her bed, noticing that her jailors were still sleeping.

When Christian came to her she would give her the letter, and Christian had promised that it should be smuggled across to the mainland and given to a trustworthy messenger.

Would the English Queen be so incensed by the indignity done to royalty that she would offer help? Or would she smile and say: This was the woman who once called herself the Queen of England!

. Mary, who quickly forgot grudges she had once borne, gave Elizabeth the credit for sharing her forgiving nature. So she was hopeful on that sunny May morning.

Later in the day when she walked with Seton down to the lake's edge she saw a boy near the boats, and as she approached he looked up giving her a frank grin.

Mary cried in sudden pleasure: 'Why, it's Willie Douglas.'

'Back now in the castle, Your Majesty,' said Willie, looking about him searchingly. He went on: 'Walk on, Your Majesty, and don't appear to be talking to me. But I have something to say and I've been waiting the opportunity. But pass on, please, and come back. When you do, I'll be lying in this boat and no one will see me. Stop close by and listen to what I have to say.'

The Queen and Seton walked on. Willie watched for a second or two and then busied himself with the boat. After five minutes or so the Queen and Seton came back to the spot. Willie was now lying in the boat and out of sight from the castle.

'Is there anyone within earshot?' he asked.

'No,' answered Seton.

The Queen sat down on the grass and Seton sat with her.

'Listen,' said Willie. 'We're going to free you any hour now. You must be prepared for when I come for you. Lord Seton and Lord Semphill are on the other side of the lake . . . and George is with them. All I have to do is to get you out of the castle.'

Mary said. 'Now . . .?'

'No, no. If you as much as stepped into a boat you'd have the garrison out. You're being watched at this moment. You're never out of their sight. We wouldn't stand a chance. You must not stay here too long or they'll be suspicious. Rise now and stand for a few minutes looking at the mainland while I tell you the plan. It'll be tomorrow. I shall try to get the keys while they're at supper. You will be dressed as one of your maids. . . . I shall come to you. The boat will be ready . . . I can arrange that, now that the boatman is injured. You will follow me out of the castle. I shall lock the gates behind us. I will give you the word. Be prepared.'

'But how can it be done, Willie?' demanded Mary desperately.

'Only while they are at supper. It is the only time they are not on guard. I must find some means of getting the keys from Sir William. If I could do that we could be out of the castle before they realize it. And once on the mainland, your friends will be waiting with fleet horses. They are waiting now. I have come back to do this. I have sworn I can do it, and I will.'

'If only you can!'

'I must do it soon . . . while the boatman is sick. If only Drysdale were sick too! He is the one I fear. Do not linger here any longer. Walk on now. It would be the end of the plan if they began to watch me too closely now.'

'Come Seton,' said Mary. 'Bless you, Willie. I will be watchful . . . and ready when you come.'

When they had left Willie lying in the boat, he stared up at the blue sky, his light eyes screwed up in concentration. He *must* do it. He had boasted to George and all those grown-up lords that he would. But how was he going to spirit those keys away from Sir William?

He waited on him at table, and so had those keys under his eyes all the time the company was at the meal. Sir William kept them by his plate so that every second he could assure himself of their safety.

How could he get those keys into his possession while the guards were at table? When he had heard the plan it had not seemed an insuperable difficulty. How different was the reality.

* * *

Now that Willie had inspired her with hope, Mary's optimism had returned. She knew that, across that small strip of water, friends were waiting for her. Surely it was not impossible to slip across to them.

At any moment Willie might be ready for her. She must be prepared. This time there must be attention to detail. When she thought of how easily she might have escaped with the

93

laundresses she was ashamed of her inability to play her part for such a short time.

She sent for Will Drysdale. She had an idea of luring him away from the castle, which might possibly work. There was one thing she had noticed about Will Drysdale, and that was his love of gambling. Therefore, she reasoned, money would tempt him. He was loyal to his masters so bribery was no use. She must use other methods.

When he came to her presence she said: 'I called you because, although it may seem strange to you, I am grateful to you. You have been appointed commander of this garrison which keeps me prisoner, but I do not hold that against you because in your dealings with me you have always been kindly and respectful.'

Drysdale bowed; he was a little under the spell of the Queen and he often regretted that his duty made it necessary for him to have her watched so closely.

'I want to reward you with a small gift. It is not as much as I would wish but, as you doubtless know, many of my possessions have been taken from me.'

'Your Majesty is good to her humble servant.'

'I have no money here, but if you will take this draft to my state treasurer in Edinburgh he will honour it. And I have a list here of articles of which I am in dire need. Good Master Drysdale, would you please bring these to me with as much speed as you can muster?'

Drysdale's eyes gleamed. It was pleasant to have the money and do a service to this beautiful woman at the same time.

'He bowed. 'Your Majesty can rest assured that I shall do my utmost to bring you what you desire as quickly as possible. And I thank you for your kindness to your servant.'

Mary gave him a dazzling smile and he bowed himself from her presence.

She was delighted less than an hour later to hear him giving orders to his men, and from her windows she saw him rowing across the lake to the mainland. Will Drysdale had left for Edinburgh, and he would consequently be absent from Lochleven for some little time.

Willie too had seen the departure of Will Drysdale and heard from some of the men that their commander was making a trip to Edinburgh.

The boatman incapacitated; the commander absent from the castle; assuredly the moment had come.

94

But how to make Sir William so bemused by wine that his keys could be stolen from him? That was the question.

* * *

Sir William was dozing in his chair. He had eaten well and the sun was warm. In his pocket were the keys of the castle; even though the guards were on duty he kept one hand on them as he slept.

'Sir William?'

He opened his eyes; Willie was standing before him.

'What is it?' asked Sir William.

'Sir William, I want your permission to give a feast.'

'What!' cried Sir William.

'To everyone in the castle . . . everyone,' explained Willie. 'I've been away and now I'm home again. It is something I rejoice in, and I would have everyone rejoice with me.'

Sir William's mouth twitched slightly. In spite of an effort to repress his feelings he could never quite do so where this boy was concerned, and he was secretly delighted to know that he was back in the castle. The page who had waited on him at table was a clumsy oaf, he always said; he was more critical of him than he might have been because he missed Willie.

Now he said: '*You* give a feast? How would you manage that?'

'I have money, Sir William. George gave it to me when he said goodbye.'

'And when do you propose to have this feast?'

'Today.'

'On a Sunday!'

'A good day for a good deed,' said Willie raising his eyes piously. 'I have already had meat and vegetables brought from Kinross, and with them several bottles of good wine which would not offend even your palate.'

'And suppose I give you permission to hold this feast, whom will you ask? The Queen, I suppose.'

'I shall ask everyone, Sir William. The Queen, Sir William, Lady Douglas . . . everyone who cares to come. It is to be a banquet equal to that which the Queen has enjoyed at Court, and I shall be the Lord of Misrule.'

Sir William burst out laughing. 'And Willie Douglas will do all this?'

'Willie Douglas will.'

'I don't believe it.'

'Then I must prove it!' Willie stood back a few paces and bowed low.

'I thank you, Sir William, for your permission. I offer you a formal invitation to Willie Douglas's feast.'

Sir William was laughing.

It's good, he thought, to have the young rogue back in the castle.

* * *

The feast took place in the early afternoon. Mary was present; so were Sir William and Lady Douglas; in fact all who could be spared from their posts were at the great table. Willie presided, plying his guests with wine; aping the manners of the nobility in such a manner that he had the entire company laughing at him. He minced about the room; he gave orders in arrogant tones; he was gallant to the ladies, his freckled face wrinkled in simpering admiration; and all the time his alert eyes were on Sir William, who kept his keys in his pocket and, although he drank heavily and complimented Willie on his good wine, was none the worse for the amount he took.

Willie was also watching the Queen. He was eager to get a message through to her. He wanted her to be ready to leave during supper this evening. He knew that she was expecting some signal, but how difficult it was when he could not find an opportunity to have a word with her.

The company was becoming drowsy and the feasting could not be prolonged, so Willie suddenly announced that he was going to take advantage of his position as Lord of Misrule. Picking up a green branch which he had acquired for the occasion he approached the Queen.

'I am the Lord of Misrule,' he chanted. 'I touch you with my rod. This day you must follow me whither I command.'

Mary answered: 'Lord of Misrule, this day I will follow you wherever you lead me.'

Willie danced into the centre of the room and beckoned the Queen, who rose from her chair and made to follow him.

Willie tripped from the room, with Mary behind him.

When they were outside, Willie turned and whispered: 'It must be during supper tonight. Be watchful.'

'Willie . . . are you sure?'

Willie shook his head and laid his fingers on his lips. Lady Douglas was coming towards them.

'I am a little weary after the revelry,' said the Queen. 'I think I will rest awhile.'

Lady Douglas's eyes were alert. She had not forgotten the part Willie had played in the laundress scheme. 'I will accompany Your Majesty,' she said.

Willie returned to his guests while Lady Douglas went with the Queen to her own apartments.

Mary lay on her bed; she was too tense to feel tired; she closed her eyes, pretending to sleep, and Lady Douglas seated herself by her bed. It was clear that she did not trust Willie and had been made suspicious by the feast. Mary knew that Willie had hoped to lure all the guards to the feast and during it manage to steal the keys: he had been disappointed in that, and all he seemed to have done was arouse suspicion.

Lady Douglas bent over the bed to see if she were asleep, and Mary gave no sign that she was aware of this. She heard Lady Douglas sigh deeply and go to the door.

Someone said: 'My lady, I felt I should tell you without delay.'

'What is it?'

'My lord Seton was seen close to the lake on the mainland. He rode by with a party of horsemen.'

'Was that so?'

'I thought I should tell you.'

Mary did not recognize the voice which was speaking, but she guessed it to be that of one of the kitchen maids.

'You did right.'

'And, my lady, it is said that Master George has not gone to France, but is with my lord Seton in Kinross.'

'Is that so?' said Lady Douglas slowly. 'Then . . . off with you. You will awaken the Queen.'

Mary's heart was beating so fast that she was afraid Lady Douglas would notice. But the older woman gave no sign of this and returning to the bed continued to sit beside it. It seemed a long time before she rose and went to her own apartments.

*   *   *

The afternoon was coming to its close when Mary rose from her bed and declared that she was rested from Willie's revelry and would take a walk. She put on a cloak and went out of the castle in the company of Seton.

'This suspense is becoming intolerable,' she whispered to Seton. 'I am afraid they are too suspicious of us. We expect too much from Willie. He is after all only a boy.'

'I am sure his plan was to do something during his feast. Now it is to be while supper is in progress.'

'We are being followed now,' said Mary.

Lady Douglas came up with them and as she fell into step beside them they were startled by the distant sound of horses' hoofs, and looking up saw a party of horsemen on the mainland.

Lady Douglas watched them intently and with some misgiving; Mary guessed she was eager to report what she had seen to Sir William, and she felt dejected; for after Willie's unusual behaviour, the gossip of the kitchen-maid and the actual appearance of horsemen on the mainland, she felt that it must be obvious that some plan was in the air.

She sought to turn Lady Douglas's thoughts from what she had seen by complaining bitterly of the way in which Moray had treated her.

Lady Douglas could never bear to hear her favourite son attacked. When this happened she immediately forgot all else in her defence of him.

'His one thought,' she insisted, 'is the good of this land.'

'His one thought,' retorted Mary, 'is to rule this land.'

'Your Majesty wrongs him.'

Mary then began to enumerate all that he had done against her, and Lady Douglas grew warm in his defence.

All was now quiet on the mainland and it seemed that Lady Douglas had forgotten what a short while ago she had seen there to disturb her. She talked in glowing terms of the cleverness of Moray, how like his father he was, and therefore a little like Mary. 'For, Your Majesty, I see your father in you.'

Lady Douglas was back in her glorious past when she had been a King's favourite mistress. So that the suspicious activity on the mainland completely slipped from her memory.

She was still talking when Sir William appeared.

'The Queen's supper is about to be served in her chamber,' he said. He bowed to Mary. 'May I escort you there?'

She went into the castle with him, and never had the place seemed so gloomy, never so much a prison as it did on that Sunday evening.

She went to her room and took her supper.

For a short while she was alone with her friends whom she could trust: Seton, Marie Courcelles and Jane Kennedy. Jane said suddenly: 'If Willie can procure the keys, it is still possible.'

'How *can* Willie procure the keys?' Mary asked. 'Yet w
must be prepared. I will change clothes with you, Seton, for
you are more my height than the others. And I will do it now,
for if the moment should come, we must be ready.'

They changed clothes.

'I will keep my veil,' said Mary, 'because I must wave this
from the boat as a signal, so that my faithful defenders may
know I am on the way.'

So in Seton's gown and cloak, with her own white veil with
its red and gold border and red tassels, Mary waited tensely
for what would happen next.

*　　*　　*

Sir William was feeling drowsy. The wine Willie had provided at his feast had been very potent. He could go to sleep
there on the dais. All was well. The guards were at supper with
him and the rest of the household; the castle gates had been
carefully locked; and beside his plate lay the keys, without
which no one could leave the castle.

Lady Douglas was talking indignantly of the Queen's accusations against Moray, and defending him; but Sir William had
heard his mother on the perfections of Moray before, and it
added to the soporific effect of the wine.

Behind Sir William's chair stood Willie, ready to fill his plate
or his goblet. It was good to have Willie back in place of that
clumsy oaf who had served him during the boy's absence.

As for Willie, he could not take his eyes from that bunch of
keys which were lying on the table. His fingers itched to seize
them. He had to resist an impulse to snatch them and run –
which would of course be the utmost folly.

Sir William sat yawning and Willie poured more wine into
his goblet. On and on went Lady Douglas. And Willie stood,
only half hearing what was said, his impatient fingers pulling
at the napkin in his hands.

The meal would soon be over and then it would be too late.
Shortly Drysdale would be back; the boatman might be well
enough to take over his duties; and there would never be an
opportunity like this. Now the boat was ready, the oars in
place, and how could that possibly have been prepared unless
Willie had charge of the boats!

Yes, he must spirit those keys away five minutes before it
was noticed that they were gone . . . enough time to go to the
Queen's apartments, to bring her out, to hurry down to the

castle gates, unlock and lock them again; then down to the boats and away. But he must have the keys.

Willie leaned forward to remove Sir William's plate and, as he did so, he let his napkin fall over the keys. When he picked up the napkin and Sir William's plate, the keys were no longer on the table.

This was the most difficult part – to walk out of the hall holding the plate, the napkin and the keys, unhurried and without concern, knowing that at any moment the absence of the keys might be noticed. If so, he would be stopped, all would be discovered and that would be the end of Willie Douglas's hopes of saving the Queen – and perhaps the end of Willie Douglas.

Past the long table, past the noisy soldiers and the servants ... and out.

Willie was taking the stairs two at a time. He unlocked the room which led to the Queen's apartment. He was standing before her. He did not speak but held up the keys.

Now Mary was following him down the stairs and out of the castle.

Jane Kennedy, who it had been arranged should go with her, had been putting on her cloak in the ante-chamber when Willie had arrived and, as there was no time to lose, Mary had started after Willie without Jane.

It was a glorious feeling to be in the fresh air and the short distance to the castle gates seemed one of the most exciting journeys Mary had ever made. Willie ran ahead. He was unlocking the gates, holding them for her to pass through; then he locked them again behind them.

At that moment Jane Kennedy emerged from the castle. Mary looked back, but Willie shook his head. They had overcome the biggest obstacle. They were outside the castle and everyone else was locked inside. He was not going to run any risks by unlocking the castle gates. At any moment the loss of the keys might be discovered and the hue and cry would start. Those soldiers would find some means of coming after them.

The plan had not yet succeeded.

Willie ran ahead to where the boat was ready and waiting. Mary stepped into it, Willie took the oars, and they were slipping away from Lochleven.

'We have succeeded!' cried the Queen.

'We have to reach the mainland yet,' Willie grimly reminded her.

'We will,' replied Mary, and she took an oar and began to row with him.

There was a sudden splash in the loch close by and, to her horror Mary saw a dark figure swimming towards them.

'Why,' she cried, 'it's Jane! Stop, Willie. It's Jane Kennedy swimming after us.'

Jane had gone to one of the castle windows from which she had jumped into the loch and encumbered by her clothes was making slow progress towards the boat. But Willie would not stop even for her. Eventually however she reached them and Mary eagerly leaned over the side of the boat to help her scramble in.

'I could not let . . . Your Majesty . . . be without one of us to serve you,' she panted.

In a few seconds she had recovered her breath and ignoring her dripping garments, insisted on taking the oar from Mary, and she and Willie pulled with all their might for the shore.

Each stroke took them farther and farther from Lochleven and nearer to freedom. Mary took off her veil and waved it and when she heard a shout from the mainland and the clatter of horses' hoofs she believed she had rarely been so happy.

The boat touched ground and someone had come forward to kneel at her feet.

'Why, George,' she said, 'so you are the first to welcome me back to my kingdom.'

Now others were crowding round her. Horses were waiting and it would be unwise to stay in Kinross.

Friends were with her now: Seton, Semphill, John Beaton, George Douglas and the humble people of Kinross who had sheltered the Queen's loyal subjects secretly in their houses awaiting this great day.

The horses were ready. Mary was helped into the saddle. Willie watched her, grinning with delight as he turned and threw the keys of Lochleven into the middle of the lake.

Then he took the horse which was waiting for him; and so the Queen escaped from her prison of Lochleven.

CHAPTER THREE

LANGSIDE

THE QUEEN WAS galloping through the night, George Douglas beside her, exultant with the knowledge that at last they had succeeded.

Not far behind them rode Willie, laughing to himself as he contemplated what was happening in the castle, where Sir William and the guards would now be endeavouring to break out and raise the alarm.

Mary was thinking that so many times she had undergone this urgent riding through the night, that it became almost like a pattern of her life; yet never on similar occasions had she felt this lifting of her spirits; she knew this was because she had come out of captivity and was riding to freedom.

Danger was still in the air. She was realist enough to know that she had taken but the first tottering steps towards victory; but at last she was no longer a prisoner; she was free to command, to plan, to wrest her kingdom from those who sought to keep it from her.

Now they were swerving from the route to the coast that they might avoid the territory of Kirkcaldy of Grange who it was well known was her enemy; she could smell the sea and she knew that they could not be far from the Firth of Forth.

Once they had crossed it they would be a little nearer to safety, but as they rode down to the sea and Mary saw the small open fishing-boat in which she must cross the Firth she felt a tremor of misgivings; yet she knew that this was no time to look for comfort. George was at her side, helping her into the boat, and with her company of faithful friends in similar craft, the crossing took place.

It seemed as though the ill fortune which had been her lot for so long had changed, for the crossing was made in safety and as they came ashore a party of horsemen was waiting for them, led by Lord Claud Hamilton, all ready to fight for the Queen.

Lord Seton, who helped the Queen into her saddle said as he did so: 'Your Majesty, I think that you should take a few hours' sleep before morning. And I suggest we ride on to my

castle of West Niddry that you may rest in comfort there
before pursuing the journey.'

Mary bowed her head.

'I doubt whether I shall sleep,' she answered; 'but I should
certainly welcome the chance to rest my weary limbs.'

So, on through the night to West Niddry.

*   *   *

In the chamber which the Setons had prepared for her in
West Niddry Castle, Mary found it impossible to sleep. Jane
Kennedy, rid at last of her wet clothes, lay at the foot of her
mistress's bed and fell at once into deep slumber.

Mary was not eager to sleep, for that might mean to dream
she was a prisoner in Lochleven; freedom was too precious,
too recently come by to be lost, even in her dreams. So she
lay trying to plan for the future, but finding the immediate
past intruding into her thoughts, so that she was again waiting
in her chamber for the coming of Willie, walking out of the
castle, while Willie locked the gates behind her . . . riding
through the night, tossing on the Firth of Forth.

But that is all past, she told herself. Now it remains for me
to regain my throne.

Could it be done peacefully? Was that hoping for too
much? She thought how strange was her life, when her little
son, who should have been with her, was the symbol for which
her enemies would tell the world they were fighting.

As she lay between waking and sleeping the first streaks of
dawn showed in the sky; and with them came the distant sound
of pipes and bugles.

Mary lay listening, as nearer and nearer came the sounds,
and unable to remain on her bed, she leaped up and, her chestnut hair falling about her shoulders, snatched a robe and went
to stand at the window.

She saw them then . . . marching towards the castle and she
felt tears of joy sting her eyelids as she recognized Lord
Livingstone at the head of his men.

Now they were filing into the courtyard; and they were
almost below her window when Livingstone, seeing her there,
called a halt to his men and shouted: 'Long live the Queen!'

Over the sweet May air their voices rang out and it was
some time before Mary could speak to them and tell them
how she welcomed them and how it warmed her heart to see
such loyal subjects.

Even as she spoke, the pipes of other companies could be heard, and she saw the Bruces advancing and it seemed to her that from all directions the clans were converging on West Niddry Castle to offer themselves in the Queen's service.

*   *   *

The Castle of West Niddry was intended to be only a resting place and Mary with her followers – now swollen to a considerable size – left for Hamilton Castle where she had heard that more clans were coming in from all parts of the country to welcome her.

Here she was received by Archbishop Hamilton, and when she had made her speech of welcome to all those who were rallying to her cause, she was delighted to hear that Sir Robert Melville had arrived at the castle.

She sent for him and when he came to her she greeted him warmly.

He was a little shamefaced, in view of the fact that he had been present when she had been forced to sign her Abdication, and he apologized for this.

Mary immediately forgave him; if she wondered whether he had changed sides rather hastily she dismissed the thought because she was so happy to be free and to have friends. Moreover, Sir Robert had sound advice to give her.

'Your Majesty's first task should be to repudiate the Abdication,' he told her. 'And you have two witnesses with you here at Hamilton who can verify the fact that you were forced, on pain of death, to sign those documents.'

Mary recognized the wisdom of this and summoned George Douglas, and when he came to her she held out both hands to him in her impulsive way. George took them and kissed the delicate fingers.

'George,' she cried, 'you are so self-effacing that I feel I have to tell you every time I see you that I shall never forget what you have done for me.'

'It is enough reward for me to see Your Majesty free,' murmured George.

She told him that she was going to repudiate the Abdication and that he, with Melville, was to be a witness to the fact that she had signed under pressure.

George's face brightened at the prospect of being of further assistance to her; she immediately called a council and made her formal declaration that the Abdication was null and void.

104

Immediately afterwards, for all were aware of a great urgency knowing that Moray would act swiftly, there was a meeting at which the next step was discussed.

Seated round the council table with such tried friends as Lords Seton and Livingstone, were Lord Claud Hamilton and Lord Herries with Sir Robert Melville; and Mary had insisted that George Douglas should be present.

'We seem strong,' said Mary, 'but we must remember that Moray is strong also, and that in his hands are the royal arsenals of Edinburgh and Stirling Castles, also Dunbar. He has the revenues at his disposal and all my most precious jewels are in his possession. I have little with which to pay those who fight for me, although in good time I hope to regain all that I have lost and so pay my debts. The first step I propose is to write to France and ask for help. I believe that the King of France would be eager to help me, although I am not sure of his mother. I suggest therefore that we send, without delay, a trusty messenger to France who will lay this matter before King Charles and ask his help in my name.'

This was agreed to be wise and John Beaton was chosen for the mission. He agreed to make his preparations and set out immediately.

'Your Majesty,' said Lord Seton, 'we must prepare for battle without delay.'

A slight frown touched Mary's brows. 'I had hoped that we could settle our differences without resort to violence,' she said. 'I propose to send a letter to the Regent Moray with a copy of my revocation of the Abdication, which was forced upon me during my imprisonment, and to assure him that if he will restore my rights to me peacefully, I will forgive him all that he has done against me; and because I have respect for his powers I shall wish him to work with me in the government of this realm.'

Melville shook his head; Seton was disturbed.

'Your Majesty,' said the latter, 'we must remember that the Regent has shown himself to be your enemy. It was on his instructions that you were kept in rigorous confinement.'

'I know,' replied Mary; and she looked round the company with a smile that held some exasperation. How could she explain to them: I understand Jamie. He even has my sympathy. There is not a more ambitious man in Scotland – and we must remember how frustrating it must be to have been born a bastard when you long to wear the crown. Oh poor frustrated Jamie! He made me a prisoner; he wished to rule Scotland. He shall no longer do so, but I could make him happy with some post worthy of his exceptional abilities.

No, they would never understand her.

He is my brother! she wanted to cry. The Stuart blood runs through our veins. He was unjust to me, but I could never be so to him. The matter would lie on my conscience. I should remember it all my life.

Therefore she would not listen to their advice. At least she would give James a chance to confer peaceably. The idea of a civil war in Scotland was abhorrent; but that it should be war between brother and sister was doubly so.

No. She must give Jamie a chance to be her friend. She must forgive and try to forget.

So she wrote to Moray.

*　　*　　*

When Moray heard the news of the Queen's escape he was dumbfounded. He let out an exclamation of rage – something he had rarely done in his life; but in that moment of dismay he was beyond self-control.

Escaped from Lochleven, and now at Hamilton Castle where supporters were rallying to her banner!

He sought out Morton at once.

'This is disastrous!' cried Morton.

'Nay,' answered James, almost his calm self again. 'It is bad, but we must not be over-disconsolate. Deeply as I regret what has happened, there may still be a chance to settle this matter once and for all.'

'They say supporters are rallying to her side.'

'She will not have the money to pay them.'

'Doubtless she will receive help from France.'

'I am afraid of that. But it will take a little time before aid can reach her. In the meantime we have the arms. We also have her jewels. I shall immediately offer her pearls to Elizabeth of England.'

'You think she will buy them?'

'I know she will. She has wanted them ever since she heard that Mary was a prisoner in Lochleven.'

Morton looked at Moray. A sly one, thought Morton; so he had already been in negotiation with Elizabeth over the pearls! You could trust Moray to be one step ahead of his enemies –

106

and his friends. Morton believed – in spite of rumours that were in the air – that he was on the right side.

'She will offer twelve thousand crowns for them,' went on Moray.

'I had heard they are worth sixteen thousand.'

'It is so. But the Queen of England dearly loves a bargain and it is to our advantage to please her. Moreover she has an obsession about her cousin of Scotland and constantly longs to outshine her in all things. She is the vainest woman in the world, and there have been too many reports of my sister's beauty and charm which have reached her. She hates her rival. In truth she was delighted to hear she was a prisoner in Lochleven, robbed of her comfort and luxury. She constantly inquires about the health of her *dear* cousin, and professes concern that imprisonment may have impaired her beauty, fervently hoping all the time that it has. She wants the pearls so that Mary cannot have them and she will pay for them without delay. We shall need the money.'

'You think we can rely on her help?'

Moray nodded slowly. 'She will offer congratulations to Mary; she will rage against the indignity done to Royalty; and she will turn a blind eye and a deaf ear while her minister, Cecil, supports the Protestants of Scotland against the Catholics. Throckmorton assures me of this.'

'But meanwhile Mary may receive help from France.'

'It is wrong, I believe, to wait for help from England. By then Mary may have received help from France. There must be a battle if we are to preserve the throne for James VI; we must prepare for that battle and it must take place without delay. In the meantime I will write humbly to my sister so that she will think I am considering her proposals. But make no mistake about it. The time to strike is close at hand. If we delay we shall have the Highlanders marching South. I doubt not that when Huntley heard the news he began shouting the battle cry.'

'You are right,' agreed Morton. 'To delay would be to give the Queen the advantage.'

*　　*　　*

Mary was disconsolate because Moray had now shown his true intentions. After seeming to be considering a reconciliation he had put in irons the messenger whom she had sent to him in Glasgow.

There must be a battle. Her advisers were optimistic because she had now a force of six thousand, while Moray had under four thousand. Victory seemed inevitable and she was glad that the battle would not be delayed because, having at Carberry Hill seen how rapidly an army could turn against its leaders, she was afraid of a similar occurrence when those who had rallied to fight for her knew that she had – until she gained the victory – no means of paying them for their services.

There was trouble within her ranks. She had given the command of the army to the Earl of Argyle who was the husband of a half-sister of hers – one of her father's bastards. Mary, who had always longed to be one of a large family, had constantly shown indulgence towards her father's bastards. However, Lord Claud Hamilton thought that the command should have been offered to him. This was an unfortunate state of affairs particularly as neither of the contestants was noted for his military genius, and against them Moray would have the best general in Scotland – Kirkcaldy of Grange, one of the Queen's most bitter enemies.

The Queen's ill luck seemed to have returned, for it started to rain heavily and, so violent were the storms, that the progress of the Highlanders, who under Huntley were hurrying to her banner, was halted.

Moray, aware that delay could cost him his future, determined on immediate battle. Mary, however, still hoping to avoid bloodshed, decided to march with her followers to Dumbarton, which was in the loyal hands of Lord Fleming. But the Hamiltons were eager for battle; they had old scores to settle with Moray and it was largely for this reason that they had rallied to the Queen; they did all possible therefore to impede the departure for Dumbarton.

Moray had set spies among the Queen's men and was kept informed of her movements. Thus the news that she was making her way to Dumbarton, to join with Fleming and doubtless pick up other supporters on the road, was brought to him and, as he was discussing tactics with his General Kirkcaldy, at the time, Kirkcaldy hit on the plan that he and his army would intercept the Queen and hers on the road to Dumbarton. In this way he would be able to choose his battlefield and position – always an important factor in victory; and as it was necessary to engage in an action as soon as possible, the time had come.

Moray was confident that he had the finest general in Scotland and he agreed at once. So Kirkcaldy selected his battle-field at the little village of Langside close by Govan Moor.

* * *

On her way to Dumbarton Mary stayed the night at Castle-milk as the guest of her kinsman Sir John Stuart.

She slept well for she was confident of eventual victory; and when it was hers she would send for Moray and reproach him for all that he had done against her. She would remind him of the blood ties between them and she would of course forgive him; and, she hoped, that then there would be an end of strife between them. 'Jamie,' she would say, 'I understand and you have my sympathy. I am our father's legitimate daughter; you are his illegitimate son. It is sad for you who are so ambitious, but you must learn to accept that.'

And he would agree because, whatever else James was, he was a man of sound common sense.

How wonderful to be at peace again – a Queen on her throne! And the years of violence and tragedy would not have been in vain, because she had learned so much through them, and she would profit from those lessons. She would be a good Queen to her Protestant subjects no less than to her Catholic ones. There should be freedom of religion in Scotland, freedom of opinion, prosperity and peace.

She dozed, for she was worn out with emotion and physical exhaustion. She dreamed that she was in Lochleven and her joy was great when she opened her eyes in the large room with the three embayed windows which gave her wide views over the countryside.

Not Lochleven but Castlemilk on the road to Dumbarton!

But in the morning when she arose and went out to the battlements to gaze down on the magnificent view of her beautiful country she saw troops encamped in the distance; and she felt sick with apprehension because she knew that they were not her own soldiers but those of the enemy.

She believed then that the battle could not long be delayed.

* * *

She had just completed her toilet, and was wearing a crepe coif and simple dress, which fitted her figure closely and which was made of white taffety, when she heard that Lord Living-stone was asking for an audience with her.

He looked disturbed, and when she asked the reason, he kissed her hand and told her that all augured well for this day and that he believed that before nightfall their enemies would be defeated. There was a small trouble however. Two captains of her musketeers were quarrelling as to who should have supremacy over the other.

Mary sighed. 'There is no time for private quarrels on such a day. Who are these men?'

'Arthur Hamilton of Mirrinton and John Stuart of Castleton. They are bitter enemies, and are ready to draw swords against each other. I warned them that if they did not desist I should be forced to lay the matter before Your Majesty. They persist in their quarrel, so I have come to ask you to give a decision.'

'Is one a better captain than the other?'

'They are both good fighters, Your Majesty; but arrogant, stubborn and proud.'

'Then I suppose I must perforce give the command to the Stuart . . . for the sake of the name.'

Livingstone bowed. 'It is one way of solving the problem, Your Majesty.'

Mary said: 'The enemy is massing against us. I can see them in the distance.'

Livingstone nodded. 'The battle will surely take place this day. Will Your Majesty come now to the chamber in which your generals and councillors are gathered?'

Mary went with him; and there it was decided that, on account of their superiority in numbers, they should surround the rebel army and annihilate it in a short time.

'We will call for surrender,' insisted Mary. 'If they surrender there will be no need for slaughter. I do not wish the blood of Scotsmen to be shed unnecessarily on this day. I am sure that many who now stand against me may well become my good friends when they learn that I intend to rule well, to forgive them and bear no malice that they once ranged themselves against me.'

One of the guards at the door of the council chamber slipped away from his post. None noticed his departure because there was so much coming and going; moreover many of those who had rallied to the Queen's cause were friends of his.

He had no difficulty in procuring a horse and soon was speeding across country to the headquarters of Mary's enemies.

There he went straight to Kirkcaldy who was conferring

with Moray, and received their congratulations when he was able to tell them the form in which the enemy's attack would be made.

* * *

Kirkcaldy was exultant. He was certain of victory. The inferiority in numbers concerned him little for throughout the Queen's army were his own men. He had taken the precaution of sending them to declare their loyalty to the Queen, with strict instructions as to how they were to act. He did wonder uneasily whether a similar strategy had occurred to the other side. Hardly likely. The Queen would have notions of fighting fairly. As if any battle was ever won through fairness! Argyle? Not a brilliant rival. Moreover he was Moray's brother-in-law and they had been allies at one time. He did not think Argyle would prove a very good general for the Queen. She should have remembered that while he was related to her he was also related to Moray; and Moray was a shrewd and competent statesman, whereas Mary was an emotional woman.

He, Kircaldy, was never so much alive as when he was planning a battle or winning it. He would now post his hag-butters behind the hedges and in the gardens and orchards of Langside, and they should have orders to hide themselves in trees, behind bushes . . . anywhere, making sure that they were not seen by the approaching army. They were to shoot as the Queen's men marched by. That should account for a few of them. And the Queen planned to surround him! Well, he would take possession of the hill which was above the village and here place his men, so that as Mary's army tried to advance they would have to climb the hill and thus could more easily be mown down.

There was another hill close by, known as Hagbush-hill, and here, protected by a body of horsemen was a cradle in which the little James VI was sleeping unaware of the excitement which was going on about him.

It had been deemed necessary to remove him from Stirling, in case some of Mary's supporters stormed the castle; if the child fell into his mother's hands, this could prove disastrous for those who declared they were fighting to keep him on the throne.

It had been a good idea to bring the baby to the battlefield, mused Kirkcaldy. The sight of that cradle would, in a way, be an inspiration to his men; and if there should be any danger of

111

defeat – which Kirkcaldy did not anticipate for a moment – those whose duty it was to guard the cradle would swiftly carry the child away.

Kirkcaldy was waiting, well satisfied. Soon the Queen's army would begin to move.

* * *

Kirkcaldy was right. Almost before he had succeeded in placing his men the Queen's army was seen marching in the distance, their pennons flying in the breeze; their glistening pikes reflecting the sunlight.

Kirkcaldy watched them. Moray was stationed by the bridge with his men and Morton was in charge of the vanguard. Kirkcaldy felt the utmost confidence in his generals. They had so much to lose with this battle.

On the Queen's men came. They were passing the gardens and orchards, and the hagbutters were doing their work. Men were falling as they marched, their comrades looking about startled since there was no sign of the enemy.

Now they were approaching the hill on which Kirkcaldy was stationed, and Arthur Hamilton, leading his troop and smarting under the humiliation of John Stuart's being given precedence over him because he bore the same name as the Queen, suddenly shouted: 'Where are now these Stuarts that did contest for the first place? Let them come forward and take it now.'

John Stuart was close by, and heard, as Hamilton had intended he should.

'And so *will* I,' he retorted. 'Neither you nor any Hamilton in Scotland shall set foot before a Stuart this day.'

John Stuart ill-advisedly spurred his horse and leading his men tried to storm his way up the hill. The effect was disastrous. But not to be outdone Hamilton followed him with the same dire results.

The fighting was furious for a few moments and men used their dirks because they were too close to each other to draw their swords.

Argyle, who was in command of the Queen's army was seen to fall forward on his mount; yet did not appear to be wounded but slid to the ground and lay there writhing as though in a fit.

His men watched him in dismay for in that section of the army there was no one else to give them orders. None was

112

quite sure what had caused Argyle's malady. Some thought it was a fit, which seemed a bad omen; others that he had merely fainted at the prospect of disaster; some that he feigned sickness in order to play into the hands of his old friend Moray.

Mary had ridden with Lord Livingstone on one side of her and George Douglas on the other; and immediately behind her was Willie Douglas, carrying a two-handed sword which required all his attention to maintain. Willie's eyes were alight with enthusiasm; and Mary believed that none would fight more earnestly for her cause.

But she was disturbed, because she was aware of disaffection in her ranks, and could not help being reminded, with something like terror, of Carberry Hill.

Lord Livingstone was remonstrating with her. She should not go too near the battle zone, for if aught should happen to her, her soldiers would lose heart. It was better to wait some distance away and watch the progress of her soldiers from comparative safety.

George added his pleas to Lord Livingstone's, and eventually she realized the wisdom of their words and agreed to wait beneath a hawthorn tree until the heat of the battle was over. With her were Lady Livingstone and Jane Kennedy; and Lord Livingstone and Lord Herries with George and Willie remained by her side. Livingstone ordered that fresh horses should be brought.

'For what reason?' the Queen demanded.

'In case we should need them . . . in a hurry, Your Majesty,' answered Livingstone.

Mary's throat was suddenly parched. She knew that all was not going well.

*   *   *

A rider dashing up to the little party brought news of the battle. What he had to tell was disturbing: Argyle was incapacitated; Lord Seton was seriously wounded; fifty-seven of the Hamiltons had been slain.

He reported that Mary's baby son was on the battlefield in his cradle; and when she heard this Mary gave a cry of horror. Her son . . . her baby . . . exposed to danger and in the hands of her enemies who pretended that they supported him against her!

She felt weak suddenly and the tears were rushing to her eyes. Slipping from the Spanish jennet which Livingstone had

113

suggested she mount in case she should need it, she stopped to drink from the little burn which flowed from the brae.

When she had drunk she silently remounted; the excitement of the day was turning to anguish. Now she could see riderless horses, bleeding from pike wounds, running hither and thither in their bewildered agony. She was glad of the distance which separated her from that fearful scene; but her heart yearned for the child in the cradle.

Herries laid his hand on her arm and said quietly: 'I think, Your Majesty, that it is unwise to stay here longer, and the time has come for us to move on.'

That was enough. She understood. The battle of Langside was almost over. Kirkcaldy and Moray were the victors; and the captive Queen had become the fugitive.

*   *   *

To Dumbarton – where she could count on loyal supporters! But before she reached it she must cross the Clyde.

Lord Herries, who was riding beside her, while the rest of the little band followed behind, said: 'We must get down to the shore. There we shall find a boat. We must hope to find horses on the other side; but get to Dumbarton we must.'

To reach the river bank they must cross the estates of the Earl of Lennox – strong supporter of Moray; and when the men who were working in the fields saw their approach and guessed who the riders were, they brandished their scythes and uttered such curses that the Queen turned her horse and commanded that Herries did the same.

Then they abandoned hope of crossing the Clyde.

'We will make our way into Galloway and Wigtownshire,' said Herries. 'It is my native ground and the people there are Catholics and loyal to Your Majesty. You will find the going rough, but there are few who know the ground as well as I, and I shall lead you to safety.'

So along the beautiful banks of the River Doon they rode; through mountain passes and across moors and small, swift streams. The white taffety gown was splashed with mud, the crepe coif askew; yet Mary was not thinking of her appearance as she rode, but of the child who was lost to her, together with her kingdom.

All through the night they rode and at length they reached Herries' house at Terregles; and there they tarried for a rest, but only a brief one. All Mary's fathful friends knew that,

114

after the defeat of Langside, Moray would not rest until he had made her his prisoner once more.

* * *

At Terregles a follower of Herries, who had hoped that he might find his master there, had come riding from the battle-field. He brought the news that Lord Moray was sending parties out in all directions to search for the Queen and all the efforts of the conquerors were now being concentrated on her capture.

So the stay at Terregles was very brief.

Herries believed that there was one way in which the Queen could hope to regain her throne, and that was by escaping from Scotland to France, where her relatives and friends would provide her with money and perhaps soldiers to fight for her crown. Meanwhile loyal supporters in Scotland would wait for her return.

There was no time to discuss such matters now, but he knew that Livingstone and Fleming agreed with him. Their objective was the coast. If they could have crossed the Clyde and arrived at Dumbarton the flight to France would have been comparatively easy, for there ships worthy to cross the seas would have been in readiness for them. As it was they would strike the coast farther south, and who could tell what vessels would be at their disposal?

But there was no time for regrets; they must move quickly because Terregles would be one of the first places in which Moray would expect to find the Queen sheltering, since it belonged to Herries.

So the journey began again with Herries leading the way through the lonely passes of the Glenkens until they at length came to the banks of the River Ken.

Mary was almost asleep in her saddle when Herries announced that they had arrived at the Castle of Earlston.

Earlston! As Mary stared at the castle she forgot her exhaustion, for memory had brought vividly to her mind the picture of a burly man, crude and brutal, who shouted: 'I will take you to my castle of Earlston . . . and there in that lonely spot far from your courtiers you shall learn who is the master.'

Had he need to take her there, to show her what he had proved in her Court when she had been surrounded by her courtiers?

115

She began to shiver. 'No, my lord Herries,' she said, 'I will not stay at Earlston.'

'Your Majesty, there is no other refuge for miles, and you are exhausted.'

Mary shook her head. 'No,' she repeated coldly.

She turned her horse and as she did so she seemed to throw off her exhaustion. 'Come,' she said, 'we can ride on a few more miles.'

And as they rode the memories of Bothwell came flooding back. In this wild country he would have hunted and made sport. It was as though his spirit rode beside her, as though he mocked, as though he said: So even now, when I am miles away across the sea, you are afraid to enter a place which was once a home of mine. Why, Mary?

Why? she asked herself. He was far away. He could do no harm to her. Did she believe that the presence of one so vital could never be completely eradicated and must linger on in spirit when the man himself had departed?

Why was it that she could not endure to enter a place which must be full of reminders of him, where she would be afraid of encountering something which would bring back memories that were too bitter to be borne? Did it mean that she longed for him still?

She was not sure. But she believed that her abhorrence of Earlston meant that she no longer cared to be reminded; that memories brought back too much that was shameful; that there was a superstition in her mind that he it was who had brought her to disaster, and that some evil force within him could harm her still.

No, she could not be entirely sure. She only knew that, exhausted as she was, she would rather ride on than enter a house in which he had once lived.

So on they rode until at length they came to Kenmure, an estate belonging to the Laird of Lochinvar.

*   *   *

The Laird of Lochinvar had bad news for her. Her pursuers had discovered the direction in which she was travelling, and were not many miles away. It could be fatal if she tarried; so, pausing just long enough to take refreshment, she and her faithful band were on their way again. On they rode through miles of wild and beautiful country; and eventually they came to a bridge which crossed the River Dee.

116

Here Herries, calling a halt, said they would cross the bridge and then break it down so that when their pursuers reached this spot they would be delayed in their crossing of the river.

Lord Livingstone looked with compassion at the Queen. 'Your Majesty,' he said, 'rest here while we demolish the bridge. At least it will be a small respite.'

So Mary dismounted and Willie Douglas tied her horse to a tree and she stretched herself out on the grass and closed her eyes. She was thirsty and, realizing how hungry she was, she called Willie to her.

'I would give a great deal for some food and wine,' she said.

Willie grinned and laid his hand on the sword, which he would not give up although it impeded him considerably. Willie felt that he was no longer a boy since he had left Lochleven; he was ready to work like a man and fight like a man for his sovereign.

'I'll go and forage,' he told her.

George, who was busy at work on the bridge, called after Willie: 'Where are you going? If you're not here when we're ready to go, you'll be left behind.'

Willie answered: 'Dinna fach yourself, Geordie Douglas.' He drew out his sword and brandished it as though to show what he would do to any who stood in his way.

Mary could not help smiling, and when the men's attention was on the bridge she rose and followed Willie.

'Willie,' she called.

He stopped and she came up beside him.

'Why dinna you rest?' he demanded, 'You're weary.'

'So are we all,' she said. 'Where are you going?'

'There's smoke in yon trees,' said Willie. 'It means there's a cottage there. I'm going to ask for food for you.'

'I shall come with you.'

Willie looked dubious, but she smiled and said: 'I wish it, Willie; and I am your Queen, remember, although I sometimes think you forget it.'

'Oh ay,' said Willie, 'Your Majesty's such a bonny lassie that it slips the mind ye're a Queen as well.'

It was impossible not to be amused by Willie. He was so loyal, and so frank. She trusted him to work for her as she could never trust some who overwhelmed her with their flattery.

So she and Willie came to the cottage, and when Willie knocked on the door a woman opened it.

'What is it you want?' she asked.

'We're travellers in sore need of food,' Willie told her. 'This lady needs to rest and eat if we are to continue our journey.'

The woman peered at the Queen.

'Oh you poor creature!' she said. 'Come you in and you shall have some of that that's in my cupboard.'

Into the small room stepped the Queen with Willie, and the woman bade them sit at her table.

'Have ye come far?' she asked, turning to the cupboard.

'Very far,' answered Mary.

'Ah . . . these are troublous times.'

'You live alone?' Mary asked.

'Nay, there's my good man who works up at Culdoach Farm.'

'Is that far?'

'Oh no. We're on the farm land now.'

The woman had brought oatmeal and sour milk from her cupboard. She had scarcely enough for herself but her heart was touched by the plight of the travellers and she was willing to share with them all she had. At any other time Mary would have been unable to eat such fare, but so great was her hunger that it tasted good.

The woman was looking at the Queen's hands and had noticed the dainty way in which she ate.

'If I had more and better fare,' she said, 'you should have it.'

'What you have given us was good indeed,' said the Queen. 'I shall always remember you with gratitude.'

The woman started up. She had heard the sound of galloping horses and, running to her window, she saw that her cottage was surrounded.

'Mercy on us!' she cried. 'What does this mean?'

The Queen went to the window, Willie beside her, his sword drawn. Then he laughed suddenly because he had seen that those who surrounded the cottage were Herries. Fleming, Livingstone and the rest.

'All is well,' he said, 'You have nothing to fear, good woman. These are our friends.'

'Your friends!' she cried. 'Then who are you?'

Mary said: 'I am the Queen.'

The woman stared at her disbelievingly and then her eyes went to the table on which the empty bowl now stood.

'The Queen!' said the woman. 'Sitting at my table . . . eating my oats!'

Mary laid her hand on her shoulder. Then she turned to Willie: 'Go out and tell our friends that all is well, and ask Lord Herries to come here.'

'Lord Herries!' cried the woman, for in her eyes he was as grand a personage as the Queen, more to be feared perhaps because he was the laird of the land on which her cottage stood – whereas the Queen was merely a name to her.

'If you could ask for something,' said Mary, 'what would it be?'

'Ask for something?' stammered the woman.

'Some gift. Tell me what you would rather have than anything in the world.'

The woman looked about the walls of her cottage; lovingly she raised her eyes to the ceiling. 'I'd ask that this cottage was my very own,' she said.

Mary was about to say, It is yours, when she remembered that she was a Queen flying for her life, that she had been robbed of most of her possessions, including her crown. Was she in a position to say: This is yours?

She felt disconsolate. It was characteristic that she was more hurt now by the loss of her power to grant this woman her small wish than she had been by the confiscation of her precious jewels.

Lord Herries was at the door and the woman made a deep curtsey.

'I have enjoyed hospitality under this roof,' said Mary, 'and I should like to show my gratitude. I should like to give this woman the cottage in which she lives and for which she now pays rent. It is on your land, Lord Herries.'

'The cottage is hers, Your Majesty.'

The woman stared from one to the other and in the emotion of the moment tears gushed from her eyes.

'My lord Herries . . .' she began.

'Your thanks are due to Her Majesty,' Herries told her.

The woman cried: 'But I only gave her that which I would give any hungry traveller. Oatmeal and sour milk . . .and for that . . .this cottage is mine.'

'Not for the oatmeal,' answered Mary gently, 'but for your kindness to a weary traveller. Kindness is not always easy to come by and I value it highly.'

Herries said: 'What is the name of your cottage, that I may know which one it is?'

'It's Dunn's Wa's, my lord.'

'Dunn's Wa's,' Herries repeated. 'Now tell me where I can find fresh horses.'

'Up at the farm of Culdoach, my lord. They have horses there.'

So the Queen departed and in the cottage its new owner sat by her table and covered her face with her apron, rocking herself to and fro, because in that moment she could not bear to look at those beloved walls which would henceforth be her own. And all because she had given a stranger a share of her sparse supper! There'd be a little less to eat at her next meal – but she could not have enjoyed it if she had denied a weary, hungry stranger a share.

And for this . . . Dunn's Wa's was hers.

*   *   *

The fugitives had put fifty miles between them and the battlefield of Langside and had now come to Dundrennan Abbey.

Here they halted, for on the other side of the Solway Firth was England. Looking across the water Mary could see the mountains of Elizabeth's country and she felt a great longing to be there. In Scotland she must remain a fugitive until she could raise a large enough army to win back all she had lost; and she could not do that while she was flying before the enemy. She needed respite which only refuge in a foreign country could give her.

So at the Abbey of Dundrennan she called together her faithful band, and with Gordon of Lochinvar who had joined them, they sat round a council table to discuss further plans.

Among those who talked with her were Lord Herries, Lord Fleming and the Laird of Lochinvar, Lord Livingstone, Lord Boyd and George Douglas.

Herries began by saying that he believed the Queen could stay in Dundrennan and there hold out against the enemy. The place would make a good fortress and would not be difficult to defend. There was no doubt that Huntley was on the march and would join them shortly. When he arrived with his Highlanders they would be ready for battle again, and this time they would defeat the enemy.

It was Livingstone's opinion that they should move to a

more doughty fortress than Dundrennan. There were stronger places not very far distant and they should make one of these their headquarters without delay and prepare for a siege.

Lord Boyd with Lochinvar considered that the Queen was in danger as long as she remained on Scottish soil. In France she had powerful relations; she could enlist the help of the King of France. They believed that without delay she should set out for France.

Mary listened, considering each proposal as it was offered. To stay in Scotland? To risk capture and another long imprisonment such as she had suffered at Lochleven? She could not endure that.

Go to France? She thought of her ambitious uncles and the Queen-Mother of France who had always hated her. How could she return to that country where she had once reigned as Queen, where she had been beloved – except by the Queen-Mother – where she had been so happy? How could she return, a miserable fugitive, begging for help, seeking a refuge?

She could imagine the reception she would get from Catherine de' Medici. She shivered; and as she looked through the window at the distant mountains of England, she spoke firmly: 'I am going to England. I shall throw myself on the mercy of my cousin Elizabeth.' The men about the table stared at her in dismay, but Mary went on: 'She will help me. She is angry, I have been told, to hear that I am so treated. She will give me her sympathy, and more. She will help me to regain my kingdom. We are of an age – though she is a few years older than I. We are both women, both Queens. There is a bond between us.'

'Your Majesty,' said Herries, 'I implore you to reconsider your decision. You know that Elizabeth has been helping Moray to defy you?'

'He sought her help and she gave it.'

'It does not seem as though she feels herself to be Your Majesty's friend.'

'If I can go to Hampton Court, and confer with her there. I know I shall win her sympathy. We are two women; we are cousins.'

'Your Majesty,' began Livingstone, 'can you trust the Queen of England?'

'I have never had any reason not to.'

'The English have always been our enemies. They killed your father.'

'I know, but that was not the present Queen.'

'May I recall to Your Majesty's mind how your illustrious ancestor, James I, ventured to England in a time of peace; he was made prisoner for many years.'

'This is a woman, a Queen like myself. She is no hard-hearted man who wants to go to war and pillage and kill. The Queen of England hates war. We know that.'

'She likes the spoils of war and prefers others to fight for them.'

'She hates war,' said Mary firmly.

'Your Majesty,' said Livingstone, 'when your royal father was invited to York to meet Henry VIII of England he was warned by his nobles, after setting out on the journey, that he would be wise to turn back. He did.'

'I cannot see,' said Mary, 'that any good will come of my staying in Scotland or going anywhere else.'

'To France . . .' began Herries.

' A perilous journey, and how can I be sure what my reception will be?'

'But . . . to the Queen of England!'

They were studying her in dismay. Had she forgotten that long ago, secure under the sheltering wing of the royal house of France, she had assumed the title, Queen of England? Elizabeth was not the woman to forget that.

She was weary of being a fugitive and across the Firth the country looked beautiful and at peace. She could never rest easily on Scottish soil. Her sleep would be broken by the slightest noise. She would be continually on the alert for the coming of the enemy who would carry her away to a prison like that of Lochleven.

She had made up her mind. She was a Queen and would insist on their obedience to her wishes.

Calmly she faced them.

'I am going to England,' she said.

* * *

She sent for George Douglas.

'Ah, George,' she said, holding out her hand. 'It is such a short while since I walked out of Lochleven, yet it seems like a year. What will you do now that I am going to England?'

George gulped because of the lump in his throat; his eyes were earnest as they met hers.

'Whatever Your Majesty commands.'

122

'I would not command you, George. I would have you act of your own free will.'

'My will is to obey Your Majesty's orders.'

She sighed. 'Oh, George,' she said, 'if I were not myself ... I could be very happy with you. But are you wise to link your fortunes to those of an exiled Queen?'

'Yes, Your Majesty, since I am only happy serving her.'

'You cannot stay in Scotland now, George. Your life would not be worth much if you did. You should go to France. I will give you letters of commendation which you could take to my uncles. They would reward you well for all you have done for me.'

George was silent.

Mary continued: 'Christian told me that before I came to the castle there was talk of your betrothal to a French heiress. That was true, George?'

'Yes, Your Majesty.'

'And you are no longer eager for that match?'

'I am eager only to serve my Queen.'

'Then, George, there is nothing for it. I shall have to give you your orders.' She laughed and, because she could not bear to see the anguish on his face, she said quickly: 'I order you to come to England with me, George Douglas.'

The relief shone from his eyes as he said: 'Yes, Your Majesty.'

'My friends do not trust the Queen of England, George. But I shall visit her, and when I talk to her I will make her understand. The sooner I am in England the easier I shall sleep. George, I wish you to go down to the Solway and arrange for a boat to carry us to England.'

George bowed low and eagerly went to perform his task.

* * *

While George went off on his quest with Willie as his companion, Lords Herries, Fleming, Livingstone and Boyd conferred together.

Herries said: 'As we cannot persuade the Queen not to go to England, there is only one course open to us. We must go with her.'

The others agreed, and Livingstone added: 'There can be no greater peril for us all than to stay in Scotland; and I doubt that the young Douglases will find such a craft as could

123

carry us to France in safety. It may be that this plan to visit England is the best after all.'

The others were silent. The position was full of dangers. They distrusted Elizabeth; in her realm they might lose their liberty; but if the Moray faction captured any of them it would be their heads that would go.

'Then,' said Herries, 'I will write to Sir Richard Lowther who is the Deputy-Governor of Carlisle and I will ask him for a safe conduct for the Queen and her party.'

'Do so without delay,' said Livingstone. 'I shall feel much happier when we receive it.'

So Herries wrote at once and dispatched a messenger to England.

*　　*　　*

Awaiting the return of George Douglas, Mary found it difficult to rest. She had in her possession a ring which Elizabeth of England had once sent her. This she had lost for a time but Melville had restored it to her with other possessions, and she took it out now and examined it.

It was delicately made and had two joints which, when put together, formed two right hands supporting a heart made of two diamonds which were held in place by a spring. When this was opened the ring could be divided into two halves.

Mary had been delighted to receive such a ring from her cousin of England. The symbolism implied by the ornament pleased her; believing Elizabeth to be of a nature similar to her own – warm, generous, forgiving, tolerant – she had thought that such a gift must mean the desire for her friendship.

Therefore merely to look at the ring comforted her.

She decided to write to her and send half of the ring, which she was sure would touch a tender chord in Elizabeth's heart, as it did in hers.

She sat down at a table and wrote:

'My dearest sister, You are not ignorant of my misfortunes but these which induce me to write at present have happened too recently yet to have reached your ear. I must therefore acquaint you as briefly as I can, that some of my subjects whom I most confided in and raised to the highest pitch of honour have taken up arms against me and treated me with the utmost indignity. By unexpected means the Almighty Disposer of all things delivered me from the cruel imprison-

ment I underwent; but I have since lost a battle in which
most of those who preserved their loyal integrity fell before
my eyes. I am now forced out of my kingdom, and driven
to such straits that, next to God, I have no hope but in your
goodness. I beseech you therefore, my dearest sister, that I
may be conducted to your presence, that I may acquaint
you with all my affairs. In the meantime I beseech God to
grant you all heavenly benedictions, and to me patience and
consolation, which last I hope and pray to obtain by your
means. To remind you of the reasons I have to depend on
England, I send back to its Queen this token of her promised friendship and assistance.

'Your affectionate sister. Mary R.
'From Dundrennan.'

She put half the ring with the letter and sealed it; and as
she was doing this Lady Livingstone came to tell her that her
husband wished to speak to the Queen.

Mary received him immediately, when he told her that in
case the rebel army should have received word that she was at
Dundrennan Abbey and attack during the night he, with
Herries and the rest had thought it best for her to leave the
Abbey and spend the night in a mansion close by. This was
Hazlefield, the home of a family named Maxwell who were
kinsfolk of Herries and eager to help her.

Mary agreed to this. 'With good luck, it may be for one
night only,' she added, 'for if George Douglas succeeds in
finding a vessel we shall leave for England tomorrow.'

'We cannot hope yet, Your Majesty, to receive a safe conduct from the Deputy-Governor of Carlisle. Herries' request
can scarcely have reached him.'

Mary laughed. 'Rest assured we do not need such a safe
conduct. We shall set out as soon as the vessel is found.'

Livingstone was less sure, but Mary added that delay was
dangerous. She would not sleep easily until she had left Scottish soil.

Shortly afterwards she left Dundrennan in the company of
a few of her female attendants and went to Hazlefield, there
to await news of what vessel George had been able to find to
convey them to England.

* * *

The Maxwells greeted her with respectful enthusiasm and
had already prepared their best suite of rooms for her use.

Jane Kennedy suggested that she should retire early and sleep while she could, for at any moment she might hear that the journey must continue.

Jane and Lady Livingstone were helping her to retire when the door of the chamber was silently pushed open. All three turned somewhat startled. There was no one at the door; but while they stared at it, it was gently opened further and a child came into the room. He was little more than a baby, and he was chuckling as though he were enjoying himself. He stopped a short distance from the group at the mirror and then, with a gurgle of laughter, darted at the Queen and threw himself against her.

Mary picked him up and sat him on her lap.

'And who are you?' she asked.

He stared at her wonderingly.

'So you have come to see me?' she asked.

He nodded and caught at one of the rings on her fingers which completely absorbed his attention.

He was beautiful and, as she looked at the plump wrists with their creases of soft flesh, Mary was overcome with emotion. This child was about the same age as her little James. In that moment she forgot all ambitions, all desires but one – to have her baby with her again. She caught at the boy and held him against her so tightly that he wriggled in protest while she kissed the soft hair and the rounded cheek. He submitted, not without some displeasure, and when she loosened her embrace he seized her fingers again and returned to his examination of the ring.

There were sounds of consternation outside the apartment, and when Jane Kennedy went to the door she found the child's nurse there.

'He is safe,' Jane told the woman. 'He is now on the Queen's lap examining her jewels. Come in. The Queen will wish to speak to you.'

So the nurse entered and, at the sight of her, the child turned towards Mary and gripped her hand tightly, and began to chant 'No – go away. He wants to stay.'

'You are his nurse and come to look for him?' said the Queen with a smile. 'Do you know, I think he would prefer to stay with me.'

The nurse made an embarrassed curtsey and said: 'Now that he can toddle about he's more than one body's work, Your Majesty.'

'I am glad he toddled into my apartment,' said the Queen. 'And you, my little man, are glad you came to see me?'

The child regarded her solemnly and chuckled. 'He stay,' he announced.

'Could you leave him with me for a while?' asked the Queen.

'Why . . . yes, I suppose so, Your Majesty. It was just that . . . it's his bedtime and —'

'Leave him for a while,' said the Queen. 'I will tell his parents that he is with me.'

As the nurse curtsied and went out, Mary said: 'My little one must be very like this. While I hold this child in my arms I can almost believe that he is my own son.'

Then she saw that about the child were attached leading-strings, and she thought of those which little James had once worn and how, when she had visited him in Stirling Castle and knew that she had to be parted from him, she had taken his leading-strings with her and kept them as something precious. They had been lost to her after Carberry Hill, but she often thought of them with regret.

The little boy was absorbed with interest in the Queen's fingers; he then examined her face and, as his plump fingers explored it, Mary caught them and kissed the little palms.

The boy wriggled off her lap and toddled over to a table behind which he hid himself, to emerge after a second or so almost choking with laughter. Then he hid himself again, and the Queen and her women pretended to hunt for him.

This game was in progress when the boy's mother appeared.

'You have come for your son?' asked Mary.

'I fear he is disturbing Your Majesty.'

'He is giving me much pleasure. May I keep him awhile?'

'If it is Your Majesty's wish.'

The child had come out and threw himself at his mother's skirts. He pointed to the Queen, as though to draw his mother's attention to her.

'Look!' he cried. 'Look!'

His mother lifted him up and he continued to cry: 'Look!' turning to point at Mary.

'Come,' said his mother, 'it is time you were in bed. I am sorry, Your Majesty. I know you wish to rest.'

'It was a pleasure to meet your son,' Mary answered.

The little boy, sensing that he was about to be taken away, turned in his mother's arms and held out his own to the Queen.

'He wants to stay with that one,' he cried.

'Hush! Hush!' said his mother.

But Mary went to him and again took him in her arms. 'I should like to keep him with me this night.'

'Your Majesty, he will disturb you.'

'I do not think so. If he is agreeable, it would please me to have him in my bed this night.'

The child's mother was secretly delighted at the Queen's pleasure in her son, so she kissed him and left him. As for the boy, he was delighted to be with Mary and her ladies; and when the Queen lay in bed, the boy was beside her.

He slept almost at once and Mary slept too, although several times during the night she awoke and remembered the child; and she wept a little out of longing for her own little James who had been taken from her.

In the morning she left Hazlefield for Dundrennan Abbey, but before she went she took a little ruby ring from her finger and gave it to the boy's mother.

'I pray you,' she said, 'give him this when he is a little older, and tell him that it is a gift from the Queen to whom his company gave such pleasure on what may well be her last night in Scotland for many a long year.'

*   *   *

Mary waited with her friends at the secluded Bay of the Abbey of Burn-foot on the Solway Firth. The vessel which George had been able to procure was nothing but a fishing-boat, and there was great misgiving among those assembled there.

Mary uttered a prayer as she stepped into the boat: A safe passage across the water, a warm welcome from the English Queen, the help she needed, and soon she would be back in Scotland.

Several of her friends were looking at her anxiously reminding her that there was still time to change her mind; but Mary had no intention of doing that. She was filled with hope on that beautiful May morning.

The surf in the Abbey Creek impeded the boat for some minutes, and then they were out on the Firth.

Scotland lay behind them – before them was England and what Mary believed to be the way back to her throne.

CHAPTER FOUR

CARLISLE

THE ENGLISH COAST was in sight. For four hours the fishing-boat in which were the Queen and her sixteen followers, together with four sailors, had been on the Solway Firth endeavouring to battle its way against a strong breeze. There had been an occasion during the trip when Mary had thought that they would be blown out to sea; in which case she knew that her friends would have taken that as an omen that their destination should have been France.

But now they were within a few minutes of landing, and already the inhabitants of that stretch of coast had noticed the ship and were coming down to the shore to see who was descending upon them.

These simple people stared in astonishment at the strangers, and immediately all eyes were focused on the tall woman who carried herself with such dignity and whose beauty, in spite of her tattered and soiled gown and the fact that her hair was escaping from her coif, was such as to startle them.

It was Herries who spoke. 'This is the Queen of Scotland. Who is the lord of these parts?'

While some of the people pointed to a mansion on an incline a little distance from the coast, one or two of the younger men began to run in that direction, and with satisfaction Herries understood that they were going to acquaint someone of importance of the arrival.

Livingstone came to stand beside the Queen. 'Perhaps we might walk towards the house,' he said. 'It is not seemly for Your Majesty to remain here among these staring people.'

The others agreed and Herries announced: 'We will go to your master's house. Lead us thither.'

The people continued to stare at the Queen, but some of their number were ready to lead the way and the little party set off.

A strange manner, thought Mary, for a Queen to travel. And she thought of other journeys with the pomp and richness of royalty all about her.

Before they had arrived at Workington Hall, its owner, Sir Henry Curwen, now having been warned of her approach, came out to meet the party.

When he reached the Queen he bowed and bade her welcome to Workington. Then he led the way into a wooded park, and Mary felt a great relief as the gracious mansion with its castellated towers and turrets loomed before her. As she passed through the embattled gateway Sir Henry's wife and mother were waiting to greet them.

When the younger Lady Curwen had made her curtsey she told the Queen Workington Hall was at her disposal for as long as she wished and that, having heard of Her Majesty's arrival, she had immediately ordered that the finest apartments in the house should be made ready for her.

'We are sixteen,' said Mary with an apologetic smile; 'and we come unannounced. But I know you will feel pity for us when you hear of our misfortunes.'

'Let me conduct you to my own rooms while yours are being prepared,' said Lady Curwen. 'There perhaps I can help you with a change of linen and a clean gown while food is made ready.'

'You are very kind.'

'We count it an honour to have the Queen of Scotland under our roof,' said Sir Henry.

'I am sure,' put in the Dowager Lady Curwen, 'that *our* good Queen would be most displeased if we showed aught but warm hospitality to her kinswoman.'

'I hope soon to be with her,' Mary answered. 'Then I shall tell her how happy I was to be so warmly received as soon as I stepped on her soil.'

Lady Curwen led the way to her own rooms, and, while water was brought and Mary and her ladies washed the stains of the journey from their persons, clothes were sent in for them.

For Mary there was a gown of crimson brocade slashed with white satin; it was fortunately loose, which helped to hide the fact that the fit was not perfect. Jane Kennedy combed the long chestnut hair back from the high forehead and a small round cap was placed at the back of Mary's head, over which was a veil, edged with gold; this draped gracefully over her shoulders.

When she was dressed in these garments Mary felt almost gay. The worst was over, she told herself; the next step would be the journey south to Hampton Court or Windsor, or whatsoever meeting place Elizabeth suggested – and then, with England's help, would begin the regaining of her throne.

There were clean clothes for her female attendants and, when they had changed, they felt their spirits rising. It was only three days since the defeat at Langside, but those had been spent in almost continual travel, frequently by night, and it was a great relief to put on clean garments.

When Mary went to the apartments which had been prepared for her she found food and wine waiting for her there because, explained Lady Curwen, her servants were endeavouring to prepare a repast which would, they hoped, be more worthy of their royal guest.

Mary's warm-hearted thanks immediately won the friendship of the Curwens, and when they had made sure that the Queen had everything she needed and was resting in her apartments they left her to concern themselves with arrangements for her entertainment.

It was a few hours after the Queen's arrival at Workington Hall and while she was still resting, when a messenger came riding into the courtyard demanding to be taken with all speed to Sir Henry Curwen.

When Sir Henry received the messenger he was informed that the man came from the Earl of Northumberland, the lord of the district.

Northumberland had heard that the Queen of Scots had arrived in England; he was not as surprised by this as Sir Henry Curwen had been, because he had heard from Sir Richard Lowther that Lord Herries had written to him asking for Mary's safe conduct. He was therefore on the alert; and he knew his duty. He did not wish the Queen to know that she was again a prisoner, but this was what she must be until instructions were received, in the name of Elizabeth, as to what was to be done with her. Northumberland's commands were that on the following day Curwen's royal guest was to be conducted from Workington Hall to Cockermouth Hall. Northumberland, not being in residence at his castle, could not entertain her there, and it was for this reason that she was to be lodged at Cockermouth Hall, the home of Henry Fletcher, a rich merchant of the district. He was sending guards who, the Queen must be made to believe, were to protect her on the short journey and to conduct her thither; actually they would be there to make sure she did not escape.

Curwen, listening to these instructions, was indignant, but he dared not disobey Northumberland; and when the Queen appeared for supper he told her that the Earl of Northumberland had heard of her arrival and wished to entertain her in his castle. Unfortunately he was not in residence, but invited her to go to Cockermouth, where she would be entertained until he could reach her.

Mary was not displeased and without suspicion. She knew that Northumberland was a Catholic, and therefore she believed he would be an ally.

'But,' she said, 'I shall be very sorry to say goodbye so soon to you and your family, Sir Henry. You have made me so welcome and I shall never forget that you were my first friends in England.'

It was a merry supper which was eaten in the dining hall at Workington. Mary looked very beautiful in her crimson brocade; and when Lady Curwen brought her a lute, she played and sang a little.

She was full of hope and high spirits when she retired to her apartments. She slept long and deep. The nightmare of Langside and the three days of exhausting travel seemed to have happened a long time ago.

I was right, she thought, to come to England.

*   *   *

The rising sun awakened her and it was some seconds before she realized where she was.

She raised herself and looked out of the window. England! she thought. This time yesterday she had been in Scotland, and already she had good friends here, in the Curwens and Northumberland. Soon she would be calling Elizabeth her friend.

She would write to Elizabeth; then she was sure there would be no delay. She would receive a warm invitation to ride south with all speed, and how wonderful it would be to meet the Queen in that Hampton Court of which she had heard so much! How long would it be? She was impatient for the meeting.

She found that the writing materials for which she had asked had been set out on a table and, rising from her bed, she sat down and wrote to the Queen of England.

'I entreat you to send for me as soon as possible, for I am in a pitiable condition, not only for a Queen but even for a

132

gentlewoman, having nothing in the world but what I had on my person when I escaped. . . .'

She sighed and looked at the crimson brocade almost lovingly. Soon, she believed, she would have some clothes becoming to her station. She had a feminine interest in them and had enjoyed adding little touches to make them entirely her own, and if she could only have some of her own clothes sent to her she would feel more like herself.

'. . . I hope to be able to declare my misfortunes to you if it pleases you to have compassion and permit me to come and bewail them to you. Not to weary you, I will now pray God to give you health and a long and happy life, and to myself patience, and that consolation I await from you, to whom I present my humble commendations. From Workington this 17th of May. Your very faithful and affectionate good sister and cousin and escaped prisoner,

'Mary R.'

She sealed this letter and went back to her bed to await the arrival of her attendants.

*   *   *

The sun was high in the sky when Mary left Workington Hall for Cockermouth. The distance the cavalcade had to travel was only six miles but it was across country which enchanted Mary. She saw the winding Derwent and the English mountains with the peak of Skiddaw, dominating all others, stretching up to the blue sky, while her own Scottish mountains rose like grim guards on the other side of the Solway.

She was confident. She had received such kindness from her hosts; Sir Henry and his son rode with her now and the people of Workington had come out of their houses to see her ride by. They gave her a cheer and stared in admiration now that she was in red brocade and flowing veil.

Cockermouth Hall was as pleasant a residence as Workington Hall and its owner, Henry Fletcher, who was as eager to make her welcome as Sir Henry Curwen had been, was waiting to receive her. He bowed low and told her that he had had apartments made ready for her on the first floor, where the most spacious rooms in Cockermouth Hall were situated. He considered it an honour to entertain the Queen of Scotland in his house and if there was anything she lacked he begged her to make him aware of this.

133

Mary thanked him and her gracious charm had the same effect upon him as it had had on Sir Henry Curwen. Her pleasure was increased when she found that she had been given three large rooms, leading from each other, which would be her ante-chamber, presence chamber and bedchamber.

Henry Fletcher, who conducted her thither, expressed a hope that they would suffice during her brief stay on her way to Carlisle Castle, where she would be lodged in a manner more fitting to her estate.

Mary thanked him and added that she could not have been more comfortable in any castle; and if only she had some of her own clothes she would feel completely at home.

Fletcher bowed himself from her presence and Jane Kennedy and Lady Livingstone set about examining the apartments more closely in order that they might make their mistress comfortable.

While they were thus engaged there was a knock at the door and a servant entered with a large parcel which he set on the bed, with the words that it came with the compliments of his master.

When he had gone the women gathered round while Mary unwrapped the parcel; and there were exclamations of delight as thirteen ells of scarlet velvet cascaded over the bed.

Henry Fletcher had sent a note with this in which he expressed his hopes that the Queen had good seamstresses in her party who would be able to make a gown for her.

Mary stood for some seconds holding the rich material against her, her eyes filling with tears because she was deeply affected, as always, by the kindness of people towards her.

Then she burst into laughter instead of tears and, flinging the velvet about her, embraced Lady Livingstone and Jane Kennedy.

'You see how we are treated by the English!' she cried. 'They are kind, as I knew they would be. And all the consideration I am now given by Elizabeth's subjects is but a foretaste of what I shall receive from my good sister.'

She watched Jane Kennedy fingering the material and speculating as to how the gown should be cut; and she was happier than she had been since that morning in Castlemilk when she had looked from the battlements and seen the gathering forces of her enemy.

*   *   *

The stay at Cockermouth was as brief as that at Workington had been, but before she left Mary had the pleasure of meeting some of the noblest ladies of this district. These, led by Lady Scrope, who was the Duke of Norfolk's sister and therefore one of the noblest ladies in England, called at Cockermouth Hall to pay their respects to her; and Lady Scrope told the Queen that she would accompany her to Carlisle Castle and act as a maid of honour to Her Majesty of Scotland. Mary had only one regret at this meeting; there had not been time to make the thirteen ells of velvet into a gown, and she was forced to greet the ladies of England in her borrowed red brocade.

However, her natural beauty and queenly bearing stood her in good stead, and in spite of their fine garments Mary stood apart, undoubtedly Queen, undoubtedly the loveliest creature any of the ladies had ever beheld.

But during the journey to Carlisle Castle Mary's spirits were temporarily dashed, for on the road she met the French Ambassador to Scotland who, hearing that she had escaped to England, had followed her there.

Eagerly she asked for news of Scotland, but he could tell her nothing for her comfort. Many of her friends had died and others were in danger of losing their lives and possessions because they had befriended her.

Sobered, Mary continued the journey with the French Ambassador riding beside her and as they passed under the portcullis of the red stone castle of Carlisle, Herries glanced at Livingstone and he saw concern on the latter's face similar to that which he himself was feeling.

They had no need to express their thoughts. This was a fortress indeed. They were as far north as they had been on the day they arrived in England.

If the Queen of England was eager to see her sister of Scotland, should they not be travelling south?

They could not share Mary's elation as they entered Carlisle Castle.

*　　*　　*

Sir Richard Lowther, Deputy-Governor of Carlisle, to whom Lord Herries had written, arrived at Carlisle Castle to see the Queen. It had been on his instructions that she had been lodged there for, on hearing that she had arrived in England, he had immediately dispatched a messenger to Elizabeth and her ministers asking for instructions. In the meantime he had decided that it was his duty to hold Mary in his custody.

He was courteous to Mary and told her that he hoped soon to receive instructions from his Queen; until that time he would give orders that she should be made comfortable in the castle.

Mary's apartments there, were indeed comfortable with the May sunshine warming the place. In winter it would be a different story, but the winter was a long way off and by that time, Mary believed, she would either be living in luxury at Elizabeth's Court or, better still, would have regained her throne and be back in Edinburgh.

Her spirits had been considerably lowered by the news of the suffering which must be endured by her faithful friends who had remained behind in Scotland. She must not allow George or Willie Douglas to go back until she had regained her throne; as the two who had delivered her from Lochleven, their lives would doubtless be forfeited.

But her hopes were still high as she sat in the seat of her window in the tower and looked out at the pleasant meandering River Eden.

One of her first visitors to Carlisle Castle was Thomas Percy, Earl of Northumberland. Mary was delighted to receive the Earl because she believed that, as a good Catholic, he would be eager to give her his support against Protestant Moray.

The Earl bowed low and told her that it gave him great pleasure to meet her, but that his pleasure was tempered with sadness because of the reason for her presence in Carlisle.

'I am very eager to meet the Queen of England,' she told him. 'I have been treated with great kindness by all in England, but I do find the delay irksome and I wonder why I must wait in this manner.'

The Earl replied: 'Your Majesty, if I were in charge of your comfort it would not be so.'

'Then, my lord, how I wish that you *were* in charge of my comfort.'

'I will see what can be done in the matter,' he told her, all his chivalry aroused by the plight of this beautiful creature.

'Then,' said Mary softly, 'it would seem that each day I become more indebted to Englishmen.'

When Northumberland left her he went to Sir Richard Lowther and said in a somewhat arrogant manner: 'Your duties towards the Queen of Scots are now ended. I will take over the charge of her.'

Lowther answered: 'No, my lord Earl, you forget that, as Lord Warden, that duty is mine.'

'I disagree. As chief magnate of this district the task of the Queen's safe custody should be in my hands.'

The two men faced each other. It was true that Northumberland was the lord of the district, but Lowther knew that he himself would be responsible for the Queen of Scots to the Queen of England. Moreover Northumberland, on account of his religion, was no great favourite of Elizabeth and her ministers. Northumberland was a simple-minded man; he was unusually lacking in political ambitions; but being utterly devoted to the Catholic Faith, he felt it his duty to aid the Queen of Scots with all his power. As a Catholic he doubted the rights of Elizabeth herself, and it seemed to him that Mary was not only the Queen of Scotland but had a very strong claim to the throne of England also.

Lowther was aware of this, so in spite of his adversary's rank he remained adamant.

He drew Northumberland to the window and showed him the troops stationed outside. 'They obey my orders,' he said. 'It would go ill with any – noble earl or not – who sought to prevent me from doing my duty.'

Northumberland's face turned a dull red as he glared down at the soldiers.

'You varlet!' he cried. 'You are too low a man to pretend to such a charge.'

'It is true,' answered Lowther, 'that I am not a noble earl, but noble earls have been known to part with their heads on the scaffold for disobeying their Sovereign's orders.'

'And how do you propose to prevent my taking charge of the Queen?'

Lowther knew that Northumberland was no strategist.

He said coolly: 'By putting you under guard and sending you to London.' He nodded towards the courtyard. 'There are my soldiers . . . waiting. Attempt to take my charge from me, and you are the Queen's prisoner.'

Northumberland, turning away, muttered: 'It's a sorry day for England when low-bred varlets threaten noble earls.'

So might it have been, thought Lowther grimly, but he had won the day. The Queen of Scots remained in his charge.

*　　*　　*

It was a few days after the visit of Northumberland, when Mary was eagerly awaiting a summons from Elizabeth, that she was surprised and delighted to receive a visit from the Duke of Norfolk.

He had good reason for being in the district; his sister, Lady Scrope, was with the Queen, and what more natural than that he should call on her. Moreover, his third wife, who had recently died, had been the daughter of Sir Francis Leybourne of Cunswick Hall in Cumberland and widow of Lord Dacre. He certainly had business in the North.

Having heard a great deal about the charm and beauty of the Queen of Scotland he wished to discover whether these reports had been exaggerated. He saw at once that they were not, and he was enchanted.

Mary bade him sit beside her while she told him how eagerly she waited for a message from the Queen of England.

'It will come,' he told her. 'All in good time. The Queen has always expressed great interest in Your Majesty's affairs and doubtless will be most eager to meet you.'

'I had thought to be well on my journey south by now. I cannot understand why it should be considered necessary for me to stay so long in Carlisle Castle.'

'Has Your Majesty suggested that you should move south?'

'Why yes,' she told him. 'Sir Richard Lowther is very courteous but he is firm on this matter. He asks me to be patient until he has commands from his Queen.'

'He does well to wait.'

'Of a certainty he would not wish to offend his mistress, but . . . since as you say she is eager to meet me . . . and I most certainly am to meet her, it is hard to stomach this delay.'

'Ah, our Queen has a high temper. Lowther will be remembering that. Doubtless he will receive a reprimand for not speeding your journey to the English Court.'

'I shall make a point of telling my cousin how kind he has been in every way; and I am sure the delay is only due to his desire to obey her wishes in every detail.'

Norfolk's mind was busy. How gentle she was! How forgiving! And what a beauty! He was an ambitious man; he was also the premier peer and richest man in England. The Howards were of course a noble family and a rich one, but his marriages had been wise ones and, although he was now only thirty-two, in a little more than ten years he had been thrice widowed. His first wife, Lady Mary Fitzalan, had been the heiress of the Earl of Arundel. She had died when only sixteen, leaving him a son Philip who had inherited his grandfather's title of Earl of Arundel. His second wife had been Margaret, heiress-daughter of Lord Audley; that marriage had lasted five years and had ended in the death of Margaret. In a little over three years later, early in 1567 he had married once more; this time Dacre's widow, who had died before the year was out. These heiresses had added to his own considerable fortune; but as Elizabeth Dacre had had a son and three daughters when she married him and he was eager to keep the Dacre fortune in the family he was endeavouring to arrange marriages between his own children and his step-children.

He had not found great favour at Elizabeth's Court since he had resented her friendship with the Earl of Leicester, but even the Queen could not ignore the premier peer who was also the richest man in the country.

As he talked pleasantly with Mary a certain speculation entered his mind. She was undoubtedly marriageable. It was true her husband Bothwell was still living. What had happened to him? There had been many rumours, and the fellow would never dare to return to Scotland if he valued his life. There could be a divorce. A dispensation from the Pope might be obtained.

His three wives had been heiresses. Well, here was an heiress of another kind – the greatest heiress of them all, if she regained what was hers.

These thoughts made Norfolk's eyes shine and the gallantries trip from his tongue. Mary found pleasure in them particularly as they could mean that this powerful Englishman was ready to be her friend.

The visit was all too brief, and when Norfolk departed he kissed her hand with a certain emotion which was significant.

There had been numbers of men in love with Mary. She was not yet twenty-six years old, but she had felt very old during the last weeks and burdened with responsibilities.

The Duke of Norfolk had made her feel young again and she was grateful to him.

*　　*　　*

There was excitement in the castle because of new arrivals from Scotland. The Queen had been sitting in her window looking out over the countryside and had seen them approaching; she had called Jane Kennedy and Lady Livingstone to her side, and they had all stood watching until as the party came nearer they recognized familiar faces.

'It is!' Mary murmured. 'I really believe it is!'

Jane cried out: 'That's Bastian and his wife Margaret Cawood. I remember the night they were married. . . .'

She stopped. Bastian, the valet, had been married to Margaret Cawood, the maid, on the night when Darnley was murdered.

Mary said, as though she had not heard: 'There are Lord and Lady Fleming . . . and yes . . . Marie Courcelles and my dear . . . dear Seton.'

Mary could wait no longer; she went down to the courtyard to greet the newcomers.

There had been no mistake; she was almost weeping with joy. She would have no ceremony; she took these dear people one by one into her arms and embraced them all.

'Your Majesty is not more happy to see us than we are to come,' Seton told her.

'My dearest Seton!' cried Mary. 'How can I tell you all how much I love you!'

Now it seemed that she had a suite worthy of a Queen. There were twenty-eight people in her entourage, for they had brought with them a cook, a pantler and a pâtissier.

'There will doubtless be more coming to your service,' Marie Courcelles told her, 'for when it was known that we proposed to follow you to England, there were many who wished to join us and announced their intention of following in our wake.'

'If this were but one of my own palaces I should order a banquet such as I never gave before,' Mary told them.

'The welcome you have given us brings us more pleasure than aught else could ever do,' Lord Fleming replied on behalf of them all.

It was wonderful to sit with Seton and Marie Courcelles and hear news of Scotland. The first subject they discussed was Lochleven and what had happened when Mary's flight had been discovered. Seton told of the rage and despair of Sir William and how Lady Douglas could not help showing her pride in George who had had a hand in it all, and while condoling with William was obviously hoping that George would not suffer because of the help he had given the Queen.

'Nor shall he,' murmured Mary fervently, 'if I can prevent it.'

It had been some time before Sir William noticed the loss of his keys and gave the alarm; by that time Mary was on the mainland. The commotion in the castle had been tremendous. Sir William's great concern had been how to break out and give the alarm, and to send guards in search of the escaping party.

'As for Will Drysdale,' went on Seton, 'when he returned he swore that if George and Willie Douglas ever fell into his hands he would cut them into collops and wash his hands in their hearts' blood.'

Mary shuddered. 'I must make sure they never do,' she answered.

There was little good news Seton had to impart, so she changed the subject of what was happening in Scotland and expressed her displeasure at the Queen's appearance.

'Your Majesty's hair!'

'Yes,' Mary agreed. 'It has suffered without you. I know you are the best busker in Scotland – and, I doubt not, in England also. Seton, when we go to Hampton Court you must not let Elizabeth lure you from me.'

'As if anyone could ever lure me from Your Majesty!'

'They say she is very vain, Seton. She will doubtless envy me my busker.'

'Then she may envy all she wishes. I should like to get to work on your hair at once.'

'All in good time, Seton. You must not let Jane Kennedy notice your contempt though. She believes herself to be a very good busker. So we must have a care.' Then Mary sighed. 'Why do I talk of frivolous things when my heart is so full? But I must go on or I shall weep. So Seton, how will you dress my hair? What are you going to say when you see that I have but one red brocade dress, given me by Lady Curwen who took pity on my poverty? And thirteen ells of red velvet . . . also a gift of pity. How shall we make up those thirteen ells . . . eh, Seton?'

Then Mary took her closest friend in her arms and they laughed and cried together.

* * *

The next day, sitting alone with the Queen, Seton spoke of Bothwell.

'There is news of him,' she told Mary, 'and I have been wondering whether it would grieve you to hear it.'

'It may grieve me,' said Mary, 'but I must know it.'

'He is alive.'

Mary was silent. Speaking of him brought back such vivid memories; and yet she was not sure that she wished to see him. Her experiences since Carberry Hill had changed her so much; how could she know what the woman she had become would feel towards the bold Borderer?

'And,' went on Seton, 'the prisoner of the King of Denmark.'

'A prisoner! That will not please his bold spirit.'

'Moray has made efforts to have him sent back to Scotland.'

'That he might kill him,' said Mary expressionlessly.

'I have heard that the King of Denmark is a little inclined in his favour because Bothwell wrote to him after he had been seized, saying that he was on his way to him to lay before him and the King of France the wrongs you had been forced to suffer, and to ask their help. He assured the King of Denmark that he had been acquitted of the murder of Darnley; therefore that King would not send him back to Scotland, but satisfied himself by keeping Bothwell in prison.'

'He will suffer in prison,' Mary murmured. 'I believe he would endure death rather.'

'I heard too that he had promised the King of Denmark the Islands of Orkney and Shetland in return for his liberty.'

'Ah! He would risk his life for freedom, I am sure, so should we be surprised that he offers the islands? And the King of Denmark?'

'Doubtless he knows that it would be too difficult to hold those islands. So Bothwell remains a prisoner. It is said that he has now been moved to a new prison at Malmoe – to one from which it would be well nigh impossible to escape.'

Mary was silent thinking: Tonight I shall dream of him. It will be as though he is beside me, as though we are back in the days before Carberry Hill.

Thus it had always been when others had talked of him with her, and she believed that she would never escape from her memories as long as she lived. But that night she did not dream of Bothwell. She dreamed of arriving at Hampton Court and being embraced by Elizabeth who said: 'Give me Mary Seton to dress my hair and I will return your kingdom.'

She awoke laughing.

Then she knew that she was indeed changed. She had escaped from the spell of James Hepburn, Earl of Bothwell.

*　　*　　*

News came to the castle that Queen Elizabeth was sending two trusted noblemen to the Queen of Scotland that she might be assured of her dear sister's comfort. These were Lord Scrope and Sir Francis Knollys.

When he heard that they were coming, Lord Herries discussed the meaning of their appointments with Livingstone and Fleming.

'I do not like the sound of this,' said Herries.

Fleming and Livingstone agreed.

'The delay is too long,' added Fleming. 'Something is afoot. I would I knew what.'

'At least we know,' put in Livingstone, 'that if the Queen attempted now to go back to Scotland, she would be prevented from doing so.'

'And therefore,' went on Fleming, 'she is virtually a prisoner. Carlisle is a little more pleasant than Lochleven, but it is imprisonment all the same – even though the Queen is unaware of it.'

'We can only say that she appears to be a prisoner,' said Herries. 'Do not let us make her aware of our suspicions until we know them to be justified. She has suffered so much already, and is hoping for so much from this interview with the Queen.'

'Why do you think Scrope and Knollys are being sent?' asked Fleming.

'To replace Lowther who has offended the Queen by allowing Norfolk to visit Her Majesty.'

'Elizabeth is notoriously jealous of our Queen,' said Livingstone. 'She does not wish her to receive the gentlemen of England in her apartments. It may be that Norfolk has prated of her beauty. Oddly enough that could upset Elizabeth more than anything else.'

'I feel sure it is the reason for Lowther's dismissal from his post as jailor,' Herries said. 'I suggest that I go out to meet them. If I can have a quiet talk with them before they arrive, it may well be that I can discover the true state of Elizabeth's feelings towards the Queen.'

The others agreed that it would be an excellent idea if he set out at once and made contact with the new jailors before they reached Carlisle Castle.

*   *   *

Lord Herries met Sir Francis Knollys and Lord Scrope about six miles from Carlisle Castle. He introduced himself

143

and told them that if they were willing he proposed to make the journey back with them, as there were certain matters he wished to discuss on the way.

Both Knollys and Scrope were uneasy. They had their instructions direct from Sir William Cecil. They were to keep watch over the Queen of Scots and prevent her slipping back over the Border to Scotland; they were to intercept all letters which came to her; they were to report any remark which might be used against her and give the Queen and her ministers an excuse for holding her a prisoner; they were to prevent her seeking help from foreign powers; and while they performed these duties it was considered desirable to make her believe that she was not being held prisoner.

It was by no means an easy task, and both men would have been happy to avoid it.

Sir Francis Knollys was a favourite of Elizabeth, partly because he had married her maternal cousin, Catherine Carey; she had made him her vice-chamberlain and he was a member of her Privy Council.

Henry Scrope, Baron Scrope of Bolton, was also a man of whom Elizabeth had a high opinion; he had been an intermediary between Elizabeth and Moray and was aware of facts not known to many. He also was a member of the Privy Council.

Herries regarded these men anxiously, wondering what their arrival was going to mean to his mistress; but they greeted him cordially and told him that they appreciated his coming to meet them.

'You will find my mistress in a sorry state,' Herries told them. 'She has been treated with great disrespect and has been accused of crimes of which she is innocent.'

Neither Knollys nor Scrope offered comment on this, but replied by saying that they were eager to meet the Queen of whose beauty and charm they had heard much.

'I and her friends are hoping that you bring her an invitation to the English Court.'

Herries was looking eagerly into the faces of the men as he asked this important question.

Knollys answered: 'There are matters which have to be settled before such an invitation could be given.'

'How so?' demanded Herries. 'Should not these matters be settled between the Queens at their meeting?'

'There have been evil rumours concerning the Queen of

Scots. She has been accused of playing a part in her husband's murder.'

'Lies! Calumnies! The Queen is completely innocent.'

Scrope said: 'Our Queen is jealous of her reputation.'

Jealous of her reputation! It was all Herries could do to stop himself shouting: I seem to remember a little matter in which your Queen was concerned. Her lover, Dudley, had a wife who was found dead at the bottom of a staircase. Oh, she did not marry Dudley then. . . . She was too wise. Too cold, too hard, too determined to stay on the throne. But is she in a position to question what part the Queen of Scots played in the murder of Darnley while there is a doubt as to what part Elizabeth of England played in the mysterious death of Amy Robsart?

But he must be careful. To alienate the sympathies of Elizabeth and her subjects now could be fatal to Mary's cause. Of one thing he was certain. There was going to be no easy way for Mary to reach the English Court.

Knollys went on: 'It might be necessary for the Queen of Scots to clear her name before the Queen of England could receive her.'

'I must go to the Queen of England as soon as it can be arranged,' said Herries. 'I must myself make her understand the innocence of my Queen.'

'That might be an excellent plan,' admitted Scrope, looking at Knollys. And Herries wondered: Are they eager for me to be gone? Do they want to see me out of the way? And what would happen to me when I reached London? Should I be sent to a lonely cell, there to regret my zeal for what they hope to make the lost cause of the Queen of Scots?

'Our mistress has heard that her cousin of Scotland has need of garments. We have with us a box of clothes – a present to the Queen of Scotland from the Queen of England.'

'I am sure my mistress will receive this gift with pleasure.'

And as they came nearer to Carlisle Castle Herries' spirits sank still further. It seemed to him that the arrival of Knollys and Scrope confirmed what he had always feared; it had been a mistake to expect help from the Queen of England.

* * *

Mary received Scrope and Knollys in her apartments in the tower of the castle. She was wearing the red brocade dress, having no other, but Mary Seton's work on her hair had

145

transformed her appearance. She looked very beautiful, and Knollys to a large degree, Scrope to a lesser, felt a sudden loathing of the part they had to play.

Rumour had certainly not lied about the Queen's appearance; and the sweetness of her expression and the gracious way in which she received them made them understand why so many of her servants had wished to come to England to be with her.

'Well,' she said, 'I trust you bring me news of my good sister.'

'The Queen of England sends affectionate greetings to Your Majesty.'

'I hope soon to thank her for them with my own lips.'

Knollys and Scrope hesitated, and Mary said sharply: 'Do you bring me an invitation to her Court?'

'No, Your Majesty.' Scrope was leaving Knollys to explain. 'Your Majesty will understand. . . . You come to England under a sad suspicion.'

'Suspicion?' cried Mary.

'Your Majesty, your second husband died mysteriously, and rumour has it that, since you married so quickly after his death. . . .'

Mary lifted a hand. In that moment she was very regal and almost forbidding. 'Say no more,' she said. 'All who know me are certain of my innocence in that matter, and I have not come to England to defend myself.'

'Your Majesty, the Queen of England is jealous of her reputation.'

'She has need to be,' answered Mary promptly.

'As a virgin Queen she is eager that no scandal shall attach to her name, as might be the case if she entertained at her Court one who —'

Mary laughed. She wanted to say: It is not so long ago that Robert Dudley and the Queen were concerned in a similar matter. But she did not mention this, because she understood that one of the reasons why Elizabeth was so eager to protect what she called her good name was because there must be many who remembered the Amy Robsart mystery and were asking themselves if that name was so spotless, if the Queen, who so eagerly proclaimed herself a virgin, was not too emphatic on this matter.

But she was hurt, and the tears of anger momentarily gleamed in her eyes.

Knollys felt his pity touched by the sight of her, and he said gently: 'Our Queen is sorry that she cannot do you the honour of admitting you to her presence as yet. But the time will come when Your Majesty is purged of this slander of murder. But the affection of our royal mistress towards Your Majesty is very great and you may depend on her favour. But she would not be pleased if you brought strangers into Scotland. If you do not do this she will use all her means to make you comfortable during your stay in her realm.'

'But do you not see,' persisted Mary, 'that I have come here for a temporary refuge, that I hope for help to regain my kingdom? If the Queen will not see me, how can I hope to make her understand my case?'

'Her Majesty of England will admit Your Majesty of Scotland to her presence when you are cleared of the slander, which we all trust you will be ere long. To show her friendship Her Majesty has sent you a gift.'

Lord Scrope said: 'My servants will bring it up at once.'

Knollys felt sick with shame. He did not know what was in the box, but Elizabeth had sent for him and Scrope and told them that she was eager to know exactly what the Queen of Scotland's reactions were on opening the box; and because of the malicious smile which had been on Elizabeth's face when she had said this, he was apprehensive.

The box was brought in and Mary called for Seton to come and help unpack it.

While this was done Knollys and Scrope stood by.

Seton gasped as she lifted out two shifts that were frayed at the edges and in holes. Mary looked with astonishment from these garments to Scrope and Knollys, neither of whom could meet her gaze. There were some pieces of black velvet almost rusty with age; there were shoes scuffed at the toes and almost falling to pieces; and undergarments badly in need of patching.

'Is this what the Queen of England sends me for my wardrobe?' asked Mary, and the quietness of her tone betrayed to those who knew her what restraint she had to exercise to subdue her anger. She had had a vision of herself at the Court of France in blue velvet and gold, and the courtiers and the King of France with Madame de Poitiers, and young François telling her that she was the loveliest girl at the Court; that she had a way with a gown which transformed it into a thing of beauty when it clothed her form. Then she heard the cheers of the crowds as she rode through the streets of Paris. 'Long live the Dauphine! Long live the Queen of England!'

How careless she had been then! What had her red-headed rival in England said of her, thought of her, when she had heard that in Paris she, Mary, was being called the Queen of England? Was she determined on revenge? Was this that revenge? Two pieces of mangy velvet, patched shifts, worn-out shoes! Was this a symbol of the help she must expect from the Queen of England?

She scarcely glanced at the things in the box and Knollys began to stammer: 'The Queen of England understood that your maids were in need of clothes. These were intended for them.'

'Perhaps she intended them for my scullions,' said Mary sharply. 'But do you know, when I had my own Court, I wished to see my lowest servants decently clad.'

She signed that the interview was over, and Knollys at least was glad. He felt ashamed.

Scrope eyed him warily. That remark about the contents of the box being intended for the maids was extraordinary. Was Knollys, like so many others, about to become a victim of the fascinating Queen of Scots?

Shortly after Knollys and Scrope had left her, and before she had recovered from her anger, the Lords Herries and Fleming were asking for an audience.

She admitted them at once and saw from their grim looks that their fears equalled her own.

She smiled wanly at Herries. 'You do not say, my lord, that you warned me not to come to England. But I remember that you did.'

Herries shook his head sadly. 'Who can say what would have befallen us if we had tried to reach France, Your Majesty?'

'Nothing worse than that which could happen to us in England. Why, my lords, I feel almost as much a prisoner here as I did in Lochleven. Remember how long I have been here. I have made no progress through England at all. I have merely changed Lochleven for Carlisle.'

'We have a suggestion to put to Your Majesty,' said Fleming. 'Someone must plead your cause with Queen Elizabeth and, since it cannot be yourself, we propose that one of us should go to London and try to obtain an audience with her.'

Mary looked from one to the other.

'I should go, Your Majesty, with your permission,' Herries told her.

'I shall miss you, my good and faithful counsellor.'

'You have a bigger retinue than when you came – all faithful friends,' said Herries. 'I can now leave Your Majesty with confidence, knowing that you have about you those who will protect you with their lives.'

'God bless you,' Mary replied emotionally. 'When do you propose to set out?'

'Immediately.'

Fleming said: 'I have come to ask Your Majesty's permission to go to France . . . if that is possible.'

'To France!' Mary's eyes widened. 'Ah, that is where I should have gone when I left Scotland. I see it all now. The King of France would have been a good friend to me. He is older now and, it may be, not so completely under the control of his mother. And you will go to him, my lord Fleming, and tell him of my plight.'

'Herries and I have talked of this matter,' Fleming went on. 'I shall tell Your Majesty's Uncles, the Duke of Guise and the Cardinal of Lorraine, what is happening to you in England. I shall explain to His Majesty of France that we do not trust the English and I shall ask for their help and advice.'

'We can trust them, I know,' said Mary. 'They are indeed my friends.'

'It will be necessary for the Queen of England to give me a safe conduct,' Fleming pointed out.

'Which she will not do if she believes you are going to ask for French help,' added Herries. 'The last thing she wishes to do is to bring the French into Scotland. It would not be a difficult matter then for them to cross the Border.'

'My plan, Your Majesty,' went on Fleming, 'is to tell the Queen of England that the King of France has offered help – which he has – but that as you are not yet in a position to receive it you wish, while thanking him to ask if you may call on it later if and when you should be in a position to make use of it.'

'You think she will believe that?' asked Mary.

'We must hope that she will,' answered Herries. 'We must take *some* action. If we do nothing we may be here for months.'

'You are right,' Mary told them. 'We must act – even if by

so doing we merely discover the true nature of Elizabeth's feelings towards me.'

Shortly afterwards Herries and Fleming set out for the English Court.

*   *   *

Sir Francis Knollys was more pleased than he admitted to himself to see five small carts arriving in the courtyard accompanied by heavily laden pack horses. He went down to make a closer inspection, although he guessed whence these came.

'You come from Lord Moray?' he asked one of the drivers.

'Yes, my lord. With these goods which are for the use of the Queen-Mother of Scotland.'

'Then unload them with all speed,' ordered Sir Francis.

While this was being done, he made his way to Mary's apartments and asked that he might see her.

She received him immediately, hoping that he brought news from his royal mistress; he was smiling and she began to believe that he would have been pleased to help her.

'I see that travellers are with us,' said Mary. 'I trust they come from Queen Elizabeth.'

'No, Your Majesty, they come from Lord Moray in Scotland.'

Mary's expression changed. 'Then they can bring no good to me.'

'Yet I do not believe Your Majesty will be displeased when you see what has been brought.'

'I cannot conceive of any good coming to me from my bastard brother.'

'I have asked that these articles be sent to Your Majesty,' said Knollys. He smiled. 'I have a wife, and I know how important such things can be.'

'Do you mean that some of my possessions have been returned to me?'

'I sent word to Moray, asking him not to withhold your clothes but to send them to you here that you might have the pleasure of wearing them.'

'That was good of you, Sir Francis; but you remember that, the last time such a request was made, he sent me only things which I had long discarded . . . ruffs and coifs which were quite out of date, and dresses which were almost in rags. Indeed, what Moray sent me was only slightly better than those which your Queen sent . . . to my maids.'

Knollys looked uncomfortable for a few seconds, then he brightened. 'I do not think you will be disappointed this time. May I have the articles brought to you?'

Mary's smile was dazzling. 'At least,' she said gently, 'I rejoice that one of my jailors has a kind heart.'

'You must not think of me as such,' insisted Knollys.

'Nor shall I, when I receive my invitation to your Queen and we travel south,' was the answer. 'When that will be, who shall say? So in the meantime let us content ourselves with seeing what my bastard brother has sent from my wardrobe.'

Mary summoned Seton, Jane Kennedy, Lady Livingstone and Marie Courcelles, and the packages were brought to the apartment.

This time they were not disappointed. Having received a request from an Englishman of such importance Moray had thought it wise not to ignore it.

The women cried out with pleasure as they unrolled eight ells of the finest black velvet, and thirty each of grey and black taffety. There were twelve pairs of shoes and four of slippers as well as stitching silk and jet buttons.

'Now,' cried Seton, 'we shall be busy.'

*   *   *

In spite of the absence of Herries and Fleming, Mary had a larger retinue than she had had since leaving Scotland. Now and then some Scotsman would arrive at the castle with the request to be given a place in her household, in preparation for the day when she would return to Scotland to fight for her crown.

George Douglas, with Willie, was constantly on guard; she told them that she felt safe when they were near, and that constantly in her thoughts was the memory of what they had done for her at Lochleven. She now had her own two private secretaries, Gilbert Curle and Monsieur Claud Nau, as well as carvers, cupbearers, cooks and scullions. A little Scottish Court was rapidly being formed in Carlisle Castle.

One day Sir Nicholas Elphinstone arrived at the castle with letters to Scrope and Knollys from Moray. This caused great consternation throughout Mary's retinue, for Elphinstone was notoriously antagonistic to the Queen.

George Douglas swore that if he came face to face with Elphinstone he would challenge him and nothing but combat would satisfy him; Willie was brooding on a scheme for taking Elphinstone prisoner; and several of the lairds declared their intentions of challenging him to a duel.

Scrope, disconcerted, went to Knollys and was a little re-proachful.

'You see what is happening. You have shown too much friendship towards the Queen of Scotland. You have allowed her to collect this entourage which is almost like a small court about her. Therefore, when a messenger from one with whom we have no quarrel arrives, they behave as though Carlisle Castle belonged to them and they had the right to say who should or should not be entertained here.'

Knollys saw the point of this and, as he was afraid that complaints might be made to Elizabeth, and as he knew that her chief feeling towards Mary was jealousy, he realized that he must in future act with more caution.

In the company of Scrope he went to her apartments; and Scrope opened the attack by protesting at the conduct of people like George Douglas, who had challenged a peaceful messenger who came to the castle.

'Your Majesty must remember that you are the guest of the Queen of England, and that you have no power to order who shall or shall not venture into the Castle of Carlisle.'

Mary haughtily replied: 'This man is a Scotsman, and one of my subjects.'

'Your Majesty forgets,' went on Scrope, 'that all Scotsmen do not call you their Queen.'

Mary flushed hotly. 'This state of affairs shall not be allowed to last.'

Scrope looked doubtful, Knollys uncomfortable, and Mary went on in the impulsive way which was characteristic of her: 'You do not think this so, my lords. I see from your expressions that you believe Lord Moray to be the ruler of Scotland in the name of my son. It will not long be so. Huntley, Argyle and others are with me. They assure me that very soon I shall be back in Edinburgh, the acknowledged Queen of Scotland. Ah, I see you do not believe me.' Determined to prove the truth of this statement she crossed the room and opened a drawer of her table. 'Look at these, my lords. Letters, you see, from my friends. Huntley has the whole of the North behind him. I can picture him now . . . planning my return. I'll swear his Highlanders are already marching to the lilt of the bag-pipes.'

She was thrusting papers into their hands, and Knollys would have liked to warn her, but Scrope was scrutinizing the letters.

'Interesting,' he murmured. 'Very, very interesting.'

'So you see,' said Mary, 'I am not so deserted as you . . . and perhaps your Queen . . . have thought me to be?'

'No, Madam,' answered Scrope grimly. 'I see that you are not.'

*   *   *

Scrope said to Knollys: 'You see what intrigue goes on under our noses. Why, it would not be impossible for her to be carried back into Scotland before we could prevent it. Huntley and Argyle writing to her thus! Do we see the letters? We do not! Yet it is our Queen's command that we see all letters which pass into the hands of the Queen of Scotland, and all those that she sends out.'

Knollys shook his head. 'I would to God we had never been given this task.'

'I confess to certain misgivings. But perforce we have this task, and perform it we must . . . or be in trouble ourselves.'

'What new rules do you propose to put in force?'

'Firstly I shall write to Cecil and suggest that Carlisle Castle is too near the Border for my peace of mind. There is my castle of Bolton —'

'Ha! A fortress if ever there was one.'

'I should feel happier there with this captive of ours than I do in Carlisle. Then I like not all these servants about her. I believe that none of the men of her court should be allowed to sleep in the castle but should find lodgings outside. The rooms leading to her bedchamber should be filled with our guards – and perhaps ourselves – rather than her friends. The castle gates must be kept locked through the night and not opened until ten of the clock in the forenoon and closed at dusk. Then it might be difficult for Huntley and Argyle to whisk her away without our Queen's consent.'

'Ah,' sighed Knollys sadly, 'little did she know when she escaped from Lochleven that she was changing one prison for another.'

*   *   *

There was no news of Herries, no news of Fleming. That boded ill, for Mary knew that if they had succeeded with their missions she would have heard from them. She was beginning to suspect the goodwill of Elizabeth, and was wondering whether the shadow of Elizabeth of England would darken her life now, as that of Catherine de' Medici had her childhood.

One day a certain Henry Middlemore called at Carlisle on his way to Scotland with dispatches from Elizabeth to Moray and, hearing of his arrival, Mary asked that he be brought to her.

The demeanour of this man should have been enough to show Mary the hopelessness of her case with Elizabeth, for he treated her with a deliberate lack of respect.

'Have you brought me news of when your mistress will grant me an interview?' asked Mary passionately.

'Madam,' was the answer, 'I can only tell you what you know already. The Queen of England cannot receive you until you have cleared yourself of suspicion of murder. And that you have not done, and facts are black against you.'

'How dare you say such things to me?' demanded Mary.

'Because they are the truth, Madam. Her Majesty, my mistress, asks you to prevent those Scotsmen in Dumbarton and other places in Scotland from accepting help from France should it be sent.'

'Why should I prevent others from helping my cause when your mistress refuses to do so?' asked Mary.

'You have put yourself in my mistress's hands and if, when she has judged your case, she finds you guiltless, doubtless she will help you. I go to Scotland now to ask the Earl of Moray to suppress all signs of civil war in Scotland at the request of the Queen of England.'

Mary was slightly mollified at this and Middlemore went on: 'Her Majesty believes you would find better air away from Carlisle and that it would be to your advantage to go to some other castle which shall be placed at your disposal.'

'Does the Queen of England intend to have me taken there as a prisoner or for me to go of my own free will?' Mary asked.

'I am sure the Queen of England has no wish to make you her prisoner. She will be happy if you accept her plans for you without demur. It would please her if you were lodged nearer to herself. That is the main reason why she wishes you to move from Carlisle.'

'Then if that be so, let me go to her without delay. Let me have apartments next her own at Windsor or Hampton Court.

she could not then complain of the distance which separates us.'

Middlemore ignored this. He said quietly: 'Her Majesty had in mind the Castle of Tutbury in Staffordshire . . . a goodly place, Madam, and one which you would find convenient.'

Convenient, thought Mary hysterically. Conveniently far from the Border, conveniently far from Hampton Court! What was the Queen of England planning against her? And where were Fleming and Herries now?

Middlemore took his departure and Mary could only ease her disquiet by writing a long letter to Elizabeth in which she passionately demanded justice, an opportunity to see her, a chance to assure her good sister and cousin of her innocence. She asked that Lord Herries be sent back to her as she needed his good counsel; and she would like to have news of Lord Fleming.

When she had written the letter she sat at her table staring moodily before her. As each day passed hope seemed to fade farther and farther away.

Meanwhile Middlemore went on his way into Scotland, where the Regent Moray and Lord Morton were preparing translations from the original French of those letters which they alleged were found in a casket under Bothwell's bed when he fled to the North.

These translations would prove to Elizabeth, and the world, that Bothwell and Mary were lovers before Darnley's death, that Bothwell had raped the Queen, and that since then she had no desires for any man but him; that they had plotted together to murder Lord Darnley, the Queen's husband, so that marriage between Mary and Bothwell might be possible.

*   *   *

In spite of the vigilance of Scrope and Knollys more men from Scotland arrived at the castle. Mary was walking in the grounds with Seton when she saw George Douglas coming towards her.

He bowed low and his earnest eyes were on her lovely face as she gave him her affectionate smile. She was thinking: Poor George, what life is this for a young man! If I am to remain a prisoner, what will become of him?

'Your Majesty,' he said, 'I have a packet of letters which have been stolen from Moray's secretary. I believe you would wish to see them. One of the new arrivals brought them and

155

gave them to me that I might pass them to you at an opportune moment.'

'You have them with you, George?'

'Yes, Your Majesty, but I fear we may be watched.'

'You are right. They watch me here even as they did at Lochleven. We will go into the castle and, when Seton has taken me to my apartments, she shall come out to you again. Could you be at this spot and hand them to her? They do not watch her as they watch me.'

'I will do that, Your Majesty.'

With that the ladies turned and went back to the Queen's apartments, and soon afterwards Seton returned to the grounds where George was waiting for her.

When Seton went back to Mary's chamber, the Queen eagerly seized what she had brought. It was a packet of letters from Moray's secretary, John Wood, to Elizabeth's ministers; and as she read them, Mary's indignation was fierce for there was no doubt that Elizabeth's advisers were in league with Moray against her, Mary; and that their main objects were to prevent her receiving help from France and to keep her a prisoner in England that Moray might rule in her stead.

Even now it did not occur to her that Elizabeth was a party to this scheme, and she believed that the reason she was being kept from the Queen of England was because her ministers, in collaboration with Moray, were preventing the meeting.

Without consulting her friends she sat down and penned an impulsive note to Elizabeth.

She told her of the letters which had come into her possession and wrote:

'They assure him that I shall be securely guarded, never to return to Scotland. Madam, if this be honourable treatment of her who came to throw herself into your arms for succour I leave other Princes to judge. I will send copies of these letters, if you permit it, to the Kings of France and Spain and to the Emperor, and will direct Lord Herries to show them to you, that you may judge whether it be right to have your council for judges, who have taken part against me. . . .'

She paused and looked out of her window from which she could see the blue hills of Scotland. If only she could go back to Langside, if only she had listened to the advice of the good Herries and her friends, she would not be here now. She would be with her friends in France; and although Catherine de Medici might be her enemy, there would have been powerful uncles to help her, and the King of France who had been so desperately in love with her would surely not have failed her.

She turned to her letter and continued:

'. . . I beseech you not to allow me to be betrayed here to your dishonour. Give me leave to withdraw. . . .'

Yes, she thought, I will go back to Scotland. If I could take boat to Dumbarton, there would be faithful friends waiting for me. I could join with Huntley and Argyle. She could see them – those brave, bold Highlanders; she could hear the skirl of their pipes.

'God grant that they lessen not your authority by such practices, as they have promised Moray to lead you as they will, to lose the friendship of other Sovereigns, and to gain those who loudly proclaim that you are unworthy to reign. If I could speak to you, you would repent of having so long delayed to my injury in the first place, and to your prejudice in the second. . . .'

She went on writing rapidly and, sealing her letter, sent for a messenger and bade him begone with all speed.

* * *

Life at the castle was changing. There was little pretence now of treating her as anything but a prisoner. No man of her suite was allowed to have his quarters in the castle; Lord Scrope slept in the room adjoining hers; with him were his hagbutters who occupied the rooms leading to her apartments.

Mary was grateful for the company of her women. 'Yet,' she said, 'I cannot help wondering when they will deprive me of your company.'

'They never will,' Seton declared. 'We shall simply refuse to leave you.'

'You forget, my dear, that we are in their power.'

One day when she walked in the grounds Knollys came to walk beside her. She was pleased to see him because his gentleness was comforting. She could not complain of disrespectful treatment from Lord Scrope, but he was the more severe jailor of the two. When she remembered the crude manners of Lindsay and some of the Scottish lords, when she thought of Bothwell himself, she felt she owed some gratitude to Scrope and Knollys who, determined as they were to keep her their prisoner, never failed to remember that she was a woman.

Knollys said: 'I have good news for Your Majesty. You are to leave Carlisle for a more congenial place.'

She caught her breath. 'You call that good news?'

'Bolton Castle is admirably situated.'

'For what?' she asked. 'For prisoners?'

He turned to her. 'I am sorry,' he said, 'that I have the unfortunate task of insisting that you leave this place – but that is the case.'

'So I am to be taken from one prison to another! This is not strong enough; is that the case? I am too near Scotland, and the people who give you your instructions are anxious that I shall not escape them.'

'We shall endeavour to make you comfortable in Bolton Castle. There, Lady Scrope will be waiting to welcome you.'

'I am not sure that I shall go,' retorted Mary. 'Here I am not far from home. Unless I receive an invitation to visit the Queen of England I do not feel inclined to leave Carlisle.'

Knollys sighed. He knew that it was not for her to decide. He also knew that the Queen had refused Fleming a safe conduct to France, that she had kept Herries in London because she was anxious to move Mary while he was away; Knollys believed that the cause of the Queen of Scots was a hopeless one; and he was deeply sorry for her.

*　　*　　*

During the next few days Mary thought constantly of George Douglas, and she longed to reward him for his devotion to her, for she knew that he was in love with her and that it was love born of chivalry.

'Poor George,' she said to Seton in whom she confided most of her thoughts. 'He is wasting his life with me.'

Seton who was dressing the Queen's hair, paused, the comb in her hand and said:

'When the time comes for you to fight your way back to the throne and he is with you, he will not consider he has wasted his time.'

'If ever I return to the Scottish throne there shall be honours for George . . . and for Willie. Never, never shall I forget what they have done for me. Willie is but a boy and his lot here is no more uncomfortable than it was at Lochleven . . .

but George is different. He is a young man who should be making his way in the world. He should find a beautiful wife and live happily with her, not spend his days in semi-captivity, sighing for a queen who can never be aught else to him. Seton, I wish there was something I could do for George.'

'You do all that he asks, simply by existing,' replied Seton with a smile.

'It is not enough. I want him to go from here, Seton.'

'George . . . leave you! He would never obey that command.'

'He would if I made it . . . in a certain way. Do you know that he was betrothed to a French heiress? Christian told me, and I have seen a portrait of her. She is very beautiful. I am sure George will love her.'

'George is faithful to one and one only.'

'Do not smile, Seton. I will not allow him to waste his manhood here in Carlisle . . . or Bolton . . . and perhaps other castles to which one day I shall be taken – for I begin to fear I shall never be allowed to visit Elizabeth.'

'Your Majesty is sad today.'

'Yes, because I know that soon I must say goodbye to George. There is something else, Seton. The men of my suite are no longer allowed to have their quarters in the castle. Since I read John Wood's letters and have some idea of the correspondence which passes between the Regent and Elizabeth's ministers, I suspect that ere long some of my faithful friends will be sent back to Scotland. What do you think their fate would be? If George were sent back, all that he has done for me would most certainly cost him his head. I am determined to prevent that. And there is only one way in which this can be done. I shall try to send George to France.'

'Lord Fleming, it seems, cannot obtain a safe conduct. Would George?'

'I think he might succeed where Lord Fleming has failed. His more humble status would make him seem less important in their eyes. And I should not make the mistake of sending letters with George.'

'Are you determined on this? You would miss him sadly.'

'I have thought of that. The parting will be a sad one for us both, but I am so fond of that young man, Seton, that I cannot let him waste his life for me. He is so young. He will in time outgrow his love for me. I shall be his Queen, and he will always be my faithful subject. But he would be happier with a

159

wife . . . with children and some hope of making his way in the world.'

'But when Your Majesty regains the throne?'

'The first thing I shall do will be to send for George Douglas and offer him honours which are his due.'

'So you are determined to see George. When will you do so?'

'There seems little point in delaying further. Let it be now, Seton. Send him to me.'

* * *

George stood before her, and when she saw the desolation in his eyes, she wavered.

Let him stay with her. It was what he wished; it was what she wished. Let the future take care of itself.

'Oh George,' she said, stretching out a hand to him which he took and covered with kisses, 'do not think that I want you to go. I shall miss you very much. Do not think that I shall ever forget what you have done for me.'

'I ask only to be allowed to stay near you, to defend Your Majesty if need be, to be at your side . . . to serve you in victory or defeat.'

'I know, George. No Queen ever had more faithful subject; no woman more loving friend. But you have seen what has happened since our coming into England. It is very necessary that my friends in France should know what is happening to me. George, I begin to feel that is the only direction in which I can look for help. You will be on my service. I want you to go to France. I do not think the Queen of England will deny you a safe conduct as she has Lord Fleming. I want you to see the King, who is my very good friend. My uncles, the Duke of Guise and the Cardinal of Lorraine will be your friends and take you to the Court. There you can do more for me than you can here in England.'

An eager look had come into George's face. He believed her; and if he could serve her best by being denied the joy of her presence he was willing enough to accept the sacrifice.

'I shall give you no letters to take to them, but I am writing through the French ambassador to tell them of your coming. So they will be expecting you; and when you are there, George, I know that you will plead my cause as few others could, because all you do for me is done for love of me and not hope of any honours I might one day be in a position to

160

give you. Willie shall remain with me. Have no fear that I shall not reward him when the opportunity arises. Never, never shall I forget those days in Lochleven and all I owe you two.'

George knelt before her to hide his emotion. He wanted to tell her how he adored her, to repeat again and again that he longed to give his life for her.

She understood and, making him rise, kissed him tenderly.

'You do not have to speak, George,' she said. 'I understand. And it is friendship such as yours that makes it possible for me to endure my misfortunes with a good heart.'

George said: 'Once Your Majesty gave me an earring. I treasure it always. Shall it still be a symbol, should the need arise to send it?'

He took the earring from a small pouch which hung on a chain under his doublet and showed it to her.

'Ah yes, I remember it well. I have its fellow, and think of all you have done for me every time I see it.'

She wanted to give him the other earring – a present for his bride. But no, that would be to tell him the real reason why she was sending him away. He must not be allowed to guess that. Later, perhaps, she thought, when he is betrothed, when he realizes that a man needs more from life than the love between us two.

'I will give you something else, George, to set beside that earring. A memento of me.' She went into the ante-chamber and came out with a portrait of herself. It was a charming picture, a good likeness in which she looked serene and beautiful; diaphanous material falling from her coif draped her shoulders; her ruff was of finest lace and the delicate white fingers of her right hand fingered the jewel which hung about her neck.

George was so moved that he could not speak; as for Mary, she was finding it difficult to control her emotions. Impulsive as she knew herself to be she believed that if he did not go she would throw herself into his arms and beg him to stay, to say to him: Why should we think of the future . . . either of us? What has the future for us? You are young and I am not much older.

She turned away from him and as she looked towards the Scottish hills, she thought of the guards about this castle and the plans to move her to a stronger fortress. She thought too of other men who had loved her – of her three husbands, whom tragedy had overtaken. To only one had she brought happiness – to little François, delicate, clinging François to whom she had been nurse and playmate. But that had been a childhood friendship rather than marriage. Then Darnley who, after their brief and stormy union, had been the victim of murder. Had he not married Mary Stuart he would certainly not have met violent death in Kirk o' Field. And Bothwell . . . what fate could be more unendurable to him than that of a prisoner! And this had befallen him because he had married Mary Stuart.

I bring ill luck to those who love me, she thought. But it shall not be so with George. George was innocent as none of the others had been – except perhaps François. No, she knew she was an impulsive woman. governed by her emotions rather than sound common sense. But she could learn some lessons; and she had learned this one.

I could only bring suffering to him if I kept him with me to become my lover. I will not do it. You must fly away, George . . . to freedom and a life that is not too closely entwined with that of ill-fated Mary Stuart.

'Take this picture of me, George,' she said steadily, 'and go now. Make preparations for your departure. I shall see you before you leave.'

He bowed, and she did not look at him as he went from the room.

*   *   *

Sir Francis Knollys came to her apartment and asked for an audience.

He looked harassed and she guessed that he had bad news.

'Your Majesty,' he said, 'I regret that I have orders here. You are to prepare to leave at once for Bolton Castle.'

'Whence come these orders?' she asked.

'From the Queen's ministers, Your Majesty.'

'May I see them?'

Knollys handed them to her.

'I do not see the signature of the Queen of England.'

'Secretary Cecil signs for her.'

'I will not be commanded by the Queen s ministers,' retorted Mary. 'Without your Queen's express warrant I shall not stir from Carlisle.'

Knollys sighed and went to consult with Scrope, while Mary sat down and wrote one of her passionate letters to Elizabeth, explaining that she was sure Elizabeth would not order her to go where she did not wish, and imploring her to remember that, as Queen of Scotland, she was an equal of the Queen of England.

       *   *   *

But Mary knew that she was in Elizabeth's power when word came from her that the Queen of England was sending her own litter and horses to convey the Queen of Scots from Carlisle to Bolton.

There was also a letter from Elizabeth for Mary, which the latter seized on with eagerness.

'My lord Herries has told me two things which seem to me very strange. One, that you would not answer before anyone but myself; the other, that without force you would not stir from the place where you are, unless you had license to come to me! Your innocence being such as I hope it is, you have no need to refuse to answer to some noble personage, whom I shall send to you, not to answer judicially, but only to assure me upon it by your answers; not making them to your subjects which would not be considered proper, but sending to lay before me your defence, that I might publish it to the world, after having satisfied myself, which is my principal desire. Then as to the place I have ordained for your honour and safe keeping, I beg you not to give me cause to think all the promises you have made were but as wind, when you sent word to me that you would do whatsoever might seem best to me. . . .'

The letter dropped from Mary's hand. She knew, without reading further, that she would be obliged to obey the wishes of Elizabeth.

'It is my intention,' continued Elizabeth, 'to keep Lord Herries here till I shall receive an answer on both these points. . . .'

So until she left Carlisle she would be deprived of the services of one of her most faithful friends.

Mary put aside the letter and covered her face with her hands.

It was two months since she had fled from the battlefield of Langside, so full of hope, certain that she could rely on Elizabeth's help.

Now had come that Queen's orders. From Carlisle to Bol-

163

ton – from that refuge, whose windows looked on the bonny
hills of Scotland, to Bolton to which she had heard Sir Francis
Knollys refer as 'the highest walled castle I ever did see'.

Why? What did the future hold for the captive Queen?

CHAPTER FIVE

BOLTON

GREAT WERE MARY'S misgivings when she first saw
Bolton Castle. Set in beautiful Wensleydale in the North
Riding of Yorkshire, it was indeed a fortress; and she was not
surprised that Knollys had remarked that it was the highest
walled castle he had ever seen.

It had been three days ago that, most reluctantly, she had
left Carlisle. How happily she would have done so had she
been going south to the Court of the Queen of England! But
she knew the reason for this move. She was going farther
away from Scotland, out of reach of those loyal lairds who
were planning how to set up her standard again and bring her
back to her own.

Lord Fleming had returned to Carlisle before she left; Elizabeth had refused to grant him a safe conduct to France, but
Mary had been right when she had believed that George Douglas would not be denied one. George was allowed to go,
ostensibly to make his home there and to see that heiress to
whom he had been affianced. Lord Fleming had now gone
back to Scotland, his object being to visit Dumbarton first –
that loyal stronghold – and then join forces with Argyle and
Huntley.

Before she left Carlisle Mary sent certain of her followers
back to Scotland, among them the energetic Lord Claud
Hamilton, for she realized that if she were to be a prisoner in
England, these faithful friends could be of greater service to
her cause in Scotland where she knew that men were rallying
every day to Huntley's banner.

So it was a depleted party which set out from Carlisle.
Willie Douglas rode near Mary's litter and threatened to draw
that enormous sword if any tried to shift him. Now that
George had gone he whispered that he was taking over Geor-

die's duties as well as his own, and she had no need to fear as the Douglases were with her.

She was grateful to Willie, because he never failed to make her smile, and it was so much easier to reconcile herself to her fate when she could do that.

The journey from Carlisle had taken two days and nights, the first night being spent at Lowther Castle where she had been treated with respect and sympathy – for which she was grateful – by the entire Lowther family; she had spent the next night at Wharton, and the following day reached Bolton Castle having come twenty miles south from Carlisle.

The castle was built round a great court and, standing as it did on a hill, gave the occupants wonderful views of the surrounding country, which at this time of the year was startingly beautiful.

Waiting to greet Mary was Lady Scrope, and this was a great pleasure because Mary had taken a liking to her when they had met at Carlisle; moreover this lady was the sister of the Duke of Norfolk who, during his interview with Mary, had managed to convey to her, amid his gallantries, his desire to help her.

'It is a pleasure to meet you again,' said Mary.

Lady Scrope made a deep curtsey and expressed herself honoured to have the pleasure of entertaining Her Majesty of Scotland.

She led the way into the castle which Mary noticed was sparsely furnished; and it was clear to Mary that her hostess was a little concerned for her guest's comfort.

Mary tried to set her at ease by telling her how pleased she was to find a friend waiting to greet her.

Lady Scrope gave her a look which implied that she was gratified to be called such, and Mary's spirits rose. Friends were of more importance to her than fine tapestries.

On their way to the apartments which had been prepared for the Queen in the south-west of the building Lady Scrope showed her the great clock, of which the family were very proud, for it not only told the time but also the movements of the sun and moon, and day of the week. She explained also how the chimneys were tunnels in the sides of the walls, thus during the cold weather the chill was taken from the apartments.

Mary listened with interest and all the time she was thinking: Lady Scrope will be a go-between for myself and the

165

Duke of Norfolk. How sincerely did he mean those veiled promises to help me, when I saw him at Carlisle?

* * *

There was more freedom to be enjoyed at Bolton Castle; and providing she was surrounded by those whose duty it was to guard her, Mary was able to hunt in that exhilarating countryside. Her appetite increased and it was clear to all that her health had improved since she had come to Bolton.

English manners, although less courteous than the French, were nevertheless gracious when compared with those she had experienced in Scotland. All those who were in truth her jailors seemed determined to show her that they were not, wishing her to believe that they guarded her solely for her own protection and not to prevent her escaping to Scotland or receiving enemies of their own Queen.

Sir George Bowes, who had arrived at Carlisle in order to escort her to Bolton, accompanied by a hundred armed horsemen, expressed the greatest sympathy for her and, when he saw how inadequate was the furniture in her apartments, he immediately sent to his own house for bedding and hangings that they might be set up in Bolton for the Queen's use. Never once did he imply that he was guarding her for the Queen of England and her ministers; and Mary, whose great misfortune was her too trusting nature, could easily forget that she must be continually on her guard against her jailors.

It was a different matter with Lady Scrope. She was pregnant and, liking to rest often, she would sit with the Queen in her apartments overlooking those glorious hills and dales, and they would talk together; and Margaret Scrope would always seek to lead the conversation to her brother, the Duke of Norfolk.

'He mentions you constantly when we meet or in his letters,' she told Mary. 'He is so anxious that you should be well treated and is delighted that you have now come to Bolton.'

'How pleasant it is to know that I have friends in England,' answered Mary.

Margaret would bring out the tapestry which Mary loved to work, and as their fingers were busy, so were their tongues.

'Thomas believes that you should not put too much trust in Secretary Cecil,' Margaret told Mary.

'I am sure he is right.'

'The Queen is apt to be guided by her ministers, particularly Cecil and Leicester. She is very vain and imagines that they are all in love with her. It is Your Majesty's reputation as a beauty that makes her so interested in you.'

Mary told of the tattered garments Elizabeth had sent her. 'Master Knollys said they were for my maids, but I do believe she meant them for me.'

Margaret looked over her shoulder. 'She, in her rich satins and velvets ablaze with jewels listening to the flattery of the courtiers, likes to believe herself the most beautiful woman in the world! She knows this is not so and wants to make sure you do not have the advantage of wearing becoming garments.'

'Is she indeed so petty?'

Margaret, plying her needle, nodded; and Mary remembered that Elizabeth was royal and that it was not becoming in one Queen to tattle of another so she changed the subject to Margaret's brother. Would he be coming to Bolton?

'Who can say? I'll dare swear the Queen will not wish him to, while you are here. I believe he must have spoken admiringly of you.' Margaret laughed and rethreaded her needle. 'Thomas is a handsome man,' she went on with sisterly affection. 'It is a pity that he is a widower, for he was such a good husband to his three wives. How sad that death should have claimed them all and so soon!'

Margaret Scrope did not look at the Queen. She was thinking: Thomas married three heiresses; why should there not be a fourth? This heiress was a most romantic one. He would have to fight to reinstate her and that might mean rebellion, but Thomas had already quarrelled with Leicester and was resentful of those men with whom Elizabeth surrounded herself and on whom she conferred favours. Nor could Elizabeth afford to ignore him, because he was the premier peer and one of the richest men in England. Cecil did not like him, nor he Cecil. As for Mary, she was not only Queen of Scotland but, if Elizabeth should not marry and have an heir, Mary was next in succession to the throne of England.

Margaret felt dizzy with ambitions on behalf of her brother and she regarded it as great good fortune that the Queen of Scotland had come to Bolton.

Mary was thoughtful. He had married three times, and so had she. But how different his marriages must have been from hers! If Lady Scrope could be believed her brother's matrimonial life had been one of continual bliss. Mary felt a little

167

envious as she listened to Margaret Scrope's eulogies of her brother, and because she looked a little wistful Margaret said: 'Your Majesty, one day you will marry again. You will regain your throne, and then you will live in serenity.'

'Sometimes I think that the serene life is not for me.'

'It would be,' Margaret assured her, 'if you married the man who could give you it.'

The seed was sown. Mary's interest in Thomas Howard was growing, and when they sat together, or walked about the castle, Margaret Scrope talked so often of her brother that Mary felt she knew him, and was growing fond of him.

She missed George Douglas. The passionate days and nights spent with Bothwell were so far away that they seemed like dreams.

She was a woman who needed love.

*　　*　　*

News was smuggled to her from France. It was easier now to receive such letters, for she had a strong ally in the castle – the mistress of the house herself.

George Douglas wrote that he had not been negligent in her service. He had been received by the Cardinal of Lorraine and the King of France, who assured her of their love. He had raised a thousand men who were armed and in training, waiting for the day when she should send for them.

Mary kissed the letter. 'Dear George,' she murmured, 'but I sent you to France to make your fortune, to marry your heiress and live happily there!'

There was also news from Scotland. Huntley and Argyle had ten thousand men assembled, waiting for orders to make an attack on Moray. Fleming was working zealously on her behalf. The Hamiltons were gathering in strength.

Moray must sleep very uneasily these nights.

Hope was high in Bolton Castle during those lovely summer days, and Mary's health and spirits were at their peak. She was gracious and friendly to familiarity with all who served her. Her guards were susceptible to her charm, and Bolton Castle during those weeks could not have been less like a prison.

Then to crown her pleasure Lord Herries arrived back from London.

Mary embraced him when he came to her apartments. He was decidedly pleased and she guessed that he brought good news.

'You have seen the Queen?' she asked eagerly.

'Yes, Your Majesty, and talked long with her.'

'And what news do you bring?'

'That if Your Majesty will commit your cause to be heard by her order, not as your judge, but as your dear cousin and friend, and to commit yourself to her advice and counsel, she will see that you are once more set upon your regal seat.'

Mary clasped her hands with pleasure.

'It seems that she is aware of our relationship, and is indeed my friend. What plans does she set forth in this matter?'

'She will send for certain of your enemies and, before noblemen of England – who shall be chosen with your approval – they shall explain why they have deposed you. If they can give some reason for this, she will reinstate you, but there will be a condition that they are not deprived of their estates. If on the other hand they should not be able to give a reason, she promises to restore you by force of arms if they should resist.'

'But this is the best news I have heard since I left Scotland.'

'There is one other condition. If she helps you to regain the throne of Scotland, you must renounce any claim to the throne of England during her lifetime or that of any issue she may have.'

'I never wished to claim the throne of England,' said Mary. 'It is true the title "Queen of England" was bestowed on me in France, but that was not my wish.'

'There is something else. You must break your league with France and enter into league with England; you must abandon the Mass in Scotland and receive the Common Prayer after the manner of England.'

Mary was silent. 'I am not anxious to interfere with the religion of my people.'

Herries said: 'It seems that at last the Queen of England is ready to help you. It would be possible to receive the Common Prayer and allow those who wished to celebrate Mass privately to do so.'

Mary still hesitated.

'She could put Your Majesty on your throne more easily than any other. She could doubtless do it without bloodshed. Moray would never dare stand against the English. The French have to come from overseas and it is not easy to make a landing in a foreign country. But the English are on our Border. Moray would never dare risk a war with England and a civil war at the same time. He would be crushed between two strong forces and could do nothing to help himself.'

'I have always believed in negotiation round the council table rather than battle. But . . . George Douglas is raising men for me in France. He already has a force of a thousand armed men in training. That is but a beginning, I am assured. And you say the Queen of England declares that I must not accept help from France.'

Herries assured her that this was so. He had been deceived by the Queen of England who was one of the wiliest rulers of her day. She had made it her business to know a great deal about Herries. He was one of the most loyal of Mary's adherents. Elizabeth knew that, because Leicester had sought to win him to Moray's cause, while he was in London, with promises of great honours to come, and Herries had not even treated Leicester's overtures seriously. A sentimental man, thought the Queen of England; she admired him for his loyalty and wished that he were a subject of hers. At the same time she knew how best to deal with such a man. So, when he had been brought to her, he had met a woman, completely feminine, deeply sympathetic to her dear cousin of Scotland, a little emotional and anxious to do what was right. She fervently hoped, she had told him, that the Queen of Scotland's innocence would be established; she wished more than anything to receive her dear sister and cousin, to comfort her, to talk with her in private. But her ministers were in some ways her masters. They were jealous of her reputation. They insisted that Mary's innocence must be proved before she was received by their Queen.

Herries was as completely duped as she had intended him to be, so now he told Mary: 'The Queen of England sincerely hopes to prove your innocence. She has assured me that she is on your side.'

'Yet,' said Mary, 'I am a Queen even as she is, and it is not for her to sit in judgement over me.'

'She does not wish to. She only wishes to show her ministers that these evil foundations which have been circulating about you are without foundation.'

'Tell me how you were received by her. I would hear everything.'

So Herries told of how he had waited for an audience – waited and waited – and later realized that it was her ministers who had made it impossible for him to see her. But when he did so, she had convinced him of her love for the Queen of Scots. 'She is my kinswoman, my lord,' she had said. 'And do you think that I, a Queen, wish to see another Queen treated so disrespectfully by her subjects? Nay, I wish to restore to her all that she has lost; and I swear that once her innocence is proved, no matter what any man say, she will find me her firm friend.'

Mary smiled. She was picturing that meeting. Her cousin whom she had never seen, but who she knew was red haired, occasionally arrogant, sometimes gay, at times frivolous, loving to dance and be flattered, holding her little court of favourites to whom she liked to give the impression that they could become her lovers, seemed a very human person.

Mary endowed Elizabeth with the more pleasing characteristics which were her own – generosity, impetuosity, eagerness to help those in distress.

Thus she made one of the most ruinous mistakes of her life when she said: 'I will write to George and tell him to disband his men; I will tell Argyle, Huntley and Fleming the same. I will put my trust in Elizabeth and do as she suggests.'

*   *   *

No sooner had Mary agreed to fall in with Elizabeth's wishes than misgivings beset her.

She heard of George Douglas's bitter disappointment when he was forced to disperse his little army. Argyle, Huntley and Fleming were shocked beyond expression, but there was nothing they could do since the Queen ordered them to disband their forces. In the decision of a moment Mary had destroyed all that her friends had been carefully building up since the defeat at Langside. She was no match for her wily enemies.

She had written to Elizabeth telling her that as she had given her consent to the plan, she believed she should have Elizabeth's own agreement in writing. She was sure the Queen would instruct Secretary Cecil to write to her confirming the offer which Herries had delivered orally.

Each day she waited for the Queen's reply; but none came; yet she heard that Moray and Morton were preparing the case against her, and that it was accepted that she had agreed to have her case tried in England.

Sometimes she cried out in anger: 'Who are these people to judge me? I will answer to one judge only and that judge is

171

God, before whom I shall not be afraid to stand and declare my innocence.'

But it was too late to protest. Copies of the casket letters had already been translated, and Moray and Morton, in collusion with Cecil and his friends, were building the case against her.

Her friends in Scotland deplored this state of affairs. There was a little brightness in the immediate future however. Although she never went out unless accompanied by guards, and although the castle gates were carefully locked at night, Scotsmen were still allowed to come and go; and this meant that news could be brought to her from the world outside Bolton Castle.

While Herries walked with Mary in the grounds one day he said. 'I think we have been too trusting.'

Mary nodded. 'No word from Elizabeth. Do you think her ministers are preventing her from putting in writing what she told you?'

Herries was thoughtful. It was difficult to imagine the woman he had seen, taking orders from her ministers. She had appeared to him in the role of compassionate friend of his mistress, but he could not forget the demeanour of her courtiers, the docile manner in which they – and her foremost ministers – never failed to speak to her, as though she were a goddess. Could such a woman be waiting on the word of ministers who were so clearly pre-occupied in discovering new ways of flattering her and winning her approval? Herries had begun to wonder whether he had been duped by the English Queen.

In any case while Mary was in England she was to a great extent at the mercy of Elizabeth; and knowing that ten thousand Scotsmen had rallied to Huntley's banner, and that Frenchmen had been ready to come to her defence, he had been considering that if Mary were in Scotland she might have a better chance of bargaining with Elizabeth.

That was why he was thoughtful now. A scheme had been put before him. It was simple as he believed all good schemes should be. What could have been more simple than the escape from Lochleven? It could work.

'Your Majesty,' he said, 'I and others of your friends begin to think that we could more likely win Elizabeth's help if you were not her prisoner. And let us face it – although she calls you her guest, you are in fact her prisoner.'

172

'You mean, if I were back in Scotland it would be easier to bargain with her.'

'I believe that to be so now, Your Majesty.'

'What would happen if I told Knollys and Scrope that I intended to return?'

'Your Majesty would be very politely and courteously prevented from doing so. That in itself should make us realize how necessary it is for you to return.'

'I see that you are as disturbed as I am because the Queen of England has not put her offer to me in writing, and has announced my willingness to have my case judged in England, without making it known what concessions she promised if I should do so. Oh yes, my dear Lord Herries, you are right, as you so often have been in all this wearisome business.'

'I fear I put too much trust in the Queen of England.'

Mary laid her hand on his arm. She understood how he had done that; she herself had been failing all along by putting her trust in those of whom she should have been wary. It was not in her nature to reprove others for faults which she herself possessed in greater measure. Nor would she have blamed any who made mistakes, if their intentions were good.

'So Your Majesty will perhaps listen to a plan for your escape,' went on Herries quietly.

'With pleasure,' she answered.

'Your servant, the Laird of Fernyhirst, has suggested that if you could cross the Border his castle would be at your disposal. Everything is being prepared to receive you there . . . providing you could leave Bolton Castle.'

Mary's eyes began to sparkle. The thought of action after so much inactivity was inviting. Moreover she was weary of having to make continual requests to the Queen of England, who either ignored them or made promises which it seemed she was reluctant to keep. That box of worn-out shoes and rusty black velvet was not easily forgotten.

'How could I leave Bolton Castle?'

'Only after dark.'

'But there are guards at the doors.'

'The only way to escape would be through one of the windows of your apartments. If you could slip through the coppices, and down the hill, we could arrange for horses to be waiting there; and then . . . we are not so many miles from the Border.'

'Then let it be done,' cried Mary impulsively.

173

'There must be few in the secret, and few to go with you. Perhaps Mary Seton . . . Willie Douglas . . . myself. . . . For a number of us to leave might mean our betrayal. Others could follow you once you were safely away. I am sure there would be no wish to detain them after you had gone.'

'Then let us decide how it shall be done.'

'First we will stroll round the castle to that window of your apartments which looks down on the grounds.'

They did this and, without appearing to pay much attention, carefully noticed the distance from window to grass below.

'You see,' said Herries, 'it would be possible, once you reached the ground, to slip out through the coppices and if the horses were in readiness at the bottom of the hill you would be away in a matter of five or ten minutes.'

'What of the guards, and Scrope and Knollys?'

'They will be fast asleep in the ante-rooms. They will not think it possible for anyone to descend through that window. As long as the affair is conducted quietly you could be almost at the Border before the alarm is given.'

'Willie Douglas will doubtless have ideas of how this can be accomplished.'

'I had thought to enlist his help, Your Majesty. In spite of his achievement at Lochleven he is not taken seriously here; which is doubtless what he intends in order to be ready for an occasion like this. He is a smart young fellow. Strutting about with his sword, showing that disrespect for people in high places, amuses everyone. Yes, Willie can help in this. I thought of sending him away to procure the horses. He is less likely to be missed than anyone else for, as Your Majesty knows, he sometimes goes off into the country and stays away for hours. We will send him off to find horses immediately.'

'Immediately?'

'Why not, Your Majesty? Fernyhirst is ready and waiting. As soon as you are safely in his castle he will send word to Huntley and the rest. I do not think that we shall then have to concern ourselves greatly about the conscience of the Queen of England.'

'I will take Seton with me,' said Mary.

'But no other maid. The entire success of this venture depends on its simplicity.'

'And you will be waiting for me with Willie and the horses.'

174

'I . . . or Livingstone . . . or one of us who can most easily be there. It matters not as long as you are away. You must make for the North without delay.'

Silently they continued their walk. Each was thinking of the plan.

It was so simple, they were sure they would succeed.

* * *

The Queen had retired for the night, and her faithful women who shared her chamber were alert. Mary did not undress. Instead she helped Jane and Marie who were knotting sheets together. They did not speak, for each knew the importance of making this appear to be like any other night the Queen had spent in Bolton Castle. In the next room Scrope and several of his men were sleeping. The low murmur of voices which had reached the waiting women had now ceased, and this meant that the moment had come, for the earlier the escape could be made the more time there would be for putting distance between the fugitive and Bolton Castle.

The window was high in the thick wall and a stool was silently brought so that the Queen could stand on it to climb to the scooped out aperture. Marie Courcelles firmly tied the knotted sheet about Mary's waist. Jane Kennedy tested it and nodded.

Then the escape began. Mary reached the window and peering down saw a dark figure below. Herries? She said nothing, but as silently as possible clambered out of the window.

Behind her the sheet was held firmly by her waiting women; then she was swinging in mid-air, only her skirts protecting her from the rough castle wall as she was lowered.

She was seized in a strong pair of arms and with a rush of triumph, felt her feet touch ground.

Hastily she untied the sheet about her waist. There was no time for more. Then she and her companions were running towards the coppices, down the slope to where Willie was waiting with the horses.

Willie grinned at her and helped her into the saddle. She felt a great joy surge over her as she whispered to her horse: 'Away!' And the gallop through the soft night air began.

As they started off she thought she heard a shout from the castle; then there was silence.

She heard Willie's chuckle beside her and for a few moments there was no sound other than that of the thudding of horses' hoofs.

*　　*　　*

It was Seton's turn to follow. She knew that she had to catch up with the others, for the plan was that there was to be no waiting; and as soon as Mary reached the horses she was to mount and ride away.

'Quickly!' cried Seton. The knotted sheets were hauled up, but as this was done one of the women fell backwards, and in her fall, taking the stool with her, went crashing to the floor.

There were a few seconds of shocked silence as she lay there. Then Seton said: 'Hurry. There is no time to lose.' Marie Courcelles was tying the sheets about Seton's waist, when the door opened and Lord Scrope stood on the threshold of the room.

He took it all in at a glance: the knotted sheets and Seton preparing to descend through the window. Then his dismay was apparent, for he had noticed the absence of the Queen.

He said nothing, though he must have guessed that had he come in a few minutes earlier he would have caught the Queen in the act of escaping.

He went back to the ante-room, and the frightened women heard his shouted orders.

*　　*　　*

Mary looked over her shoulder.

Where was Seton? She should have been close to them by now, because it took only a few moments to descend from the window.

Willie shouted: 'She'll catch us up. If not in England, in bonny Scotland. We'll almost be there by morning.' They thundered on; but when they had ridden some two miles there was still no sign of Seton; but the night was dark, Mary told herself, and it might well be that Seton was not far behind.

They had reached a gap in the hills and, as they were about to pass through this, a horse and rider confronted them.

Mary thought: Seton! Then she must have come by another road to the gap.

But almost at once she saw that it was not Seton.

Lord Scrope said: 'Well met, Your Majesty. Had you told me you wished to take a midnight ride, I should have arranged for a suitable escort to accompany you.'

Mary was speechless with dismay. She heard Willie let out an oath.

'And,' said Lord Scrope, 'your descent from your window must have been very uncomfortable.' He laid his hand on her arm. 'It shall be my pleasure now to escort you back to the castle.'

Mary had rarely felt so mortified. Her companions said nothing as the three of them, surrounded by the guards whom Scrope had brought with him, were conducted back to the castle.

* * *

Scrope did not retire to his bed on returning to the castle. He went to Knolly's bedchamber and, awakening him, told him how he had prevented the Queen's escape.

Knollys started up from his bed in consternation.

'You may well look alarmed,' said Scrope grimly. 'If this plan had succeeded – as it so nearly did – it could have cost us our heads.'

He hastily explained what had happened. He had had an intuition that all was not normal in the women's chamber and consequently he had not dropped off to sleep quickly, as he usually did. He had thought the women were whispering together and this was followed by a too sudden and unnatural quiet; then when he had heard a stool overturned and gone to investigate he had discovered the knotted sheets and that the Queen was missing.

Knollys congratulated him on his speedy action.

'I can tell you,' said Scrope, wiping his brow at the memory, 'I had some uneasy moments.'

'What have you done now?'

'Posted guards at the door of the Queen's chamber and others below her window. In future we shall have to make sure that she is guarded in every possible way. I cannot imagine what will be said when our Queen knows of this.'

'It is my belief that she will take the Queen of Scots from our care and place her in the custody of someone else.'

'I have heard Tutbury mentioned in this connexion, and that would doubtless mean that she would pass into Shrewsbury's care. He would be more than welcome to her.'

'What do you propose to do?'

'Write to Secretary Cecil without delay. He has asked for a full account of all that happens here. He must be told of this

177

attempt. It clearly indicates that some action must be taken sooner or later, because there will be other attempts to free her.'

There was a knock at the door at that moment and, to the astonishment of both men when Knollys called 'Come in,' Lady Scrope entered.

She had wrapped a loose gown about her and had clearly come straight from her bed.

She cried: 'What is this? I was awakened by the commotion, and now I am told that the Queen almost escaped.'

'That is so,' her husband replied. 'And you should return to your bed. You will catch cold. Remember your condition.'

'I am not cold,' answered Lady Scrope, 'and as our child is not expected until the end of the year you need have no qualms about my condition. But *I* have qualms on another matter. Tell me what measures are you going to take?'

Knollys said: 'Pray sit down, Lady Scrope.' And Scrope brought a stool for his wife, who sat down near the bed.

'We are doubling the guard of course,' her husband told her.

'But you must not let it be known that she almost eluded you!'

'My dear,' began Lord Scrope indulgently, 'you do not understand. . . .'

'Do not understand Elizabeth!' she cried.

Both men looked uneasily towards the door, and Lady Scrope acknowledged their furtive glances by lowering her voice. 'What do you think Her Majesty will say when and if she hears of this night's doings?' she went on. 'Two members of her Privy Council, and as many men as they care to employ, to guard one woman – and they almost fail! Do you think she will say "Well done!" If you do, you do not know Elizabeth. *I* know that if you had allowed the Queen of Scots to escape, the Tower of London might very well be your destination. As you prevented that calamity . . . but only just . . . you might avoid the Tower, but you would not win Her Majesty's approval, I do assure you.'

Both men were silent. There was a great deal in what Lady Scrope was saying. Naturally she was agitated; she had no wish to see her husband fall into disgrace.

'This must be hushed up,' she said. 'If you are wise you will certainly not write to the Queen or her ministers about what has taken place tonight. You will stop the news being spread. The fewer who know, the better. As for the extra guards you

178

intend to put on duty, do so, but let it be done with stealth. If you value Elizabeth's good opinion and her favour, for the love of God do not let her know that you almost failed in your duty.'

Scrope came to her and laid a hand on her shoulder. 'You must not allow yourself to become too excited,' he cautioned.

'I shall only recover my serenity when you tell me that you will take my advice in this matter.'

Scrope was looking at Knollys, and Margaret Scrope was clever enough to know that her words were being considered. She guessed that both men realized the wisdom of them.

'We are thinking of this matter,' Scrope told her.

And the gallant Knollys added: 'And we should always consider your advice, which we know of old is sound.'

Margaret sighed. 'Then I will return to my bed satisfied that at least you will consider this matter.' She rose and Scrope led her to the door. She hesitated there, and looked back at Knollys who was a little discomfited to be in his bed. 'Thank you both,' she said. 'I feel at ease because I know that when you consider this matter you will see that I am right.'

Back in her own room Margaret Scrope threw off her robe and lay down on her bed.

They had understood that this attempt to escape from Bolton Castle should be hushed up. That was well, for if Elizabeth decided to move Mary to Tutbury and take her out of the charge of Scrope and Knollys what chances would Lady Scrope have of furthering a match between Norfolk and the Queen of Scots?

That was something Lady Scrope had set her heart on; and she believed that her visit to Knollys and her husband had prevented the destruction of this cherished plan.

*   *   *

Although there was now a stronger guard at the castle, both day and night, Mary's attempt to escape was never openly mentioned, although it was whispered about among the guards and serving men and women; and the spot where she had been intercepted by Lord Scrope became known as 'The Queen's Gap'.

The friendship between Mary and Lady Scrope was growing fast, and one day when they were stitching their tapestry together, Lady Scrope asked Mary if she had ever seriously considered the Protestant Faith.

179

Mary replied that she had been born a Catholic and that during her childhood and girlhood, which had been spent in France, she had been brought up among Catholics and had therefore always been led to believe that that was the true faith.

'Yet there are many good men who are Protestants, Your Majesty,' Lady Scrope reminded her.

Mary agreed that this was so. 'My own Lord Herries is a Protestant; so is George Douglas. Indeed yes, I have much for which to be grateful to Protestants.'

Lady Scrope's eyes sparkled. Her brother, the Duke of Norfolk, was a Protestant, having had John Foxe as tutor; and if there was to be a marriage between them, it would be wise if they both conformed to the same religion. Norfolk had written to his sister, suggesting that if Mary could be induced to change her religion she would find it easier to regain her throne, because one of the biggest grudges many of her Protestant subjects bore against her was that she was a Catholic.

'I could answer Your Majesty's questions on the subject as far as I am able,' Lady Scrope continued. 'I also have books which might interest you.'

Mary was enthusiastic about the project. It would be one way of occupying her mind and making her forget, temporarily, to wonder what sort of morass she was falling into, for since her attempted escape had been foiled, there could be no doubt whatever that she was Elizabeth's prisoner.

So now those occasions when they sat over their tapestry were enlivened by discussions between Mary and Margaret Scrope; others of the ladies joined in; and soon it became known throughout Bolton Castle that the Queen was considering becoming a Protestant.

*   *   *

When Sir Francis Knollys heard the rumours he was delighted. As a stern Protestant, it pleased him that the Queen should be considering conversion to what he believed to be the true religion.

He himself offered to give her instruction, and soon Mary was reading the English prayer book with him.

He was persuasive, and Mary was enjoying her lessons.

While they read together Knollys, acutely aware of her charms, thought how sad it was that she should be in her position. He would have liked to see her back on the throne; she would need a husband to help her rule, and he did not see why she should not have an English husband.

He grew excited, believing he knew the very man for the position. This was his nephew, George Carey, a handsome young man who was surely eligible because of his relationship to Queen Elizabeth. Knollys' wife was first cousin to the Queen, and her brother, Lord Hunsdon, was the father of George Carey. It was true that the relationship came through Anne Boleyn rather than the royal house; nevertheless the ties were there.

He could not refrain from mentioning his young nephew to her, and immediately began to plan a meeting between them.

'I look upon my nephew as my own son,' he told Mary. 'He will shortly be in the district and will wish to call on his uncle.'

'Naturally,' Mary agreed.

'And if he should come to Bolton Castle, have I Your Majesty's permission to present him to you?'

'I should take it ill if you did not,' Mary told him; and Knollys was satisfied.

*　　*　　*

George Carey knelt before the Queen of Scots. He was young and extremely personable, and when Mary told him that she was pleased to see him, she was speaking the truth.

'I pray you be seated,' she went on. 'Have you news from the English Court?'

'None, I'll swear, that Your Majesty does not know already,' answered the young man.

'But I know so little. Tell me, is my sister and cousin in good health?'

'Her health is excellent, Your Majesty.'

'And did she, knowing you were about to visit your uncle and therefore would come to my lodging, give you any message for me?'

'She gave me none, Your Majesty.'

Mary was despondent, but only momentarily; it was such a novelty to have a visitor, and such a charming young man, who could not hide his admiration for her, was very welcome.

'Her Majesty Queen Elizabeth is displeased with Scotsmen at this time,' she went on. 'I have had complaints that on the Border some have been carrying out raids on English territory.

I am sorry for this, but she must realize that at this moment I am in no position to enforce my rule.'

'Her Majesty would know that, I am sure,' answered George.

'I wonder if you would be good enough to carry a message from me to the Queen?'

'I could take a message to my father who would see that it reached her.'

'Then tell him that if any border robbery has been carried out by any of my followers I could have them punished. If their names are sent to me, my friends would see that, since they injure my cause, they should be suitably dealt with. But if they belong to my enemies – which I think certain – it is beyond my power to prevent their ill conduct.' She went on confidingly: 'You will have heard talk of me.'

'I have, Your Majesty.'

'And much that is ill has been said of me, I'll swear.'

George flushed slightly and then said vehemently: 'I would never again believe aught against Your Majesty.'

She smiled ruefully. He had told her so much in that remark; she guessed that gossip, concerning Darnley's murder and her hasty marriage to Bothwell, was rife and that the scandal touching herself was boundless.

'Ah,' she said, 'it is sad when evil stories are spread regarding a lonely woman who has no means of defending herself.'

'I shall assure all I meet of your innocence,' he told her.

'Which has not been proved to you,' she reminded him.

'But it has, Your Majesty. Ever since I came into your presence I have known those tales to be false. I know that your conduct could never be aught but good and noble.'

Here was adoration similar to that which she had received from George Douglas. Her spirits were raised. George Carey would be her good friend – even as that other George had been.

She told him of her adventures since she had arrived in England. 'It is August now, and it was May when I came south. I thought to go straight to Hampton Court that I might meet the Queen and lay my case before her. Alas, here I remain – the guest of the Queen of England, but in truth her prisoner.'

'If there were aught I could do . . .' began George passionately.

'You could speak with your father who I believe has some influence with the Queen of England.'

182

'I will do this. And if there is aught else I can do to serve Your Majesty. . . .'

When Sir Francis Knollys asked permission to enter the Queen's apartments and found his nephew still in her company, he was well pleased.

He could see that it had been an excellent plan on his part to bring the young man to Bolton Castle.

*   *   *

During those late summer days bad news came to Bolton Castle. Rumours of Mary's possible conversion to Protestantism had reached Moray and filled him with panic. Nothing could have caused him greater disquiet.

The Queen a Protestant! If that were indeed true, before long there would be a clamour for her return. The only reason why so many had flocked to his banner was because he was of their religion and the Queen was not.

Moray never delayed when he thought action was necessary. The greatest boon he could ask for was that Mary should remain Elizabeth's prisoner, an exile from Scotland.

This was indeed a blow. And he must take immediate counter measures. So the result of Mary's brief flirtation with the Reformed Faith was that a vicious attack was made on her supporters in Scotland; and the Regent's forces seized their lands and possessions so that those who might have rallied to Mary's aid would not be in a position to do so for a very long time.

*   *   *

All through September Mary waited to hear news of when the Conference, at which her future would be decided, was to take place.

She knew that some of her friends deplored the fact that she had allowed matters to go so far in such a direction. Seton was one who believed that the Queen of Scotland should never have put herself in such a position as to allow herself to be judged by a court set up by the Queen of England and her ministers.

How right Seton was! thought Mary. And yet, what could she do? When she had fled to England she had placed herself in Elizabeth's power.

Lady Scrope, now far advanced in pregnancy, came to her one day with news that Elizabeth had named her Commissioners.

The Earl of Sussex was to be one, and Sir Ralph Sadler another.

Mary was horrified to hear that the latter had been appointed. Sadler had been one of Cecil's agents, and she knew that he had long been engaged in negotiations with Moray. Cecil was her enemy and sought to keep her in England, she knew, so that Moray might hold the Regency. And this man – who was assuredly one of her most bitter enemies – had been appointed a Commissioner of the Queen!

Why therefore was Lady Scrope – who had always shown herself to be a friend – looking so pleased?

'There is one other who has been appointed with these men,' Margaret Scrope explained. 'It is natural that he should be. Even the Queen must realize that he is the premier peer of England.'

A smile was slowly spreading across Mary's face. 'You mean?'

Margaret nodded. 'His Grace the Duke of Norfolk is also among Elizabeth's Commissioners, and Your Majesty may be sure that he will apply himself to your cause with all the zeal of which he is capable.'

In her relief Mary embraced her friend. Margaret smiled, well content.

She was certain that a marriage between them would not be displeasing to Mary.

*　　*　　*

Now that Mary heard that Elizabeth's Commissioners were chosen she decided on her own: Lord Herries should be one, and he, with Livingstone and Boyd, should be assisted by Sir John Gordon, the Laird of Lochinvar, Sir James Cockburn of Skirling and Gavin Hamilton, the Abbot of Kilwinning.

There was one other whom she was anxious to consult – the Bishop of Ross, John Lesley – and she lost no time in sending a messenger to London, where she knew he was, asking him to come to her with all speed.

Lesley arrived at Bolton Castle during early September, and as soon as she talked to him Mary realized what a grave view he took of her case.

He had been endeavouring to obtain permission from Elizabeth for the Duke of Châtelherault to come to England that he might be present at the inquiry; but Elizabeth had made continual excuses not to grant this.

Lesley shook his head sadly. 'The reason being of course that she fears the appearance of one of royal blood at the hearing might sway opinion in your favour.'

'You believe then,' said Mary, 'that it is the Queen of England's desire that I should appear guilty?'

Lesley lifted his shoulders noncommittally, but he continued to look grave and Mary went on impulsively: 'But this hearing of the case is being conducted that the disobedient lairds shall answer before the Queen of England's Commissioners for their ill-treatment of me. When they have admitted their offences, it is agreed that they shall be forgiven, and we shall all be reconciled and I regain my throne.'

But Lesley, a man of wider experience than Herries, was not so easily deceived by Elizabeth; and he did not believe in evading the truth for the Queen's comfort.

'It was a grave mistake, I fear,' he told her, 'to have allowed the English to interfere in this matter. This reconciliation which we all fervently hope will come about, should be a matter between you and Scotsmen, and should be achieved without meddling by the English. I fear Your Majesty has many enemies and they will do all within their power to defame your character.'

'Alas, I fear you are right. But I rejoice to hear from Lady Scrope that her brother, the Duke of Norfolk, has been appointed one of Elizabeth's Commissioners. I know him to be my friend. I have had friendly messages from him, which have been delivered through Lady Scrope. And with you and my friends to represent me and yet another good friend at the head of the English Commissioners, I do not see how the verdict can fail to be in my favour.'

'Sadler will do his best for Moray against Your Majesty.'

'But it will be necessary for one of his standing to listen to a noble Duke,' replied Mary complacently.

Lesley was less confident. Sir Ralph Sadler was an able and cunning man, and he was unsure of the ability of the Duke of Norfolk to stand up against him.

However they must make the best of a bad business, and Lesley gave himself up to the task of advising the Queen.

* * *

The Conference opened at York early in October when Mary's Commissioners began by complaining, on her behalf, of those of her subjects who had conspired against her and imprisoned her in the Castle of Lochleven. They accused Moray of taking over the Regency and ruling in the name of Mary's baby son, while he took unlawful possession of her personal effects such as her valuable jewels, as well as the arsenals of Scotland. Mary wished these rebel subjects to confess their faults and restore the throne to her.

Moray, Maitland and Morton were disturbed. The prevarication of the Queen of England made them unsure of what help they could expect from her. Moray had already sent to Elizabeth, asking whether the power to proclaim Mary guilty of murder should lie in the hands of the Commission. Unless it did so they were reluctant to make the accusation. Elizabeth replied that everything which took place at the Conference was to be made known to her and that judgement was to be given according to her orders.

Moray was at a loss to know how to proceed. He was eager not to offend Elizabeth who might object to the public accusation of murder and adultery against a Queen. Therefore his answer to Mary's statement was that Bothwell had murdered Darnley, had raped the Queen and kept her captive at Dunbar until he had divorced his wife, and a so-called marriage had taken place between him and Mary; and that he, Moray, and the Scottish lairds had taken up arms to protect Mary from this tyrant.

Meanwhile Moray had in his possession translations of those letters which Mary was reputed to have written to Bothwell in French, and he was wondering how best he could use them.

He began by showing them privately to Norfolk, who had been appointed president of the Conference.

When Norfolk read those letters, with their suggestion of great passion and abandon, he felt more than ever attracted to the Queen of Scots. If she had written them she was a murderess and adulteress, but what an exciting wife she would be! He had seen her and he knew her to be beautiful; to him she had seemed generous and ready to be affectionate. He had not been unaware of the fire beneath the kindly exterior. Norfolk was a man of great vanity, and he believed that he would succeed with Mary where Darnley and Bothwell had failed.

If the letters were not genuine – and Mary would most certainly declare they were not – she was still the most attractive woman he had ever met, and it would be piquant to endeavour to discover the truth of what had happened in Holyrood House and Kirk o' Field during those eventful days.

Norfolk's desire for marriage with the Queen was intensified. He would not look too far ahead, but he was certain that she would through him regain the Scottish throne. And what of England? He was related to Elizabeth, on her mother's side. And Elizabeth was no longer a young girl; she had not married; and there were many who said she never would. What if there were no heirs to the English throne? Mary would be next in the line of succession.

The prospect was even more dazzling after reading those erotic letters. Not only would he have a wife who could bring him a crown – perhaps two – but a voluptuous mistress skilled in the arts of love.

*　　*　　*

Maitland of Lethington sought out Norfolk. Maitland had his own reasons for not wishing the circumstances of Darnley's murder to be brought into the light. Darnley had been no friend of his, for it was due to Darnley that at one time his life had been in danger; and but for Mary's intervention he might have lost it. Mary would never forget that he was the husband of Mary Fleming – one of the four Marys who had shared her childhood – and for his wife's sake, if not for his, she had done everything possible to save him. Therefore Darnley's murder had been something he would not have moved a step to prevent; indeed he was strongly suspected of being in the plot to murder. Much better, thought Maitland, not to delve into the matter.

Moreover, although a shrewd statesman, he was deeply in love with his wife and he knew that she was concerned about the Queen's plight because she was constantly imploring him to do what he could for Mary.

Maitland believed that he could serve himself best by preventing the accusation of murder being brought against the Queen; and he saw that the man who could be most useful was Norfolk.

He summed up Norfolk immediately: Vain in the extreme, arrogantly aware of his position as premier peer, eager for power, anxious to add another heiress to the three he had already married and from whose estates he had benefited.

'My lord,' said Maitland, 'I have come to talk to you in secret. I believe you to be the wisest of your Queen's Commissioners, and as you are the most highly born I am of the opinion that the plan which I shall suggest may not seem impossible of achievement.'

Norfolk was alert.

'The Queen of Scots is a young woman who has not yet celebrated her twenty-sixth birthday. She is inclined to frivolity and needs a husband to guide her.'

'I believe you to be right,' answered Norfolk.

'I am sure that there is not another more fitted for the role than yourself.'

Norfolk could not hide his elation. That his secret ambition should be suggested by one of the most powerful Scots might have been astonishing to one less vain. But Norfolk could immediately explain to himself: But it is true. She does need a husband. And who is more suitable to be the husband of a Queen than the premier peer of England?

'The project is not distasteful to Your Grace?' asked Maitland.

'Distasteful! Indeed not. I have seen the Queen and thought her most comely. And I agree with you that she is in need of a husband to look after her. She is delightfully feminine . . . and, as you say, she is inclined to frivolity . . . in urgent need of a guiding hand.'

'Let this matter remain a secret for a while,' suggested Maitland, 'but I would have you know that I shall do all in my power to further it.'

Norfolk nodded. 'I shall not forget your friendship,' he said a trifle pompously. 'There is of course . . . Bothwell.'

'There would be no difficulty about that. A divorce could be arranged. There are many who believe that the marriage was no true marriage.'

'And the Queen?'

'Will be ready enough to rid herself of Bothwell for ever at the prospect of marriage with Your Grace.'

'You believe this to be so?' Norfolk was smiling; he believed it wholeheartedly. His sister Margaret had told him frequently that Mary enjoyed talking of him, and had asked many questions about him. With Margaret to help him at Bolton, and Maitland of Lethington secretly in favour of the match, what could prevent it?

'I do indeed. I believe too that we should proceed with care in this inquiry. It would be well if the case brought against the Queen were merely her hasty and unseemly marriage with Bothwell. I do not think it would be wise to continue with this charge of murder. If the Queen's innocence were not proved it could well be that the Scottish right to succession might be endangered, and that could of course be harmful to the Queen's future.'

'I see that you are right in this,' replied Norfolk readily.

Maitland smiled. 'We must work together in this matter, Your Grace, and, I repeat, in secret. Others may not see the great good which could come out of the success of this plan.'

Norfolk smiled his agreement.

He was well pleased.

*　　*　　*

Maitland's next task was to see Moray.

'I have sounded Norfolk on a possible marriage to your sister,' he said.

'And the young coxcomb is delighted at the prospect of being husband to a Queen?'

'That is so. And a good prospect it is, for it provides a solution to our problems. Married to Norfolk she would reside in England and it would be necessary to appoint a Deputy to take charge of matters in Scotland.'

Speculation was in Moray's eyes.

It was a way out. He was determined to cling to his position of Regent; but he did need peace in Scotland. While the Queen was a prisoner in England there would be factions in her favour springing up throughout the length and breadth of Scotland. But if she were kept out of the way through marriage, that would be a different matter.

'It would be necessary to suppress the more vile charges against her,' said Maitland.

Moray was disappointed. He had looked forward to the wide circulation of those 'casket' letters.

'Norfolk could scarcely marry a murderess, even though she is a Queen,' insisted Maitland.

Moray was thoughtful. There was a great deal in what Maitland suggested.

*　　*　　*

Lady Scrope was beside herself with excitement. She had heard from her brother that certain of the Scottish lairds were in favour of his marriage with Mary. In that case she believed there could not fail to be success.

She was preoccupied with thoughts of the coming child; and Mary, although being with Lady Scrope reminded her poignantly of her own little James whom she had lost, threw herself wholeheartedly into the plans for the new baby.

She was with Lady Scrope in the nursery, inspecting the cradle, the clothes which were being prepared, and listening to details of preparations which were being made for the lying-in, when Margaret whispered: 'Who knows, perhaps ere long Your Majesty will be making similar preparations.'

'Ah, who can say,' replied the Queen; and she thought of those months when she had been expecting James. What sad, violent months they had been! She remembered sitting at the supper table, with David Rizzio singing and playing his lute . . . and how his murderers had stormed into the room and dragged him from her side to plunge their knives into his quivering body. Poor David! And that had happened during the months of waiting for little James!

But how different it would be to wait in serenity as Margaret Scrope waited . . . thinking of nothing but the coming of the child and the possible romance of her brother and a captive Queen.

Yes, such serenity was enviable. Would it ever be her lot? she wondered. And wondering she found a yearning within her. She was weary of her loneliness. If this marriage ever came about she would welcome it.

A servant came to them and announced that Lord Herries wished to see the Queen immediately.

'It is news of the Conference,' said Mary to Margaret. And to one of the servants: 'Bring him to me without delay.'

One look at Herries' face told Mary that he was far from pleased.

'What news, my lord?' she demanded.

'It is simply this, Your Majesty. The Queen of England is not pleased with the manner in which the Conference has gone at York, and she is disbanding it. There is to be a second, which will take place next month at Westminster.'

'I see,' said Mary slowly.

'She is not pleased that those vile accusations were withheld, I fear,' said Herries.

Mary's eyes narrowed. 'If there is to be a conference at Westminster,' she said, 'and accusations are to be made against me, I wish to go in person to answer them.'

Herries did not reply, but continued to look sadly at his mistress.

*　　*　　*

190

Sir Francis Knollys found the Queen taking exercise in the grounds of the castle, and asked if he might join her. She gave him her gracious permission and told him that he was looking a little anxious lately.

'My wife is ill,' he said. 'I am worried about her.'

Mary was immediately all concern.

'But you must go to see her. I am sure she would like to have you with her at such a time.'

'Alas, I cannot do that.'

'But . . .' began Mary and stopped. There was a silence for a while and then Mary went on: 'So your Queen refuses to allow you to leave Bolton?'

'She feels that my duty lies here at this time.'

'But that is heartless.'

Knollys was silent, and Mary lapsed into thoughts of her own. She felt that, although she was not allowed to come face to face with the Queen of England, that woman's character was gradually being unfolded for her. Had she known more of Elizabeth, would she have been so eager to ignore the advice of so many of her friends and take that trip across the Solway Firth?

She was sorry for Knollys who, in addition to having this rather objectionable task thrust upon him – and she was sure it was objectionable, for he was not a natural jailor – was not allowed to visit his sick wife.

He seemed eager to change the subject, and Mary said: 'Do you think that it is your Queen's intention to have another conference?'

'Indeed yes. It is to be held at Westminster.'

'And do you think she really wishes to see me reconciled with my subjects?'

'It is Her Majesty's desire that this should be so. Your Majesty, I pray you forgive me asking this question . . . but . . . would you consider a proposal of marriage?'

Mary was silent for a while. She immediately thought of Norfolk as he had been at Carlisle. Young, handsome, ardent, he had implied that he would be her staunch ally; and she believed he was. She was certain that the reason the conference at York had gone so much in her favour was due to him.

Knollys went on eagerly: 'If a proposal came from a close relative of the Queen of England, would that be to Your Majesty's liking?'

Mary smiled faintly. 'I would not greatly mislike it,' she answered.

She did not realize that Knollys was not thinking of the same man who was in her thoughts. Both Norfolk and George Carey were related to Elizabeth through Anne Boleyn, for Lady Elizabeth Howard had been Anne's mother; and George Carey was the son of Mary Boleyn, Anne's sister.

Knollys was delighted with the reply. It was invigorating to plan for his family; it took his mind away from the anxieties about his wife.

When he left Mary he went to his own apartments and there wrote at once to his brother-in-law, Lord Hunsdon, and told him that Mary Queen of Scots was very favourably disposed towards his son George, and a royal marriage for George could be changed from a possibility into a certainty.

* * *

It was the 25th November before the Conference was opened at Westminster. Elizabeth had refused to allow Mary to appear in person; and the atmosphere of the court was quite different from that of the one which had taken place at York, for Elizabeth intended this to be a criminal court and was determined that Mary should be tried for the murder of her husband. The Earl and Countess of Lennox, Darnley's parents, had been begging her to see justice done, and her desire was to find a legitimate excuse to keep Mary her prisoner, to avoid meeting her, and to sustain Protestant Moray in the Office of Regency.

Elizabeth could not forget that there were many Catholics in England who did not believe she was the legitimate daughter of Henry VIII, and, if this were indeed the case, the true Queen of England would be Mary Queen of Scots. This doubt of legitimacy which had hung over Elizabeth all her life – especially so in her youth, when with sickening regularity she had been in and out of favour, never certain what was going to happen next – made her suspicious of any who might contest her right to the throne.

She would never forget that Mary had called herself the Queen of England while she was in France. That was reason enough in Elizabeth's opinion to send her to the scaffold. Elizabeth could not however send her to the scaffold . . . yet;

but she could hold her prisoner. That was what she determined to do.

Therefore she would intimate to Moray, who dared not disobey her, that every means at his disposal was to be used to defame the Queen of Scots. She heard most of what was going on; she had alert spies. She had those minsters to whom she playfully referred as her Eyes, her Lids, her Spirit. . . . There was her dearest Leicester whom she would always trust. There were shrewd Cecil, and Walsingham who served her so ardently that he had a spy system, which he maintained at his own expense, and it was all in order to preserve her safety.

It was not surprising therefore that she heard that two bridegrooms had been proposed for Mary Queen of Scots: George Carey and Norfolk!

She was furious, being determined that Mary should have no bridegroom. Unlike Elizabeth Mary was no virgin – all the world knew that; and Elizabeth could well believe that the lecherous creature yearned for a man. Well, she should have none; she could be as celibate as her cousin Elizabeth because this state for them both was the choice of Elizabeth.

She sent a sharp note to Hunsdon expressing her deep displeasure that he should have thought fit to scheme for a marriage between his son and the Queen of Scots. She was considering whether it smacked of treason.

She sent for Norfolk, and shrewdly looking him in the eyes asked bluntly if he were planning to marry the Queen of Scots.

Norfolk was terrified. He remembered how his father, the Earl of Surrey, had lost his head for the flimsiest reason by the order of this Queen's father. Ever since, he had determined to walk warily; and now he saw himself caught in a trap.

He promptly denied that he had any desire to marry the Queen of Scots and that he knew anything of such a plan; and if Her Majesty had heard rumours of it, then it was put about by his enemies.

'Would you not marry the Queen of Scots,' asked Elizabeth artfully, 'if you knew it would tend to the tranquillity of the realm and the safety of my person?'

Norfolk, feeling he was being led to betray a desire for Mary and the marriage, replied vehemently: 'Your Majesty, that woman shall never be my wife who has been your competitor, and whose husband cannot sleep in security on his pillow.'

This remark appeared to satisfy the Queen; and she dismissed Norfolk with a smile. She even allowed him to resume his presidency of the Conference.

Norfolk was in a cold sweat when he left her presence. He had decided not to dabble in dangerous affairs again. He must be careful during the Conference not to give an impression that he cherished tender feelings for Mary.

*   *   *

Knollys was alarmed. Mary sensed it. And it was not only his wife's illness which disturbed him. Margaret Scrope had told her that he had had a sharp reprimand from the Queen because he had been too ambitious for his nephew George Carey. Knollys was afraid he was out of favour, and that could be a dangerous thing at Elizabeth's Court.

'I have not heard recently from my brother,' went on Margaret. 'I'll warrant he is busy on your behalf at Westminster.'

Letters had been coming frequently from George Douglas in France, where he was longing to gather together another army for Mary's defence.

She thought of him tenderly and often wished that he were with her. But she was glad that he was in France. There he would be leading a more normal life than he could in captivity with her; and she knew that her uncles would make it a point of honour that he was given every chance.

She wished that she could do the same for Willie. Then an idea occurred to her.

She sent for the boy.

He came into her apartment still wearing the sword which no longer looked quite so incongruous as it had when they had escaped across the Solway Firth, because Willie had grown considerably in the last months.

'Willie,' she said, 'you are no longer a boy.'

Willie gave his grin. 'I'm glad Your Majesty recognizes the fact,' he said.

'And I have a mission for you.'

She saw the pleasure leap into his eyes.

'A dangerous mission,' she went on, 'but I trust you to complete it.'

'O ay,' said Willie.

'You are going to France, taking letters from me to George and my uncles.'

194

Willie's eyes sparkled.

'First it will be necessary for you to obtain a safe conduct from London. So you must make your way there. Send word to me through the Bishop of Ross when you have received it. Then I shall know that you will shortly be in France. And I shall wish to hear from you and George that you are together.'

'And am I to bring back letters to Your Majesty?'

'We shall see. First go to George. He will give you your instructions.'

'We'll get an army together,' cried Willie. 'Ye'll see. We'll come and win England from the red-headed bastard and give it to Your Majesty.'

'Hush, Willie. And pray do not speak of a royal person in such a manner in my hearing.'

'No, Your Majesty, but that won't alter my thoughts. When do I start?'

'I leave it to you, Willie.'

She knew it would be soon. She saw the desire for action in his face.

He left next day. She watched him set out, and she felt very sad.

'Yet another friend has gone,' she said to Seton.

'If it saddens Your Majesty to lose him, why let him go?'

'I think of his future, Seton. What future is there for any of us . . . in this prison?'

'But we shall be back in Scotland one day.'

'Do you think so, Seton?' She sighed. 'If you are right, the first thing I shall do is send for George and Willie and try to recompense them in some measure for all they did for me. In the meantime, I like to think of them . . . over there . . . making their way in the world. Because there must be one prisoner, that does not mean there have to be hundreds.'

Seton was silent, thinking: She is melancholy today. She is wondering what is happening at the Conference. Knollys' depression affects her.

She looked out of the window and saw that the snow had begun to fall.

*   *   *

This was a special day. Twenty-six years before, in the Palace of Linlithgow, a baby had been born. That baby was Mary, Queen of Scotland and the Isles.

Mary opened her eyes to see her women round her bed, all come to wish her a happy birthday; she embraced them one by one.

They had presents for her which delighted her – little pieces of embroidery mostly, which they had managed to hide from her until this morning.

There were tears in her eyes as she cried: 'The best gift you can give me is your presence here.'

But it was a birthday, even though it must be spent far from home in a castle which was a prison. For today, thought Mary, she would forget everything else but the fact that this was her birthday. They would be merry.

They would have a feast. Was that possible? She was sure her cook could contrive something; they would invite everyone in the castle. They would all wear their best gowns and, although she had no jewels to wear, Seton should dress her hair as she never had before. They would dance to the music of the lute, and they would forget that they were in Bolton and imagine they were dancing in those apartments which in Holyrood House had been known as Little France.

So the happy day progressed. It was too cold to go out, and a great fire was built up to warm the apartments. Everyone in the castle was eager to celebrate the birthday, and there was an air of excitement from the cellars to the turrets.

Seton dressed her mistress's hair by the light of candles, and the face which looked back at Mary from the burnished metal mirror seemed as young and carefree as it had before the days of her captivity had begun.

It was her duty, Mary told herself, to throw off gloom, to forget her exile from her own country, that little Jamie was being kept from her, that in London a Conference was being held and perhaps the most evil charges were being brought against her.

The meal was prepared; she heard the laughing voices of her servants as they scurried to and fro; she smelt the savoury smells of cooking meats.

And when the table was set in her apartments the whole household assembled there, and she received them like a Queen in her own Palace.

She sat at the centre of the table and Knollys insisted on handing her her napkin; Lord Scrope and Margaret looked on with pleasure.

Margaret was getting uncomfortably near her time, and her

husband was anxious that she should not tire herself, but she declared she was happy to be there; and when the meal was over, she sat with the lute players and watched the Queen lead the others in the dance.

Mary, flushed with the dancing, her chestnut hair a little ruffled with the exertion, seemed like a very young girl in her excitement.

Knollys watching her thought: How easy it is for her to forget. She was meant to be joyous. When will this weary business end?

It was while they were dancing that messengers from Elizabeth, delayed until now by the bad weather, arrived bringing letters for the jailors of the Queen of Scotland.

Knollys and Scrope went down to receive them. Knollys was startled when he read the letter which was addressed to him; he could only read it again, hoping he had been mistaken.

Elizabeth was displeased with Mary's jailors. They had shown too much leniency towards their prisoner; and had indulged in schemes for her marriage. Elizabeth therefore proposed to deprive them of their duties, and they were to prepare to conduct the Queen of Scots to Tutbury Castle, where the Earl and Countess of Shrewsbury would be her new keepers.

'Tutbury!' he murmured. And he thought of that bleak Staffordshire castle which was one of the most comfortless places he had ever seen, lacking the chimney tunnels which were a feature of Bolton Castle and which had helped so much to make the large apartments bearable during this bitterly cold weather.

Knollys was filled with pity for the Queen of Scots who was so surely at the mercy of the Queen of England; he was even sorrier for himself. He had offended Elizabeth, and who could know where that would end! How could he have guessed that she would have taken such a view of his attempt to marry his nephew to Mary? George Carey was a kinsman of hers, and she had always favoured her relations – particularly those on her mother's side, for those on her father's might imagine they had more right to the throne than she had.

There was a postscript to the letter. He was not to leave Bolton until he did so with the Queen of Scots. It would be his duty to conduct her to Tutbury and place her in the hands of the Shrewsburys.

He thought of Catherine, his wife, who was so sick and asking for him.

197

He let the letter drop from his hands and sat staring ahead of him; then he noticed that Scrope was as agitated as he was himself.

He tried to thrust aside his personal grief and said: 'But Tutbury . . . in this weather! We could not travel there while the blizzards last. It is too dangerous.'

'Tutbury . . .' said Scrope as though repeating a lesson.

'Yes, I suppose she tells you what she tells me . . . that we are to be relieved of this task, and that it is to be handed to the Shrewsburys?'

'Yes,' said Scrope as though dazed, 'she tells me that. But . . . how can I move her? How could she go now?'

'We shall have to wait until the weather has improved a little,' said Knollys. 'She will be reluctant. Remember how difficult it was to remove her from Carlisle.'

'I was thinking of Margaret. . . .'

'Margaret!'

Scrope tapped Elizabeth's letter. 'The Queen orders that Margaret is to leave Bolton without delay. She expects to hear that she has gone before Christmas.'

'But in her condition!'

Anger blazed into Scrope's eyes. 'She suspects Margaret of meddling to make a match between the Queen of Scots and Norfolk; therefore she says, pregnant or no, Margaret is to leave Bolton without delay.'

'But where . . .' began Knollys.

Scrope spread his hands in desperation. 'I do not know. I cannot think. But unless I am to displease the Queen still further I must set about finding a lodging for Margaret without delay.'

Outside the wind howled. Knollys was thinking of his wife, who was dangerously ill and asking for him; Scrope was thinking of his, who would very shortly bear their child. Elizabeth was telling them that their personal affairs must not be put before their duty to her. Not that they needed to be reminded of how implacable could be the wrath of a Tudor!

They did not return to the birthday party.

Knollys said quietly: 'There is no need to tell her tonight that she is to be moved to Tutbury. Tomorrow will suffice.'

*   *   *

'Tutbury!' cried Mary, looking from Scrope to Knollys. 'I cannot go to Tutbury in weather like this!'

'Those are our Queen's orders,' said Scrope. Mary noticed that his expression was blank, his face grey, and she believed that he was afraid because this meant that he had failed and for this reason the charge of her was being transferred to others.

'I shall refuse,' retorted Mary. 'I think there are occasions when your Queen forgets that I am the Queen of Scotland.'

Knollys looked at her dully. What did rank matter to Elizabeth! All she cared was that her desires be gratified.

'We can make the excuse of the bad weather for a while,' answered Scrope. 'But we should begin to make our preparations.'

'I have heard that Tutbury is one of the bleakest places in England and that Bolton is full of comfort in comparison.'

'Doubtless much will be done to make Your Majesty comfortable.'

'I refuse to consider making the journey until the winter is over,' said the Queen.

Neither Scrope nor Knollys attempted to advise her; they were both thinking of their personal problems.

Later that day Mary discovered the reason why, when one of Lady Scrope's attendants came to her and asked if she would go to her ladyship's apartment as she was too unwell to come to her.

Her pains cannot have started yet, Mary thought. It is too soon.

She hurried to Lady Scrope's bedchamber and there found her lying on her bed.

'Margaret!' cried Mary. 'Is it indeed . . .?'

'No,' said Margaret. 'But I have bad news. I have displeased Elizabeth and . . . for my punishment I am to be banished from Bolton.'

'Banished! But you cannot go from here in weather like this . . . in your state.'

'Those are her orders. I am to leave at once.'

'For where?'

'We do not know. But Her Majesty insists that I am to go . . . presumably because she does not wish us to be together. She has heard of our friendship and. . . .'

Mary clenched her hands together. 'Has she no pity!' she cried. And it was characteristic of her that she could feel more angry over the harsh treatment of Margaret Scrope than over any injustice that had been done to herself.

'No,' answered Margaret. 'She has no pity when she feels that her subjects have worked against her. She must have learned that I have been giving you news of my brother. . . .'

'But this is monstrous. I'll not endure it. You are to stay here, Margaret. You are to have your baby here, as you have arranged.'

Margaret put up a slim hand to touch her neck. She smiled grimly. 'I am in no mind to lose my head,' she said.

'Oh Margaret, Margaret, how can she be so cruel!'

'You do not know her, if you can ask that,' replied Margaret bitterly. 'But I am being foolish. I have to go.' She had suddenly become calm with the serenity of pregnant women. 'I'll swear the child will be born as easily elsewhere as here.'

'But the journey! I have heard the roads are almost impassable.'

'Still, it must be, Your Majesty.'

'Then we must say goodbye, Margaret?'

'I fear so.'

'You know I am to go to Tutbury.'

'I do. And that means that you will pass into the care of the Shrewsburys. But we shall meet again . . . soon. My brother will not forget, and one day. . . .'

Mary did not answer. She was looking at Margaret's swollen body, and her indignation was so great that she could not trust herself to speak. She thought of all the mistakes she had made as ruler of Scotland; and she thought of wily Elizabeth who was shrewd and, if ever she found herself in a delicate situation, managed to extricate herself with the genius of a born statesman.

They accuse me of murder and adultery, thought Mary. Yet I would not care to have her sins on my conscience.

*   *   *

How wretched were those days before Christmas! Mary missed Margaret Scrope who had been moved to a lodging only two miles from the castle, but the bad weather and her condition made it impossible for her to visit the Queen. It was some comfort, though, that Lord Scrope had managed to find a lodging that was not too far away.

What was happening in Westminster she had no means of knowing, for the bad weather held up messengers and it might have been that those of her friends who knew were reluctant to tell her that the damning 'casket' letters had been produced and that the case was going against her – since it was the will of Elizabeth that it should.

There was only one episode that lightened those dark days. That was when a messenger did get through to bring her letters from the Earl of Northumberland.

Northumberland had been converted to the Catholic faith and having heard rumours that there was a plan to marry Mary to Norfolk who was Protestant, he had become busy trying to prevent this. Mary's recent flirtation with the Protestant religion had alarmed him; but that had not been of long duration and she had said on more than one occasion that she believed every man should worship God according to his conscience, and when she returned to rule her country she would endeavour to see that this was the law.

Northumberland however yearned not only to free Mary but to bring England back to Papal rule; and he had believed the best way of doing this was to arrange a marriage between Mary and Philip II of Spain. This plan had been simmering in his mind for some time; and he had been in communication with Philip about it. Philip however had now remarried, and he suggested that a marriage be arranged between Mary and his illegitimate brother Don Jon of Austria, who was both personable and a popular hero.

So during those sad weeks Mary had letters from Northumberland about this project; and although she had made up her mind that her next husband would be the Duke of Norfolk – so eulogized by his adoring sister that Mary had begun to see him through Margaret's eyes – she could realize the advantages of being married to the dashing hero, who would not rest until he had won back her kingdom for her.

But Margaret's letters brought back to her so vividly the conversations they had shared together, and Mary wrote to Northumberland that he must tell the King of Spain that, as she was in the hands of Elizabeth, she was in no position to enter into a matrimonial engagement at this time; for before it became possible to do so she required help in order that she might regain the throne of Scotland.

To the anxiety for Margaret was added another; there was no news of Willie Douglas, and this was overdue.

Christmas was a melancholy season at Bolton Castle.

*   *   *

The weather was slightly warmer and some of the snow had thawed in the roads to and from the south.

Letters came from the Bishop of Ross. He told Mary how the Conference was progressing, and it did not make happy reading. But there was one fact which worried her more than any other: The Bishop did not mention Willie Douglas.

Deeply disturbed Mary wrote at once to the Bishop asking him to have inquiries made concerning Willie, and a week later she heard from him again. Willie had been seen in London; he had received a passport in the Queen's name and from that day had been seen no more. Inquiries had been made at his lodgings; but he had not returned to them; his landlord was indignant because Willie had left owing money.

The Bishop wrote that Willie's landlord had been paid and that further inquiries were being made.

Now Mary was really uneasy, feeling certain that some calamity had befallen Willie. It was known that he had been shrewd enough to make possible her escape from Lochleven; did this mean that someone believed he was too sharp a boy to be allowed to go about on the Queen's business?

Elizabeth had written letters expressing her displeasure to Scrope and Knollys. She had given orders that the Queen of Scots was to be removed to Tutbury, and she could not understand why there should be this delay. Knollys wrote back that the delay had been due to the bad condition of the roads and the fact that there were no horses.

Elizabeth's retort was that horses must be borrowed from neighbours and the journey made as soon as the roads were sufficiently cleared to make the journey possible. She added that she was well informed as to the state of the roads and was not pleased with dilatory servants.

'There can be no more delay,' said Knollys to Scrope. 'We shall have to set out.'

Scrope was as unhappy as Knollys; he was hoping that his child would be born before they must leave for Tutbury; but both men agreed that preparations must go ahead. The two of them were so much out of favour that, if they offended their Queen further, they might be in serious trouble.

Scrope's troubles lightened a little during the next days, for his wife was delivered safely of a son. Knollys was less fortunate.

When news came to the castle that his wife had died, asking for him, he shut himself in his own chamber and remained there for some days. He no longer cared what happened to him; temporarily he hated Elizabeth who had prevented his being at his wife's bedside, and he was afraid that if he spoke to anyone he would give such utterance to his wrath that he would be in danger of being named as a traitor.

When he emerged he was subdued, but there was a terrible bitterness in his face which Mary noticed and understood. All her sympathy was for him; and she felt: he is that callous woman's prisoner, even as I am.

'My dear Sir Francis,' Mary said, 'I would there were something I could do to comfort you.'

'Your Majesty is good,' he answered listlessly.

'At least you know she suffers no more.'

He turned away, his sorrow, choking him, prevented speech.

'Have you written to the Queen asking permission to go to her?' she asked gently.

'Of what use now?' he murmured.

'You will wish to bury her,' Mary told him.

He nodded.

Mary laid a hand on his arm. 'Then write to her. There are others who can take me to Tutbury. She cannot refuse you this.'

'I will write to her,' he said. 'I thank Your Majesty for your sympathy.'

He looked into that lovely face and saw that the long eyes were wet with tears; and he was so moved that he could only turn and stumble away.

* * *

Elizabeth's retort was sharp. Knollys' duty would not end until the Scottish Queen was safely delivered into the hands of her new keepers at Tutbury, that mission which, to her amazement, had not yet been carried out.

Knollys could not believe that she had refused him this. But there was no mistaking her meaning.

'Ah well,' he murmured, 'what does it matter now? What does anything matter?'

* * *

Seton and Mary were together looking out onto the snowy landscape.

'There will not be many more nights when we shall look from these windows at that scene,' Mary was saying. 'We shall miss it. It is very beautiful. Oh Seton, we are going farther into the heart of England. Each mile we go south means a mile farther from Scotland.'

Seton was silent. She had no comfort to offer. Like her mistress she was beginning to understand that the Queen of England was extremely capable in the art of double-dealing.

At last she said: 'Perhaps it will be less of a fortress than this one.'

'I doubt not we shall be well guarded. And I am to lose Knollys and Scrope.'

'For the Earl and Countess of Shrewsbury, who may become your true friends. Your Majesty has a way of finding friends.'

'Let us hope I find a friend who will help me to regain my kingdom. But they say that Tutbury is one of the bleakest castles in England.'

'We will do our best to make you comfortable; we have not done so badly here.'

While they talked, messengers arrived with letters from London.

Willie's whereabouts remained a mystery. There was one however, she was told, who might have more opportunity of discovering what had happened to him than Scotsmen who were treated with some suspicion in London, and that was the French ambassador, Bertrand de Salignac de la Mothe Fénelon. Mary's friends in London had mentioned the matter to him, but if she herself wrote he might be inclined to double his efforts.

Mary said: 'I will write at once. I cannot rest easily until I know what has become of Willie.'

*   *   *

It was late February when Mary was preparing to leave Bolton Castle. The weather was bitterly cold and the roads only just negotiable. Progress would be very slow and uncomfortable, but Elizabeth was growing impatient and neither Scrope nor Knollys dared delay longer.

While the last preparations were being made, a note from the French ambassador was brought to Mary, and when she read it she grew pale and called to Seton.

'Is it Willie?' asked Seton.

Mary nodded.

'They have not. . . .'

204

Mary smiled. 'Oh no. . . . He is alive. But he is in prison in the North of England. He must have been arrested as soon as he acquired his passport.'

'And all this time he has been a prisoner. What will become of poor Willie?'

'He will be freed. I shall insist on it. I shall not rest until he is free. What has he done but be a loyal subject to his Queen!'

'You think that something can be arranged?'

'Yes, through Fénelon. Elizabeth will not wish the French to know that she is clapping my supporters into jail simply because they are my supporters. I shall not rest, I tell you, until Willie is free.'

'And then?'

'And then,' said Mary firmly, 'he shall remain with me until it is safe for him to join George in France. I shall write at once to Fénelon. He must do this for me.'

Mary sat down at her table and wrote an impassioned appeal which she knew would not fail to move the heart of the King of France. She reminded him of those long ago days and how happy they had all been together. Now she asked his help because his ambassador could more easily than any other friend of hers obtain the release of one of her most faithful servants. She implored Charles to help in this instance. The release of Willie Douglas – her saviour of Lochleven – was the greatest boon she could ask of him; and she knew he would instruct his ambassador that this was a task in which he must not fail.

She sealed the letter and dispatched it; then she wrote another to de la Mothe Fénelon.

There was nothing more she could do but continue with her preparations for departure.

* * *

The Queen of England was pleased with the outcome of the Conference. Nothing had been clearly defined – which was what she had hoped for – but Mary's character had been completely blackened; Elizabeth herself had declared that she could not, without manifest blemish of her own honour, receive her into her presence. The ruling had been that nothing had been proved against Moray and his supporters that might impair their allegiance and honour; and nothing had been sufficiently proved against the Queen of Scots.

The affair had ended in a stalemate. But Elizabeth had a satisfactory excuse for not receiving her cousin at her Court. Moray could return to Scotland and still hold the Regency, while Mary remained in England at the mercy of Elizabeth.

It had all been a splendid example of procrastination such as Elizabeth desired.

Now Mary should remain in captivity; for Elizabeth could never feel entirely at peace while one, so close a claimant to the English throne, and of undoubted legitimate birth, was free. The picture of Mary Queen of Scots being hailed as the Queen of England – as she had once dared to be in France – still haunted Elizabeth's dreams. It was pleasant therefore to visualise her on the weary journeys from one bleak castle to another.

*　　　*　　　*

So, on a bitterly cold day in the middle of winter, the cavalcade left Bolton Castle. Mary was carried in her litter over the rough roads which were often icy and dangerous. She had insisted on a litter for Lady Livingstone who was indisposed and unfit for travel. But it was no use pleading that excuse. It had clearly been commanded that there were to be no more excuses.

The snow began to fall and settle on the litter and the hoods of the ladies who rode on horseback.

Mary closed her eyes and longed to reach Tutbury. And when she did, she asked herself, what then? To what would this new journey along the road of her misfortunes bring her?

CHAPTER SIX

TUTBURY

ELIZABETH, Countess of Shrewsbury, had been delighted when she had heard that her husband was to be the new keeper of the Queen of Scots. A sign of Elizabeth's favour, she believed; and to the strong-minded Countess that was very important.

She bustled about Tutbury Castle, giving orders which she herself made sure were carried out. There was not one person in the castle – even the Earl – who was not in awe of her. The Countess – Bess of Hardwick, as she was often called, for she was the daughter of John Hardwick of Hardwick in Derbyshire – although in her fifties was as handsome as she was energetic. She had been married to the Earl only about a year but he already knew who was master. Not that he minded. Bess had had three husbands before him and they had found her a stimulating partner. She was completely happy as long as she could have her way; and as her great desire was to promote the fortunes of all her family – sons, daughters and husbands – and as she was extremely efficient in this endeavour, they were all prepared to place the management of their affairs in her capable hands.

Her father had often said 'Our Bessie should have been a man.' Bess herself did not agree. She did not believe that her sex should be a handicap. She might have the mind of a man but she was determined that her woman's body should not hinder, but further her ambitions.

Tutbury! she was thinking as she waited the arrival of the Queen of Scots on that bleak February day, not the most delightful of our homes.

But she was shrewd enough to know why the Queen had chosen this for Mary; it was doubtless because she believed her rival had been too luxuriously housed at Bolton.

This was certainly a chilly place. Not that energetic Bess noticed that; but she could not prevent herself from concocting schemes for improving the place; building houses was a passion with her. It was far more interesting though, to build a fresh one than attempt to improve an old place. Her most ambitious endeavour to date was the mansion of Chatsworth and the thought of her achievements there made her glow with pride – and long to repeat them. Bess never believed in standing still. She was determined to add several such mansions to her possessions before she died. Not that she ever thought of dying. Had she not been so practical, so bursting with common sense, she would have said that she was immortal. That being absurd, since after all even Bess was only human, she contended herself with acting as though she were.

Now she was considering what sort of welcome should be given the Queen of Scots. George would leave the matter in her capable hands, she knew. But it was a delicate matter since Queen Elizabeth was dismissing Knollys and Scrope for their too favourable treatment of the captive Queen; whatever else the excuse, Bess knew this to be true. Therefore the Shrewsburys must not emulate Knollys and Scrope. On the other hand the Queen of Scots was no ordinary prisoner, inasmuch as the fate of Kings and Queens could change in a very short time. They must never forget – while obeying the wishes of the Queen of England – that the Queen of Scots might one day, not only regain her throne, but take that of Elizabeth also.

'Ah yes,' Bess had told George, 'this is indeed a delicate matter. Leave it to me.'

She would therefore make a cautious friendship with Mary, while she let her know that she must needs obey the will of Queen Elizabeth. And any suspicious conduct on the part of Mary must at once be reported to Elizabeth and not left to be discovered by others.

They should do well from this new task – provided Bess of Hardwick was in charge.

Bess could look back on the triumphs which her own cool brain and determination had brought her. The daughter of John Hardwick had come far since, at the age of fourteen, she had been married to Robert Barlow. Robert, who was about her own age, had been a delicate boy too young for marriage. He had not long survived it, but he had left her a large fortune and when barely fifteen she had had the experience of being a considerable heiress. She had enjoyed her independence and had not married again until some sixteen years later – this time to Sir William Cavendish who had been thirteen years older than herself and had already had two wives. Those had been happy years with Cavendish. Bess had learned how to charm and govern at the same time – a rare accomplishment, but she was a rare woman. She had imbued Cavendish with her passion for building, and together they had planned Chatsworth, though he had died before it was completed, and she had had to finish it alone. The building of that mansion had been a great joy to her.

Cavendish had been a satisfactory husband; he was the only one who had given her children, and for that she would be grateful. More lives to govern! More to scheme for. She had three sons and three daughters and she was determined that they should follow their mother's example and succeed in life. Of her sons there was her eldest, Henry, then William and Charles; and her daughters were Frances, Elizabeth and Mary.

She had persuaded Cavendish to sell his estates in the south and acquire land in her native Derbyshire; this he had done, and the result had been the building of Chatsworth.

Alas, Cavendish had died, and she then took as her husband Sir William St. Loe, a knight of Gloucestershire, who showed himself as willing – and even eager – to be governed by his wife as her previous husbands had been. It was true that there had been some unpleasantness with his family, who called her a masterful woman set on having her own way. Bess snapped her fingers at them; little did she care for their gibes; all that mattered was that St. Loe was an obedient, affectionate and adoring husband.

When he died all his vast possessions were hers, and that was another matter which annoyed his family. But what did Bess care, since she was now one of the richest women in England; and as such naturally she looked to one of the leading peers of the realm and found George Talbot, Earl of Shrewsbury, greatly to her liking.

George Talbot behaved exactly as Bess could have wished. He was so eager for the marriage that she could feign a certain aloofness; and thus, before their nuptials took place, she succeeded in arranging two excellent marriages for her children. Her eldest son Henry was married to Lady Grace Talbot, Shrewsbury's youngest daughter – a good match for Henry. But Bess was never one to be satisfied when she saw further advancement for her family within reach; and as George Talbot had an unmarried son, she did not see why he should not be paired off with one of her daughters; thus Gilbert Talbot, Shrewsbury's second son, was married to Bess's youngest daughter, Mary. A very satisfactory linking of the families. These two marriages celebrated, Bess graciously gave her hand to Shrewsbury, so cementing the family alliance still further, and satisfying Bess's passion for arranging the lives of others.

The union of Bess and Shrewsbury had been smiled on by Queen Elizabeth and, doubtless to show her approval, she was now appointing them guardians of the Queen of Scots. So Bess, determined to continue in the Queen's favour, bustled about her castle giving orders.

The party must soon arrive, although the inclement weather was doubtless the reason for the delay. She climbed the stairs to those apartments which had been set aside for the use of the Queen.

209

'H'm!' she murmured with a grim smile, for they were two miserable rooms very sparsely furnished. There were patches of damp on the wall where the rain had seeped through the broken roof; and as there was no tapestry or hangings of any sort to cover the cracks in the walls the general effect was depressing.

Even Bess shivered slightly, although she prided herself on no coddling and was passionately devoted to fresh air.

Fresh air! The air in this chamber was far from fresh. That unmistakable odour came from the privy, immediately below the window, which was emptied every Saturday; then, of course, the stench was unbearable. There was always an unpleasant smell in these apartments; it was merely increased when the process of emptying was carried out.

But she will soon become accustomed to it, Bess decided.

The point was that Queen Elizabeth knew what Tutbury was like and she had expressly ordered that Mary was to be taken there.

But she will have the view, Bess told herself. The view? Well, the Queen, looking from her window, would see the marshes; they were not considered very healthy and doubtless the dampness of Tutbury was in some measure due to them, but the River Dove was charming enough, and Bess thought it pleasant because she could look across it to her beloved Derbyshire and felt when doing so that she was not far from home.

Bess went to the window. The smell of the privy made her draw back slightly, but as she did so she caught sight of a party of riders in the distance. Yes, and surely that was a litter she saw. The Queen would be travelling in a litter. At last they were approaching Tutbury.

Bess left the room and started on her way down to the hall. She saw one of the servants about to enter a room as she did so and called: 'Come here, girl.'

The girl looked startled, but that did not displease Bess. It was how she expected her servants to look when she turned her attention to them.

'Come here!' she repeated.

The girl came shyly and, when she reached her mistress, she dropped an embarrassed curtsey. A flush stained her cheeks, giving them a soft, peach-like bloom. She was inclined to be plump and was rather more comely than Bess liked her maids to be.

210

'You are Eleanor Britton,' she said, for she made a point of knowing the names of even her humblest servants and would expect an account of their efficiency or lack of it from those whom she put in authority over them. This Eleanor Britton was a newcomer to the household and had been among the extra staff engaged for the coming of the Queen.

'Yes, my lady.'

'And why are you not in the kitchens?'

'My . . . lady,' stammered the girl, 'I was sent to prepare one of the rooms for the Queen's party'

'I see. I believe my lord Earl to be in his bedchamber. Go to him now and tell him that the Queen will be arriving very soon. I have sighted her party less than half a mile away.'

Eleanor Britton bobbed another curtsey and made off with all speed, delighted to escape. One of the main occupations of the staff, both male and female, was to avoid claiming the attention of the lady of the house, and when they failed to do so, they rarely escaped without some reprimand.

Eleanor hurried to the Earl's apartment. He called to her to enter when she tapped and she found him seated in his chair, dozing. He would have liked to stretch out on his bed, but Bess did not approve of sleeping during the day. It was a lazy habit and Bess, who was never lazy, deplored the fault in others.

The maid dropped a curtsey: 'Begging your pardon, my lord,' she said, 'but my lady says . . . you're to. . . .'

She stopped, because it hardly seemed right to her that a noble Earl should receive commands from his wife.

George Talbot understood the girl's feelings and he smiled faintly, and because she seemed an intelligent and perceptive girl, he looked at her with interest and noticed the colour in her cheeks and how soft her skin was.

She was very young of course – little more than a child, younger than his own daughters. A pretty creature.

'What were my lady's orders?' he asked gently.

'My lord . . . my lady has seen the Queen's party. She says they're not half a mile away.'

George Talbot rose. 'Is that so then?' he said. And he went towards the girl, smiling.

She dropped a low curtsey and said in a frightened voice: 'Is there aught your lordship wishes?'

'You must not be frightened, you know,' he told her. 'There is nothing to fear.'

Then he wondered that he had bothered to say such a thing to a servant; it was most unusual. Why had he done it? he wondered. Was it because she seemed sorry to bring him one of Bess's peremptory messages? Was it because he guessed that her recent encounter with Bess had terrified her? Was it because she looked so young and pretty in her embarrassment?

On impulse he said. 'What is your name? I do not think I have seen you before.'

'It is Eleanor Britton, my lord.'

'Well, Eleanor, go on your way. I will tell the Countess that you gave me her message.'

'Thank you, my lord.'

She took one fleeting look at him as she hurried away.

The Earl went down to the hall, where his wife was already waiting to greet the Queen of Scots.

*　　*　　*

Mary felt despondent as she rode nearer to Tutbury. It had been a tiresome and tedious journey, eight days having elapsed since she left Bolton. It had not however been an uneventful journey. Lady Livingstone, who had been ill before they started, became worse as they travelled over those ice-bound roads; as for Mary herself, she found that her limbs were stiff with the cold, and when she tried to move them felt excruciating pain.

They had spent the first night at Ripon and, because Mary and Lady Livingstone were so ill, it was impossible to leave the next day. Knollys and Scrope, believing that if they delayed longer Elizabeth would accuse them of deliberately prolonging the journey they had obviously been reluctant to undertake, assured Mary that they could give her no more than a day in which to rest.

But there was a whole day's respite and this Mary spent in the room which had been provided for her, writing letters; and during the second night she lay at Ripon she listened to the howling wind and dreaded the resumption of the journey on the next day.

As the cavalcade travelled from Ripon to Wetherby, Mary was startled by a beggar who thrust his way to her litter and began begging for alms.

Knollys and Scrope were frowning and the guards made to drag the man away, but Mary would not have this. She said: 'Heaven knows how we suffer, yet we do enjoy a modicum of comfort. I pity those who are homeless on days such as this.'

She turned to the man. 'My good man,' she said, 'I have little to offer you, but I would it were more.' As she took a coin from her purse the beggar put his head close to hers and whispered in a voice which was so unlike that of the whining beggar that Mary almost showed how startled she was: 'Your Majesty, I am here on the orders of my Lord of Northumberland. He bids you be of good cheer. He wishes me to tell you that he will be in touch with you at Tutbury. He has plans . . . and men of influence are ready to stand with him.'

Mary's spirits could always be raised by incidents such as this; unostentatiously she took a gold enamelled ring from her finger and pressed it into the man's hand, with the words: 'Take this to your master. Say that I look to him to keep his promise.'

Northumberland's messenger moved away from the litter and for the rest of that day Mary was scarcely aware of her discomforts, telling herself that because she had noble and influential friends in England, as well as Scotland, she could not long remain a prisoner.

But later when they arrived at Pontefract Castle, where they were to spend the night, even the memory of Northumberland's message could not prevent the depression which descended on Mary as she entered that place of tragedy; and as she looked at the tall walls flanked by the seven towers, at the deep moat, the barbican and drawbridge, she could not help shivering at the thought of Richard II.

'Oh, Seton,' she said, when they were lodged in the apartment which had been put at their disposal, 'I would not wish to dwell long in this place. I would rather face those bitter winds than live within these walls.'

'Your Majesty should be careful not to betray your revulsion; otherwise. . . .'

Mary finished for her: 'My good cousin and dear sister might seek to make me her prisoner here. Yes, you're right, Seton. I will take care.'

It was a restless night that was spent within those walls. Mary dreamed that she was a prisoner in the terrible dungeons to which, she had heard, there was no entrance except through a trap door above them, and from which escape was impossible.

Escape! Her mind was for ever occupied with the thought of it. And that night it was as though the ghost of Richard II, who had met his mysterious and bloody death within these walls, came to her and warned her to escape from this prison – and any prison in which it might please the English Queen to incarcerate her.

How relieved she was to set out on her journey again; but depression descended on her when, at Rotherham, Lady Livingstone's malady increased and all agreed that she was unfit to proceed; but as both Knollys and Scrope agreed that they dared not delay longer, Lady Livingstone was left behind while the rest of the party went on.

Mary's head was aching, her limbs stiff and painful; but she was able to travel, and that was enough.

Her thoughts were with her dear friend Lady Livingstone, as she travelled on and spent the following night at a mansion near Chesterfield. This was a pleasant experience following on the stay at Pontefract, for here was a comparatively simple country house, presided over by a kindly hostess, Lady Constance Foljambe, who was determined to make the Queen of Scots as comfortable as possible.

The next morning, when Mary said goodbye to Lady Foljambe, she thanked her warmly for her hospitality and said how she would have liked to linger as her guest.

'Our house is always at Your Majesty's disposal,' Lady Constance told her; and there was compassion in her expression. She knew what the Queen would find at Tutbury.

*   *   *

Mary saw the castle in the distance. Set on a ridge of red sandstone rock, it was impressive, and she could see that it would be almost impregnable, for surrounded by a broad and very deep ditch, it was a natural fortress. She was shivering, not only with the cold, as she drew nearer.

The party crossed the drawbridge; this was the only means of entering the castle and Mary noticed that the artillery in the gateway towers would make escape difficult.

That set her thoughts on Willie Douglas, and she wondered where he was now, and if he would ever be with her in Tutbury. If he were, she could be sure that he would begin to plan her escape.

The Earl and Countess of Shrewsbury were waiting to receive her. She noticed with relief that the Earl had a kindly face and that he was a little embarrassed to receive her as his prisoner. He was a man of some forty years. And there was his wife. Mary was not sure of the Countess whom she judged to be some ten years older than her husband, a woman who was undoubtedly handsome; but there was a severe aspect in her features which was faintly disturbing. As they came forward to make their bows and curtseys it occurred to Mary that the Countess was not quite the kind of woman to whom she would have looked for friendship.

'I trust Your Majesty will be comfortable at Tutbury,' said the Earl, almost apologetically.

'We shall *see* that Your Majesty is comfortable at Tutbury,' the Countess quickly affirmed.

'I thank you both. It has been a long and weary journey, and I am very tired.'

'Then allow me to conduct you to your apartments,' said the Countess. 'There you may rest for a while, and I could have food sent to your chamber.'

'That is kind and would please me,' answered Mary.

The Countess went with Mary up the cold stone staircase.

There were two rooms allotted to Mary, one above the other, and these were connected by a short spiral staircase.

In the lower chamber Mary looked about her with distaste. She noticed the cracked, damp walls and she could already feel how very cold the place was.

'Perhaps Your Majesty would prefer the upper room,' said the Countess briskly; and they mounted the staircase.

Mary saw the vaulted ceiling with the damp patches and the moisture trickling down the walls; she could feel the icy wind blowing through the ill-fitting casement and door. She went to one of the two small windows cut out of the thick walls and looked out over the bleak and snowy countryside.

Suddenly she wrinkled her nose distastefully. 'What is that I smell?' she asked.

Bess sniffed and looked blank. 'I smell nothing unusual, Your Majesty.'

'It is most unpleasant. Seton, what is it?'

Seton who was looking out of the other window, turned and said: 'It seems, Your Majesty, that the privies are situated immediately below this window.'

Mary looked sick, and indeed felt so.

'One soon becomes accustomed to the odour, Your Majesty,' Bess consoled her.

'I never shall.'

'But I assure Your Majesty that you will. It would be advisable on Saturdays, when the privies are emptied, to keep away from the windows. That is a day when the stench is really strong.'

Mary put her hands over her eyes in a gesture of horror, and Seton turned to the Countess. 'Her Majesty is very tired. I am going to help her to her bed. Perhaps you would be good enough to have her food sent up.'

Bess bowed her head. 'If that is Her Majesty's wish, so shall it be. We wish to make her comfortable here.'

Then she left the apartment. Mary did not look at her; she was studying her new prison, and there was desolation in her heart.

*　　*　　*

It was impossible to keep warm during that first long night.

'Oh Seton, Seton,' Mary moaned. 'This is the worst that has happened to us.'

Seton had covered her with all the clothes she could find, and lay beside her hoping to keep her warm. She had noticed Mary's fits of shivering on the journey, and the fact that they had not abated on their arrival worried her.

'The weather is so bitterly cold,' soothed Seton. 'It cannot last. Also I think that the Earl and his Countess were not prepared for your coming.'

'I think they were well prepared, Seton. Shall I tell you what else I think? Elizabeth no longer makes the pretence that I am her guest. I am nothing more than a state prisoner. You see, they did not have to make special preparations for my coming; I may be put in damp, cold and evil smelling rooms. It is of no importance because to them *I* am of no importance.'

'That is not so, Your Majesty. I am sure, if I speak to them and tell them that you must have some comfort, they will be ready to help.'

'The Earl looked kind,' Mary admitted.

'And the Countess too,' Seton added. 'She appears to be sharp tongued but I am sure she has a kind heart. I will see what can be arranged tomorrow. You will feel better then.'

'Oh yes, Seton, I shall feel better.'

'Do not forget the message from Northumberland.'

'You are right, Seton. I have some good friends in England. Norfolk will not forget me. Nor will Northumberland.'

216

'Tomorrow, everything will seem different,' said Seton. But it was a long time before they slept.

* * *

The next day Mary was not well enough to leave her bed. She had a fever and her limbs were stiff and painful.

Seton announced that the Queen would spend the day resting, and while she lay in her bed her women came into her chamber and set out some of the tapestry which they had brought with them from Bolton. These were inadequate to cover all the cracked walls, but they did add a little comfort; and Mary felt happier to have them, and also to see her women.

Knollys and Scrope came to say goodbye to her; and she was deeply sorry to see them go. She sent affectionate messages to Margaret Scrope through her husband; and she was sorry to see Knollys looking so sad. Poor Knollys! His was not an enviable fate. He had lost the wife he loved, and his Queen's favour at the same time. Yet he had been a kindly jailor. She would always remember that.

'I trust Your Majesty will be happy under the care of the Earl and Countess,' said Knollys.

'Thank you,' Mary replied. 'I hope you have explained to the Earl that I am allowed certain privileges – for instance, my own servants and my friends to visit me when they come to Tutbury.'

Knollys answered gravely: 'The Earl will make his own rules, I fear, Your Majesty. You know that those of myself and Lord Scrope were not considered to have been adequate.'

'It is bad enough to live in this cold and dreary prison, to endure that perpetual odour. I do not know how I shall go on living here if those small privileges are to be taken from me.'

'Speak to the Earl about these matters,' Knollys advised.

'Not to the Countess,' Scrope added.

'Certainly I should speak to the Earl. I suppose he is in charge here.'

Scrope and Knollys exchanged glances and Scrope said: 'I have heard that Bess of Hardwick is always in charge wherever she finds herself.'

Mary smiled. 'I believe that I shall be able to win their friendship,' she said confidently.

Then Scrope and Knollys took their leave. Mary heard their departure but she did not go to the window to watch them.

She felt too emotional, too weary, and she knew she had a fever.

*   *   *

During the first week at Tutbury, Mary scarcely left her bed. At the end of that time the fever had left her; she still suffered acutely from the draughts, but she fancied she had grown a little accustomed to the smell. She had seen little of the Earl and Countess; her servants brought her food, of which she ate very little, and looked after her as well as possible. She supposed the Earl and Countess were waiting for her to leave her bed, or perhaps for instructions from Elizabeth.

One day, when the wind was slightly less keen, several heavily laden packhorses lumbered into the courtyard. Eleanor Britton who had seen them arrive ran out to discover what they were.

A man who had leaped from his mule called to her: 'Hey, girl. Take me to the Earl of Shrewsbury without delay.'

'And who are you then?' asked Eleanor.

'Never you mind, girl. Do as you're told.'

'But I must say who you are,' Eleanor insisted.

'Then say we come on the Queen's business.'

Eleanor, suitably impressed, ran into the castle, eager to carry this important message to the Earl before anyone else could do so. Already some of the grooms had appeared and were asking questions of the newcomers.

Eleanor did not go to the Countess's apartments although she had to pass these to reach the Earl. It was so much easier to talk to the Earl than to the Countess, because he was a kind man and had a smile which seemed to say that he was aware of her even though she was only a lower servant. Whereas the Countess. . . . Well, one did not speak to the Countess if one could avoid doing so.

The Earl was in his apartments and he was alone, so that Eleanor was not made to pass on her information to one of the servants.

'My lord,' she stammered, 'there are men in the courtyard with laden horses. They came on the Queen's business.'

The Earl strode towards her and stood looking as her as though he had not quite heard what she had said.

'The Queen's business, my lord,' she repeated.

'They have come heavily laden?' he asked; and he smiled suddenly. 'Ah, if this is what I believe it to be I shall be very pleased.'

'Yes, my lord.'

He put out a hand as though he would grip her shoulder but he changed his mind and his hand fell to his side. 'Comforts for the Queen of Scotland,' he murmured. 'Poor lady, I fear she suffers much from the cold. I sent for them but I did not expect to receive them so soon.'

Eleanor smiled with him. It was pleasant to feel she shared a secret with him. How strange that he should have told her what the messengers had brought!

'Come,' he said, 'we will go down and see what they have brought, and then, my child, you can help carry the comforts –if this they be – to Her Majesty's apartments.'

He signed to her to go before him. It was an odd sensation going on ahead of the Earl, aware of him, close – very close behind. Eleanor hoped that none of her fellow servants would see her. They would think it so strange. And what if the Countess saw!

Eleanor quickened her pace, and very soon she was in the courtyard where now several servants had gathered. They were chattering, until they saw the Earl, and then fell silent. But they did not realize that he had come down with Eleanor.

*   *   *

The Earl was asking for admittance to the Queen's apartments.

'I bring Your Majesty good news,' he said. 'I have sent to Her Majesty, Queen Elizabeth, for articles which will give you some comfort. May I have them brought up?'

'This is good news, my lord,' Mary replied. 'Pray do not hesitate to bring them up.'

The Earl turned and signed to the servants to carry in the packages.

'They come from the royal wardrobe of the Tower of London, I believe, Your Majesty; and if they are what I asked for, I am sure they will please you.'

Mary called her women to her as the packages were carried in, and they helped unroll them.

There were several pieces of tapestry hangings lined with canvas.

Mary clapped her hands. 'I cannot wait to hang them,' she cried. 'They will keep out the draughts a little.'

Seton spread them out and saw that they were not only

useful but decorative, portraying as they did the history of Hercules. Next there were four feather beds with bolsters.

'They make me warmer even to look at them!' said Mary.

This was by no means all. There were more pieces of tapestry – one set depicting the story of the Passion; there were cushions, stools and Turkey carpets. There were even hooks and crochets with which to hang the tapestry.

Mary turned to the Earl, her face radiant. 'How can I thank you?' she asked.

He smiled. 'Your Majesty, it grieved me that you should come to Tutbury which as you know is too ill furnished to receive you. When I knew that you were to be here, I asked that these objects might be procured for you. I am only sorry that they have been so long in coming. The bad state of the roads is the cause.'

'I shall certainly sleep more comfortably now,' she told him, and my thanks are due to you.'

Everyone in the room was now looking towards the door which had been left open. The Countess stood there.

Mary said: 'My dear Countess, I am thanking your husband. I must thank you also, I know. These things are going to make a great deal of difference to my comfort.'

The Countess sailed into the room. Eleanor, watching her, thought: She did not know. He did it without asking her.

She dared not look at the Earl; she felt there would be fear in his face, and she did not want to see it. It was brave of him, she thought, to do it without telling her. Anyone must be brave who stands against *her*.

'I am delighted that Your Majesty is pleased,' said the Countess, her sharp eyes taking in the tapestry, the beds, the rugs and all the furniture.

'Such a difference!' sighed Mary. 'I really do not think I could have endured the cold without something to keep out the draughts.'

'I trust the servants are doing all you require of them?'

'Yes, thank you.'

'Then the Earl and I will beg your leave to retire.'

'But of course.'

The Countess looked at the Earl, and her eyes were expressionless.

She curtseyed and the Earl made his bow.

As they went out together Eleanor wanted to whisper: You

should not be afraid of her. You are the Earl. You should tell her so.

When they reached her apartments Bess turned to her husband; now she was smiling because she prided herself on always being in complete control of her feelings.

'So you sent to the Queen for those fripperies?' she asked.

'I thought they were necessary for our guest's comfort.'

'I dare swear that if Her Majesty had thought them necessary she would have sent them without being asked.'

'She does not know how comfortless Tutbury can be.'

There was a brief silence while Shrewsbury thought of his first wife, Gertrude, eldest daughter of the Earl of Rutland. What a gentle person she had been! He was beginning to remember her with increasing regret.

'I hope she does not think you are going the way of Knollys and Scrope.'

'Because I ask for a carpet, a bed and some hangings to keep out the draughts?'

Bess gave a sudden harsh laugh. 'Our Queen knows Mary's reputation,' she said. 'It is rumoured that she bewitches all men who set eyes on her. Is this the beginning of bewitchment?'

'Nonsense,' retorted the Earl. 'The poor woman is ill. Her Majesty would not be very pleased with us if it were said she died through neglect.'

Bess nodded her head slowly. 'So, without consulting me, you sent for comforts for her.' Again she gave that hard laugh. She slipped her arm through his and she was smiling. 'George,' she went on, 'I think, in view of the disgrace of Knollys and Scrope, we should be careful. Of course if she is in danger of dying of neglect, *I* shall see that she does not do so. Perhaps it would be better if such matters were left to me. No one could accuse me of being bewitched by the charm of the Queen of Scots, I fancy!'

Shrewsbury was beginning to hate that cold laughter of hers. What she was saying was: Next time leave it to me to make arrangements. I am the one who makes decisions here.

He was pleased that he had managed to procure the comforts before she had had a chance to interfere. Then, as he looked into her domineering, handsome face, he thought of Eleanor Britton; which seemed unaccountable. It's the contrast he told himself. One so arrogant; the other one so meek.

221

But of course Eleanor Britton would be meek. Was she not a servant?

* * *

Two pleasant occurrences quickly followed the arrival of the comforts from the Tower of London.

Lady Livingstone, who had been so ill on the journey, had recovered and came on to Tutbury. Mary who had thought it possible that she might never see this dear friend again was overcome with joy.

Lady Livingstone however was shocked by the Queen's appearance.

'I have recovered more quickly than Your Majesty did!' she said aghast.

'Ah,' laughed Mary. 'But you have not been at Tutbury.' She was serious suddenly. 'You should not stay here. It is a foul place. The stench at times is unbearable. Why do you not return to Scotland? I still have friends there, and you and your husband could return to your estates and live in comfort.'

'And leave you!'

'My dearest friend, I do not know how long I shall be here. Sometimes I think it will be for years.'

'Then if we must remain prisoners for years, so be it.'

Mary embraced her friend. 'It seems meet and proper,' she said, 'that I should have a Livingstone with me. In my youth it was your sister-in-law, Mary. She would be with me still, as Seton is, if she had not married. But if at any time this becomes too much for you, you must not hesitate to return to Scotland.'

'One day we shall go together,' was the answer.

* * *

It was shortly afterwards when a young man was admitted to her apartments. In the first seconds she did not recognize him. Then she cried out in great joy: 'Willie!'

Willie Douglas bowed and, as the light fell on his face, she saw how thin he was.

'Oh Willie, Willie!' She took him into her arms and held him tightly against her. 'This is such joy to me.'

'And to me, Your Majesty.'

'You have suffered since I last saw you, Willie.'

'Oh ay.'

Releasing him she laid her hands on his shoulders and looked searchingly into his face.

'But you are back now, and I thank God.' She drew him to one of the stools which had been sent from the Tower of London and bade him sit.

There he told her that he had travelled jauntily to London, had received his passport and had been ready to make his way to the coast of France. But as he walked through an alley in the City of London, where he had his temporary lodging, he had been set upon.

'They came upon me from behind, Your Majesty, and I never saw their faces. There I was walking along that alley where the houses seemed to meet at the top, when I was attacked. I woke up in a dark cellar, trussed up and with my head bleeding. I'd lost all my papers. I knew I'd been robbed then. I lay there for what seemed days and nights, but I had no means of telling. But at last they came for me . . . rough men I'd never seen before. They put me in chains and set me on a mule, and I knew we were coming north. I thought I was being brought back to you, but I soon learned that was a mistake. I was taken into a place like a castle and put in a cell there. There were bars at the window, and now and then a crust of bread and pitcher of water were thrust in at me. Other than that the only companions I had were the rats and beetles.'

'My poor Willie! I had evil dreams of you. I knew something fearful had befallen you. That was why I asked the French King to command his ambassador to discover what had become of you. You must have spent many weeks in that prison.' She thought: But for my French friends it might have been for the rest of your life, and that, for Willie in those conditions would not have meant more than a year or so.

'I used to lie there thinking of how I could get out,' went on Willie. 'There didn't seem any way, but I went on trying to figure something out. Then it got so that I couldn't walk very well and I could only think of when I was going to get my next portion of bread and water.'

'I fear you have suffered much for my sake, Willie.'

He gave her a return of the old grin. 'Oh ay,' he murmured.

But she knew that he would never be the same jaunty urchin he had been before he set out for London. Willie had grown up considerably since they had last met.

*　　*　　*

Lord Herries arrived at Tutbury from London with those who had been acting as her Commissioners at the Conference. They were very grave, realizing fully how Mary's position had deteriorated since the Conference.

At the little council meeting held in those evil smelling apartments, Herries said: 'We cannot go on in this way. We should try to bring Your Majesty out of England. I do not think that any good purpose can be served by your remaining here.'

'But how can I leave?' Mary wanted to know.

'Only by a demand from your Scottish nobles that you should do so. I do not think Elizabeth would risk war. Moray is her ally; we must depose him and his party and, once that is done, there can no longer be an excuse for keeping you here.'

'What do you propose?'

'That I return to Scotland with my brother-in-law Cockburn.'

'Then I shall lose two of my most faithful friends.'

'Not lose them, Your Majesty. But merely allow them to be of greater service to your cause. Livingstone and Boyd will be here to advise you; and the Bishop of Ross can act as your envoy at the Court of Elizabeth. I am of the opinion that we could not serve you better.'

'I am sure you are right,' she told him. 'Oh, my dear good friend, one thing I ask you, help to bring me out of this noisome place, for I believe that I shall not stay here long. I must either leave it soon on my two feet or be carried out in my coffin.'

Herries begged her not to despair, but he himself was very anxious, for he could see how the place was affecting her; and she had not recovered yet from the long journey through the ice-bound country from Bolton.

Herries and Cockburn left within a few days. Mary watched them from her window until they were out of sight. Herries, who had been her trusted friend; and as for Cockburn, his mansion and his village of Skirling had been completely destroyed by Moray in vengeance on one who was the very good friend of the Queen of Scots.

* * *

Mary would sit at her tapestry with her women; occasionally she would sing or play the lute. But each day she was more easily fatigued, and her friends watched her with misgivings. The Earl spoke to the Countess. 'I am anxious,' he said. 'Her health does not improve and she might well fall into a mortal sickness.'

'Nonsense,' retorted Bess. 'She has but to adjust herself. What does she do all day but amuse herself! Look at me. Think of what I do. I am years older than she is.'

'I fear the rigours of Tutbury ill suit her.'

'We live at Tutbury, do we not? I'll admit it is not the most sweet of our houses – but there is nothing to harm in a stink. If she had more to do she would be well enough.'

There was a knock at the door and, when Bess commanded whoever was there to enter, Eleanor came in.

She looked fearfully at the Countess but she was very much aware of the Earl.

'Well, girl?' said Bess sharply.

'My lady, there is a messenger below. He is asking for the Earl.'

'I will see him without delay,' said Bess. 'Send him to me.'

Eleanor curtseyed and retired, returning shortly with the messenger.

Bess imperiously held out her hand for the documents he had brought.

'Take this man to the kitchens and see that he is refreshed,' she commanded Eleanor who, curtseying once more, caught the eyes of the Earl on herself and flushed deeply.

Bess was too eagerly examining the documents to notice the demeanour of her serving-maid.

'Orders from the Queen,' she said, and the Earl came to stand beside her and look over her shoulder.

'Ah!' went on Bess. 'So her friends are suspected of planning her escape. You see what you have done by showing your desire to pamper her. You have aroused our Queen's suspicions. Depend upon it, George Talbot, we have to tread very warily if we are not to find ourselves in disgrace along with Scrope and Knollys.'

'What does Her Majesty require?'

'That Boyd and the Bishop are not to be allowed to remain with her or come to see her. They are to be banished at once to Burton-on-Trent.'

The Earl sighed. Poor Queen Mary! he was thinking. Here was another blow.

*　　*　　*

The Earl met Eleanor Britton on the staircase near the Queen's apartments.

She flushed and curtseyed.

'Do you serve the Queen of Scots then?' he asked.

'I help her servants, my lord.' She added quickly: 'It is the order of the Countess that I should do so.'

He nodded. 'Poor lady, I fear for her health.'

'She is not happy at Tutbury Castle, my lord.'

'She has told you so?'

'We have all heard that it is so, my lord.'

There was the briefest of silences, and each felt drawn to the other through their sympathy for the Queen of Scots. This young girl, thought George Talbot, is aware of the Queen's charm as Bess never could be. But then, of course, Bess never saw people or circumstances through any but her own eyes; it was an impossibility for her to put herself in any other's place.

'I wish she could be moved to a healthier place,' he said, as though speaking to himself.

'Yes, my lord.' The girl was looking at him with an odd expression in her eyes. Was she telling him that he was the lord of Tutbury, the first guardian of the Queen? She made him feel strong, more powerful than he had felt for a long time . . . surely since his courtship of Bess of Hardwick.

He passed on, but he could not dismiss the maid from his thoughts. She was so young, scarcely more than a child, without doubt a virgin. She would not remain so long, perhaps. Even Bess could not prevent the men servants and the maid-servants frolicking together.

He felt angry that a young girl should be exposed to such contamination.

Strange, this preoccupation with a serving girl – and a Queen. It was having an odd effect on him. He went straight to his private apartments and there wrote a letter to Elizabeth of England, in which he told her that he feared for the life of Mary Queen of Scots if she remained at Tutbury. Would Her Majesty agree to a removal to his nearby seat of Wingfield Manor where he felt sure the health of the Queen of Scots would be improved.

This he dispatched, telling Bess nothing of what he had done.

*   *   *

Bess stormed into her husband's apartments, and with an angry wave of her hand dismissed his servants.

When they were alone she held up a letter and cried: 'Her Majesty writes that, in answer to your letter, she is agreeable that the Queen should be removed to Wingfield Manor until further notice.'

'Ah, I am glad. It is what Queen Mary needs.'

'So you wrote to Elizabeth?'

Although he had rehearsed this scene many times, knowing it was inevitable, now that the moment had come to face Bess, he found it difficult to do so.

He stammered: 'I thought she would be ill pleased if the Queen were to die of her malady soon after coming under our care.'

'Die!' snorted Bess. 'She has many years left to her.'

But she was not thinking of the Queen of Scots and her dilemma; what astonished her was to be confronted by such a disobedient husband.

She went on: 'Do you think it was wise to suggest this move?'

'It was wise and humane,' answered the Earl firmly.

'The Queen will have a poor opinion of us if we continually present her with complaints.'

'The Queen knows us both well. She has long since formed her opinions of us.'

'She chose us for this task, and it is one well within our compass, if we are wise and do not allow ourselves to be duped by the wiles of one who, I understand, has but to give a man a smile to make him obey her.'

'She has not been very successful in making men obey her, poor lady.'

'Poor lady! Not so poor! She is waited on hand and foot. I am surprised, George, that you should have taken this step without consulting me.'

He shrugged his shoulders. 'Well,' he said mildly, 'it is done. What we have to do now is prepare to leave for Wingfield Manor.'

Bess was watching him covertly. She had thought he would always be obedient to her wishes as her three earlier husbands had been. It was disconcerting to find him asserting his independence.

What could it mean?

Was he a little enamoured of the Queen of Scots? She must be watchful. Bess was a woman who demanded a husband's affection and devotion as well as obedience. She would not

227

allow it to be said that Shrewsbury ceased to be a devoted husband when the Queen of Scots came under his roof.

That woman might bewitch other men but, Bess was determined, never George Talbot, Earl of Shrewsbury.

CHAPTER SEVEN

WINGFIELD

MARY WAS DELIGHTED to arrive at Wingfield Manor. She could not feel grateful enough to Shrewsbury for arranging the removal for, in comparison with Tutbury, Wingfield was charming. Situated as it was on a steep hill it commanded a beautiful view of the valley of Ashover and seemed to be shut in by hills.

The manor house had been built some hundred years before by Ralph, Lord Cromwell and, because he had been Treasurer of England, bags and purses had been carved in the stone over the gateway which led to the quadrangle. Having been built at that period when the comfort of castles was being questioned, and desirability of building palaces realized, this was an excellent example of what a hundred years before had been considered a new type of architecture.

The house was built round two square courts and as soon as Mary stepped into the spacious hall with its Gothic windows, one of a very unusual octagonal shape, her natural optimism took possession of her. Tutbury was left behind and she was telling herself that nothing so unfortunate as her stay in that noisome place would ever happen to her again. She should rejoice that that evil was behind her.

Countess Bess took her to the rooms which had been allotted to her.

'They are on the west side of the north court, Your Majesty,' she said, 'and this is generally judged to be the most beautiful part of the building.'

Mary stood for a while looking out over the hills.

'It is undoubtedly beautiful,' she said. 'A change from the marshlands of Tutbury. And how pleasant to have lost that appalling odour.'

The Countess gave her a quick, sudden laugh. 'I am sure

Your Majesty will be comfortable at Wingfield. Allow me to show you these stairs. They lead up to the Tower which will be part of your quarters.'

Mary mounted the spiral staircase to the top of the Tower, and from there she had a wider view of the countryside than that from the windows of her bedchamber.

She stood looking into the far distance.

One day, she thought, my friends will come riding here to rescue me.

She turned away and smiled at the Countess who had followed her to the Tower.

Yes, she could certainly rejoice that she had come to Wingfield Manor.

*　　*　　*

Even now that she was in more salubrious surroundings Mary needed time to recover from the harm which had been done to her during that journey through the snow from Bolton to Tutbury and her stay in the damp apartments of the latter. She was never free from twinges of pain in her limbs and sometimes when she attempted to rise from her bed she found it impossible to do so without assistance.

'Ah, Seton,' she would often say, 'I left my youth behind me in Tutbury.'

She spent those first weeks in Wingfield writing letters and recuperating, promising herself that when the spring came, and she could go hunting or hawking in this beautiful countryside, she would feel young again.

The Countess seemed to soften at Wingfield and was solicitous of Mary's comfort; she implied that she was in charge of the household and any request Mary wished to make should be made, not to the Earl, but to herself; and Mary quickly realized that as long as she accepted the Countess's supremacy, Bess was ready to be her friend. Seton had said that she would be happier with the Countess as a friend rather than an enemy, with which statement Mary had agreed.

Spring was now on the way and, although its coming must remind Mary that she had been almost a year in England, she was pleased to see it.

One evening after supper Mary complained of sudden pains and as she rose from the table began to shiver. Her women, startled by her pallor, crowded about her, and she told them that she felt alarmingly sick and dizzy.

Seton, taking charge, hastily conducted her to her bed-chamber and as Mary lay writhing on her bed a horrible suspicion came to Seton that her mistress had been poisoned.

She turned to Jane Kennedy and said: 'Go at once to the Earl and Countess and tell them that I fear the Queen is grievously ill.'

Jane hurried to the Earl's apartments and, finding him alone there, told him of Seton's fears. The Earl went at once to Mary's bedchamber and when he saw her he was deeply disturbed.

'Her Majesty's apothecary is preparing a remedy for her,' said Seton. 'But I think she may need greater skill than his.'

At that moment the Countess came into the apartment.

'What is wrong?' she demanded. Then she saw the Queen. 'I shall send at once for Dr Caldwell,' she said. 'I do not like what I see.'

For once Seton was glad of the Countess's methods when, in a very short time, the doctor for whom she had sent arrived in the Queen's chamber.

He spent the night at her bedside and in the morning, much to the surprise of all those who had seen how ill she was and the nature of her illness, Mary still lived.

*   *   *

Bess talked in private with her husband.

'I do not like the look of this,' she said.

'Nor I.'

'I believe someone tried to poison her.'

The Earl nodded. Bess looked at him in silence for a few moments, then she said: 'Do you think *she* has commanded this to be done?'

'Never!' The Earl was emphatic. 'If the Queen of Scots were to die of poison, the first person to be suspected would be Elizabeth. She would not want that. If there are men and women in this country who would wish to set a Stuart on the English throne, there is nothing more likely to advance their cause than such a murder. The Queen of Scots would become a martyr while the Queen of England would be reckoned a monster. I am sure this has nothing to do with Elizabeth.'

'Then it is clearly one of Moray's people.'

'And how can we say who? Scotsmen come and go. They declare themselves to be friends of Queen Mary, but depend upon it, there are spies among them. If she were to die. . . .'

230

His wife interrupted: 'We should no longer enjoy Elizabeth's favour. She would blame us for allowing poisoners to have access to her.'

'But how can we prevent that?'

'By being more watchful of course, and making sure that this does not happen again. I am going to send for Dr Francis who is as good a physician as Caldwell. The two of them together will pull her through.'

The Earl bowed his head, and Bess put up one of her strong white hands to ruffle his hair. She could be affectionate at times; she liked to have a man about the house as long as he obeyed her. And George was being sensible over this matter.

He took her hand and kissed it. 'I am glad that you are sending for Dr Francis.'

She laughed almost roguishly. 'You would not like this to be the end of our romantic captive?' she asked.

'In point of fact,' he said, 'I was thinking I should not like this to be the end of the Shrewsburys.'

Bess laughed. 'Leave this to me. I shall see that she does not die.'

The Earl was certain that Bess would succeed, and was glad at that moment that he had such a clever, forceful and capable wife.

*　　*　　*

When Mary recovered within the next few days, after, as everyone admitted, coming near to death, many were convinced that there had been an attempt to poison her. This seemed certain when news came to Wingfield that in Scotland the Regent Moray was taking military action against all her friends, robbing them of their lands and riches and levying exorbitant taxes on those whom he allowed to keep some of their possessions.

So rigorous had been the measures taken, and so great was his power now throughout Scotland, that Argyle had thought it wise to accept his authority and had signed a treaty acknowledging this. When Huntley and Herries did likewise it seemed that Mary's cause was lost; and the fact that these events were taking place in Scotland while Mary had had her mysterious sickness at Wingfield, confirmed the suspicion of many that this had been an attempt by Moray's agents to poison her.

Willie Douglas was insensed at what had happened and, coming unannounced into the Queen's apartments one day, had implored her to allow him to keep a closer watch on all who came near her.

'You have my permission, Willie,' said the Queen. 'Indeed, I shall only feel safe if you do so.'

So Willie was often to be seen at the door of her chamber, and he kept his eye on all who came into her presence and who conferred with each other in the castle. Previously he had been concerned with finding a method of bringing the Queen out of captivity; now he had an additional task. He had to save her from those who planned to murder her.

It was startling and significant when news came from London that Mary's death had been reported there.

'It would seem,' said Seton to Willie, 'that some were so eager to announce it that they did not wait for it to take place.'

'If I can find the man that harms her,' Willie growled, 'I'll cut his head off with my sword, I will, and I'll march round the castle with the bauble dripping on my sword.'

'We will watch over her together, Willie,' said Seton.

'We'll never leave her while she needs us,' answered Willie.

'I have sworn an oath that I never will,' Seton said solemnly.

And it was as though they had made a pact together.

*   *   *

Mary was better now and able to walk in the grounds; the May sunshine was warming and she quickly showed signs of regaining her health.

But she soon found herself in a predicament which caused her alarm and was desperately seeking a way out of it.

As she walked with Seton on one side and Jane Kennedy on the other she spoke to them of her troubles.

'I am becoming very short of money, and the doctors whom Shrewsbury summoned are asking for payment. The fact is, I have no money with which to meet their demands, and I do not know how I can raise it.'

Seton began taking stock of their valuables, but most of the Queen's possessions were now in Moray's hands.

'Even if we sold everything we have there would not be enough,' said Mary. 'And I wonder how I am going to continue to live. I owe you all so much.'

Jane and Seton declared that she owed them nothing. But Mary sighed and said there was nothing she could do but write to Lesley, Bishop of Ross, in London and tell him of her embarrassment.

'Do this, Your Majesty,' advised Seton, 'and I will summon Borthwick to convey your letter to London with all speed. The sooner Lesley begins to deal with it, the easier you will sleep.'

So they retired to Mary's apartments where she wrote her letter, and Borthwick left with it at once for London.

He returned before they expected him; and to their surprise and pleasure he brought money with him.

There was two hundred pounds which would relieve her of her immediate anxieties, and more would be following.

Mary was astonished by this ready response. Then she read the letter which Lesley had written and which, Borthwick said, was to be delivered into her hands alone. Her benefactor was one from whom it was most meet and fitting for her to receive assistance: the Duke of Norfolk to whom she was almost – though in secret – betrothed.

Norfolk was true to his word. Within the next few weeks more money arrived and very shortly Mary had received nine hundred and sixty-six pounds from the man who hoped to become her husband.

There was however a letter from Lesley who, having heard of Norfolk's generosity, was a little uneasy. He believed that by accepting the money, Mary was entering into an intrigue from which she might find it difficult – supposing she wished – to extricate herself. He advised her to ask for money from France and to look upon that which Norfolk had sent her as a loan.

Mary, completely generous, accepted as readily as she would have given. But she did trust Lesley's judgement. She therefore made an endeavour to obtain money from France and sent her secretary across the Channel with that purpose. His efforts failed, but meanwhile rumours of her pecuniary difficulties became known in certain quarters, and those who were carefully watching the political state of affairs in England decided that this matter might be turned to advantage.

*   *   *

Lesley received a call from the Spanish ambassador.

'I have heard,' said the ambassador, 'that the Queen of Scots needs money, and I have had instructions from His Most Catholic Majesty that I am to do all in my power to assist the Queen.'

233

Lesley was exultant. It seemed to him that if Mary must accept money it were better to do so from a friendly power than from a private individual. Mary's secretary, Raulet, had been sent to France to try to raise a loan; and here was one being offered by Spain.

'I know His Most Catholic Majesty to be the good friend of the Queen of Scots,' murmured the Bishop.

'He desires to help her in her need,' went on the ambassador, 'and I will give you a bill of exchange which you may draw on the banker, Roberto Ridolfi.'

'I tender you my most grateful thanks and I know that the Queen will do the same.'

'Then come to my lodging in an hour's time and you shall have it.'

Lesley said that he would do so, and when they had parted the Spanish ambassador went to the Italian banker and talked with him for a while. He knew that Ridolfi was a Papal spy; and that both the Pope and the King of Spain were determined to prevent at all costs the marriage of Catholic Mary with Protestant Norfolk. 'If she accepts our money,' said the banker, 'she will have taken the first step. The Northern Catholics assure me they are ready to revolt under Northumberland. We will set the Queen of Scots at their head. And then . . . with luck we shall drive the bastard Elizabeth from the throne.'

'She will accept the money. She needs it; and she realizes that it is not meet for her to take it from Norfolk. It will be for ten thousand Italian crowns . . . a sturdy sum, which will show her that we are her friends. Doubtless she feels the need of friends at this moment. And I'll swear she has no notion of how ready Northumberland is to march on the Protestants of England.'

The two men conferred further together, and when Lesley arrived he was greeted warmly by the banker, who hinted that he was aware of Spain's desire to help the Queen. He was certain too that the Pope deplored her present plight.

Lesley left, with the money which seemed like a fortune to him; and, what seemed almost as good, the knowledge that Mary had powerful friends.

*　　*　　*

Lesley, Bishop of Ross, came to Wingfield to talk with the Queen.

234

Mary received him eagerly and was pleased to see how optimistic he was, for Lesley was never a man to disguise the true state of affairs.

'Your Majesty,' he said, 'I come in person because there are some matters it is better not to trust to letters. I have great hopes that your captivity will soon be over.'

'My dear Bishop,' cried the Queen, 'you could not bring me better news.'

'Your marriage with Norfolk will bring you freedom, and the project is now receiving the support of men of standing.'

'Yes?'

'Leicester himself.'

'Leicester! Then this means that Elizabeth herself gives her consent.'

Lesley was thoughtful for a moment. 'I am not sure that we have come as far as that. In her bad treatment of you, Elizabeth has been advised to act as she did by Cecil, who is determined to keep a Protestant ruler in Scotland. Cecil's influence on the Queen does not please her ambitious ministers. But for Cecil, Leicester might have been Elizabeth's husband. I believe that at the time of the Amy Robsart affair he came near to it. Leicester never forgave Cecil, and he sees now a chance of flouting his authority by giving his support to the marriage with Norfolk.'

'They say the Queen is still enamoured of Leicester.'

'I believe it to be true. I have seen them together, and although she encourages others to admire her, there is a shade of difference in her manner when she is near him. If Leicester approves of the match with Norfolk, I am of the opinion that he will persuade Elizabeth to do so. I have letters here from Leicester and certain other noblemen in which they praise Norfolk and tell you that they will give their support to a marriage between you.'

'Give me the letters,' said Mary; and when Lesley did so she opened them with hands which shook with excitement. What Lesley had said was true. There was the letter, written in Leicester's own hand, commending the Duke of Norfolk, persuading her to marry him, and assuring her that he had the nobility behind him when he told her that, should the Queen of England die without heirs, they would support her as the rightful heir to the throne. He went on to say that he was sure the Queen of England could be persuaded to see the wisdom and justice of this.

When Mary had finished reading, she looked at Lesley with sparkling eyes. She felt young again; full of hope. 'I shall soon be free of my prison,' she murmured.

Then she thought of another prisoner. Bothwell. What hope had he of ever being released! The French would insist on his remaining shut away; they would never allow one who had played such a devastating role in her life to go free; and if he were free, where would he go? To Scotland, where certain death awaited him at Moray's hands? To England? Elizabeth would never tolerate him there. What were his thoughts at this time? How much had he changed?

These months of imprisonment had for her been at times almost intolerable. But what of him? She at least had her friends, and a certain consideration must be shown a Queen even by her enemies. But what did Bothwell suffer, and how would one so bold and vital endure such suffering?

She had ceased to yearn for him as she had a year ago. She knew that he had disappeared completely from her life and she would never see him again. Indeed, if they did meet they would not be the same people because the Mary, who had lost her crown for love of him, had gone for ever. A woman grown sober by captivity and suffering had taken the place of that headstrong girl. Bothwell must have changed too. What was that blustering, fascinating, irresistible adventurer now?

She was aware of Lesley, waiting for her to speak. 'Bothwell?' she murmured.

'We do not anticipate any difficulty in having that marriage annulled,' said Lesley.

*   *   *

The Earl of Shrewsbury was anxious. It was all very well for Bess to say that she would manage their affairs, but he was the one who would be blamed if they failed in their duty. The guarding of such an important political prisoner was a constant anxiety, and he had never been a man who could stand up against perpetual worry. His head ached continually; he found that when he rose from his bed in the morning he was giddy. It was no use complaining to Bess of these matters, or even mentioning them. 'All you need is a little fresh air,' she would say, 'and you'll be better tomorrow!'

Bess was alert however. She knew as well as he did that messengers from the North and South were finding their way to the Queen's apartment. Intrigue was rife and, if it ever was brought into the light of day, the Shrewsburys must be on the right side.

Which *was* the right side? The Queen of England was strong; but if it were true that men such as Leicester, Arundel and Pembroke were eager to promote the marriage of Norfolk and Mary without having first obtained Elizabeth's consent, who could be sure what would happen next?

Shrewsbury was a man who wished to remain poised cautiously between two factions, so that he might leap onto the winning side at an opportune moment.

He had already reported to Elizabeth that a young man named Cavendish – who was connected with Bess through her second husband, Sir William Cavendish – was bringing letters to Mary from Norfolk. Elizabeth's reply had been that she was aware of this and that she wished Cavendish to be allowed to carry messages to the Queen. This sounded as though Cavendish were a spy for Elizabeth while feigning to work for Norfolk. Who could know who was a friend, who was an enemy, in such a morass of deceit?

It was small wonder that he found the task too much for him and sighed for the old days of comparative peace before he had been singled out to guard the Queen of Scots.

He went to his bedchamber and there, risking discovery by Bess, he lay on his bed; but when he did so the room seemed to rock as though he were on board ship.

He lay for some time and gradually the giddiness left him. I never felt thus before, he thought. Is this an illness brought on by worry?

There was a knock on the door, so quiet that he was not sure whether he had imagined it. He ignored it, and then he saw that the door was slowly opening, and the serving girl, Eleanor Britton, was standing in the doorway watching him.

'What is it?' asked the Earl.

'I come to ask if there is aught you want,' she answered.

'Why? I did not send for you.'

'But I saw how sick your lordship looked and, begging your pardon, I came to see if there was aught you needed.'

'Come in and shut the door.'

She came slowly to his bedside and the light from the Gothic window shone on her round young face. She was comely; he noticed her neat yet plump figure beneath her serving maid's gown; but it was the expression on her face which held his attention. She looked enraptured, almost angelic, he thought.

What a strange girl she was! No wonder he had singled her out for his attention.

'My lord is well?' she asked; and that mobile face was suddenly filled with sorrow.

'I am well enough,' he answered.

'Is there aught I could do, my lord?'

'Nay.'

They looked at each other in silence for a few seconds, then he held out his hand.

'You are a comely girl,' he told her. 'It pleases me to see you in my house.'

She lowered her eyes and dropped a curtsey – he was not sure why.

He wondered what would happen if Bess came in and saw the serving girl standing by his bed. The girl would be dismissed – and he . . . he would never hear the end of the matter. She could taunt him with what she called his bewitchment by the Queen of Scots. She did it half jokingly, although there was a certain malice in her words. She was displeased but not outraged that he should find Mary attractive; but what would she say if she knew that he, one of the noblest Earls in England, was a little fascinated by one of her humblest serving girls?

He was feeling a little lightheaded, and in this unusual state he did not care.

'Come nearer,' he said.

She came, her lips slightly parted showing good teeth; he knew then that he had only to order and she would obey.

He took her hand and drawing her to him kissed it, not with passion, but with gentleness while a soft flush spread from her neck to the roots of her hair.

She knelt beside the bed and pressed her lips against the hand which held hers.

He was aware of a rising passion such as he had never known before; he wanted to seize her roughly, to embrace her, but he knew that if he gave way to such feeling he would be too giddy to stand.

He thought then: She is so young and I shall not always be sick.

There was a sudden clatter of horses' hoofs below. They were both startled, and the girl rose to her feet.

'You must go and see who has arrived,' he told her. 'Come back and tell me.'

238

She left him and he lay still listening to the clamour below.

*　　*　　*

It was not Eleanor who came back to his apartment but Bess.

She came in without knocking and was startled to see him lying on the bed. He thought: She might have come thus when I was talking to Eleanor. And the thought made his heart beat fast.

'So you are lying down!'

'I felt unwell.'

'You look a little pale. You do not take enough fresh air. I came to tell you that Leonard Dacre is here.'

The Earl raised himself on his elbow. 'Dacre!'

Bess nodded. 'I think we should go down to greet him. In view of his connexion with Norfolk we cannot know what he may be up to.'

The Earl passed a weary hand across his brow. 'Not more trouble, I hope.'

Bess gave her short laugh. 'Trouble! There will always be trouble while we have your romantic Queen under our roof. Did you not know that?'

'I am learning it.'

She gave him a sharp look. 'And I'll warrant you think such a beauty is worth the trouble.'

'I'd gladly give the task back to Scrope and Knollys,' he retorted, 'for all her beauty.'

She appeared almost arch, but her gaze was searching. 'I shall not tell her what you say,' she replied. 'It would appear ungallant.'

He thought then that she would be a jealous woman if she discovered infidelity in her husband; and he wondered what form her jealousy would take.

Rising from his bed he tried to fight off his giddiness, and as he followed his countess down to the hall he felt it receding. By the time he was ready to greet Dacre it had left him.

Leonard Dacre would have been a handsome man but for the fact that one of his shoulders was higher than the other. He was very conscious of this as he was that he was the second son of Lord Dacre of Gilsland, and therefore not his heir. His elder brother had died leaving a son George, and George's mother, Lady Dacre, had become the wife of Thomas, Duke of Norfolk. On her death Norfolk had, in

239

Leonard Dacre's opinion, concerned himself over much with the affairs of the Dacre family and, as there was a great deal of money involved, had arranged marriages between his three step-daughters and his sons. As these girls were co-heiresses with their young brother George, Norfolk thus made sure that a large part of the Dacre wealth did not pass out of the Howard family.

This was a source of great annoyance to Leonard Dacre and he did not feel too kindly towards Norfolk in consequence.

Now he bowed low over Bess's hand and expressed his hope that he found her in good health.

'My health is excellent,' answered Bess.

'And my lord Earl?'

'Oh, he does not take enough exercise. It is my continual complaint.'

'I have, it is true, been less well of late,' explained the Earl.

'He did not like Tutbury. He will be happier now that we are here at Wingfield Manor.'

'And you look less happy than when we last met,' said the Earl.

'I have had bad news,' Dacre replied. 'My young nephew has died. I received the news this day.'

'Young George!' cried Bess. 'But he can't be more than seven! We are truly sorry. My poor Leonard! You must come to my private chamber and I will have wine brought. This is indeed sad news.'

The Earl slipped his arm through that of Dacre, and the Countess summoned a servant and gave orders.

'How did it happen?'

'While he was practising vaulting at Thetford. A bad fall on his head. He died soon afterwards.'

'What tragedy! First the father . . . then the son. . . . So you are now the heir.'

'It is of this matter that I come to talk to you and the Countess.'

When they were all seated in the Countess's private chamber, Dacre explained why he was angry.

'The barony is one which descends to the female members of the family,' he said. 'So that not only do his young sisters inherit the Dacre fortune, but the title also.'

'Norfolk was wise,' commented the Countess, 'in betrothing his sons to the three Dacre girls.'

'Very wise, very sly,' added Leonard. 'I intend to contest the case.'

Bess nodded. She doubted whether he would stand much chance of winning.

They talked for some time of family affairs and eventually Bess said: 'I must present you to the Queen of Scots. She would take it ill if she knew you had been here and not called to pay your respects.'

'I should be pleased to speak with Her Majesty.'

Thus it was that Mary made the acquaintance of Leonard Dacre.

* * *

The young man, Cavendish, had brought Mary a letter from the Duke of Norfolk.

Mary seized on it delightedly. The intrigue with which she seemed to be surrounded since coming to Wingfield Manor had brought new liveliness and she welcomed it.

Taking the letter to her bedchamber, Mary sat at the window and opened it.

The Duke wrote that he was deeply disturbed because he had heard rumours that the Papal spies in London, together with the Spanish ambassador, were planning to marry her to Don Jon of Austria. He needed reassurance. He must have it by return. He was sending her a diamond which was intended to pledge his troth to her and he was asking that a contract be drawn up between them without delay.

Why not? thought Mary. The sooner marriage with Norfolk became a fact, the sooner she would be free of her prison. She had come to see marriage with him as the only way out for her. Moreover she wanted marriage; she was weary of living without a man. She assured herself that she had forgotten Bothwell and that he no longer meant anything to her.

She took up a miniature of herself and a tablet of gold. She would write, sending these to Norfolk as her pledge, and she would ask Lesley to draw up the contract of marriage without delay.

She answered Norfolk's letter in most affectionate terms and, enclosing the letter with the tablet and miniature, dispatched Cavendish back to the Duke.

Shortly afterwards the contract was drawn up between Mary and Norfolk, although those English peers who had given their support to the marriage were not made aware of this.

Norfolk was unsure who was his friend, who his enemy, and was therefore uncertain whom to trust. As he saw it, all that mattered was that the contract had been signed.

He was sure – and so was Mary – that before long she would be his wife.

* * *

The Earl and Countess were discussing the ill luck of Leonard Dacre.

'It seems to me that he has little love for my lord Norfolk,' said Bess.

'That is easily understood.'

Bess nodded. Both she and her husband agreed on that point. To see title and fortune, to which one felt one had a right, taken by others was intolerable!

'I believe Leonard plans to contest the matter,' said the Earl, 'but he'll not have a chance.'

He walked to the window to look out over the country, and as he did so he reeled slightly.

'You have drunk too much wine,' said the Countess with a laugh.

The Earl turned, feeling a sudden wave of anger against her. He was about to utter a protest when he felt very faint; he stretched out to catch the hangings; that was the last he remembered for some time.

* * *

When he was again conscious, he was lying in his bed, and Bess was in the room, with the doctors, Caldwell and Francis.

The Earl tried to call out but he appeared to have lost his voice; he tried to lift his arm but could not move it.

Bess was beside his bed. 'Do not try to move, my dear,' she said gently.

His mouth formed words which he could not utter and she went on: 'You have been ill; but you will be all right now. I am going to see to that. The doctors are here. They are very hopeful of your recovery.'

She laid her hand on his brow; it was very cool and it seemed to him as though some of that tremendous vitality of hers flowed into him.

'B . . . Bess. . . .' His lips formed the word and his eyes filled with tears. He felt so weak that he rejoiced in her strength.

'You must rest for some time,' she told him. 'Close your eyes now and try to sleep. All will be well in time. I have told the doctors that they are not to leave Wingfield until I am satisfied with your condition.'

He obeyed her, and it seemed that he slept awhile.

*　　*　　*

It was a week or so after his attack before the power of speech returned to the Earl, and although he could move his limbs he was still slightly paralysed.

Bess rarely left the sickroom; she herself prepared gruels and potions for her husband; she guarded the sickroom and would allow him no visitors except the doctors. With them she was in constant conference, and all agreed that the Earl owed his life to the indefatigable Bess of Hardwick.

When she judged him to be well enough to listen to her plans she sat beside his bed and talked to him.

'My dear,' she said, 'you have suffered from inflammation of the brain. The doctors think it is a condition which has been brought on by your anxiety. Your dear captive, by the way, has sent affectionate messages to you every day and insists on hearing of your progress. I am sure that will help you to get well.'

'Why Bess,' he said, 'nothing could help me get well more than your loving care.'

Bess laughed. 'You do not think I would allow a husband of mine to become an invalid, do you? You are going to get better, I tell you.'

'I feel better.'

'Of course you do. All the time you have been lying on that bed you have not been worrying about the messages which are going to and from your precious captive. You have ceased to think of the charming creature. Let me tell you, George Talbot, that is why your health has improved. There is one thing you need above all others now. That is to leave all this behind and pay a visit to the baths of Buxton. I know that will cure you completely. And I propose to take you there.'

'But what of the Queen. . . .'

'Which? Your Queen or . . . the other? But I forgot they are both your Queens are they not? Do not fret about the Queen of Scots. She is still here even though you have not been able to guard her. You see, there are others who can carry out

243

the task of jailor as well as the Earl of Shrewsbury. No, my love, you are going to Buxton. I have quite made up my mind to take you there.'

'Do you not remember that, when Knollys' wife was dying, the Queen would not allow him to visit her?'

'I am not Knollys. I say you are in need of the Buxton baths and you are going to have them. I have already written to the Queen, telling her of your state of health and asking for permission to take you to Buxton.'

'And you have had no word?'

'I have had no word . . . although I expected it ere now.'

'Bess, even you will not get consent. She will give the same answer to you as she gave to Knollys.'

Bess's face hardened suddenly. 'You are my husband,' she said, 'and it is my duty to cure you. I know that this can be done by a visit to Buxton, and Queen or no Queen, you are going to Buxton.'

He smiled up at her. She seemed invulnerable. But he did not believe they would go to Buxton.

* * *

Leonard Dacre had been a constant caller at Wingfield during the Earl's illness and, since the Countess was continually occupied with the sickroom, it was not difficult for Dacre to visit the Queen whenever he wished.

Dacre was a very bitter man. He had received no satisfaction regarding his claim to the family fortune, and he was furious contemplating how wily Norfolk had been in marrying his brother's widow and arranging matches with his nieces, so that he had manoeuvred the vast Dacre estate into his greedy hands. Norfolk was – without the Dacre fortune – the richest peer in England. He hated Norfolk.

With the Earl sick and the Countess occupied in nursing him, it had been easy to discover something of the intrigues of the household – a little friendship here, a little bribery there – and he knew that Norfolk was not only anxious to marry the Queen of Scots but that he had already a secret contract with her.

Dacre was going to do his best to stop that marriage.

He knew also that there was another faction in England which was eager to prevent it. This was the Catholic party of the North who were determined that Mary should never marry with Protestant Norfolk. The fact that this party was headed by Dacre's cousin, the Earl of Northumberland, made it easy for Leonard Dacre to become a member of it; and, since he was on visiting terms with the Queen of Scots, he was in a position to be very useful.

Dacre was determined that Mary should reject Norfolk and agree to the plans of the Northumberland faction, which were that she should make an alliance with Don Jon of Austria, who would come to England and fight for her cause – and not only her cause. There was another, very dear to the hearts of the Catholics of the North – the dethroning of the Protestant Queen whom they looked on as a bastard and no true Queen of England, and the setting up in her place of the Catholic Mary Queen of Scots.

It was while Countess Bess was with her sick husband and preparing to leave for Buxton – for although she had not yet received Elizabeth's permission she had gone ahead with her preparations – that Dacre called at Wingfield Manor and asked for an audience with the Queen. Mary was working on her tapestry with Seton and Jane Kennedy, and when she received him these two remained with her.

Dacre knew that they were in her confidence and to be trusted, and that if he were alone with the Queen it would give rise to suspicion, so he decided to lay his plan before the three of them.

'I believe, Your Majesty,' he said, 'that it would not be difficult for you to leave this prison.'

Mary, who had continued her work, held her needle poised while she looked at Dacre. He noticed the quick colour in her cheeks. Talk of escape could always excite her.

'How so?' she asked.

Dacre went on: 'I have a perfect plan to lay before you. Do not think that I have not given a great deal of thought to this, nor that I am the only one behind it. Your Majesty, not far from this place armed men are waiting to help you. You have only to escape from this manor, gallop a few miles, and you will be with them. They are ready to put hundreds of men in the field to fight for you.'

'You mean . . . Norfolk?'

Dacre could not help the note of anger creeping into his voice. 'I mean my cousin Northumberland.'

'Ah yes,' said Mary quietly.

'You know that he is working for you. He has the Pope and the King of Spain behind him.'

'They are too ambitious,' said Mary. 'They want to give me not only Scotland but England. I can be content with Scotland.'

'They will meet your wishes in every way. Westmorland is with Northumberland. They cannot fail. But first they wish for your release. Once you are free, every Catholic in England will demand that you be given your rights. Your throne will be yours once more.'

'And how do you propose to bring about my release?'

'Since the sickness of the Earl, rules have become a little lax at Wingfield Manor.'

'It's true,' Mary agreed.

'I have not been idle. I have made friends among the guards and servants here. I do not think it would be a major task for you to walk out of this Manor in the dress of one of your women.'

Mary looked at Seton and Jane Kennedy who were sitting tense, their needles held above the canvas, and she knew they were as excited as she was.

'It would be Lochleven all over again,' Mary murmured.

'It was done there,' said Dacre. 'It can be done here. Only here you have more friends to help you. I tell you, we cannot fail.'

He looked across at Seton. 'The Queen could wear a headdress like yours. She could wear your gown and cloak. You could wear hers. You could be seen together in the great hall ... and the Queen – in your gown, in your cloak – could walk out, leaving you in her clothes in the hall.' He turned to Jane Kennedy. 'You could be there also, talking as you would talk to the Queen, addressing her as "Your Majesty" ... and so you two could walk back to these apartments while the Queen walked out of the Manor ... out to the horses which would be waiting for her. The deception could be kept up for hours ... perhaps a day or more. It would not be so difficult, particularly if the Earl and Countess should leave for Buxton.'

'But if they left,' said Seton, 'someone would surely be sent to take their places. And a new jailor would most certainly be watchful.'

'It must happen before the new man arrives,' declared Dacre.

'In that case,' said Jane, 'before the Shrewsburys leave.'

'If necessary. But they will be busy with their preparations.

246

There could not be a better moment to put this plan into action. What does Your Majesty say?'

'I will think of it.'

'There must be no delay.'

'I shall give you my answer within a few days.'

Dacre was excited. She would agree. There was nothing she longed for so much as escape. This would be the end of Norfolk's ambitions to marry the Queen. He would learn what it cost to meddle in the affairs of the Dacres.

As for Northumberland and Westmorland, they chafed against delay. But he would be able to tell them that the Queen liked the plan.

In a short time the Catholics of the North would be in revolt against the Protestant Queen of England.

* * *

As soon as Dacre had gone, Mary put aside her tapestry.

'What does Your Majesty think of the plan?' asked Seton.

'It is a good one. You know, Seton, you and I are of the same height. If you dressed my hair as yours is dressed, and I put on your clothes, I'll warrant I could impersonate you so that many would be deceived.'

'I am sure you could.'

'And you could impersonate me, Seton. Who could know me better than you? When I have gone you could take to my bed for a day or so – and nothing would be discovered.'

Jane Kennedy said: 'We could rehearse it, It is so simple. I know it would succeed.'

'I wondered,' put in Seton, 'why Your Majesty did not at once agree to the plan.'

'You have forgotten, Seton, that I am affianced to the Duke of Norfolk. I could not agree to do this until I had consulted him.'

There was silence. Then Seton asked: 'You think it is wise to commit this plan to paper?'

'As you know, I write to him in code. As my affianced husband I could not dream of acting without his approval. But I will write to him now and my letter shall be taken to him with all speed. Seton, bring my writing materials, and we will not have a moment's delay.'

* * *

Bess fumed about the Manor. She was ready to leave for Buxton, but there was no answer to the request she had made to the Queen.

Bess believed it imperative that the Earl should be removed from Wingfield, for as he grew better his worries were returning and she was not going to risk another attack which, she was well aware, could be fatal.

She had explained the details of her husband's illness to Elizabeth, but it seemed that the Queen believed that the task she had assigned to Shrewsbury was more important than his life.

She is wrong there! Bess told herself. Queen or no Queen, I shall not stand by and see poor Shrewsbury suffer such another attack which will doubtless kill him or leave him an invalid for the rest of his life. We are going to Buxton.

Bess went to the window, as she did every few minutes, to see if there were any sign of the Queen's messenger. She clenched her fist in anger. No sign of a rider!

She summoned certain of her servants.

'We are leaving for Buxton this day,' she told them. 'Have all made ready for our departure.'

She then made her way to the Earl's bedchamber where he was lying on his bed, still very weak.

'All is well,' she told him. 'We are leaving for Buxton.'

'So . . . she has given her consent? Oh, Bess, you are indeed a wonderful woman. When I think of the way she behaved towards Knollys.'

Bess smiled complacently. To tell him the truth would very likely bring on another attack. The thing she must do was get Shrewsbury well and then consider how they would meet the Queen's anger.

'I told you you had only to leave matters to me,' she said. 'Now your servants are coming to prepare you for the journey. We could leave within the hour.' She laughed. 'You will want to say farewell to your dear Queen, so the preparations should start without delay. I will leave you now because there is so much to do.'

*   *   *

The Earl and Countess had taken their leave of Mary who stood at her window watching their departure. She could hear the Countess's authoritative voice giving orders. The guards had been put on their mettle. On pain of death they were to guard the Queen of Scots until her new keeper arrived, which would be ere long. In the meantime all was to go on at the Manor as if the Earl and Countess were in residence.

The Earl was placed in a litter because he was too weak to ride, and as he was being carried away from the Manor he looked back and, from the group of servants watching, he picked out one desolate figure. Little Eleanor Britton was sadly watching his departure.

So the Shrewsburys left for Buxton, the strong-minded Bess alone being aware that they did so without Elizabeth's consent.

* * *

There was alertness in Mary's apartments. No guardian had been sent to take the place of the Shrewsburys and it was inevitable that rules were relaxed with the absence of the sharp-eyed Bess. Never had there been such ideal conditions for escape. Dacre called. The time was now, he insisted. Why delay? With each passing hour their plans could become more difficult to carry out.

'I will give you my answer very soon,' Mary told him.

This she was able to do, for Norfolk had answered her letter as soon as he received it and had commanded his messenger to take his reply to the Queen without delay.

Certainly she must not fall in with this scheme which Dacre was proposing, he wrote. It would be the utmost folly, for Dacre's one idea was to take her out of England to Flanders or Spain – either to the Duke of Alva or King Philip – and the plan was to marry her to Don Jon of Austria.

Norfolk explained that Dacre was no friend of his on account of a dispute between them concerning the rights of the late Lord Dacre's daughters to inherit the family wealth, and that Dacre's aim was not so much to aid her as to foil the plans for that marriage to which both he, Norfolk, and she, the Queen of Scots, were pledged in secret.

When Dacre next called at the manor, Mary told him that she had been in touch with Norfolk to whom she was affianced and that he advised her not to attempt to escape.

Dacre found it difficult to hide his chagrin; and his hatred for Norfolk intensified.

Mary was however disturbed to learn of the discord between him and Norfolk and asked him for details. With much bitterness Dacre told her how he had, in his opinion, more right to the family fortune than his nieces who, through their betrothal to Norfolk's sons, would allow the Dacre wealth to pass to Norfolk's family.

Mary was sympathetic. 'It certainly seems unjust,' she said. 'Will you allow me to write to the Duke and give him my opinion? I am sure he would listen to me, and it would give me great pleasure to bring about some agreement between you.'

Dacre smiled ruefully. 'Your Majesty must do as you wish. But I would warn you that Norfolk is a hard man where lands and wealth are concerned.'

'I believe that he will wish to do what is right,' replied Mary; and because she knew that she had deeply disappointed Dacre, she determined to persuade Norfolk to make some concessions to his benefit.

*   *   *

When Elizabeth heard that the Shrewsburys had left for Buxton without her consent she was very angry, and had they been on the spot would have committed them to the Tower without delay.

As they were out of reach she immediately commissioned Walter Devereux, Viscount Hereford, to go to Wingfield Manor to take charge of the Queen of Scots. She wrote to Buxton telling the Shrewsburys to return at once to Wingfield Manor where they would find Hereford installed; and at the same time sent orders to Hereford that he was to take charge of the Shrewsburys who were to be as much his prisoners as the Queen of Scots.

When Bess received the Queen's instructions, she knew that she would have to tell her husband what she had done. But this did not perturb her as much as it would have done previously, for the baths and air of Buxton had done a great deal to restore the Earl to health; and, removed as he was from the anxieties of Wingfield, he had, as Bess had prognosticated, rapidly recovered.

She gently broke the news to him.

'Here are orders from the Queen,' she said. 'I fancy she is somewhat displeased with us.'

'But why so?'

Bess laughed. 'Because, my lord, we are at Buxton.'

'But she gave her permission.'

Bess shook her head.

'Bess! You mean that you —'

'It was very necessary. Had I not done so, my dear George, you would not be alive today.'

'But . . . to desert Wingfield . . . without her permission!'

'If it is a matter of disobeying my Queen or losing my husband,' retorted Bess, 'I choose the former. Now there is no need to become agitated. I know Elizabeth and she knows me. If we were on the spot she would be so furious with us that we might tremble for our heads. But we are not on the spot. And she knows that had she been in my place she would have done the same. We are alike in some ways and understand each other. Why, we even share the same name. This matter which angers her now will amuse her in a few days. We need time. You will write to her and so will I. We will tell her . . . in detail . . . how ill you have been, that your life was in danger, and that I considered it essential for you to leave Wingfield when you did. We left the Queen of Scots well guarded. No ill has come to her because of my decision and great good has come to us. Now . . . write. And I will do the same.'

The Earl did as he was told. He marvelled at the boldness of his wife, but he could not help admiring her; and he was touched that she had risked her life to save his – for that was what she had done.

He felt remorseful because of late he had been comparing her with other women – women such as the Queen of Scots and Eleanor Britton – and, it seemed, to her detriment. Now he was thinking of her as he had during the days before their marriage.

When he had finished his letter to the Queen, Bess read it through. She herself had written in more detail, telling of every symptom which had beset the Earl and how near he had come to death.

When Elizabeth received their letters she read them and smiled grimly.

This was the work of Bess of Hardwick. Deliberately flouting the Queen because she *wished* it! Elizabeth admitted to herself that had she been in Bess's position she would have done exactly the same. She understood Bess and Bess understood her.

She sent for one of her own physicians and said to him: 'Shrewsbury is very ill at Buxton. Go and see what you can do for him.'

Elizabeth had secretly forgiven Bess, but the Shrewsburys. must believe that they were still in disgrace.

*　　*　　*

A further shock awaited Elizabeth. News was brought to her that her favourite man, the Earl of Leicester, was grievously sick at his manor at Titchfield and was asking for her to visit him there. In view of all they had been to each other and the fact that at one time in their lives they had been on the point of marriage, Elizabeth lost no time in hurrying to Leicester's bedside.

She found him in a sad state and was moved to pity by the sight of his handsome face on the pillows; but when he saw that she had indeed come, Leicester brightened and she quickly discovered the real reason why he had asked her to visit him.

Leicester was in a panic. He had placed himself on the side of those Protestant nobles who had tried to arrange a marriage between Norfolk and the Queen of Scots. He knew that the Queen's spies were going back and forth between Wingfield Manor and the Court; he knew that Cavendish, who was a messenger for Mary, was also Elizabeth's spy, and he believed that Elizabeth was aware of a great deal which was going on, and that if she knew he had been intriguing without her knowledge she would regard him as a traitor.

When he considered all these points he did not have to feign illness; the prospect of her wrath, if she ever discovered that he, of all men, had worked against her, was enough to make him want to take to his bed.

But here she was, all solicitous concern for her Gay Lord Robert, as she sometimes called him.

He took her hands as she sat by his bed. 'My Queen, my love,' he said, 'you know that I would die for you.'

'Now, Robert,' replied the Queen gently, 'do not speak to me of dying. You and I are too close to think happily of a world which does not contain the other.'

There were tears in Leicester's eyes. 'I want to assure you of my love and devotion. It is as firm now as it was in the days when we were in the Tower together and I loved you so madly . . . so hopelessly.'

'You were never without hope, Robert,' she told him.

'I hoped then . . . and I hope now, my Queen. I hope for your forgiveness.'

'There is only one thing for which I should never forgive you, Robert,' she told him. 'That is – if you die and leave me in this world without you.'

Leicester then knew the answer to the question which had tormented him for the past weeks: Dare he confess? Yes, he might.

'My dearest,' he said, 'there is a plot to marry the Queen of Scots to Norfolk. I am not guiltless. I have made myself a party to this. I felt it the lesser of two evils. The Catholics of the North have been restless since the Queen has been in England and are ready to rise. I thought it wiser for Mary to marry a Protestant and, as Norfolk was willing, I believed it the best way in which to protect Your Majesty.'

'So you entered into plots without my knowledge, Robert?'

'I confess my fault, sweetheart.'

'H'm. Here's a pretty state of affairs when a Queen's ministers – and those whom she believes she has more reason to trust than most – begin to plot and scheme without her knowledge.'

'It has caused me great disquiet. It is the reason why I am brought to this sick bed. But I could no longer bear to keep this secret from you.' He reached for her hand and covered it with kisses. 'I would give my life for you, as you know. It was for your good that I entered into this plot. But now I tell you, for I can no longer bear to have a secret which you do not share. You must punish me as you will. I shall insist always that all I do is out of love of your sweet self.'

'Who else was in this plot with you?'

'Pembroke and Arundel.'

Elizabeth rose from the bedside.

'My love . . .' began Leicester anxiously.

She stooped over him and laid her hand on his forehead.

'I fear you are displeased with me . . .' he went on.

'And what do you expect when you plot behind my back?'

'What can I do to win back your regard?'

'Get well. I like not to see you sick abed.'

She kissed him, and when he would have taken her in his arms she laughed and eluded him. 'Remember you are a sick man, Robert. Remember too that the Queen commands you to be well. I expect you at Court ere long.'

Leicester was still smiling when she had left him. He felt limp with relief. He thanked his stars, his good looks, and his charm by which he had extricated himself from that dangerous situation.

*　　*　　*

Arriving back at Court Elizabeth was thoughtful.

Pembroke, Arundel, Norfolk, she was thinking. And so Norfolk fancies himself as her husband, does he? And doubtless she fancies Norfolk. She has been without a husband so long that she will be eager for one, I'll swear. But she can go on panting for a man, for she'll not get one!

When she was with her ministers, the Spanish ambassador found his way to her side.

He told her – as he did on every occasion they met – that His Most Catholic Majesty was deeply concerned about the imprisonment of the Queen of Scotland, and he requested Her Majesty to give the matter her attention.

'I give the matter attention,' retorted the Queen. 'And I tell you this, that if the Queen of Scots does not bear her condition with a little more patience she may find some of her friends shorter by the head.'

A silence followed this remark. Those who were friends of the Duke of Norfolk sought the first opportunity of making their way to his apartments.

They warned him that he was in mortal danger. Someone had betrayed to Elizabeth his intentions towards the Queen of Scots, and Elizabeth's remark was almost certainly directed towards him.

Norfolk, always on the alert for danger, was far from the Court before that day was over.

*　　*　　*

Elizabeth summoned the Earl of Huntingdon to her presence.

'I am sending armed guards to Wingfield Manor,' she told him. 'I consider it an unsuitable residence for the Queen of Scots. You will go to Tutbury Castle whither the Queen is being removed. Shrewsbury and his Countess will be with you there. You will keep a watch on them also. There has been too much intrigue. See that there is no repetition of such happenings at Tutbury.'

Huntingdon assured her that he would leave without delay and that her orders should be carried out.

So Huntingdon set out for Tutbury, while the Earl and Countess of Shrewsbury left Buxton for the same destination.

CHAPTER EIGHT

RETURN TO TUTBURY

MARY WAS WORKING at her tapestry at Wingfield Manor, with her ladies about her, when Lesley's letter was brought to her. She read it and, noticing her pallor, Seton rose from her work to come to her side.

'Leicester has betrayed to Elizabeth that there is a contract between myself and the Duke, who has left Court with all speed. The Queen has hinted that my friends are in danger.'

'That means . . .' began Seton and stopped.

'It seems so foolish,' cried Mary impetuously. 'Why should Elizabeth object to my marriage with an English nobleman?'

'Perhaps,' suggested Seton, 'it was unwise to keep the matter secret from her.'

'Lesley advises me to burn all the letters I have received from the Duke, together with any secret documents I may have in the apartment. He feels sure that a search will be made and that if anything which they can call treasonable is found it will give them the excuse they need.'

Seton said: 'I do not think there is a moment to lose.'

Mary nodded, and she and Seton with the rest of the ladies left their tapestry. Mary then went to her table and unlocking a drawer took out certain documents which she threw into the fire.

'Is there anything else?' asked Seton anxiously.

Mary was searching through the boxes in which the few clothes she possessed were kept. She sent her ladies to their own chambers, instructing them to bring out any single thing that could be called incriminating.

The documents were still smouldering in the grate when there was a knock on her door and Hereford entered.

'Your Majesty,' he said, 'you are to prepare to leave for Tutbury without delay.'

'Tutbury!' Mary's voice rose in shrill protest.

'Those are the orders of Her Majesty, the Queen.'

'Oh, not Tutbury. Not that evil smelling place!'

Hereford answered: 'We shall be leaving within the hour.'

'But that is impossible. I am not prepared.'

'Have no fear on that account,' answered Hereford grimly.
'I and my guards will put your possessions together, and the
Queen's orders are that there must not be even an hour's
delay.'

His eyes had gone to the smouldering pile in the grate and
he understood. He was too late to find that which he had
hoped to send to the Queen. But perhaps there was something
left.

Mary gasped with indignatión to see his guards already
coming into the apartment.

'But this is monstrous! Am I to enjoy no privacy?'

'I beg Your Majesty's pardon, but I am obeying the orders
of my mistress, the Queen of England.'

It was no use pleading.

Within the hour Mary and her suite, in the company of
Hereford and his armed guard, had left Wingfield Manor for
Tutbury. Hereford was disappointed. He had come to her
apartments just too late to seize the documents which he knew
must be there. All he had to send to Elizabeth was the cipher
she had used in her correspondence with Norfolk. Still, that
might prove of some use.

*   *   *

Through the golden September day they travelled.

When Mary saw the fortress on the red sandstone rock and
the marshy lands surrounding it, her spirits drooped.

Her whole mind and body called out a protest: Not Tutbury!

As soon as she entered her old apartments that evil smell
assaulted her nostrils, bringing with it memories of sickness.

How could she endure those bleak rooms, one above the
other, connected by that cold stone staircase?

Tutbury seemed to her a place without hope.

She was anxious on account of one of her women – Margaret Cawood, wife of Bastian, who had been married at the
time of Darnley's murder – for Margaret was pregnant, and
Mary was wondering how she would fare in the cold of Tutbury during the winter months which lay ahead.

There was more to concern her than a cold and uncomfort-
able house. Hereford was handing her over to the Earl of
Huntingdon who, he explained, was to take the place of the
Shrewsburys as her keeper.

Mary was aghast at Elizabeth's choice, and she thought there was some sinister meaning behind it, for Henry Hastings, Earl of Huntingdon, the son of Catherine Pole and therefore a descendant of the Duke of Clarence, had royal connexions and a remote claim to the throne.

Such a claim might have made him extremely unpopular with Elizabeth, and she was naturally watchful of him; but she knew that he would be more eager than most people in her realm to prevent a marriage between Mary and Norfolk, that he would be very anxious to incriminate the Queen of Scots if it were possible to do so – and therefore she considered him highly qualified to have charge of Mary at this stage.

He received the Queen respectfully but coolly, and as she was conducted to those well remembered and much loathed apartments she felt that the walls of Tutbury were closing about her for ever.

*   *   *

Mary stood beneath the vaulted ceiling and covered her face with her hands to shut out the sight of the place.

Seton, close to her, whispered: 'Your Majesty, do not despair.'

'It is this place, Seton. I loathed it from the moment I entered it. I loathe it even more now that we have returned to it.'

'Let us hope there will be another move, ere long.'

'We can always hope.'

'Who knows what will happen, Your Majesty? The Duke has had to retire from Court, but there are still your friends in the North. Perhaps they will come marching to Tutbury and carry you away.'

'Who knows? Meanwhile we stay here. Oh . . . this smell, Seton! It makes me feel so ill. And what of Margaret? How is she? How did she endure the journey? Is she resting now? She should.'

'Before the child is due we shall be away from here,' soothed Seton. 'Have you noticed we never stay anywhere long?'

'It may be that I shall be carried from here to my tomb.'

'Your Majesty, it is unlike you to despair so soon.'

'Blame the stench, Seton. But listen, you see who our jailor is. I shall never feel safe while he is here. He is a claimant to the throne of England. Why, if Elizabeth were to die without heirs, I believe he would try to take the crown. And here am I at his mercy. What do you think, Seton? Will it be the poison cup? Or a dagger while I lie abed?'

Seton saw that the Queen was near hysteria and she wondered how to comfort her. Secretly she was cursing the walls of Tutbury which she hated as fiercely as Mary did.

'There is someone at the door,' she said.

'Go and see who is there and say that I am too weary to be seen this day.'

Seton went, and Mary heard her say: 'Her Majesty is indisposed and wishes to rest. . . .'

But Seton was thrust aside and when the Countess of Shrewsbury came into the room, Mary gave a cry of pleasure. Nothing could have pleased her more than to hear that the Earl and his wife were reinstated in their old posts and that the Earl of Huntingdon was to be dismissed.

'Your Majesty,' said Bess, curtseying.

'It gives me pleasure to see you,' Mary told her. 'I trust this means that Huntingdon is returning to London.'

Bess grunted angrily. 'Oh no. He is to remain here. He is to be *our* jailor. The Earl and I are his prisoners even as Your Majesty is. Have you ever heard the like! We are prisoners in our own castle!'

Mary was speechless. Not so Bess.

'I shall not allow it, of course. I will tell Huntingdon that neither the Earl nor myself will stomach any interference in our doings. I shall keep a sharp eye on Master Huntingdon. I believe he begins to understand that.'

'You are, like myself, out of favour with the Queen,' said Mary.

'I displeased her by saving my husband's life.'

Mary was smiling; it was surprising how the gloom of the last half hour was being dispersed by the dynamic Bess.

'We shall stand no nonsense from him!' went on Bess. 'Nor should Your Majesty.'

'I shall certainly not do so.'

Bess smiled. 'If there is aught Your Majesty requires, I pray you make your wishes known to *me*. I shall do my best to see that they are carried out.'

'I pray you be seated,' said Mary. 'I would hear news of the Earl's sickness and recovery.'

Bess sat down and they talked; and as they did so Mary realized that now she had a firm ally in the castle. Bess intimated that she would be watchful of Huntingdon, and she warranted that if two clever women put their heads together they had nothing to fear from meddling Earls.

When Bess had left, Seton noticed how the Queen's demeanour had changed.

*　　*　　*

Meanwhile Elizabeth had summoned Norfolk to appear before her at Windsor. She sent similar summonses to the Earls of Arundel and Pembroke, Lord Lumley and Sir Nicholas Throckmorton, whose names had been given her by Leicester, as those noblemen who, with himself, had banded together to bring about Mary's marriage to Norfolk.

Norfolk, who was at Kenninghall, wrote to Elizabeth pleading sickness which prevented him from travelling. Meanwhile Arundel, Pembroke and their friends, having obeyed the Queen's summons were promptly arrested and conveyed to the Tower, where they were questioned in the hope that they would incriminate the Queen of Scots in treason against the throne of England.

They assured their questioners that Mary had had no designs on Elizabeth's crown and that the suggestion of marriage with Norfolk had not come from her.

Meanwhile Elizabeth had sent a peremptory order to Norfolk. Sickness or no sickness, he was to present himself to her without delay.

In great trepidation Norfolk set out, was arrested on the way and taken straight to the Tower.

When the news of his arrest was brought to Elizabeth she showed grim satisfaction. She was going to teach the premier peer of England a lesson. But there was one other at whom she longed to strike. Ever since she had heard that Mary had allowed herself to be called Queen of England she had been watchful of her. She had attempted to capture Mary on her return from France to Scotland; she would never be at peace while Mary lived; and when fate (in the shape of the folly of the Queen of Scots) had delivered Mary into her hands she had been exultant.

She longed to sever that beautiful head from those graceful shoulders. She hated the Queen of Scots for many reasons. Mary was beautiful, infinitely desirable, and men were ready to risk their lives and fortunes for her. They said the same of Elizabeth; every day there were courtiers to tell her she was the most beautiful woman in the world. She was their

Gloriana, the mistress of her male subjects, all of whom grovelled at her feet and capped each other's flattering comments. Yet, thought Elizabeth in one of those rare moments when she faced the truth, how many would be prepared to worship her if she were the poor prisoner in the castle of a jealous enemy?

That was one reason why she wished to be rid of Mary. A poor reason, admitted Elizabeth the Queen. The true reason was not that of the vain and simpering woman. It was a Queen's reason: She threatened the crown. She could be a figurehead to Elizabeth's Catholic subjects. Those who questioned the legitimacy of the marriage between Henry VIII and Anne Boleyn might call Mary, not Elizabeth, the true Queen of England; therefore Mary must die.

But there must be a good reason for her death. It was not wise to set a precedent for the murder of Queens. Royalty must be respected. A case must be proved against Mary; and even then Elizabeth would not happily sign the death warrant.

She went to her council and there railed against the perfidy of Norfolk.

Timidly her councillors pointed out that in negotiating for marriage, Norfolk had done nothing in law to incure a severe penalty.

She had become suddenly furious with them. 'What the law cannot do,' she cried, 'my authority shall effect!'

Then because she suspected she might have shown her fears of Mary too openly, which would have been unwise, she played the emotional woman, pretending to faint so that the councillors brought vinegar and restoratives to revive her.

But she always knew when she had gone far enough. Recovering from her 'faint' she graciously told her courtiers that she feared at times she was but a weak woman, and she thanked them for the good counsel on which she knew she could always rely.

She left the Council Chamber wondering how she could bring about the destruction of her enemy without seeming to have played a part in it.

*   *   *

Lesley, Bishop of Ross, was disturbed by these events. He knew that the prisoners would be questioned, and he wondered how deeply they would incriminate Mary.

It was while he was in his lodgings, brooding on these

matters, that his servant came to tell him that a gentleman was without and asking to see him on urgent business. Lesley commanded that he be brought to him without delay, and the man was ushered in.

When they were alone he came straight to the point.

'My name is Owen,' he said, 'and I am a gentleman from the household of the Earl of Arundel.'

Lesley was excited. 'You bring news from your master?'

'As you know, my master is in the Tower, but before he was taken he gave me instructions to call on you and lay this plan before you. He believes the Queen of Scots to be in great danger.'

'I fear that is so.'

'And that she should be removed from Tutbury Castle at no matter what cost. If she could be taken from her prison and brought to Arundel, she could embark there for France. Once there it would be easier for her friends to work on her behalf. But she should leave Tutbury as soon as possible.'

'I am in agreement with you,' said Lesley. 'I like not the choice of her jailor.'

'You do well to doubt his designs. But there is this in our favour. The Earl and his Countess have no reason to love Huntingdon either, since he has been set up as a jailor over them as well as the Queen. It may well be that they would be ready to assist the Queen's escape.'

'And risk their heads?'

'They are no longer in charge of her. Doubtless they would be pleased to see Huntingdon fail . . . where they did not . . . even though they left their captive for the Buxton baths.'

'I will write to the Queen with all speed and tell her of this plan.'

'Pray do so. It is what my master wishes.'

As soon as Owen had left, Lesley wrote a letter to Mary and sent a messenger off with it to Tutbury.

* * *

It was not easy now for Mary to receive correspondence from her friends, for Huntingdon was a sterner jailor than had so far been hers.

This meant that intrigue in Tutbury intensified, and as there hung over the Queen the perpetual fear that she was to be murdered, the days, being full of alarms, were certainly not dull.

Mary and her devoted friends were constantly alert for a look, a gesture from even a serving man or maid which could be significant.

The letter from Lesley had been smuggled in to her through the services of one of these. The messenger had arrived at Tutbury with letters for Mary which must pass through Huntingdon's hands; but there was one which he carried secreted on his person, and this he kept back, seeking a moment when he could pass it to Seton. This was the letter in which Lesley told her of the plan to carry her off to Arundel.

When Mary had read the letter she passed it to Seton. Seton too was aware of a brooding warning within these walls. She often thought how easy it would be to slip a little poison into Mary's food, to force her to one of the windows or the top of a staircase and throw her down. Since their return to Tutbury, she had been constantly on her guard, sleeping in Mary's own bedchamber, starting at the smallest sound in the night; but even her strong nerves were giving way under the strain, and she would have been ready to risk a great deal to escape.

'What do you think, Seton?' asked Mary.

'I believe that it should be tried.'

'I would be ready to risk my life for escape from this place.'

Seton nodded. 'Northumberland and Westmorland would be ready to come to your help. It has a good chance of success.'

'I am anxious about the noblemen of the North, Seton, because their aim is not only to win me back my Scottish crown but to set me on the throne of England.'

'Perhaps it would be wise to take first things first. Escape. That is what we desire. Let us have that and see where we go from there.'

'To France, it seems, Seton.'

'We were happy in France,' Seton reminded her.

Mary was thoughtful for a few seconds, then she said: 'There is one other matter, Seton. What of Norfolk? He is in the Tower. If I escaped, Elizabeth would take her revenge on him and that could cost him his life. I do not think I could give my consent to this plan while Norfolk is in the Tower.'

Seton looked sadly at her mistress. She did not have the high opinion of Norfolk that Mary had, believing him to be selfish and avaricious. Seton often wondered whether, but for Norfolk, Mary might have escaped from her enemies by now.

'Let Norfolk take care of himself,' she said rashly. 'Here is a chance to escape from this place.'

Mary was shocked. 'You have forgotten, Seton, that he is my affianced husband.'

'He is in the Tower, but it may be that you are in greater danger.'

'But he might well be in as great danger if I angered Elizabeth by escaping. There is only one thing to do. I will write to Norfolk.'

'It is dangerous to write, Your Majesty.'

'Nay. I write in cipher . . . a new one now that they have stolen the old. We have our friends here who smuggle out our letters, and friends in the Tower who smuggle them in. Who would guess that corks of ale bottles which are taken into the Duke's cell contain my letters! We are well served, Seton.'

Seton saw that it was no use warning the Queen against Norfolk. She, who had always been so trusting, so generous, persisted in endowing others with the same qualities.

* * *

Norfolk's reply was almost frantic. She must not listen to these wild plans for her escape. She must stay where she was. He believed that those friends whom she was prepared to trust might well, in spite of their promises, desert her if they should find themselves in danger. It would be folly for him to try to leave his prison, for if he were caught in the attempt he would surely lose his head; whereas at the moment, since he had committed no crime, he was in little danger. But if *she* were to escape, she could be sure that Elizabeth would take revenge on *him*.

When Seton read this letter she felt a dull anger within her, being certain that Norfolk was serving his own cause rather than the Queen's. 'It would seem that we are working for the good of my lord Norfolk rather than the Queen of Scots,' she said bitterly.

'Our causes are one,' Mary replied. 'I should never forgive myself if he suffered through my actions.'

'Let us hope,' retorted Seton, 'that he would feel the same if harm came to you through any of his.'

'I am sure he shares my feelings,' was Mary's reply. 'Do not forget that he is my affianced husband.'

So, mourned Seton, there was another opportunity lost for bringing the Queen out of her doleful prison.

* * *

When Mary's despair threatened to become intolerable she would give her attention to the care of others; and one person in her retinue who needed care at this time was Margaret Cawood, who was expecting to give birth to a child.

Margaret was not so rigorously confined as Mary was, yet the Queen did not believe the air of Tutbury was good for anyone; and she made sure that Margaret was lodged as far from the obnoxious privies as possible and that she took regular exercise.

She asked Huntingdon – who carefully watched all comings and goings to and from the castle – if he would permit a midwife to attend Margaret. Anxious to assure the Queen that he was eager to help her as far as he could, Huntingdon agreed, and a midwife was found who paid regular visits.

One day Margaret was discovered in a faint, and when the news was brought to Mary she sent at once for the midwife, who on arriving examined Margaret, soothingly assured her that all was well and made her lie down.

When she left Margaret apparently sleeping, she asked if she might speak in private to the Queen as she was anxious about the condition of her patient. She wished to speak to the Queen alone because she did not want whispers of what she was about to say to reach Margaret's ears, for as would readily be understood, it was necessary at this stage for her to have no worries about herself.

Mary, always anxious for the welfare of her servants, had the midwife brought to her presence immediately.

'What is wrong with Margaret?' she demanded. 'Please do not hide anything from me.'

The midwife looked over her shoulder and whispered: 'Are we quite alone?'

'We are,' replied Mary.

'Margaret's condition is excellent. She pretends it is not so in order to give me this opportunity of speaking to Your Majesty in private. The Earl of Northumberland sends me to tell you that he has a plan for your escape which cannot fail. He wants you to change places with me and walk out of the castle in my clothes.'

264

Mary's eyes sparkled; then she said: 'And what of you when it is known that you have allowed me to do this?'

The midwife turned pale at the thought but she said: 'I would do it.'

Mary shook her head. It would be certain and most painful death for the woman; and not only death. They would doubtless torture her to discover who was behind the plan and, much as Mary longed to escape, she would not allow this woman to suffer on her account. Noblemen had suffered hideous deaths but there was even less respect shown to humbler persons.

'I thank you with all my heart,' said Mary. 'But I could not leave you to suffer what I know must be your fate if you played such a role.'

'I would do it for the good of the Catholic Faith.'

'Nay,' said Mary. 'And in any case we should not deceive them for a moment. See how much taller I am than you! The clothes you wear would never fit me. The impersonation would be seen through at once.'

The midwife answered: 'I will tell my master what Your Majesty has said and doubtless he will think of some other plan.'

After that messages were carried between Mary and Northumberland by way of the midwife, and a few days later Mary heard that the Countess of Northumberland, who was visiting a friend close by Tutbury, would come in the guise of a midwife, change clothes with Mary, and remain behind to impersonate her while Mary escaped.

Mary need have no fears of this impersonation's being discovered, for the Countess of Northumberland was of similar height to the Queen; and, dressed in midwife's clothes, a hood doing much to conceal her face, Mary might pass through the guards without the deception being noticed.

Moreover the Queen should have no qualms about leaving the Countess behind because, being of the high nobility, she would not be treated as a humble midwife would. There was another point: very soon the Earl intended to raise the Catholic standard, and in that case he would very quickly rescue his wife from any predicament in which she found herself.

Intrigue was necessary to Mary's existence. Now life might be uncomfortable but at least it was not dull. She allowed herself to listen to these new plans.

Huntingdon however had noticed that the midwife seemed to spend more time alone with the Queen than with her patient, so one day he stopped the woman on her way out of the castle, and she was searched. Fortunately there were no letters in her possession; but she was severely questioned and Huntingdon was not satisfied with her replies.

He ordered that the midwife was to be examined both when she entered and left the castle; and he himself would be present at her conferences on the health of Margaret Cawood with the Queen.

The plot to smuggle Mary out of Tutbury as a midwife was stillborn.

* * *

The winds of October buffeted the walls of the castle and, even though the winter had not yet come, it was bitterly cold in the Queen's apartments. Mary felt a return of all the rheumatic pains she had suffered during the previous winter, and she suddenly became so full of despair that she was stricken with sickness. Each morning she would awake to that nauseating odour to which she could never become accustomed. Seton had placed on the bed as many coverings as she could find, but still Mary shivered. She was feverish and shivering in turn, and her friends feared for her.

Bess made hot possets for her and undertook to help with her nursing. She gave brisk orders to Mary's women which they obeyed because they realized the efficiency and skill of the Countess. Chafing against the presence of Huntingdon in her home, Bess had determined to become the friend of Mary, although she was still alert when her husband was in the presence of the Queen.

When Mary was able to leave her bed for a short while she occupied herself by writing pitiful appeals to Cecil and to Elizabeth.

'You have known what it is like to be in trouble,' wrote Mary to the Queen; 'judge then from that what others suffer in like case.'

Bess also wrote to Elizabeth. She admitted her fault in taking her husband to Buxton without waiting for her consent. 'But, Your Majesty, I had to choose between your consent and the life of my husband. I found myself, as a wife, obliged to choose in favour of the latter; and knowing the good heart of my mistress, I was certain that she would understand and forgive me.'

Bess went on to remind Elizabeth that the Queen of Scots had suffered no harm when under their care and that it made her and the Earl unhappy to be forced to endure the presence of a stranger as head of their own household.

Elizabeth read these letters and was thoughtful.

Mary was ill and confined to her bed; the Shrewsburys would never dare disobey her again; she would play the lenient and forgiving sovereign.

* * *

Bess burst into the Queen's apartment.

'Good news!' she cried. 'At last we shall call our home our own. The Queen orders Huntingdon to leave Tutbury.'

Mary raised herself from her pillows, and her pleasure was evident. No more wondering whether the food she ate had been spiced with poison; no more waking in the night wondering in terror whether that was a stealthy step she had heard outside her door.

With an impulsive gesture she stretched out her arms to Bess, and the two women embraced each other.

* * *

Bess with her husband stood at the castle gates watching the departure of the Earl of Huntingdon.

'Now we are alone,' she cried, 'I pray God that never again shall our privacy be so invaded. Come, let us go into the castle. I feel we should celebrate the end of Huntingdon's rule. There shall be a banquet and the Queen shall be present.' She looked at the Earl slyly. 'You will like that, eh?'

'I am not sure of the wisdom of it.'

'Come come,' laughed Bess. 'She shall be seated on your right hand. But do not forget that I shall be watching you, so if you wish to tell her of your devotion you will have to do so in whispers.'

The Earl was about to protest but Bess was laughing loudly.

Into the kitchen she went and her voice could be heard throughout the castle issuing orders.

'Now come along, Peg. Look sharp, girl. There's work to be done. Do not think that, because my lord Huntingdon has left us, there is naught for you to do but gape about you. Eleanor, you go to the kitchens. There'll be work for you there. Go and tell the cooks I shall be with them shortly. I have orders to give them, now that my lord Huntingdon is no longer with us!'

Eleanor was aware of the Earl's eyes upon her as she obeyed the instructions of the Countess. They spoke little to each other, yet he knew of her happiness in his recovery, and she was aware that he was deeply affected by her joy.

*　　*　　*

Bess gazed contentedly about her table. It was good to be mistress in her own house. She could feel proud of her achievement. She had had her way with Elizabeth and had been taken back into favour. Now she and George were in the same position as they had been in before the trip to Buxton. George's health was wonderfully improved and he was almost himself again. She had been triumphantly proved right, and there was nothing Bess liked better.

The Queen of Scots was looking pale. Poor ineffectual creature! Bess could feel sorry for her and she could laugh inwardly at what she called George's romantic attachment. *She* would see that it never became more than it was at present. George could go on admiring the captive Queen as long as he kept his distance.

One thing I should never tolerate, Bess told herself, is an unfaithful husband.

She had no fear. Any woman who could flout Queen Elizabeth and manoeuvre herself back into favour could do anything.

Why not a little dancing? A little music on the lute or virginals?

She suggested to Mary that she should invite the company to her apartments, and Mary joyfully agreed.

There after the banquet Mary played the lute and sang to the company; and she felt so much recovered that, when the dancing began, she found her feet tapping to the tune and she was unable to resist trying a measure.

Willie Douglas begged for the honour, and graciously she consented to his wish.

Willie's eyes were full of dreams. She knew he was thinking regretfully of escapes which had come to nothing, and desperately trying to think of one which would succeed.

She felt hopeful. I have so many good friends, she told herself.

*　　*　　*

There was a commotion at the castle gates.

Bess, who immediately went down to see what was happening, was struck with dismay when she recognized the livery of Huntingdon's men.

'What is the meaning of this?' she demanded.

Before she could receive an answer she was joined by her husband. 'Huntingdon's men have returned,' she cried. 'I had thought them at Court by now.'

And as she spoke Huntingdon himself was riding towards her.

He dismounted and a groom immediately took his horse.

'To what do we owe this pleasure?' demanded Bess with sarcasm.

Huntingdon came straight to the point. 'Northumberland and Westmorland are in revolt. They are marching on Tutbury and are but some fifty miles from us. There must not be a moment's delay. I am ordered by Her Majesty to take the Queen of Scots from here at once.'

Shrewsbury said: 'And what are Her Majesty's orders concerning us?'

'You are to come with us to protect the Queen of Scots if necessary from the rebels. I have an armed guard with me. We should go to the Queen's apartments immediately. We must be gone from here before an hour has elapsed, for it is unsafe to stay longer.'

Mary was startled when the Earls of Huntingdon and Shrewsbury came to her.

She listened in dismay.

Leave Tutbury! It was what she had been praying for. But in very different circumstances from these.

CHAPTER NINE

COVENTRY

THE FIRST HALT on the flight from Tutbury was at Huntingdon's castle at Ashby-de-la-Zouch.

This castle, set in wooded country, was a magnificent building which had been erected by Alan de la Zouch in the reign of Henry III, and in such contrast to dreary Tutbury that Mary might have welcomed the change had it not been that she was once more under the guardianship of Huntingdon.

'Only three days free of him,' she said to Bess, 'and here he is again. Do you think he has brought me to Ashby to murder me?'

'He dare not. The Queen would never allow it.'

'There are some,' remarked Mary ruefully, 'who are prepared to disobey not only the Queen of Scots but the Queen of England.'

'Not Huntingdon. He values his head too much. You need have no fear,' Bess went on. 'While I am here no harm shall come to you.'

Such was the personality of the Countess that Mary took courage from her presence. Nevertheless she was relieved when that long night was over and they left Huntingdon's mansion.

There was no time for delay. Ashby was too uncomfortably close to Tutbury for the party to be allowed to stay there, and Coventry was the next destination, some twenty-six miles on.

They halted at the Three Tuns Inn at Atherstone for refreshment on their way and then rode hard for Coventry, a town where a defence might be put up against the rebels, for a strong wall surrounded it on which were thirty well fortified towers.

But no preparation had been made in Coventry for the arrival of the party, and Huntingdon and Shrewsbury consulted together as to where they could find lodgings for the Queen.

Bess said that as the Queen was very weary and far from well they should find a lodging for her and continue their conferences later. She suggested the Black Bull Inn in Smithford Street not far from the Greyfriars gateway.

'There she can be well guarded,' she went on, 'until a more seemly lodging can be found. It would be a sorry matter if we were forced to flee again, and the Queen too sick to travel.'

Mary was not displeased to find herself in a hostelry which, although infinitely smaller, had more comfort to offer her than gloomy Tutbury. There was excitement among her friends because, with the Northern Catholics on the march and herself being hustled from place to place, rescue seemed more likely than it could be while she was incarcerated within the strong walls of a fortress. She had brought with her, in spite of the hasty flight, twenty-five of her friends on whom she could rely absolutely, led by such stalwarts as Mary Seton, Jane Kennedy, Willie Douglas, the Livingstones and Marie Courcelles. There were also two members of the Beaton family – Andrew

270

and Archibald – the former her Master of the Household, the latter her usher; and she knew that they would readily give their lives for her. There were times when she believed she would never be able to express her gratitude to these people who, from choice, shared her captivity with her.

Bess, who had established herself in command of the whole company and even managed to subdue Huntingdon, advised her husband to write at once to Elizabeth telling her that Mary had been safely conveyed to Coventry and that she was now held at the Black Bull Inn.

The letter was written and, while Elizabeth's reply was awaited, Huntingdon discussed the possibility of reducing the number of Mary's servants, for if they must needs move on, it was no easy matter to convey such a large party.

'That,' said Bess, 'is a matter of less import than some. The Queen will be desolate if she is parted from her friends. This is no time to concern ourselves with the reduction of her household. Furthermore if you turn these people adrift at such a time they will join the rebels with valuable information. Let well alone.'

Huntingdon was forced to accept the logic of this, and he did not broach the subject to Mary as he had intended. He satisfied himself, during their stay at the Black Bull, with making sure that the Queen was well guarded night and day.

Elizabeth's reply was choleric, and she wrote individually to both Shrewsbury and Huntingdon. She was furious and a little frightened, as she always was when confronted by rebellion among her subjects. She was relying on the Earl of Sussex who was stationed at York, and Sir George Bowes who was at Barnard's Castle, to subdue the rebels. In the meantime she berated the Earls for so demeaning royalty by taking a Queen to an Inn. They were to remove Mary at once and find some suitable house in Coventry – a good and loyal city – where she was to remain until commanded to do otherwise; and Elizabeth expected her prisoner to be guarded day and night.

Bess, who had already been looking for a suitable residence – she herself considered it somewhat demeaning for a Countess to stay at an Inn – had discovered an old house known as St Mary's Hall, and her inspection of this had shown her that it contained adequate lodging for the Queen.

Immediately on receipt of Elizabeth's letter Mary was taken to St Mary's Hall and there a large room, which was called the Mayoress's Parlour, was given to her as her presence chamber; there were other rooms connected by a wooden gallery, which served as bedchamber and ante-chamber for Mary. Her ladies were housed in smaller rooms connected with those allotted to Mary; and in the circumstances Bess considered that they had housed the Queen satisfactorily.

Now that she was settled, Huntingdon again took up the matter of her servants, to which Mary was intensely hostile. She would not part with any one of her friends, she cried. 'Is it not enough for you,' she demanded, 'that I am kept a prisoner here, that I am not allowed to see my sister and cousin, Elizabeth, that I am treated as though I am a criminal? I will not allow you, my lord Huntingdon, to part me from one of my friends.'

Huntingdon tried to soothe her. 'You must not regard me as your enemy,' he insisted.

'When you show yourself to me as my friend I will not,' was her answer.

'I will show you that I am your friend,' Huntingdon promised her, 'and that soon.'

Mary did not take his words seriously and was as suspicious of him as ever.

*　　*　　*

It was a life of rigorous imprisonment that she was forced to live in Coventry. She was not allowed to walk out in the open air, and she pined for it. The time was passing and when she looked back she grew frantic to realize that she was more Elizabeth's prisoner now than she had been when she had first come to England.

'I should never have come south,' she told Seton frequently. 'I should never have put my trust in Elizabeth.'

During those days of late November news came of the rebels. They had acted rashly, for although they had enjoyed initial success, it was clear that they could not hold out for long against the English.

'How I wish they had never attempted this!' cried Mary. 'They will bring nothing but misery to themselves and others.'

The fear that the rebels would march on Coventry and fight for the possession of the Queen's person was each day growing more and more remote; but this did not mean a relaxation of the rigorous rules.

The Shrewsburys were as anxious that she should not escape as Huntingdon was, and although Bess remained friendly she was watchful, and it would not have been easy for any letter to have passed her scrutiny on its way to Mary.

It was a surprise one day when Huntingdon came to the Queen's apartment and told her he wished to talk privately with her. Mary sent her friends away, and when they were alone he said: 'I bring a message from my brother-in-law, the Earl of Leicester, who sends his greetings to you and wishes me to tell you how much he deplores the manner in which you are being treated.'

'I would he would speak to his mistress on my behalf. I understand that she has a special regard for him.'

'He has worked continually for your comfort.'

'Then I should have expected better results from one who enjoys such favour with his Queen.'

Huntingdon smiled almost slyly. 'The Queen, having such regard for my brother-in-law, might not be pleased to hear of his devotion to Your Majesty.'

'Tell me more of this . . . devotion.'

'The Earl of Leicester bids me tell you that, if you will break your engagement to Norfolk and take him instead, he will use all his powers to bring about your release and restore to you that which is yours by right.'

'You cannot mean that the Earl of Leicester wishes to be my husband!'

'That is what I do mean. What is your answer?'

'I am affianced to Norfolk.'

'Who can do you little good, being in the Tower.'

'I was not speaking of what good could come to me, my lord, but of my engagement to His Grace.'

'Your Majesty should consider this matter.'

'I do not need to consider. Until my engagement to Norfolk is broken I could not contemplate entering into another.'

Huntingdon bowed and took his leave.

* * *

Mary called Seton and Andrew Beaton to her and told them what Huntingdon had suggested.

'Why,' said Andrew, 'it is clear what is happening. Elizabeth is going through a pretence of taking the Duke of Anjou for a husband. Leicester is piqued and wishes to show her that he can play the same game.'

'Then,' said Mary, 'I was right to treat this offer with little seriousness.'

273

'Perhaps,' put in Seton quietly, 'it would have been well not to have made a definite refusal. It may have been that Leicester could have done you some good.'

'Oh, Seton, nothing can come right when no one person trusts another. Let us be straightforward and act honourably. I am betrothed to Norfolk, and while that betrothal exists I cannot enter into the same state with another man.'

Seton spread her hands helplessly. 'We are surrounded by people who play these double games. And we try to be honourable! Is that why we are hustled from one prison to another?'

Mary looked at her friend reproachfully. 'Perhaps Seton,' she said. 'But I would not wish to betray those who have befriended me, even if by so doing I could win my freedom.'

'This is a desperate game and we are playing it with rogues,' insisted Seton.

Mary was firm. 'I must find some means of writing to Norfolk,' she said, 'he will be sad and lonely in his prison.'

* * *

It was again her birthday, this time to be spent in St Mary's Hall at Coventry. It seemed incredible that it was only a year ago when she had celebrated her last birthday. So much had happened since, and yet so little. 'I was a prisoner then,' mourned Mary; 'I am a prisoner still.'

She would have no attempt made to celebrate the occasion.

'I have lived twenty-seven years,' she told Seton, 'and I fear I grow old. Where shall I spend my twenty-eighth birthday, I wonder? Christmas will soon be with us and then another year will begin. I cannot believe that Elizabeth has kept me so long her prisoner.'

There came bad news of the Northern rebels. Sussex was in pursuit of them. Mary wept when she heard that Northumberland, who seemed like an old friend to her, had fled with Westmorland into Scotland. Elizabeth's avenging army however, robbed of the leaders, did not hesitate to avenge themselves on their followers, and gibbets with their hideous burdens were now a feature of the northern roads – a grim warning to any who thought to follow the example of the rebels.

Now that the insurrection had been put down, there was no need for Mary to remain in Coventry. Elizabeth sent word that she was to be taken back to Tutbury and, as there would perhaps be attempts to rescue her on the way, if there were any danger of these being successful, Mary was to be executed rather than allowed to escape.

Elizabeth, deeply disturbed by the northern rebellion, believed now that there would be no peace in her realm while Mary lived; she longed for her death, yet she had no wish to be known as the one who had given the order for it.

If Mary died suddenly in an English castle there would be many to connect Elizabeth with the event. No matter what evidence was produced, suspicion would always attach itself to Elizabeth.

A letter from John Knox, written to Cecil – which that good and faithful servant immediately brought to his mistress – gave Elizabeth an idea which she determined to study.

John Knox raged against the Queen of Scots, while he congratulated Cecil on the suppression of the northern rebellion.

'But,' he wrote, 'if you strike not at the root, the branches which seem to be broken will bud again.'

That was clear enough. The root was Mary, Queen of Scots.

Elizabeth could trust Moray to know what to do with his half-sister if she were returned to Scotland, because he longed for her death as much as Elizabeth did; he had usurped her kingdom; would he greatly care if he were known throughout the world as her murderer?

First let her return to Tutbury; then a scheme could be devised for returning her to her unscrupulous brother.

In January Mary left Coventry for Tutbury.

CHAPTER TEN

TUTBURY AGAIN

MORAY RECEIVED the news from England with the calm which was second nature to him. Mary was an encumbrance of which he longed to be rid. He bore her no personal malice; had she not been a menace to his own power he could have been fond of her in so far as he was capable of affection. He wanted to see Scotland prosperous and at peace, and how could that be when rebel factions were continually springing up and making themselves felt, to the detriment of Scotland and his own dire danger?

275

Elizabeth was an uneasy ally. He believed he could trust Cecil, as much as a statesman could be trusted; for as both he and Cecil were stern Protestants therein lay the bond between them.

The time had come for the removal of Mary, and if she were returned to Scotland his first task would be to prove her worthy of death. Surely there was a good case against her. She had murdered her husband, and the just reward of murderesses – be they Queens or commoners – was surely death. True, many murders had been committed in Scotland and the victims had never been avenged. But, mused Moray, had their death been necessary for the good of the realm, and had those who would benefit been strong enough, those murderers would have gone the way he must now prepare for Mary.

Knowing Elizabeth, he realized that before long she would, with outward magnanimity, hand Mary over to her bastard brother – the understanding being that he should perform the deed with which Elizabeth had no wish to soil her hands.

Moray had many enemies in Scotland. He was a hard man and had never hesitated to act ruthlessly if the occasion warranted it. There was one incident which was characteristic of the manner in which he had shown the people his determination to be obeyed. It had taken place in the autumn when plague had struck Edinburgh, and he had ordered that when any man or woman was infected with the sickness, his or her family were to remove the sufferer without delay out of Edinburgh. That they must leave all they possessed was a condition they must accept. The Regent ordered that the family should leave, and leave it must – or incur his displeasure. There had been a husband, recently married, who, when his wife had been stricken, had kept this fact hidden, secretly nursing her in the comfort of his house, rather than take her out to die wretchedly in one of the surrounding villages where there was no suitable accommodation.

On the Regent's orders that young husband had been taken from his wife's bedside and hanged outside his own door.

To rule, one must be strong, the Regent believed. Mary had failed through sentimental weakness.

He had determined to treat Mary's followers with the same ruthlessness as he had shown to that young husband. He peremptorily ordered them to give up all their possessions, and set his Justice-Clerk, Sir John Bellenden, to make sure that the order was carried out.

In a country like Scotland, where it was not always easy to know who were one's friends, it was necessary to pay highly those who did the most unpleasant work which the Regent would rather not himself perform. Bellenden therefore looked for rewards and, as payment for his services, Moray bestowed on him the estate of Woodhouselee which belonged to one of Mary's most ardent supporters – a member of the Hamilton family, James Hamilton of Bothwellhaugh.

* * *

Alison Sinclair, wife of James Hamilton, lay in her bed, her young child, who had been born a few days before beside her. A great fire blazed in the fire place, for it was difficult to keep the rooms warm during such weather. Outside the snow was falling.

Alison was thinking of long ago days when she and her sister had knelt at the windows of this house looking out on the snow-covered countryside. She was remembering how they had been kept prisoners in the house by the weather and had amused themselves by playing hide and seek because it was such a wonderful house in which to hide. No matter where she went, she always thought of Woodhouselee as her home.

She had inherited it and brought it to James Hamilton when they married; and she believed it was as well, because now that James was more or less an outlaw, since he was the Queen's man, he had lost much of his own property; she was perpetually thankful that Woodhouselee, being her inheritance, was unassailable.

James was now in hiding with his kinsman, Archibald Hamilton. It was sad that the troubles of the time should mean so many separations; but she was sure that when he heard that their child had arrived he would find some means of coming to her.

While she lay thus musing she heard the sounds of arrival in the courtyard below, and called to her maid: 'He is here! I knew he would come. Go and bring him to me at once and make certain that no one leaves the house while he is here. I expect all my servants to be loyal, but how can one be sure in times such as these. And if Moray's men knew that he was here they would most certainly come to take him.'

Smiling down at her newly born child, she called for a mirror. It was some time since she had seen her husband and she was eager to look her best. She was delighted because

277

child-bearing had not changed her appearance, and she looked if anything younger than before. Perhaps that was because she was so happy. She had her baby . . . and now James had come to see them.

The door was flung open and a man stood on the threshold of the room. She was surprised rather than alarmed in those first seconds.

'But . . .' she stammered, 'who are you?'

'Sir John Bellenden,' was the answer, 'Justice-Clerk and owner of this house.'

'You are mistaken. This house belongs to me. My father left it to me.'

'You are wrong, Madam. It belongs to me. The estates of James Hamilton of Bothwellhaugh are confiscated by the Regent, and Woodhouselee is his gift to me for my services to Scotland.'

'This cannot be so. This house is not my husband's property, but mine.'

'Madam, that which was your property became your husband's on your marriage, and I tell you that all his possessions have passed out of his hands.'

'If my husband were here —'

'Alas, he is not. We should know how to deal with a traitor.'

'He is no traitor.'

'Come, Madam, he has worked against the King and has sought to bring back Mary to the throne.'

'You see my state. My child is but a few days old. Leave me in peace and this matter will doubtless be settled in due course.'

'I have come to take possession, and I must ask you to leave my house without a moment's delay.'

'You see how I am placed!'

'I see only that you trespass in my house.'

'Please leave me now. I am not strong yet . . . and I feel faint.'

'The fresh air will revive you. Come, Madam, rise from your bed. I shall give you five minutes in which to prepare to leave the house. If you have not gone in that time you will be forcibly evicted.'

With that he left her, and she lay listening to the sounds of heavy footsteps in other parts of the house. Her maid came to her bedside; she was weeping.

'What shall we do, Madam? What can we do?'

'They cannot mean that they will turn us out. They will take this house . . . my Woodhouselee . . . but not now. They must give me time. . . .'

She held her child tightly in her arms, and it was thus that Bellenden found her when he returned to the room.

'So you are obstinate,' he growled. 'Come, rise from that bed at once.' He turned to the maid. 'Find a cloak for her. She will need it . . . it is cold outside.'

For Alison what followed was as unreal as a nightmare, and as terrifying. Fainting, scarcely able to stand, she was forced to rise from her bed; a cloak was wrapped about her and, clasping her baby in her arms, she was turned out of doors.

The cold winds tore at her garments; the snow was falling so thickly that she could not see. The baby began to cry but she could not comfort him.

She tried to grope her way to the woods, where she believed she might find some shelter. She plunged through the snow, weeping and calling for her husband to come and help her.

There was no one abroad on such a night and, although Alison knew the surrounding country well, the heavy snow-drifts had changed its contours, and soon she was lost.

She stumbled on; she believed she had reached the woods but was not sure as, clutching the baby tightly to her, she fell into a deep drift.

*　　*　　*

When news of the fate of his wife and child was brought to James Hamilton of Bothwellhaugh, who was at that time living secretly at Linlithgow in the house of his kinsman, Archibald Hamilton, his grief was uncontrollable. But it was soon replaced by a rage that was even greater, and the only way in which he could bear to go on living at that time was to plan revenge.

Bellenden was in residence at Woodhouselee, and it was certain that there would be a strong guard about him, for it was believed that Bothwellhaugh would not be able to resist taking his revenge on the man who had sent his wife and child so callously to their death.

But, reasoned Bothwellhaugh, and the whole Hamilton clan were with him in this, there was one who was more to blame than Bellenden. That was the man who set a ruthless example to his lieutenants; it was the man who would shrug callous shoulders when he heard of the tragedy at Woodhouselee, and wish everyone to know that such a fate was to be expected by all those who disobeyed the Regent's orders.

Bothwellhaugh would assuage his grief, not by the assassination of the insignificant Bellenden, but by that of the Regent Moray.

*   *   *

On the 23rd day of January Moray would pass through Linlithgow on his way to Edinburgh, and Bothwellhaugh was ready for him. He had concealed himself in a house where the High Street was at its most narrow. At this point the cavalcade in which the Regent rode would be slowed down, and moreover it was impossible for more than two to ride abreast. The house backed onto fields; and in the fields a saddled horse was waiting.

Bothwellhaugh, spurred, ready for flight, watching behind latticed windows, was thinking of Alison – lying abed, the child in her arms, waiting for him, of her wandering blindly through the snow, of her terrible end. When he thought of this his fingers grew steady and he knew with cold certainty that when he took aim he would not miss.

At the lattice windows were hangings to conceal him; in these he had cut a hole only large enough to take the muzzle of his harquebuss. There were four bullets in that harquebuss. He intended to make no mistake.

Now the cavalcade was turning into the High Street, and Bothwellhaugh, concealed by the hangings, could peep through them and watch its progress. At its head he rode – the Regent Moray, the man who, as much as that other, was the murderer of his dear Alison. Bothwellhaugh only needed to remember that, and he could feel quite cool and calm.

The Regent was almost abreast of the window. Now was the moment.

Bothwellhaugh took careful aim; and when he saw Moray fall forward, saw the red blood staining his jacket, he knew that he had avenged Alison and their baby.

He heard the shouts as he ran from the room, down to the garden, leaped onto his horse and was a mile away before Moray's men had succeeded in breaking into the barricaded house.

Bothwellhaugh had flown to Hamilton; and the Regent Moray's turbulent life was ended.

*   *   *

Jamie dead! Mary could not believe the news when it was brought to her.

She pictured him, riding at the head of his men – vigorously living one moment; and the next slipping away to death.

She wept for the Jamie she had known as a child when she had believed him to be her friend. She had loved him then, and she had found it difficult not to go on loving him. He was clever; he was meant to be a ruler; he was his father's son; she had understood more than most, the terrible frustration he had suffered because he was not the King's legitimate son. She, who was that King's legitimate daughter and heir, could forgive Jamie more readily than most of her friends could do.

Seton came to her and found her weeping.

'Your Majesty should dry your eyes,' she said. 'This should prove no hardship to you. He was never your friend, and of late years your most bitter enemy.'

'All that is over now, Seton,' Mary replied sorrowfully. 'He is gone to his Maker, and I can only remember my big brother . . . whom once I thought to be my friend.'

'Then Your Majesty should remember his conduct to you since Carberry Hill. Most of your sufferings can be traced to him.'

'Perhaps I should, Seton, but I was never one to do what I should. My emotions will always command my actions; and I can only think of Jamie in the days when I loved him so dearly and thought I was the luckiest girl in Scotland to have him for my brother. So leave me now, and since you cannot share my grief, let me mourn in secret.'

So Seton left her with her memories of the young Jamie; and as the Queen wept for the past, which might have been so different, her faithful friends were asking each other what difference this would make to her future.

*　　*　　*

Elizabeth was horrified by the assassination of the Regent, whom she had looked upon as an ally and who was ready to obey her wishes; it had been part of her plan to keep him ruler of Scotland; she had also of late wished him to rid her of the Queen of Scots.

It had been an obsession with Elizabeth – since the rising of Northern Catholics – that she must rid herself of Mary; and to find this plan – which had seemed to her the only safe one –

foiled by Moray's assassination, made her for the time being almost frantic.

Her first action was to seize the person of Mary's ambassador to England, Lesley, Bishop of Ross, and send him to the Tower.

She saw at once that her fears had not been without grounds. Mary's friends in Scotland, led by Huntley and Argyle, marched on Edinburgh. Kirkcaldy of Grange, who was keeper of the Castle and regretted his disloyalty to the Queen at Carberry Hill when he led Moray's forces, had joined the lords of the Highlands. Fernyhirst, who had once offered Mary refuge in his castle if she could escape her English captors, marched across the border. And Leonard Dacre, on whose behalf Mary had pleaded effectively with Norfolk so that Dacre had not lost all his family possessions, gathered together three thousand men, and there was a new rising in the North.

If only Mary could escape, there was an army waiting to fall in behind her.

Huntingdon and the Shrewsburys, realizing the danger, doubled the guard at Tutbury; for they knew that fresh schemes for rescuing the Queen were being set in motion, and they believed that never had Mary's chances of escape been so good.

Mary, however, thought constantly of Norfolk in the Tower. There was one thing she needed more than freedom; and that was affection. Generous as she was, she poured out her affection on any who were ready to receive it; and although she knew Norfolk only through his letters, she was prepared to give him the devotion she had always longed to give a husband.

She wanted to be loyal; she wanted to make sacrifices; she was striving towards that perfect relationship which in her three previous marriages she had not attained.

'Mine own good Lord,' she wrote, 'I would know your pleasure if I should seek to make some enterprise. If it please you I care not for my danger. . . .'

There was no answer from Norfolk, and she wrote again:

'If you think the danger too great, do as you think best, and let me know what you please that I do, for I will be for your sake perpetual prisoner, or put my life in peril for your weal and mine. . . .'

And she signed this letter 'Your own faithful to death Queen of Scots, my Norfolk.'

When Norfolk received the letter he sweated with terror.

Did she not know that, since the death of Moray, she was being watched more closely than ever before? He was not risking his head to write love letters.

*   *   *

Mary believed that she was now living through the most dangerous weeks of her life. Her enemy and father-in-law, the Earl of Lennox, was the new Regent; and all Scotland was aflame.

But Elizabeth had no intention of allowing Mary to be reinstated; she subdued the rebellion in England as she had that led by Northumberland; and she sent Sussex to Scotland with seven thousand troops to teach Mary's supporters a lesson. Lord Scrope followed Sussex, and Sir William Drury laid waste many a Scottish community which had declared loyalty to the Queen.

Each day melancholy news was brought to Mary of the suffering of her supporters, who could not hold out against the military superiority of the English.

That winter and early spring were desperate days, and in addition to her sorrow and despair Mary suffered the return of the pains in her limbs and the sickness which seemed to her to grow out of the contaminated air of Tutbury.

She found small comfort in her tapestry and the companionship of her faithful friends. Bess and George Talbot were friendly, but she knew that they were – as they must be – spies for their Queen. They were not harsh jailors, but they were determined not to let her escape.

'How I wish,' she told Bess, 'that I could ride out into the country now and then. I should love to have my horses again; I always had my dogs, for I love the creatures. I sadly miss having no animals of my own.'

'It may be that some day the Queen will consent to your having pets if you wish for them,' was all Bess offered. Yet Mary believed that, had Bess decided she might have a little dog, she would not have thought it necessary to ask the Queen's permission.

There was some good news. When Scotland was defeated and there was no longer any hope that an army of Mary's faithful followers would come marching to Tutbury to rescue her, Elizabeth released the Bishop of Ross from the Tower.

But even when Scotland was subdued, there were continuous

arrests of those who had rebelled in the North and many were taken to London, tortured, and finally subjected to the horrible traitor's death. Mary knew that these men were tortured in the hope that they would betray her as having urged them to rebel against the Queen of England.

Each day when she arose she wondered whether it would be her last on Earth; every time there was an arrival at the castle she wondered whether an order had been brought to conduct her to the Tower.

*　　　*　　　*

The Earl of Shrewsbury had recovered from his sickness, and the gentleness Bess had shown him during his illness had disappeared. She was sharp and domineering, and there were times when George Talbot deeply regretted having married her.

Often he would find himself comparing her with two women – the Queen and the serving maid.

He was deeply aware of Eleanor Britton and it seemed to him that in the course of the day he saw more of her than he did of any other person. Perhaps he was always aware of her; perhaps he sought her out, and she was eager to be sought. When he sent for a serving girl, it was often Eleanor who came; he found himself thinking of the tasks he could give to one of the serving girls; thus she came often to his apartments.

It was dusk and when he had sent for a girl to light a fire in his ante-chamber, it was Eleanor who came, graceful, hesitant yet eager, her coarse gown cut low to show her white skin; her apron clean, having been hastily donned since she was to come to him; her hair was hidden by her cap and he felt an irresistible urge to see it.

'My lord desires a fire?' she asked in her gentle voice.

He nodded.

She said: 'I have just lighted one in the Queen's apartments, where my lady sits with Her Majesty. They are together at the tapestry.'

She did not move as he came towards her.

He took off her cap, and her hair fell about her shoulders; it was long, thick and gold-coloured.

'It seems a shame to hide it,' he murmured.

She was waiting breathlessly for what would happen next; although she knew; and he knew; for in that moment they both realized that this was inevitable. This was what they had been waiting for since they had first become aware of each other.

*   *   *

During that long winter, Mary suffered greatly from the rigours of Tutbury. She was longing for the spring to come. When she received the news that a Papal Bull had been obtained, which dissolved her marriage with Bothwell on the grounds of rape, she was devoid of emotion. There was one thing it did teach her though; she was free of Bothwell in all ways. She no longer thought of him as her husband; she thought of herself as a widow – Darnley's widow – and it was as though that most turbulent relationship had never existed.

She longed to change her state of widowhood. Sometimes she would call Seton, Jane and the others to her and discuss the gowns she would have made after her marriage. It would be wonderful, she told them, to have beautiful clothes again. 'I shall have some little dogs,' she declared. 'Oh, how I long to be free again!'

Of the desires which were nearest to her heart she spoke rarely. Most of all she longed to see her son again. He was a sturdy little fellow now and the letters she enjoyed receiving most were those which contained some scrap of news of him. He was astonishing his tutors by his cleverness, for he had a natural aptitude for book learning. He was in the charge of the Earl and Countess of Mar who, like all her enemies, did their best to make her son forget he had a mother. But he was a wise little boy, and obstinate; she learned that he asked questions only of those who he believed would give him truthful answers.

So it was a delightful daydream to picture herself in the company of her son, with her husband beside her. She had endowed Norfolk with all the qualities she looked for in a husband. It was true that she had seen him rarely, but she knew him to be young and personable; they had corresponded frequently since those days when Lady Scrope had smuggled letters in and out of Bolton Castle. She believed that he was serious, devoted, affectionate and wise – everything that she longed for in a husband. She would not believe that she had created a myth out of her own desires and desperate need.

Those were happy days which brought a letter from Norfolk or one containing news of her son; and doubly precious were those letters since there was such a risk in sending and receiving them.

One day there came a letter from an old French servant of hers who had found service in young James's household.

She wrote: 'When Lady Mar inquires of him whom he loves best, his mother or her, he replies boldly, although he knows the answer will displease: "My Mother." '

Mary sat reading those words again and again, and when Seton came to her she found her seated in her chair holding the letter against her breast while the tears fell unheeded.

*　　*　　*

Bess came into the Queen's apartment, her face alight with satisfaction.

'Good news, Your Majesty. Huntingdon has received his marching orders.'

Mary showed her relief. She understood, of course. The rebellion in Scotland was quashed; the Queen of England believed she need not fear the Catholics of the North. It was possible to relax the rigorous rules which it had been necessary to impose during such disturbances.

'I guessed that you would be pleased,' went on Bess, 'So now Shrewsbury and I are in sole charge. I can tell Your Majesty, you cannot be more pleased than I. The idea of having that man . . . in my house . . . giving his orders, enraged me.'

'It was the price you paid for disobeying the Queen's orders.'

Bess smiled triumphantly. 'I do believe that Shrewsbury would not be here today if I had not insisted on his taking the baths.' She studied Mary. 'Your Majesty would benefit from a trip to Buxton. I must speak to the Queen. Not immediately though. We are still not quite back in favour.'

'You believe that the baths would help to rid me of these pains in my limbs?'

Bess who had never felt a pain herself nodded vigorously. Let the Queen believe she was receiving the right treatment, and her pains would disappear. The only illnesses Bess believed in were those which were manifest by some outward sign. For instance, when the Earl had been unable to speak or move she accepted the fact that he was very ill. Mary's ailments, she believed, grew out of boredom produced by captivity.

'I will suggest it later. In the meantime I have written to Her

Majesty to tell her that you are melancholy in this place and that it does not suit your health. I have asked for a move.'

'And you think she will agree?'

'I have every hope that she will. I long to see Chatsworth and show Your Majesty the house which I built with Cavendish.'

Chatsworth! mused Mary. It would be good to escape from Tutbury. The summer was coming and there would not be the bitter cold to be borne; but the odours were more objectionable in the warm weather. And a move was always a matter of interest.

Then she was alarmed, wondering whether it would be as easy to keep up her correspondence with the Duke of Norfolk at Chatsworth as it was at Tutbury.

CHAPTER ELEVEN

CHATSWORTH

BESS WAS IN high spirits because her household was leaving Tutbury for Chatsworth. Not only was that mansion one of the most beautiful in England, but she herself had created it. Of course her second husband, William Cavendish, had been of some assistance, but Bess thought of Chatsworth as hers. Had she been a woman for regrets she would have regretted the death of William Cavendish because he had been the most satisfactory of her husbands. Perhaps this was partly due to the fact that he had provided her with her six children, whose affairs were of the utmost importance to her, and made her life so interesting. No, it was more than that. William had been a good husband in every way – far more so than George Talbot who, Bess must confess, was the least commendable of the four.

Of late he had changed towards her; he seemed somewhat absentminded; he accepted her reproaches almost with indifference, as though he were brushing away a fly which only mildly irritated him.

He was often in the company of the Queen of Scots. Could it really be that she reciprocated his admiration? Bess would not say that her George was the most likely man to attract a

Queen who, all her life until she had been taken into captivity, had been a magnet for the flattery and attention of the opposite sex. But Mary was now a prisoner; her retinue was restricted; it was true she had her faithful friends, and Bess believed that many of the male members of the suite entertained romantic feelings for Mary. But the Earl was the most powerful man in her circle; and there was attraction in power. Mary was a woman who needed men about her. Could it really be possible?

Bess laughed aloud at the thought. She had often teased her husband about Mary, but she had not really taken the matter seriously. And if it were true, how would she feel? Jealous? Certainly. Bess desired to possess every member of her family completely. She wanted absolute obedience from them, and all the admiration and affection of which they were capable.

No. This was no love affair. It was one of those airy romantic relationships- because the Queen, who was very beautiful, was also a helpless woman.

It did not go beyond that and Bess would make the Earl understand that it should not do so. She herself would spend more time with Mary when they were at Chatsworth; *she* was going to be the Queen's best friend . . . not George.

And she would not hesitate to ridicule George's devotion. She would let him – and Mary – see that although the Earl was ostensibly in charge, in truth that was a role which fate had assigned to Bess of Hardwick, wherever she found herself.

*   *   *

It was a bright May day when the Queen and her household, accompanied by the Earl and Countess and theirs, set out from Tutbury, their destination being Chatsworth.

Mary could not help being charmed when she saw the lovely manor of Chatsworth. She had ridden through country which was both wild and grand, and when she saw the house she understood Bess's pride in it. It was situated on the east bank of the Derwent almost at the base of a thickly wooded hill. As she approached the quadrangular and turreted building Mary was asking herself for how long it would be her new prison.

Riding up to the mansion they were joined by a party of horsemen, and the Countess told Mary that this was made up of the nobles of the neighbourhood who, hearing of the Queen's expected arrival, had come to pay their respects to her.

Mary was delighted by this attention and asked that the visitors be presented to her; and in the hall of Chatsworth she learned that these were led by two sons of the Earl of Derby, Thomas and Edward Stanley, and a certain Sir Thomas Gerard, a Mr Rolleston and Mr Hall, landowners of the district.

Because the weather was benign, because she had left the hateful Tutbury behind her, Mary was in high spirits; and it was obvious to all how much she had charmed the young men.

When they had left, Mary was conducted to her apartments, and she was grateful to Bess who had arranged that she should have a suite of rooms in accordance with her rank.

Bess, determined to win Mary's confidence, accepted the Queen's thanks with a show of pleasure.

'I would that I could offer Your Majesty a horse to ride,' she said, 'but you know that to do so would be to ignore Queen Elizabeth's express command. However, there is a little garden, not far from the house, which I can offer you and in which I think you will be able to spend some happy hours while you must remain at Chatsworth.'

Mary asked to be shown this garden and Bess led her out of the manor to a small lake which was almost concealed by thick foliage. In the centre of this lake was a tower and to approach it it was necessary to cross a stone bridge. With Bess, Mary entered the tower and climbed the spiral staircase to a flat roof. On this flowers, and even trees, had been planted. About the garden was a balustrade, beautifully carved, and from it there was a superb view of the surrounding country.

'It is very beautiful,' Mary murmured.

'Then while Your Majesty stays with us, it shall be your garden.'

'Thank you. I shall enjoy it.' Mary smiled ruefully. 'I doubt not that when I visit it I shall be accompanied by guards. They will wait for me at the bridge, but perhaps they will not come with me to my tower-top garden, because it would be impossible for me to escape from there.'

'I beg Your Majesty not to despair,' Bess comforted. 'Now that we have rid ourselves of the zealous Huntingdon, I shall sue the Queen for favours for you. I know she will agree to what I ask, in time.'

Mary laid her hand on Bess's arm.

'At least,' she said with a smile, 'if I must have a jailor, I could not have a more kindly one.'

And in a very short time she became attached to her garden and planted flowers of her own choice. She and Seton or Jane Kennedy and Marie Courcelles went there often. It was exhilarating to look across the country from the top of the tower, even though she knew that guards were stationed at the bridge, that they would take their stand all round the lake, that they would accompany her back to the manor when she went, and that they would be posted at all important spots.

She was a prisoner, but she could live more comfortably at Chatsworth than she had at Tutbury.

* * *

She had not been long at Chatsworth when Seton brought a letter to her.

'It was given to me by one of the servants who is a friend of a butler in the house of the Earl of Derby,' she was told.

Mary read the letter which contained an impassioned appeal from Thomas and Edward Stanley, who declared themselves ready to die in her cause. They were making plans for her escape. Other gentlemen who had had the honour of seeing her on her arrival were with them, and they proposed to write to her in cipher which was being worked out for them by a priest in the house of Mr Rolleston. Would she allow them to make plans? They could arrange for letters to be smuggled in and out of the house.

Mary in her reply thanked them for their good efforts on her behalf; she was, however affianced to the Duke of Norfolk and could do nothing without his consent. She would however write and tell him of their proposals, and they would be hearing from her in due course.

Norfolk's reply was noncommittal, yet he did not altogether banish the idea of using the young men of Derbyshire. He wrote that it might not be wise for those young men to meddle at this time, when Elizabeth might be prepared to treat her as she should be treated; but if such a plan were to be put into action, Derby's sons were the sort of men he would like to see at its head.

Thus encouraged, the conspirators brought Lesley, Bishop of Ross, into the plan; and because he, having lived close to Elizabeth and having been her prisoner, had a more intimate knowledge of what could be expected at her hands, he was inclined to view any attempt to escape with favour.

Thus the summer months were enlivened with these plans

and, as it was always a matter for rejoicing when letters were safely smuggled into the house, and as without this kind of excitement life would have been intolerably dull, Mary indulged once more in dreams of escape.

The plan was progressing. Mary was to escape from her window by means of a cord; horses were to be waiting and she was to be conducted to Harwich where a ship would be ready to sail for Flanders.

News of this plan leaked out and was discussed in the inns and taverns of the Duke of Norfolk's territory. He was in the Tower, and the people of Norfolk grumbled to one another that it was not justice that their own Duke should be kept in the Tower merely because he had thought of marrying.

At Harleston Fair one man stood on a platform and addressed the crowds. Where was their Duke, he demanded of them. Was it fitting that a noble Duke – their own Duke of Norfolk – should be kept a prisoner in the Tower? The Duke's place was in Norfolk with his own people.

There were shouts of agreement and very soon several hundreds had collected to shout their disapproval of a Queen who had thrown their own Duke into the Tower when he had committed no crime.

'We'll march to the Tower!' cried the man who had first spoken. 'We'll burn down the place and we'll bring our Duke back to Norfolk where he belongs.'

The march began; but before it had gone more than a few miles it was intercepted by the Queen's soldiers who promptly arrested the ringleaders and hanged them on the nearest trees, while the rest of the rioters turned and fled for their lives.

The disturbance was ended almost before it began, but when news of what had happened reached Elizabeth's ears she was uneasy. Nothing could depress her so utterly as a rising of her subjects against her. She was not afraid of her ministers; she knew how to deal with them. One step to the Tower and the next to the block were easily accomplished. But loss of popularity with the common people was her constant dread.

Whenever she experienced it – however slight, however remote – she always knew that, if only for her peace of mind, something had to be done.

*   *   *

In his gloomy prison in the Tower Norfolk was growing more and more uneasy.

Each time a letter was brought to him, very often concealed in the cork of an ale bottle, he trembled; he could not help wondering when the ruse would be discovered; it was ironical that he, who had vowed that he would never become involved in treason, should be caught up in the intrigues surrounding Mary Queen of Scots.

Marriage with her would be a big prize and therefore perhaps he would have to take a risk or two.

But there were occasions when, gazing up at the bars in his cell or leaning against the cold stone wall, he wondered if he would ever be released and whether, when he was, it would be to make that short journey, which so many had taken before him, to Tower Hill, with the blade of the executioner's axe turned towards him.

Now there was plague in the prison. All knew that in such an atmosphere it could spread like fire in a gale, so perhaps he would be taken out in his coffin.

His keeper, Sir Henry Neville, who had been specially appointed by the Queen to watch over him, treated him with the respect due to his rank; but he knew that if the Queen gave the order for his execution, Neville would not hesitate to do all that was required of him. There was little hope of his ever leaving this prison unless Elizabeth relented.

Neville came into his cell, and they sat at the small table playing cards, as they often did to pass the time.

'How goes the plague?' asked Norfolk.

'Bad . . . very bad.'

Norfolk studied the cards, but he was not thinking of the game.

'Would to God I could go back to the country. I should keep well away from Court, I do assure you.'

'And you'd be wise in that,' answered Neville. 'There have been riots in Norfolk and that does not please the Queen. Some of your men at a fair, I hear, wanted to know why you were being kept a prisoner in London.'

'The devil they did!' said the Duke with a smile. 'And what was the Queen's answer to that?'

'Short and swift. The ringleaders are now swinging on gibbets, a warning to any Norfolk yeomen who shout "A Howard!"'

'Then I fear that has done me little good.'

'None, I fear. Nor will any good be done you until there is

no longer talk of a marriage between you and the Queen of Scots.'

Norfolk nodded grimly. Yet, he thought, the project is too far gone to be lightly abandoned. Who knows from one moment to another, when Elizabeth herself might be set down and another put in her place? What if Mary were made Queen of England and he had been short-sighted enough to break his engagement with her?

He remembered an occasion when he had denied to Elizabeth that he had any pretensions to marriage with Mary. He had said that he would not feel safe on his pillow, married to such a one. That had satisfied Elizabeth at the time, he had believed; but she had referred to that phrase of his later when, full of suspicion that he might be in negotiation with Mary, she had suddenly leaned towards him when she sat at supper, nipped his arm firmly between her fingers and thumb and warned him that he should look to his pillow.

He could still feel the terror of occasions like that; it brought back memories of the day when he had heard that his father had lost his head because a sovereign willed it.

He turned to the card game and went on playing in silence.

While they were at play a messenger arrived with documents for Neville and for Norfolk.

They were from the Queen.

Elizabeth was grieved to think of my lord of Norfolk wasting his days and nights in the Tower. She liked not to hear that plague had penetrated the fortress. She was inclined to be lenient, and she was going to offer Norfolk a chance to leave his prison. He might return to his own house at the Charterhouse, whither Sir Henry Neville would accompany him, that the Queen might rest happily assured that he made no mischief. This she would grant him permission to do and asked only one concession in return. He must sign a document in which he solemnly pledged his word that he would not marry the Queen of Scots nor take part in her affairs without first obtaining the consent to do so from his Sovereign, Elizabeth.

When he and Neville had read these documents they regarded each other in sombre silence.

Neville said: 'It is the chance you have been praying for Take it.'

Norfolk's weak face was creased in almost petulant exasperation.

'Think of what she asks!' he cried. 'How can I give my word

to give up the Queen of Scots, after the solemn promises we have made each other?'

But even as he spoke he knew he would.

*   *   *

William Cecil, accompanied by Sir Walter Mildmay and Lesley, Bishop of Ross, was riding towards Chatsworth.

He was thoughtful as he rode, wondering how far he could trust Lesley; the man had been imprisoned once and managed to escape with his life, but there were so many plots and counterplots surrounding the Queen of Scots that Cecil was not prepared to trust any one of her servants. He would keep a watchful eye on Lesley.

The matter was more serious than was generally believed – although the fact that Cecil thought it worth-while making the journey to Chatsworth might cause some to realize its seriousness. While the Queen of Scots lived, his sovereign Elizabeth was in danger; and Cecil had made up his mind that if Elizabeth would not agree to the execution of her rival – and Cecil had to admit there was logic and good sound sense in her reason for this – then the lady's claws must be clipped. There must be no more Catholic risings. By great good luck these had been suppressed on previous occasions, but it was possible that good fortune might not always be on the side of Cecil and Elizabeth.

It was all very well for a Protestant Queen and her even more fervently Protestant ministers to snap their fingers when Pius V excommunicated Elizabeth. There were too many powerful Catholics in England, too many even more powerful Catholic rulers abroad, waiting for that moment when they too could add their disapproval to the Pope's.

And the trouble centre was wherever the Queen of Scots happened to be. Chatsworth at this time.

So to Chatsworth rode Cecil, with his own little plan for rendering the Queen of Scots no longer a danger to his mistress. The most disastrous turn of events could be if Mary escaped from England to France or Spain and there was married to some Catholic Prince. This must be avoided at all cost. Cecil would have felt happier to see her head severed from her body; only thus, he believed, could she cease to be a menace; but failing that, he wished to see her make a Protestant marriage to an Englishman of his and his Queen's choosing. This was the reason for his making the journey to Chatsworth.

When Mary heard that Cecil had arrived and was asking to see her, she was astonished. This was the man whom she believed to be her greatest enemy; at the same time she knew that he was the man who could do her most good if he were so inclined. It was in a mood swaying between hope and apprehension that she greeted him in that room which she called her presence chamber.

They faced each other – the tall and strikingly beautiful woman and the small, deformed statesman. Mildmay was present but from the first Mary was aware that this was a duel between her and Cecil. Mary was trembling with emotion; the steely eyes of Cecil were as cold as ice.

They bowed low and Mary told them that she was glad to see them. She was ready to be friendly, to forget all the wrong she knew Cecil had done to her; it was he who was aloof.

'I trust,' began Mary, 'that you bring me good news of my sister and cousin.'

'Her Majesty is made sad by your reproaches,' Cecil told Mary. 'She is astounded that, as she has given you refuge for so long, you should be so ungrateful as to offer her continual complaint.'

'Refuge!' cried Mary angrily. 'Is a prison refuge?'

'Doubtless Your Majesty owes your life to the Queen of England who preserved you from the anger of your own subjects.'

'That life,' Mary cried impetuously, 'has scarce been worth the living since I came to England.'

Cecil looked shocked. 'I shall be loth to report your further complaints to Her Majesty.'

'She, who has suffered imprisonment herself, will understand full well if you ask her to recall that period of her life. I should have thought one who had experienced that would have had greater sympathy for me in my plight.'

Cecil raised his hands as though in horror and turned to Mildmay, whose expression showed that he shared Cecil's horror for what they were pleased to consider the ingratitude of the Queen of Scots.

'Tell me,' she went on passionately, 'will the Queen of England restore me to my throne? She has power to do this, I am fully aware. But I would know her intentions. Is she going to help me or not?'

'Your Majesty is distraught,' murmured Cecil. 'Would you care to discuss these matters when you are a little calmer?'

'I want to hear now.'

'Well then, Her Majesty will restore you to your throne. There are certain conditions.'

'I had thought that most likely,' interjected Mary.

Cecil went on coldly: 'She would require your son to be brought to England, and to remain here as a hostage.'

The mention of her son moved Mary so deeply that she found she could not check the tears which started to her eyes.

'He should live here,' Cecil was going on, 'in some honourable place under the guardianship of two or three Scottish gentlemen. The Queen would most graciously allow you to name one of them. The others would be chosen according to the advice of his grandfather, the Earl of Lennox, and the Earl of Mar.'

The tears had begun to fall down her cheeks. She did not see these two hard-faced men. She saw only that little boy, puzzled, wondering why he never saw his mother, perhaps hearing tales of her. Where is my father? he would ask. Would anyone tell him: 'The victim of bloody murder at Kirk o' Field . . . murder in which your mother is suspected of being an accomplice!' Yet when they had asked him whom he loved best – Lady Mar who had been a mother to him, or his own mother, he had answered boldly: My mother.

She wanted to hold the child in her arms, to teach him, to play with him. And now she knew that the bitterest punishment of all had been the loss of her child.

Cecil and Mildmay were looking at her in dismay. She could only cover her face with her hands and murmur: 'Leave me. I pray you leave me.'

*   *   *

Lesley came to her apartment and she was able to see him in private, although it was an uneasy interview because every moment Mary thought they would be interrupted and prevented from speaking without the presence of a witness.

Lesley said: 'This may be our only opportunity. I think it is imperative that you escape from here. The Queen grows restive and I feel sure will do you some harm. This plot which the Stanleys are making must be taken advantage of. If you can escape from Chatsworth and get to Harwich, I feel sure that in a very short time you will be back on the Scottish throne. But let us not waste time.'

He went to the window and looked down. 'The descent could be made by means of a cord. Let Mary Seton have a word with Willie Douglas. Do not do so yourself. You are being closely watched. But you must break out of here as soon as possible. Cecil's visit shows that Elizabeth is truly alarmed.'

'I do not think the Duke of Norfolk believes an escape should be made, although he has said the Stanleys are worthy to head such an attempt.'

'He fears that you will marry Don Jon. I am not thinking of your marriage but of your life. I am going to tell the Stanleys that the attempt should be made as soon as possible. You must be ready.'

Mary was silent. She was still thinking of her little son who was being brought up away from her. How many lies were fed to him, she wondered. She had suffered much, but if he ever turned against her, if he ever believed the tales of her which no doubt were told to him, she would become so melancholy that she would long for nothing but death.

Escape! A return to her throne! It would mean reunion with her little son.

She listened attentively to Lesley.

*　　*　　*

Cecil faced the Queen once more.

'I rejoice to see that Your Majesty's condition is improved,' he said; which was his way of telling her that he was pleased she had recovered from what he would regard as a fit of hysteria.

Mary bowed her head and waited.

'Her Majesty the Queen is deeply concerned on your behalf,' he told her. 'She thinks that, having known the married state, you might be happier in it than living celibate. Therefore she is ready to suggest a marriage for you.'

Mary was attentive. She knew that Norfolk had been released from the Tower. Did this mean that Elizabeth was ready to approve of the match?

'Her Majesty proposes that you accept her kinsman, George Carey, son of Lord Hunsdon, as your husband.'

'That is not possible,' answered Mary.

'If Your Majesty is thinking of your marriage to Bothwell, that has been happily dealt with and is not regarded as a marriage.'

297

Mary was silent. She could not tell Cecil that she was pledged to Norfolk, for the contract between them had been a secret. She could only shake her head and murmur: 'It is not possible.'

Cecil was alert. The Queen of Scots was without guile. There was some reason why she was so emphatic. If reports did not lie she had been friendly towards George Carey when he had visited her. There was some plot afoot, he believed; some reason why she was so set against the proposed marriage. Had she her eyes on Don Jon? The romantic hero would undoubtedly appeal to such a woman as she was.

He did not press the point, but turned from it to talk of the kindness of his mistress, Queen Elizabeth, who sought to help the Queen of Scots, if she would but let herself be helped.

All the time he was thinking: We must increase our watchfulness. On no account must she be allowed to slip out of our hands, out of England to our enemies across the water.

*   *   *

Mary forgot the presence of the English statesman at Chatsworth, for one of her most trusted friends had been stricken with sickness. This was John Beaton, the Laird of Creich, who had been the master of her household. He had been working zealously in her cause ever since she had escaped from Lochleven, and to see him on his sickbed filled her with such anxiety that she forgot her own concerns.

Seton shared her distress and wanted to nurse him herself. Mary agreed, that she should, and added that she too would act as nurse, for John was so grievously sick that he needed the two of them.

So day and night Seton and Mary remained in the sickroom; but it soon became pitiably obvious that there was nothing they could do to save John's life.

Seton was alone in the sickroom one evening while Mary was taking a little rest, when a young man came in and stood at the end of the bed looking at the sick man. His face was so marked with anguish that Seton rose and, going to him, laid a hand on his shoulder.

'You must not grieve so much, Andrew,' she said.

'My brother is going to die,' said Andrew Beaton.

'I am going to send for the Bishop now, Andrew. I think the time has come.'

'I will bring him here.'

When he had gone Seton placed a cool cloth on the sick man's fevered forehead and sat beside his bed waiting, for there was nothing else she could do. In a short time Lesley came back with Andrew Beaton and looked grave when he saw the appearance of the sick man.

'We will leave you with him,' said Seton, and slipping her arm through that of Andrew Beaton she drew him from the room.

Outside they stood silently for a few seconds, then Andrew said: 'I know how you have nursed him . . . you and the Queen. How can I thank you?'

'There is no need to thank us, Andrew,' answered Seton. 'We are exiles . . . we are prisoners . . . we work together, and if any one of us has trouble, that is the trouble of us all.'

He took her hand then and kissed it.

He thought there was something ethereal about Mary Seton – something saintly, not of this world. It seemed to him in that moment that he had never seen a face so beautiful.

He walked slowly away; he knew that he loved Mary Seton.

* * *

Cecil was feeling that his visit to Chatsworth was a failure. He had achieved nothing through his interview with Mary except a sensation of great unease. He would return to Court and tell the Queen that he felt she should be moved from Chatsworth. A move was always a good thing at such a time – unsettling to conspirators.

It was while he was musing thus that a servant came to tell him that a young man, calling himself by the name of Rolleston, wished to see him; the matter was of great urgency.

Cecil, who had never heard the young man's name before, hesitated; then said he would see the man. One could never be sure where important information might come from, and he had not reached his present eminence by ignoring such a rule.

Rolleston turned out to be a very young man, scarcely more than a boy, with the earnest eyes of a fanatic.

'What is it you have to say to me?' Cecil asked him.

'I have to tell you, sir, that I know of a plot to rescue the Queen from Chatsworth and put her on a boat at Harwich.'

Cecil showed no sign of the excitement he was feeling.

'Tell me more of this plot,' he said quietly.

'Thomas and Edward Stanley are at its head. They plan that the Queen shall escape from her window by means of a cord. It is arranged with her servants, and will very shortly take place.'

'Are you involved in this plot?'

The boy flushed painfully and drew himself up to his full height. 'I am a loyal subject of my Queen Elizabeth. I take no part in plots against her.'

'Well spoken,' replied Cecil. 'How then do you know of this plot?'

The boy hesitated as though he were fighting an inner battle with his conscience. Then he blurted out: 'Because my father is involved in it.'

'You have done well,' said Cecil. 'The Queen will not forget one who serves her. Now the names of the conspirators . . . and all the details you have. I believe we have little time to lose.'

*   *   *

When the chief conspirators were under arrest, Cecil wrote to Elizabeth telling of what was happening at Chatsworth.

'It would seem, Your Majesty, that the Queen of Scots enjoys too much liberty at Chatsworth. It might be advisable to remove her from that place. Shrewsbury could take her to his castle in Sheffield, which to my mind would be a meet and fitting place to house her.'

CHAPTER TWELVE

SHEFFIELD

IT WAS ON a bleak November day that Mary travelled over the mountains from Chatsworth to Sheffield. Through the mist she caught her first glimpse of her new prison, which stood on a hill above that spot where the rivers Don and Sheaf met, the latter giving its name to the nearby town. The fame of this town was already known to Mary because it was noted for the mineral wealth which had enabled its inhabitants to become the foremost manufacturers of edged tools such as knives, spear and arrow heads.

The Earl had decided that she should not go at once to the castle but occupy the more cosy Manor House which was about two miles from it and in the centre of a wooded park.

Bess had pointed out that the Queen would find Sheffield less comfortable than Chatsworth, and that as the winter lay before them the Manor House would provide a more congenial lodging than the castle.

So to the Manor House came Mary. On that day when the trees were dripping with moisture, and the spiders' webs, draped over the bushes, looked as though they were strung with tiny crystal beads, Mary felt a numbing sense of foreboding. Seton, close to her as ever, understood her thoughts. Thus must it ever be when they entered a new prison. They must always wonder how long they would stay and whether this would be their last resting place.

The situation was charming enough with avenues of oak and walnut leading to the house from several directions, and in the manor, which had two courts, an outer and inner, Mary had been allotted a suite which was adequate for her needs.

Yet as she entered the Manor House she said to Seton: 'I remember hearing that it was to this place that Cardinal Wolsey came after his arrest. I seem to feel his spirit lingers still. I understand so well his feeling, for he had fallen from greatness. He went on to Leicester to die. I wonder what my fate will be.'

Seton tried to brush away such melancholy thoughts.

'It is always difficult to adjust ourselves to a new lodging,' she said.

*　　*　　*

That winter seemed as though it would never end. The air of Sheffield was not good for Mary and sometimes her limbs were so stiff with pain that she found walking difficult. She suffered acutely from neuralgia and there were times when she was convinced that she was near death.

Only the presence of her friends made it possible, she declared, for her not to die of melancholia, for when she considered their case she reminded herself that they suffered of their own free will, for there was not one of them who could not have walked out of Sheffield, a free man or woman; yet they stayed for love of her.

It was during this mournful winter that sad news reached her from Scotland. Her son was being tutored by George Buchanan, one of her greatest enemies, who had delighted in spreading slanders about her and was now teaching young James to believe them.

This news so prostrated Mary that her friends became really alarmed, and on several occasions were on the point of ordering the administration of the last rites.

It was during this sad period that Seton brought her the news that a friend had arrived at the manor and was asking to see her.

'Who is it?' asked Mary.

Seton was smiling. 'One whom I think Your Majesty will be pleased to see.'

'Then tell me. . . .'

But Seton had run to the door and flung it open.

Mary stared at the man who entered, for a few moments not recognizing him, so much had he changed. Then with a cry of joy she seized his hands and drew him to her in a long embrace.

'How can I tell you how welcome you are!' she cried.

But George Douglas did not need to be told.

*   *   *

This was indeed not the same George who had gone away. His stay in France had turned him from an idealistic boy to a man of the world. Yet he was nonetheless ready to give his life for the Queen. He told himself that he no longer dreamed impossible dreams. She was his Queen whom he would serve until death; she was as a goddess who was far beyond his reach. Unlike her he had never believed that there could be a relationship between them other than that which had always existed; and in France he had found a woman with whom he believed he had fallen in love, and it was for this reason he had returned to Mary.

Mary was delighted, and the coming of George so lightened her spirits that her health seemed to benefit; and as there were now signs of spring in the bleak Sheffield air, her companions congratulated themselves that she had recovered from what they had feared would be a mortal illness.

She wanted to hear all about George's romance, and it was characteristic of her generous nature that she could feel only joy because he had found someone to love, even though in some measure this must mean that she was supplanted in his most tender affections.

As for George he was ready enough to talk. He tried to explain to her the beauty and charm of Mademoiselle La Verrière. Mary listened, regretful only because she could not give the couple rich presents, wondering what she could do to help them to their happiness.

For George had his problems. 'She is a lady of some rank and her parents frown on our union because of my poverty.'

'My poor George! When I think of what you have lost on my account, I could weep. But we must not despair. I am a prisoner but I have some friends. I will write at once to my ambassador in Paris who is, as you know, the Archbishop of Glasgow, and I will ask that twenty-five thousand francs be settled on Mademoiselle. La Verrière. Then I am sure her parents will be as delighted with the match as their daughter and you and I are, my dear George.'

'I fear I bring trouble to Your Majesty. You cannot afford to be so generous.'

Mary touched his cheek lightly and laughed. 'I cannot afford not to make this little gift to one to whom I owe so much. Oh, George, I would it were more I could give you. Do you think I shall ever forget Lochleven and all I owed to you . . . then and after.'

George was too touched to answer, and Mary became practical.

'If you are to return to Scotland you will need a passport. I will write to Elizabeth and try to obtain this for you. If I cannot, then you must go back to France and stay there until it is safe for you to return home.'

'Your Majesty is kind enough to concern yourself with my affairs,' said George at length. 'I have been thinking since I came to Sheffield of ways in which I could be of assistance to you. I have had many a talk with Willie, who is chafing at inactivity.'

Mary laughed. 'Ah, Willie! You find him much changed?'

'He has become a man.'

'You heard of his troubles. Poor Willie. He is another who has suffered in my cause. He has never been quite the same since his incarceration in an English prison.'

'He could not be a boy for ever,' replied George. 'In one way he has changed not at all – and that is in his devotion to Your Majesty.'

'I have so many good friends, and for them I am grateful. I will tell you, George, that there are constant schemes for my rescue, yet none succeeds. Perhaps that is my fault, for there have been occasions when I have been unwilling to escape. I have not only myself to consider, and I could not blithely ride

303

away to freedom leaving others to be punished for my actions. But I never cease to hope. And I will tell you this, George: even at this moment Lord Claud Hamilton, with others of my friends, are in touch with the Spanish government. When the time is ripe I shall be lowered from my window by means of a cord and join my friends. But I must wait until I can be sure that I have enough supporters to make the attempt worthwhile. There have been too many abortive attempts to set me back on my throne, and too many have suffered because of them.'

George's eyes had begun to sparkle. Now that he was back in her presence she filled his mind. Mademoiselle La Verrière seemed like a charming dream but this was reality; this was what he lived for: to aid this woman who, when he was in her presence, commanded all his devotion.

Now he no longer wished to return to France; he wanted to free her from this prison, to ride by her side into Scotland, to lead her to her throne and spend the rest of his life in her service.

He was going to give the whole of his attention to planning her escape. He would consult Willie who was as shrewd and wily as anyone he knew. It would be Lochleven all over again; and as they had succeeded at Lochleven, so should they at Sheffield.

He began to speak of plans for her escape and she shook her head, for she understood the change in his feelings since their reunion.

'Nay, George,' she said, 'I do not wish you to jeopardize your future further. Nothing would please me more than to see your little French bride.'

'I know now,' said George simply, 'that there can be no real happiness when I do not serve my Queen.'

Seeing how deeply in earnest he was, Mary showed him the letters which she had received from Lord Claud Hamilton in Scotland and from Lesley in London; George was excited. When the Queen escaped from the Sheffield Manor House he was going to be at her side.

* * *

As Easter approached George was often seen in the company of Willie. Bess was alert. She had soon understood the nature of George Douglas's feelings for the Queen. Well, she told herself, some women get what they want through their clinging femininity – others by their dominating characters. For the first time in her life she felt slightly envious of Mary who effortlessly managed to set people working for her; Bess considered the amount of energy she had had to put into bringing about the same result. Never mind. Bess knew where she was going. Sometimes she wondered whether Mary did.

There came bad news from Scotland, where the fortress of Dumbarton, which had been held for almost four years by Mary's supporters, had been surprised and taken by her enemies; and although Lord Fleming had escaped, Archbishop Hamilton was taken and hanged as one of Darnley's murderers.

This was bad news for Mary and her friends; not only had they lost a valuable stronghold, but papers had been found in the castle which betrayed the fact that the Spanish government was ready to help Mary back to her throne – and not only to her own throne.

This information incensed Elizabeth who immediately gave orders to the Shrewsburys that their captive must be even more securely held.

When the Queen's letter came, the Earl went at once to his wife and showed it to her.

'I have been watchful since George Douglas came here,' said Bess. 'He is trying to repeat what he did at Lochleven.'

'That is so,' agreed the Earl.

'And I'll warrant,' went on Bess, 'that the plan is to let her down from her window by means of a cord. Has it struck you, George Talbot, that that would not be a difficult matter from her window in the Manor House?'

'It would be easier to escape from the manor than from the castle.'

'Then why do we delay?' cried Bess. 'I am in no mind to lose my head, even if you are. Let the Queen be at once removed from the manor to the castle.'

*   *   *

Roberto Ridolfi was on his way to visit the Duke of Norfolk. He had wrapped a cloak, which he believed was all concealing, about his person; he had no wish for it to be known that he was paying this visit. There was danger in the air, but Ridolfi was a man accustomed to living dangerously, as all spies must be.

Ardently Catholic it was his pleasure to serve His Holiness,

305

and his business as banker in London gave him opportunities of doing his duty.

It was unfortunate that he had not been able to keep free of suspicion; but in view of his activities that would have been hoping for too much. Still, statesmen such as Cecil were glad to make use of his services in the business of banking, and the very nature of that business meant that he was cognizant of English affairs.

Pius could not have had a more useful servant; and since the coming of Mary Queen of Scots into England, with its attendant discontents and hopes, Ridolfi had been on the alert.

He had come very close to danger during the Catholic rising in the autumn of 1569, when twelve thousand crowns had passed through his hands as a gift from the Pope to the rebels. Sir Francis Walsingham had sent for him on that occasion and made him a prisoner while his business premises and his house were searched. That might have been the end of a less wise man, but Ridolfi, practised spy that he was, had always known how to cover his tracks. Nothing incriminating had been discovered, and he was released, assuring Walsingham that he had merely acted in the way of business. As Elizabeth and Cecil looked upon Ridolfi as a man they could use since he was knowledgeable in European politics and they needed his services as a banker, they had allowed him to resume business.

Ridolfi was now once more engaged on his master's work which was, in effect, to drive Protestantism out of England and set up Catholicism in its place. Never could there have been a more opportune occasion. On the throne was the Protestant Elizabeth whom many believed to be a bastard; in prison, was the Catholic Mary whom many people believed to be the true heir to the throne. Such circumstances needed to be exploited. It was Ridolfi's duty to exploit them.

Ridolfi believed that all the Catholics in the country – and they were many – were waiting for the signal to revolt. There were however many who were prepared to tolerate a marriage between Norfolk and Mary, for although Norfolk was a Protestant he was not a very earnest one. If Norfolk could be persuaded to turn Catholic, how much stronger his case would be – and that of Mary – for two factions could unite; and those who supported the Norfolk union could work with those who supported the Catholic Faith. Were they not all enemies of Elizabeth?

These were his thoughts as he was ushered into the lodging of the Duke of Norfolk at the Charterhouse, where he was in the charge of Sir Henry Neville. Neville was an easy-going jailor and quite ready to leave the Duke alone with his banker, for it did not occur to him that there could be conspiracy between the Catholic Italian and Protestant Norfolk.

When they were alone Ridolfi commiserated with the Duke for the bad treatment he had suffered, and asked him if he intended to remain Elizabeth's prisoner for the rest of his life.

Norfolk, full of self-pity, told the banker that he had done nothing to warrant such treatment. He was the victim of injustice.

'Your Grace should cease to fret, for there could be a glorious future before you.'

'Marriage with the Queen of Scots!' mused the Duke. 'Will it ever come about, do you think?'

'It could with the utmost ease.'

Ridolfi then went on to explain that the King of Spain and His Holiness the Pope were interested in the cause of the Queen of Scots. 'Philip II is prepared to supply the money for the campaign. There is only one small matter which stands between you and – not only the crown of Scotland, but that of England.'

These words set Norfolk trembling with excitement. The thought of wealth and power always delighted him. He was feeling depressed because, on account of Mary's supplications, he had been forced to give up some of the Dacre fortune; yet how could he have refused without offending her? But if, through her, he were to attain the power and riches which Ridolfi was now suggesting, the entire Dacre fortune would be no more to him than the coin one might throw to a beggar.

'And this small matter?' he asked breathlessly.

'Your Grace is a Protestant. His Most Catholic Majesty and His Holiness would do nothing to help you while you cling to that faith.'

'So,' said Norfolk, 'they are asking that I become a Catholic.'

'Do so and you have the might of Spain and Rome behind you.'

The proposition was too much for the avaricious Duke. After all he was a Protestant largely because he had been brought up by Foxe and had taken his views, but there was no reason why he should not change now.

Ridolfi was rubbing his hands together. 'I will draw up dispatches which shall be signed by you and the Queen of Scots, and other noblemen whose help I can be sure of. When I have these I shall go to Brussels and there lay them before the Duke of Alva; I am sure he will agree to send at least eight thousand troops – and, with such, we cannot fail.'

Norfolk, dazzled by the prospect, threw aside his religious scruples and gave his pledge that he would stand with the rebels who must be sure of victory since they had behind them the might of Spain and Rome.

Ridolfi left the house well pleased. It had been even easier than he had believed possible.

* * *

Ridolfi, in his Brussels lodgings, continued optimistic. All was proceeding as he had hoped and he was sure that by the end of the year he would have succeeded in taking the throne of England from Elizabeth and setting up Mary in her place. He had had a satisfactory interview with Alva who, ever zealous in the Catholic cause, had seen little difficulty in the English project. It was now for him to acquaint the conspirators in England with what was happening in Brussels, so he wrote to Lesley, Norfolk and a few of the other conspirators. Then followed the task of finding a suitable messenger to convey the letters to England while Ridolfi made his way to Rome and his Papal master.

Charles Baillie, who was at this time in Brussels, seemed the man to execute this commission, and Ridolfi invited him to his lodgings. Charles Baillie, an enthusiastic supporter of Mary's, answered the summons at once.

This young man was at this time pleased with his accomplishments. He had come to Flanders in order to have printed at Liège a volume which had been written by the Bishop of Ross and was a vindication of the Queen's innocence. He had succeeded admirably and now the copies were ready to be taken back to England and Scotland where he and his friends would see that they were circulated.

When Baillie arrived Ridolfi told him of the letters which were to be taken to England.

'I know,' he said, 'that you have ever been a good friend of the Queen of Scots, and it is for this reason that I assign to you this dangerous task. The letters are in cipher which I will explain to you, for if it were necessary to destroy them you could then convey their contents by word of mouth. There have been many attempts to rescue the Queen, and they have all resulted in failure. This will be different, for behind this plan is the Pope himself with the King of Spain. It is their duty and purpose to remove Elizabeth from the English throne and put Mary there. They cannot fail. But first Elizabeth must be assassinated; and, as soon as this has been achieved, Alva will cross the Channel with a strong force to join the English Catholics. This is the gist of what lies in these letters; so you see, my friend, in carrying them into Elizabeth's country you face mortal danger.'

'I will do it willingly for the sake of Queen Mary and the Catholic cause,' Baillie answered.

'That is what I believed. Here are the letters.'

Baillie took them and set out for England.

When he left the ship at Dover, he did not notice four men who were loitering near the harbour. Relieved that he was on dry land again he was blithely making his way towards an inn where he proposed to spend the night before beginning his journey to London, when he was aware of being followed; and as he turned the four men drew level with him; in a second there was one on either side of him, one behind and the fourth had stepped in front of him.

His heart began to beat faster with fear. Cut-purses! And four of them. It was not so much that he feared to be robbed of his money; there were other things he carried far more precious than that.

'What do you want of me, gentlemen?' he asked.

The man who stood in front of him said quietly. 'You are Charles Baillie, recently come from the Continent?'

'That is so,' he answered. 'I repeat: What do you want of me?'

'You are our prisoner, Charles Baillie.'

'On what grounds?'

'On suspicion of treason. We arrest you in the name of our Sovereign Lady Elizabeth.'

'I do not understand.'

'Understanding will come later,' answered the leader of the men; he gave a sign and a man who Baillie had not previously noticed came up with horses.

Baillie was told to mount and he could do nothing but obey. A leading rein was attached to his horse's bridle and firmly holding this one of the four mounted his own horse.

'Let us go,' he said.

Thus they brought Charles Baillie to the Marshalsea prison.

* * *

Sir Francis Walsingham was watchful. Documents discovered in Dumbarton had alarmed him, Cecil, the Queen and all those who understood the gravity of the occasion. It was certain that the Queen of Scots was to be used as a symbol by their Catholic enemies; and when such included the Pope and the King of Spain the situation was without doubt highly dangerous. No petty rising this. Walsingham, proud of the spy system he had built up, rejoiced in an opportunity to prove its worth.

Thus he was determined to have all suspicious characters brought up for examination. It was for this reason that Charles Baillie had been arrested on his return from the Continent.

On the table before him lay letters and, because they were in cipher, they seemed sinister indeed. How to translate them? That was the question. There was a possibility that the messenger, who was an intelligent man and doubtless deep in any conspiracy that was going on, might be able to decode them.

He would not wish to do so, of course; but he was in their power; and there were ways of making a prisoner talk.

* * *

Baillie told himself that he would be brave. They had discovered the letters but they could not read them since they did not know the cipher.

They could kill him, he told himself; he would never betray his fellow Catholics.

He felt sick with apprehension when they moved him from the Marshalsea to the Tower. Could any man glide along those inky waters and pass through the traitor's gate without terror entering his soul! However brave a man believed himself to be he must tremble.

His cell was small and cold; little light and air came through the iron bars. He told himself he did not care. One must suffer for what one believed to be the right.

When a warder entered his cell and told him to follow whither he led, Baillie knew where he was going. As he followed the warder through the dark corridors, down stone spiral staircases and his trembling fingers touched the slimy walls, he was conscious of nothing but the fear within him. It was not physical pain that he feared; the terror came from the doubts of his own bravery.

'I will never tell,' he repeated. 'Never, never. . . .'

Now he was in the underground chamber. He saw the questioner; he smelt the dank odour of the river, the tang of vinegar. They used that, he thought, when the pain was too much to be borne and the victim passed into unconsciousness. They did not let him remain in that blessed state but brought him back and back again, until they had obtained what they sought.

The questions were beginning.

'Charles Baillie, you brought letters back with you from Flanders. Who gave you those letters?'

'I cannot say.'

'You are unwise, Charles Baillie; but let that be. To whom were you carrying these letters?'

'I cannot say.'

'And what do these letters contain?'

'You have seen them. You have read them.'

'You know them to be in cipher. Can you transcribe them, Charles Baillie?'

'I cannot.'

'You are secretive. We have ways of dealing with those who would keep their secrets from us.'

They were leading him now to the wooden trough; he saw the ropes, the rollers; and as they laid their rough hands on him and stripped him of his clothes, even before they laid him on the rack he could anticipate the pain in his joints.

Now he lay there, a frightened man, praying silently: 'Oh Holy Mother of God, help me to be strong.'

The questions began; he shook his head.

He heard a man screaming, and with surprise realized that it was himself, for the torture had begun.

'Charles Baillie, for whom were these letters intended?'

'I do not know . . . I cannot say.'

The pain came again, more excruciating than ever, to his already tortured limbs.

'I know nothing . . . I have nothing to say. . . .'

Again and again it came . . . waves of it; he lost consciousness but the hateful vinegar brought him back and back again to pain. Not again; he could not endure it again. His whole body, his mind cried out against it.

But they had no pity. How much could a man endure?

He did not know. There was only one thing that mattered. He must stop the pain.

A man was shouting: 'Norfolk . . . Lesley. . . .' And he could not believe that was his voice betraying secrets he had sworn to preserve. Water was placed at his lips. It was cool and soothing.

'There,' said a voice, 'you are wiser now. It was foolish of you to suffer so much. Now . . . tell us what the letters contained . . . and there shall be no more pain.'

But there was pain. He felt he would never be free of it. Someone touched his disjointed limbs and he screamed in agony.

'We must know more, you understand.' The voice was gentle yet full of meaning. 'The letters were for Norfolk and the Bishop of Ross . . . and others. You shall tell us all. But first, what were their contents?'

He did not answer.

'There'll have to be another turn of the screw,' said a voice.

Then he was screaming: 'No . . . No . . . I will tell all. It is Ridolfi. The Pope . . . the King of Spain. . . . Alva will come. . . .'

He was moaning, but they were bending over him soothingly.

*　　*　　*

The Earl and Countess of Shrewsbury came to the Queen's apartment and, as soon as Mary looked into their faces, she knew that they had grave news.

She asked all her attendants to leave her, and when they had gone she cried: 'I pray you tell me without delay.'

'The conspiracy with Ridolfi, of which Your Majesty will be well aware, has been discovered.'

'Ridolfi?' repeated Mary.

'Norfolk is in the Tower. Lesley is there also. There have been many arrests. You have not heard the end of this matter, Madam.'

'But . . .' cried Mary, looking appealingly at Bess, 'this is disastrous.'

'It would indeed have been, Your Majesty,' retorted the Countess, 'if this plot had succeeded. It is difficult to know what will come out of it. But we have new orders from Her Majesty.'

Mary was trying to concentrate on what they were saying. Norfolk in the Tower! Ridolfi! This meant that Elizabeth had discovered that the King of Spain and the Pope were endeavouring to interfere in English politics.

But I never wished for this, she was telling herself. I never wanted to harm Elizabeth. All I asked for were my rights . . . my own throne . . . to have my son with me . . . to bring him up as my heir. I never wanted to interfere with the English.

Norfolk! For her sake he had been trapped into treason against his Queen. And the penalty for treason. . . .

She dared not contemplate what the future might hold.

'The Queen's immediate orders,' went on Bess, 'are that you shall remain in these rooms and not on any pretext whatsoever leave them. Certain of your servants are to be sent away from you. You are to have no more than ten men and six women.'

'I will never send my friends away,' cried Mary.

Bess shrugged her shoulders. She was shaken, angry with herself and with Shrewsbury. Here was a pretty state of affairs with a conspiracy of this magnitude going on under their noses, and they knowing nothing of it.

This would be the end of Norfolk – of that much she was certain. Would it also be the end of Mary, Queen of Scots? That might well be, for if it could be proved that she was involved in a plot against Elizabeth she had indeed earned the death penalty.

It was imperative that the Shrewsburys should be able to prove their innocence.

Bess had rarely been so shaken. They lived in dangerous times and Shrewsbury could be a fool on occasions – particularly over his beautiful Queen – so that Bess had to think for them both.

'Your Majesty would do well to select the sixteen you wish to keep with you,' she said tartly. 'If you do not, it will be for us to select them for you.'

Shrewsbury said almost gently: 'Your Majesty will understand that you are in grave danger.'

Mary said impatiently: 'I have been in grave danger ever since I sought refuge with your mistress.'

'But never,' warned Shrewsbury, 'in such danger as you find yourself at this time.'

'Come, come,' said Bess, 'it is useless to commiserate with Her Majesty. If she is involved in plots against our Queen, she knows full well the risks she runs. It would be well if Your Majesty made your own selection . . . and that with speed; for

313

I must warn you again that if you do not, it will be made for you.'

She signed to Shrewsbury and together they left the Queen. Mary immediately called for Seton who from the ante-room had overheard what had been said.

Seton said nothing. There was no need for words.

Never in all her life had Seton felt such fear for her mistress.

* * *

There was deep melancholy in the Queen's apartments.

'How can I choose from all those I love so well?' asked Mary again and again. 'How can I spare one of them!'

Bess came in. She treated Mary with disapproval in the presence of others, but when they were alone she allowed a little sympathy to show. Secretly she thought Mary a fool . . . surrounded by fools. So many attempts and not one successful! Bess was thankful that they were not. She was anxious that none should be able to say that she had given any help to the Queen of Scots. Small wonder that Shrewsbury's health suffered through this task of his. There could be none more dangerous in the kingdom than guarding the Queen of Scots.

'Your Majesty,' she said coolly, 'if you will not decide who of your servants are to go and who to stay, the Earl and I will have no alternative but to decide for you.'

With tears of wretchedness in her eyes Mary turned away; but still she could not bring herself to make the choice.

* * *

Willie Douglas stood before her, all his jauntiness departed. He was one of those who were to leave her.

Willie looked bewildered; he could not believe that he was to go. Mary took him in her arms and kissed him.

'Oh Willie, never will I forget. . . .'

'Your Majesty,' said Willie, 'we must get you out of that wicked woman's hands. We must get you back to Scotland where you belong.'

'You will go to Scotland, Willie?'

A shadow of the old grin crossed Willie's face. 'They'll be remembering Lochleven up there, Your Majesty. They'll cut me into collops if they catch me.'

'That must never happen. Go to France with George, Willie.'

314

'I'll not let them get me, Your Majesty. I'm going to bring you back to your throne, remember.'

'Oh, Willie, how can I bear this! How can I! You and so many whom I love to be torn from me! Be assured though that the life you hazarded for mine will never be neglected while I have a friend living. . . .'

When Willie had left her, Seton led her to her bed and there they lay together, weeping silently – Mary thinking of all those who had risked their lives to be with her; Seton wondering what the future held for them.

*　　*　　*

Unable to leave her rooms in the castle, left to the care of only one or two of her ladies – for those servants who remained were not allowed to come and go as they once had – Mary's melancholy turned to sickness, and once again those who loved her despaired of her life.

Her French physician, who had obtained special permission before he was allowed to visit her, was in despair because he had no medicines with which to treat her. In desperation he implored Cecil, recently created Lord Burleigh, to lift the ban which prevented him from treating the royal invalid. Burleigh – shocked by the Ridolfi plot which was being slowly revealed through the torturing of Norfolk's servants and others involved – did not answer the physician's request; and when Mary wrote to the French ambassador asking for his help, the letter was intercepted by Burleigh's spies and this too brought no relief.

'If they would but send a little of the ointment which relieves Your Majesty's spasmodic pains, that would be something,' mourned Seton. 'I would I could acquire a little cinnamon water and confiture of black grapes.'

'What is the use?' answered Mary wearily. 'They have determined to kill me, and if I die what they will call a natural death, so much the better from their point of view. There is one request I will make though, and perhaps Elizabeth will answer this: I shall ask her to send me a priest, for I believe I shall soon be in dire need of his services.'

She was so weak that she could scarcely write, and she hoped this would be apparent to Elizabeth when she received the letter, and that her heart would be touched.

It was some days later when she believed that this had come

315

about, for a priest came from the Court of England to visit her.

When she heard that he was in the castle she begged that he be brought to her at once; and when he arrived she held out her hand and prepared to greet him warmly.

The priest bowed coldly, and there was no pity in his pale ascetic face as he looked at her, so wan, so helpless in her sickbed.

'It pleases me that you have come,' she said. 'I have need of your services.'

'I came from my Sovereign Lady Elizabeth,' he told her, 'not to act as your priest and confessor but to bring you this.'

He held out a book which she eagerly grasped.

The priest retired from her bedside and took his stand by the window; and she believed afterwards that he had been commanded by his mistress to watch her reactions and to report on them.

She stared in dismay at the book, for it was one written by her old enemy, George Buchanan, and in it, set down in the coarsest terms, was the fictitious account of her life since she had come from France to Scotland. In this book she was said to be a murderess and adulteress.

And this was what Elizabeth sent to her when she was asking for a priest!

Then she remembered. This was the man who had been appointed her son's tutor.

She knew that her life was in danger, but she could only think of young James in the hands of the foul-minded Buchanan. Already he would be teaching James that his mother was an adulteress and a murderess.

Never had she been so miserable as she was now, lying in bed at Sheffield Castle holding Buchanan's coarsely written libel in her hands.

*   *   *

Bess came to Mary's chamber.

'How fares Your Majesty?' she asked.

Mary shook her head. 'You find me low in health and spirits,' she answered.

Bess approached the bed and picked up Buchanan's book. She snorted with disgust. 'I will burn this without delay. I do not care to have such filth under my roof.'

Mary smiled. There were times when Bess's presence was a great comfort to her.

'I come to tell you that the Earl has left for London,' she said. 'We have Sir Ralph Sadler here in his place.'

'But why so?' asked Mary alarmed.

Bess ignored the question for the moment. 'You need have no fear. I shall not allow him to trouble you if you do not wish to see him.'

'I have little wish to see him. He is no friend of mine.'

'I myself will come to you whenever you wish it,' said Bess.

'Thank you. I trust I shall welcome you often. But tell me why the Earl has left for London.'

Bess had wandered to the window and, as she spoke, looked out and not at the Queen.

'That he may preside in his duty as Lord High Steward at the trial of the Duke of Norfolk.'

There was silence in the chamber. Then Bess turned and came to stand at the Queen's bedside.

'I pray,' she said – gently for her, 'that Your Majesty is not too deeply involved. They took Lesley, as you know, and I hear that when faced with torture he confessed all.'

'All!'

'You,' replied the Countess shrewdly, 'will know better than I how much that was.'

Mary suddenly began to shiver. She said quietly: 'It may be that they will send for me. It may be that my next prison will be the Tower of London. You should not grieve for me, for one prison is very like another.'

'I should not care to see Your Majesty conveyed to the Tower. That could have terrible implications.'

'I know that you think it is one short step from that prison to eternity. Perhaps that is so. But if that is my fate, so be it.'

Bess felt impatient with such an attitude, yet even she was touched with pity. If there was anything she could have done to comfort the Queen, gladly would she have done it. But the only thing she could think of was to keep Sir Ralph Sadler from her apartments until the return of the Earl. This she would do by her own constant attendance on Mary.

She had no wish, of course, for Mary to think she approved of plots against the Queen of England; but during that period of dread and fear, Mary and Bess were closer in friendship than they had ever been.

* * *

It was a bleak January day when Seton came into the Queen's apartment, her eyes red with weeping.

'Well?' asked Mary. 'But I have no need to ask you. He has been found guilty.'

Seton bowed her head.

'It is what we have been fearing these last weeks,' said the Queen. 'I suffer torments, because it is for my sake that he is brought so low.'

Seton shook her head; she wanted to cry: Nay, it was his own ambition which has brought him where he is. Instead she said: 'You must not reproach yourself. All he did was of his own free will.'

'Oh Seton, if only I could go back to the days when I first came to England. I would act differently. I should never have allowed him to jeopardize his life for my sake.'

Seton did not reply. When would Mary learn that men were born ambitious, that others were not unselfish as she was herself. This was not the time to tell her. All she could do now was endeavour to comfort her in her grief.

Bess came into the apartment; she took one look at Mary's stricken face and said. 'What ails Your Majesty?'

'I know your ladyship cannot be ignorant of the cause of my sorrow,' answered Mary. 'I am in great fear for the Duke of Norfolk.'

'Then the news I bring Your Majesty has already reached you. You know that Norfolk has been found guilty of high treason.'

Mary covered her face with her hands and Bess, watching her, thought: Poor foolish woman!

*   *   *

The spring had come but Mary was too melancholy to notice it. Norfolk still lived, a prisoner in the Tower, the axe hanging over his head; he would not escape it this time, she knew. And what of herself? What fate was being prepared for her?

She had no means of knowing. She was not allowed to move from her own apartments. She guessed that in London Elizabeth was conferring with her ministers as to what should be done with the Queen of Scots.

It was not until June that the news was brought to her. She was prostrate when she heard it. On the second day of that month Norfolk had been taken to Tower Hill and there beheaded.

So he was no more, this man who she had believed would be her husband. She had seen little of him but there had been many letters exchanged between them and she had built up in her mind an image. Norfolk was to have been that ideal husband for whom she had always been seeking; and it was that ideal she mourned.

So deep was her grief that she scarcely paused to wonder or to care . . . whether she herself would soon meet a like fate.

All through the long summer days there was mourning in her apartments at Sheffield Castle.

*   *   *

Rarely was her beautiful rival out of Elizabeth's thoughts. Her ministers had told her that she had excuse enough now to bring Mary to London, to lodge her in the Tower, to have her tried for treason and found guilty. Once and for all, let this be an end to the troublesome Mary Queen of Scots.

Elizabeth hesitated. Much as she desired the death of Mary she had no wish to be connected with it. She wanted someone to rid her of the woman, but in such a manner that no blame could possibly attach itself to her.

The simplest solution was what she had planned before and would have carried out but for Moray's untimely death. Send her back to Scotland, let them try her there; let them answer to the world for her death.

She tried out Morton but he was cautious. There were too many people in Scotland, anxious for the Queen's return, for his peace of mind.

He answered Elizabeth: He would take the Queen of Scots back into Scotland, where she might be tried and found worthy of death; but he would not be responsible for her execution unless Elizabeth sanctioned it.

'Sanction it!' cried Elizabeth. 'The fool! If I did that I might as well have the deed done here in England.'

This she could do, her ministers reminded her. Mary's complicity in the Ridolfi plot gave her ample reason.

But Elizabeth hesitated. Those Catholic risings had worried her. There were many Catholics in England and the nightmare of her life was that her subjects would turn against her. She cared nothing for the antagonism of the greatest foreign power; she had always known that her strength lay in the approval of her own people.

So Mary was allowed to live on – although in the strictest confinement at Sheffield Castle.

* * *

Life had become strange; Mary did not notice the passing weeks. She lived in a daze, sleeping a great deal of the time, going over the past when she was awake, constantly expecting a summons to death.

She could not go on in that state, thought Bess; but perhaps it was as well that she seemed so indifferent at this time. Shrewsbury was panic-stricken. He was wondering how much blame would be attached to him over this Ridolfi matter. He had become as he had been before his attack; Bess was a little anxious, particularly as of recent months he had seemed to be more serene.

He would grow out of this new phase, she promised herself. Each day carried them – if not Mary – farther from trouble. If Elizabeth had meant to reprimand them, she would have done so by now.

Mary's spirits were raised a little when she heard from Lesley who had now been released from the Tower and, though still a prisoner of state, had been removed to Farnham Castle in Surrey where the Bishop of Winchester was his host and jailor. He sent her a book of meditations in Latin which he himself had written.

Mary roused herself from her lethargy to write to him and tell him that the knowledge that he was no longer in the Tower and had sent her his book brought her great comfort.

* * *

August came and it was stiflingly hot in the Queen's apartments.

She lay listlessly dreaming of the past, and Seton came to sit beside her bed.

'Would Your Majesty not like to work at your tapestry?'

'No, Seton. I have no interest in it.'

'You know how it soothes you.'

'I do not think I could be easily soothed now, Seton.'

'Your Majesty should rouse yourself. This sorrow will pass like all others.'

320

'That may be, Seton. But what is at the end of it? How long have I been in England? What is the day?'

'It is the 24th day of August, Your Majesty, in the year 1572.'

'The 24th day of August, Seton. Is that not St Bartholomew's Eve?'

'It is indeed.'

'It was in June that they killed him . . . early June. It is nearly three months since he died.'

'Too long to mourn. Tears will not bring him back.'

'You are right, Seton, as you so often are. I believe now that in time I may begin to forget. Oh, Seton, if only some good would come to me! If only my French relations would do something to help me. Do you remember our days in France?'

'It is not easy to forget the happiest days of one's life.'

'Those were the happy days, Seton. I will write to the King . . . reminding him.'

'Try to sleep now.'

'I will, Seton, and in the morning I will write to dear friends in France . . . to my uncles, to my grandmother, to the King my brother-in-law . . . even to the Queen-Mother.'

'I shall remember,' replied Seton, and there was a note of happiness in her voice, 'that you began to throw off your grief on the Eve of St Bartholomew.'

*   *   *

The news came to Sheffield Castle and Mary listened to it aghast. Terrible tragedy had struck the city of Paris, and it seemed that this tragedy was being repeated in the main cities of France. On the Eve of St Bartholomew the Catholics had risen against the Huguenots and there had been slaughter in the streets such as had never been known before. The Admiral de Coligny had been brutally murdered and vile sport had been made with his body; he was but one of thousands of brave men who were dying in the streets of France on account of their Faith.

The Queen of England and her Protestant ministers expressed their horror of such butchery; all over England there were cries of 'Down with the Papists!' And it was said that one of the leaders and instigators of this most terrible massacre was the Duke of Guise, kinsman of the Queen of Scots.

In the streets of London and many cities in England men

321

and women gathered to talk of what was happening across the Channel.

'It must never happen here,' they cried. 'This is a good Protestant country. We'll have no popery here.'

Then they remembered the revolt of the Northern Catholics, and many recalled the days of the Queen's half-sister who was known as Bloody Mary because of the fires of Smithfield which, in her day, had consumed the bodies of good Protestant men and women.

There was another Catholic Queen in their midst. She was a prisoner in Sheffield Castle, but since she had been in England she had caused trouble enough.

'Down with popery!' shouted the people. 'Down with the fair devil of Scotland!'

*   *   *

It would be well, said Elizabeth, to keep a strict watch on the Queen of Scotland, for her own safety, because when the people of England had heard of the conduct of her Catholic friends and relations in France they were ready to tear her apart.

Now was the time, thought Elizabeth, to sever Mary's head from her body, for never would she be as unpopular as she was now.

But Elizabeth remembered the Catholics in the land who were perhaps at this moment waiting to rise, as their fellow Catholics had risen in Paris.

No, she would restrain herself. The Queen of Scots should remain her prisoner. It should not be said that she had agreed to her execution because she feared her greater right to the throne.

Let her rest in prison strictly guarded. That was the best place for her.

The right moment will come, Elizabeth told herself. Then the deed can be performed with a good conscience and none will be able to say that Elizabeth of England slew her rival because she went in fear of her. Nay, at a time when it would have been so easy to bring her to the block, she, Elizabeth, had cherished her, protected her from the infuriated Protestants of England, remembering the respect due to royalty, desiring to show the world that she feared no one and would not consent to Mary's execution merely because she could enjoy greater peace of mind in a world where Mary was not.

Orders were sent to Sheffield Castle. 'Keep the Queen under even stricter surveillance. Double the guard. It is imperative that she should not escape . . . for her own sake.'

* * *

So that summer passed into winter. Another birthday came and went – her thirtieth.

'I am growing old,' she told Seton. 'See how my life is passing by while I go from one prison to another.'

Christmas came, but there were no revelries in Sheffield Castle.

The winter was long and cold, but Mary scarcely noticed it, and in the spring the Earl and Countess came to her apartments to tell her that since the castle needed sweetening they proposed to move her to the Lodge in the Park.

Mary was glad of the move. Anything was welcome to relieve the monotony; but the Earl and Countess were less happy with their captive in the manor, for they believed escape would have been easier there than from the castle.

She was never allowed out of her apartments and whenever she looked out of her window she saw guards who stood beneath it all through the day and night.

'She will never escape from here,' joked the guards, 'unless she has some magic which will turn her into a mouse or a flea.'

* * *

The Earl brought the news to Mary, and as he told her he realized that she understood its importance. She turned pale and put her hand to her side where lately she had begun to feel much pain.

'The Castle of Edinburgh has surrendered, Your Majesty.'

She did not speak for a moment. She pictured the castle, high on the hill, seeming impregnable. It was the last and the most important fortress held in her name.

'English forces under Sir William Drury captured it,' Shrewsbury told her. 'Kirkcaldy should have surrendered long ago. There was no hope of holding out against the Queen's forces.'

She knew what had been happening in Edinburgh; she had heard stories of the bravery of those who had loved her, how the soldiers' wives had allowed themselves to be let down the steep rocks by ropes in order that they might go into town to buy bread for the starving defenders of the castle; how when they had been caught, which was frequently the case, Morton had ordered that they should be immediately hanged. She had heard how the soldiers had been let down to the well by means of ropes that they might fill their buckets with the precious water.

'They had to give in,' Shrewsbury was telling her now, 'when the well was poisoned.'

'Kirkcaldy would never have surrendered otherwise,' said Mary. And she thought of Kirkcaldy who was now her firm ally yet who had stood remorselessly against her and, more than any, had helped to win the day for Moray at Carberry Hill.

'Kirkcaldy will never be on any side again,' replied Shrewsbury grimly. 'He was hanged with his brother in Market Cross when the castle was taken.'

'Oh, my lord,' cried Mary, 'why are you always the bringer of evil tidings?'

'If there were aught good to bring you, I would bring it,' Shrewsbury answered gruffly.

'Then as you can bring me no good, I pray you leave me alone with my grief.'

Shrewsbury bowed and left her. He was thinking that in some respects this might not be such bad news for her.

With Edinburgh Castle lost she was no longer a formidable enemy. Her importance to Elizabeth had waned with its capture. Might it be that now the watch on her would be relaxed a little? Her supporters in Scotland were defeated; the English were still talking in horror of the St Bartholomew massacre. Elizabeth would have little to fear now from Mary, Queen of Scots. Surely she would relent a little.

*　　*　　*

'How did she take the news?' Bess demanded of her husband.

'She has heard so much bad news that even this leaves her numb.'

'Poor creature! I pity her. It is sad that she should be so confined as she has been these last months. I am sick unto death of Sheffield. How I long for the beauty of my beloved Chatsworth!'

'What have you in mind?'

324

'She has become almost an invalid in these last months. She is in need of a change. I shall ask the Queen if we may not visit Chatsworth; and who knows, if we do I might take the Queen of Scots to the Buxton baths. They did you good. I'm sure they would be equally beneficial to her.'

'You think the Queen would listen to your request?'

'Are you a fool, Shrewsbury? Now is the time for her to show her leniency. Never have the fortunes of your romantic Queen been so low. I will write to Elizabeth. I'll swear that very soon we shall be leaving Sheffield for Chatsworth . . . and it may well be Buxton too.'

CHAPTER THIRTEEN

CHATSWORTH AND BUXTON

AS SOON AS Mary was back in Chatsworth she felt happier. How delighted she was to go once more to her garden at the top of the tower and there, with Seton and Jane Kennedy, find pleasure in seeing that those plants, which she had tended with such care, were still flourishing.

Shrewsbury had been right when he had believed that she would not be allowed more liberty. Attended by guards she would walk from her apartments to the lake, and cross the bridge. She could leave them surrounding the lake, for there was no possibility of her escape; and although, when she looked over the balustrade, she could always see some of them, at least she was free to enjoy the fresh air.

Bess talked to her continually of what the Buxton baths had done for Shrewsbury, and both Queen and Countess wrote to Elizabeth begging her to allow Mary to seek a like benefit.

It was now August, and the season for taking the waters would be over with the end of the month. Mary despaired of ever being allowed to visit Buxton, and the desire to go there became a passion with her. She talked perpetually of going.

'I know, if I can but take the baths, I shall be well again,' she declared.

Seton encouraged her. Sometimes now a whole day would pass without her mentioning the death of Norfolk or the valour of the defenders of Edinburgh Castle. She still yearned for little James, but that was something she would do all her life; she still showed anxiety as to the fate of George and Willie Douglas and all those whom she called her poor wandering sheep. But her desire to visit Buxton was doing much to rouse her from her melancholy; and, thought Seton, if we could but go there, I am certain she would be well again through her very faith in the baths.

It was near the end of August when Elizabeth granted permission, maliciously commenting as she did so that, since the season was well nigh over, the visit would doubtless do the Queen of Scots more harm than good.

But when Mary received word that she might go – late as it was – she was jubilant.

She looked young again as preparations were made for her to be taken from Chatsworth to Buxton.

*   *   *

The journey from Chatsworth to Buxton was not a long one, being of some thirteen or fourteen miles; merely to be on that beautiful road which led over the hills made Mary feel almost happy.

Already the colour was returning to her cheeks and Seton was delighted to see this change in her. How ironical, she thought, that they, who had once had such lofty ideas of regaining the throne, could now be so uplifted by the prospect of a visit to Buxton.

The climate seemed more benign than even at Chatsworth and especially so when compared with bleak Sheffield.

Shrewsbury's house in Buxton was called Low Buxton and it was here that Mary stayed. It was a charming house protected from the winds by the hill at the foot of which it stood, while it benefited from the mountain air.

Shrewsbury had given orders that all visitors must leave the Spa before Mary arrived, so there could be no opportunities for making plans for her escape; thus all the social activities of that gay little town ceased immediately; and the Queen was never allowed to go anywhere unless surrounded by her guards.

She had not dared hope that it would be otherwise, but so great was her faith in the baths, so delighted was she to be in such congenial surroundings, that her health began to improve.

She made Shrewsbury tell her about the remarkable cure he had enjoyed at Buxton; and nothing loth to talk of illness, he never tired of explaining how weak he had been before taking the baths, how strong afterwards.

'You owe your recovery to your Countess,' Mary reminded him. 'If she had not been strong and risked Elizabeth's displeasure, you would not be the man you are today.'

Shrewsbury nodded sombrely. It was true he owed a great deal to Bess, but he did not care to be reminded of this. It made his conduct with Eleanor seem more reprehensible than ever. What he needed was to make excuses for it. He had told himself that no man cared to have a woman behaving like his commanding officer, however efficient she was; a man wanted sympathy, particularly when he was engaged in such an exacting task as guarding the most dangerous state prisoner of all time. He was telling himself that any man in his position would have looked for relaxation elsewhere. A man would have to be a saint not to take the comfort and pleasure Eleanor offered.

She was not with him now; he could not insist that she accompany them to Buxton, for fear Bess should begin to suspect. It was enough that she moved with them back and forth between Sheffield and Chatsworth; he consoled himself that the visit to Buxton must necessarily be brief.

So while he indulged in a morbid pleasure with Mary, dwelling on that illness which had brought him near to death, he was making excuses for himself: I was brought low because of the anxieties which weighed so heavily upon me. They are still with me. I need some form of relaxation; I need to forget my cares now and then; and how could I forget more easily than in the arms of Eleanor?

Bess joined them and he saw the smile play about her lips.

When they were alone she said to him: 'I see you found a sympathetic listener in your Queen.'

'She asked me to tell her of the benefit I had received from the baths.'

'And you did so with relish. You will never be completely well, Shrewsbury, while you dwell so fondly on your ailments.'

'It is necessary that I do not have a return of my illness,' he retorted coldly.

'Then don't beckon it back with such loving words. You talk too tenderly of your pains. What an unsympathetic wife I am! How different is your beautiful Queen; she listens and those lovely eyes are filled with compassion for poor Shrewsbury. Lovely eyes would not have nursed you back to health,

327

George Talbot, nor would sympathetic sighs. Remember that.'

He did remember. It was why he felt so remorseful now that he was away from Eleanor. Perhaps he should end the liaison. A noble Earl and a serving wench! Not the first time it had happened, it was true – but this was no passing fancy. Perhaps when he returned to Chatsworth he would break off the relationship. Yes, he would. Bess might joke about his passion for the Queen of Scots; what would she say if she knew of that for Eleanor Britton?

He dared not think. He could almost feel the lash of her tongue now. And a woman like Bess would not stop at words. He warned himself that he must seriously consider ending the liaison.

But he knew he would not.

*   *   *

The days spent at Buxton were the happiest Mary had known since her captivity had begun. She was now able to walk with her old springy step and the sounds of laughter came from her rooms in Low Buxton; she would play on her lute and sing songs with which she had once delighted the Court of France.

It needed little, thought those who loved her, to restore her spirits and make her well again. She suffered from no serious malady. She was young still, but she had always thrived on gaiety and she needed it now. The pains in her limbs would disappear if only she could enjoy a little comfort and did not have to pass her days and nights in big draughty apartments.

One day there was an expedition to Poole's Hole, and thither Mary rode surrounded by her friends and guards. The cavern at the foot of Grinlaw Hill was only half a mile or so from Buxton, and when Mary arrived there she insisted on dismounting and entering the cave. Surrounded by ladies, guards and torch bearers, and stooping almost double, she made her way along the slippery passage, crying out warnings to those who followed; some of the ladies looked down at the stream below and shuddered because it would have been so easy to falter and stumble on those slippery stones. But Mary went on until she came to a group of stalactites, and here she paused to admire and call to her friends to do the same.

It was a weird scene there in the cave, lighted by the torches of those who had gone on ahead to show the way, the Queen's animated face looking like an excited child's in that light.

'It would be dangerous to go farther,' said one of the guards, and Mary immediately agreed that they should turn back.

It was Seton who said: 'We will call that group of stalactites Queen Mary's Pillar.'

Mary laughed with all her old gaiety. 'It was worth-while coming so far to give it my name,' she added.

Then with some torch bearers going on ahead and others bringing up the rear, the party made its way out of the cavern and back to Low Buxton.

Those happy days at Buxton passed all too quickly but with the coming of September it was necessary to return to Chatsworth.

* * *

All through September and October Mary's health remained good. She would sit with her friends over her tapestry and they would recall the visit to Buxton.

'Next year,' said Mary, 'I shall hope to go for the whole of the season. How pleasant it would be if we could spend June, July and August there. . . .'

She stopped suddenly and a grave expression crossed her face. Seton, watching, understood. Mary was thinking that she had become accustomed to being the prisoner of the Queen of England.

At the end of October the weather changed and the sunny days they had spent at Buxton seemed far away.

'I am thankful,' said Seton, 'that we are at Chatsworth. Sheffield would not be so comfortable with the winter coming on.'

'Or Tutbury!' added Mary with a shudder.

And here again, she thought, I betray my resignation to my fate. I think as a prisoner, and I am grateful for a prisoner's concessions.

Bess came to her apartments in a dark mood.

'Orders from Elizabeth,' she announced, and Mary knew before she was told that Bess was angry because she was being ordered to leave her beloved Chatsworth.

'I trust we are not going to be moved from Chatsworth,' said Mary.

'I fear so. Her Majesty has heard that you have uttered complaints against her. She declares herself to be shocked by your ingratitude.'

'Should I be so grateful for my long imprisonment?'

329

'Someone has evidently carried tales to Her Majesty. She is most displeased. She writes that she fears you have too much freedom at Chatsworth. We are to return without delay to Sheffield.'

CHAPTER FOURTEEN

RETURN TO SHEFFIELD

SO BACK TO Sheffield came Mary, and those who were close to her were aware of the change in her. She was no longer the hopeful young girl who believed that shortly she would be rescued and restored to her throne. It was as though she had come to terms with life; as though she had told herself: This is how it must be and I must therefore try to make this restricted life as happy as I can for those who have made sacrifices in order to be with me; thus I can find something to make life pleasant.

Since she had been to Buxton and her health had been so much better she tried to enjoy a little gaiety in her apartments. She made plans for working elaborate tapestry and wrote to the French ambassador asking him to buy her materials in France.

'There,' she explained to her ladies, 'he can find colours which are more beautiful than those obtainable in London; and the silks are finer.'

Seton guessed that she planned to make a present for the Queen of England, knowing how Elizabeth loved to receive gifts. Perhaps thus, mused Mary, she may be persuaded to view my position with more kindness.

She longed for some little pets, for she loved all animals and in particular little dogs.

'I could be so happy if I had a few little dogs to care for. I shall write to France for them. Surely someone will send me a little dog. I would not wish for only one. He would need a companion. I would not have him lonely. And I must ask for them to be sent in baskets with warm coverlets. I would have them prepared for the cold in Sheffield Castle.'

She also asked her French friends to send her some clothes for which she would pay when she could recover some of her possessions.

'Ah, Seton,' she said, 'do you remember the caps I used to wear with crowns of gold and silver? How becoming they were! I remember the King of France once told me that they became none as they did me. I should like some more. But perhaps there are newer fashions now. I shall ask for the latest designs to be sent to me. But perhaps I should not wear them myself but send them to Elizabeth. She is always eager to see the French fashions. I heard, and to be the first to wear them.'

So the days were now spent in planning tapestry designs and hoping for the arrival of little dogs. It was less exciting but more restful than making dangerous plans for escape.

There were times when the yearning to see little James was so strong that the Queen lapsed into melancholy; and Bess, realizing this and feeling sorry for the Queen, decided to do something about it.

Bess, who had her children with her and took an active part in their affairs, could therefore understand Mary's grief in being parted from her only son; and, since that son was a King, in Bess's eyes it made the situation even more tragic.

Bess's daughter Frances had married Sir Henry Pierpont of Holme Pierpont in Nottinghamshire, and Frances had a little daughter whom she had named Elizabeth after her mother.

It was at Bess's suggestion that Mary became godmother to this child. Bess who, where her family was concerned, was extremely ambitious, believed that it could do little Bessie, who was four years old, no harm to have a Queen as her godmother. At the same time it would add a little interest to Mary's life.

She was unprepared for the warmth with which Mary greeted this project. Her goddaughter became the centre of her life; and she showered all that devotion, which she had longed to give to James, on little Bessie Pierpont. She had the child with her whenever possible, taking meals with her, having her sleep in her bed, making clothes for her.

As for little Bessie, she returned the Queen's affection and was never so happy as when she was in Mary's company.

Bess looked on with pleasure and assured Frances Pierpont that young Bessie would come to no harm while Mary remained a prisoner, and if the latter's fortune should ever take a turn great good would come to her.

During this time Mary became more serene. The affairs of her household were beginning to absorb her. She was concerned about the health of her French Secretary Roullet, who was dying of a lung complaint and had become very difficult, being often too ill to work for her and not hesitating to express his reproaches if she allowed Gilbert Curle to take over his tasks.

She was gentle and tender to him and always tried to placate him, although often she had to do his work herself – fearing to hurt him by passing it on to some other secretary. But he was one of her household, and now she lived for such friends.

She was made very sad by news of the death of Charles IX, King of France, and was temporarily overcome by melancholy, remembering the happy days when she had been a child in the French nursery.

Seton wept with her, for had they not always been together even in those days, and she remembered Charles as well as Mary did.

'I have lost another friend,' she told Seton, 'and there are so few left to me.'

'He loved you dearly,' Seton answered. 'It was the dearest wish of his heart that you should share his throne with him. I believe that might have come about but for his mother.'

'I have had so many good friends and so many enemies,' Mary replied. 'How Catherine de' Medici hated me – especially so after she heard me call her a tradesman's daughter. It was wrong of me, Seton, and I deeply regret that now. But I paid for my folly, did I not? Sometimes I think, Seton, that I am paying in full for all the sins of my youth.'

'Let us not talk of such things,' replied Seton. 'It will not always be as it is now, and then perhaps you will be rewarded for your goodness to us all. Shall we work on the embroidery for little Bessie's gown?'

He was dead and no good could be served by mourning. Poor Charles! thought Mary. Had he so much to lose? His reign had been unhappy. He was dominated by a mother who, it was said, had perverted him in more ways than one. He suffered from perpetual remorse for the fearful massacre of St Bartholomew's Eve. Poor Charles, perhaps one should rejoice that his earthly troubles were at an end.

One morning Mary sent a maid to ask after the health of her secretary Roullet who, she fancied, had looked even more sickly than usual on the previous day.

The maid returned to her in agitation, with the news that Monsieur Roullet was gasping for breath and seemed very distressed; and when Mary hurried to his bedside she saw at once that her secretary was dying.

He was too far gone to speak to Mary as she bent over his bed, but there was loving devotion in his eyes. Mary sent for priests and the last rites were administered; and that day she wept bitterly for the loss of another friend.

She was deeply touched to discover that Roullet had not spent the five thousand crowns which she had given him as a reward for his services to her, but kept them that he might leave them to her in his will.

'How strange,' she said to Seton, 'that I, who have so many enemies, should find so many to love me.'

'It is your possessions that make some your enemies,' answered Seton sagely. 'It is you yourself whom your friends love.'

'I shall need another secretary to take the place of poor Roullet, so I shall write to the Cardinal of Lorraine and ask him to send me someone whom I can trust.'

Mary carried out that intention and very soon afterwards her uncle sent her a handsome, energetic young man who had been one of his own secretaries; his name was Jacques Nau, and he was a brother of that Claud Nau who had served Mary some years before.

*　　*　　*

One day a letter from George Douglas was smuggled in to Mary. It always delighted her to hear from George and she was happy if she learned that he was alive and well.

He wrote that he had returned to Scotland and was in hiding there. Willie was with him. George had not married Mademoiselle La Verrière. Those plans had come to naught, he wrote. He thought constantly of the Queen and sought means of bringing her back to power. He believed that the Queen would be happy if her son were taken from Morton's care, where he was being instructed by the villainous Buchanan, and taken to Spain where Philip II would be very willing to supervise his education.

'If this could be brought about,' wrote George, ' I believe, and so do many of Your Majesty's friends, that it would be the first and most effective step towards regaining the throne of Scotland.'

Mary sat with the letter in her lap, her heart beating faster. She had forgotten how exciting intrigue could be. Yes, she thought, anything to remove little James from the hands of those who hated her and were endeavouring to bring him up to do the same.

George was right. If this could be successfully achieved it would be a step towards her return to power. And if only she could but see her son again, she often told herself, she would ask for nothing more. He was growing up now, that little James, having come to the end of his eighth year; and it would be so easy for a clever man to make him believe the lies against her.

Yet would Morton ever let him go? Dear George, he had always conceived such wild plans; but she remembered that it was due to Willie rather than George that she had escaped from Lochleven.

It saddened her that his marriage had come to nothing, because she feared it might be because he had set his Queen on such a high pedestal that he compared all others to their detriment, with her – quite wrongly, Mary believed.

She wrote to George. His plan interested her very much, she said; and if it could be put into execution she was sure it would have the effect they all desired; but he had suffered enough, and she begged him not to put himself in further peril for her sake.

* * *

Sheffield Castle had never been one of Bess's favourite residences, and in October of the year 1574 she took an opportunity of visiting Rufford, another of the family's stately houses. Bess took her unmarried daughter, Elizabeth Cavendish, with her and a few days after her arrival was very glad that she had, for noble travellers called at Rufford, and these were none other than Margaret, Countess of Lennox, who to Bess's joy was accompanied by her son Charles, the younger brother of Mary's husband, Lord Darnley, who had met his death so mysteriously in Kirk o' Field.

Bess warmly welcomed the visitors and made sure that the young people were often in each other's company.

Elizabeth Cavendish was a beautiful young woman, and Bess had long been looking for a suitable match; so when good fortune threw Charles Stuart in her way, the ambitious Bess felt this to be an opportunity which should not be missed.

As soon as she had seen that her guests were comfortably

settled, she sent for Elizabeth who, knowing her mother, guessed what was in her mind.

'The young Earl of Lennox is a charming fellow,' Bess began, and Elizabeth could not help laughing aloud.

Elizabeth had spirit and Bess liked to see spirit in her children, but she was always a little afraid that it might make them stand out against her. Not that Bess had any fears that she would not in time have her own way, but she did not wish to waste time and energy in unnecessary conflict.

Elizabeth said: 'He is also Charles Stuart and grandson of Margaret, who was the eldest sister of Henry VIII.'

Bess nodded approvingly. 'I see that your thoughts move in the right direction.'

'You cannot seriously mean that there might be a match between him and me!'

'And why not? You must admit he is handsome and entirely agreeable.'

'Mother! Your ambitions cloud your sense.'

'I'll thank you not to question my sense, girl. I have no wish to box your ears, but I shall certainly do so if you forget your duty to your mother.'

Elizabeth smiled. 'Nay, mother,' she said, 'do not be angry. But do you not agree that Her Majesty the Queen will wish to choose the bride of one who is so near the throne?'

'Doubtless she will. Therefore it is for others to make the choice before Her Majesty realizes it is made.'

There was perhaps little harm in allowing her mother to dream, thought Elizabeth. She knew that the Queen would never consent to a match between them. Bess, for all her arrogance, was after all only a Hardwick, and her daughter would never be considered worthy to mate with a royal Stuart.

'The children of this young Earl will be in direct succession to the throne,' said Bess, licking her lips as though some tasty dish had been set before her.

Elizabeth agreed with her mother; she had learned that it was always necessary to do that; and when Bess arranged that she should show Charles the gardens or ride beside him, she obeyed meekly.

They seemed momentous days for those two young people. Both felt that Queen Elizabeth would never allow them to marry, so their relationship began in perfect freedom, in spite of Bess's rather obvious tricks to throw them together. But their natural feelings were too strong and although the Lennoxes stayed only five days at Rufford, before the end of that time Charles and Elizabeth were deeply in love. The knowledge both enchanted and terrified them.

Bess, seeing her daughter melancholy, came to her apartments demanding the reason, and in a very short time, discovering it, was exultant.

Nothing could have suited her better.

'There is no need for melancholy!' she cried. 'You are my beloved daughter, and if you decide you are in love and cannot be happy without that young man, then depend upon it, your mother will arrange that that young man will be yours.'

'Mother, you would not dare. Remember who he is.'

But it was precisely because of who he was that Bess would dare. It was dangerous, she knew; but if the prize was great enough Bess was always ready to risk the danger. Her Elizabeth was going to be Countess of Lennox; and that meant that Bess's grandchild could – circumstances permitting – one day wear the crown of England. So, come what may, Elizabeth was going to marry the Countess of Lennox's Charles.

She sought an early interview with the Countess of Lennox, and as soon as they were alone together she took a kerchief and held it to her eyes.

Margaret Lennox, startled to see Bess in a condition so unusual with her, asked the reason. 'It is because of my dearest daughter's unhappiness. The foolish girl! Oh, how could she be so foolish!'

'My dear Bess, tell me what has happened. You cannot mean that your Elizabeth has distressed you. I think her one of the most delightful girls I have ever met.'

'She is. Indeed she is. But, Margaret, what do you think the foolish creature has done? I can scarcely bear to tell you. She has fallen in love with . . . your son Charles and he with her.'

'My Charles! So that is why he seems changed. I have never seen him quite as happy as he has been here.'

'Poor boy. Alas for him. These foolish young people! But what can you expect? They are both so young, so beautiful. Much as I have enjoyed your stay, my dear Margaret, I almost wish you had not come here.'

Margaret loved her son dearly; more so, she believed, since the tragic death of his elder brother, and it was her dearest wish to see him happy.

Bess, the kerchief still held to her eyes, was watching her companion intently, and felt like crying her triumph aloud, for she realized that it would be the easiest thing imaginable to win Margaret Lennox to her side.

'What shall we do? What shall we do?' she moaned.

'I think we should first discover how deeply our young people feel, suggested Margaret.

'I pray that their young hearts are not too strongly committed, although I fear the worst.'

Margaret was silent for a few seconds, then she said: 'But, Bess, suppose they should have fallen so deeply in love that it will break their hearts to part . . . what then?'

'I dare not think.'

'I do not want my son Charles to suffer as his brother Henry did.'

'His was a sad marriage . . . a marriage of ambition,' Bess agreed. 'Had it been a true love match doubtless Henry would be alive today.'

'I cannot bear to think of it even now. . . . It haunts me still.'

'You are his mother . . . and like all mothers who love their children, would rather see him happily married to some good young girl than dead . . . though he was once the King of Scotland through his wife.'

Margaret had covered her face with her hands. This was going well, thought Bess. All she needed was Margaret's consent and she would go ahead with the marriage. Queen Elizabeth's wrath could be faced when the marriage was a *fait accompli*. It would be like taking Shrewsbury to the Buxton baths all over again. Although this of course would be considered a far more serious matter. Never mind. The thing was to get the pair married.

'I know how you feel,' soothed Bess. 'You want Charles to have what Henry missed.'

'I would do anything for his happiness,' said Margaret vehemently.

'Then we must put our heads together. We must discover how deeply the feelings of these two young people are involved; and if it would break their hearts to be parted, are you, as his mother, prepared to face the wrath of the Queen?'

'Yes,' said Margaret, 'I would give everything I have to ensure his happiness.'

'How well I understand your feelings for mine are the same. I love my Elizabeth even as you love your Charles. If we decide this must be . . . no matter what the conseuences, we

337

might journey to Sheffield Castle. I am sure the Queen of Scots would wish to help us.'

Margaret seemed happy with this suggestion as though, if they dared not ask for the consent of one Queen, it would be as well to win that of another.

* * *

Little Bessie Pierpont was happiest when her grandmother was not in the castle, for then she was no longer in fear of being summoned suddenly to her presence. Grandmother Bess believed that all little girls, however young, should each day be given tasks and that if these tasks were not completed by the end of the day, punishment should follow.

Bessie was not a very good needlewoman and the stitches in her tapestry were rarely all of a size. They had to be unpicked and done again; but even so they rarely came out looking like the stitches of her godmother, Queen Mary. Sometimes Godmother Mary did the stitches for her; then they were perfect. It was a secret they shared; and when Grandmother saw them she would purse her lips and say: 'There, you see what comes from really trying. Next time, I wish them to be like this from the first.'

Grandmother Bess believed in whipping children who were not all she expected them to be – and of course she expected a good deal. Handwriting had to be neat and legible; history had to be learned; and Bessie, young as she was, had already been started on Latin exercises.

So it was not surprising that with Grandmother Bess away from Sheffield Castle Bessie felt free. It was a pleasure to wake each morning; to steal out of the bed she shared with her godmother and run to the window to look out at the confluence of the Sheaf and the Don, and to wonder whether she would be allowed to ride with one of the grooms this day. It was almost certain that she would, for her grandfather would be so busy when she asked him that he would say yes; and then all she had to do was tell Eleanor that she had her grandfather's permission, and Eleanor would tell the groom to saddle her horse.

But Bessie was often too sad to ride after all, because her dear godmother could not come with her and she feared that if she went riding it reminded the Queen that she was a prisoner.

338

It was a very sad thing to be a prisoner, Bessie knew, because the Queen had told her so. The Queen told her a great deal when they were in bed together; Bessie often requested stories to help her go to sleep. Then the Queen would remember the days when she was Bessie's age and tell her about the monastery on the island called Inchmahome and how she had lived with the monks there; she would tell of how she had sailed to France on a big ship and that even then the English had sought to make her their prisoner, although the great Queen Elizabeth was not Queen then, but only a little girl like Bessie herself.

It was all very bewildering and somehow sad. Bessie wished that she could do more to make the Queen happy. Although she did quite a lot, Queen Mary herself told her.

Bessie stood at the window watching the rain falling down. So she could not go riding even if she had permission. Bessie did not know what to do. There was no one to play with. She wished she had four Bessies as the Queen had had four Marys to play with her. What games they could have played in Sheffield Castle!

As she did not know what else to do Bessie decided to go along to find the Queen and see how she was getting on with the new gown she was making for her. Perhaps if the Queen were stitching with some of her ladies Bessie would ask for a story about Inchmahome or the French Court. She never tired of hearing them.

She went to the Queen's apartment, and quietly pushed open the door. At first she thought the room was empty; then she saw a man sitting at a table, writing. Bessie was about to turn and run when he said: 'I see you. It is useless to hide. What do you want?'

Bessie came into the room, trying to look haughty. Grandmother had made her walk seven times round a room regularly each morning with a book on her head. That was to make sure she kept her back straight and her head high. It was another unpleasant duty evaded in Grandmother's absence. So now Bessie walked as though she carried books on her head and, looking as haughty as Grandmother could have wished, said: 'And who are you to question me, sir?'

The man's dark eyes seemed to shine more brightly; his mouth turned up at the corners. 'Only Her Majesty's secretary, Your Grace – or should I say Your Majesty?'

'Yes,' said Bessie, laughing suddenly, 'say both.'

The man rose from the table, laid down his pen and bowed.

'You speak in a strange way,' Bessie told him.

'That is because English is not my native tongue. I am Her Majesty's French secretary, Your Majesty.'

Bessie laughed again. 'What is your name?'

'Jacques Nau.'

'That's a strange name, not like Bessie.'

'Not like Bessie at all.'

'Still,' said Bessie, 'we can't all be called Bessie.'

'I do not think the name would suit me as well as it suits you.'

Everything he said seemed to Bessie extraordinarily funny. He was less like a grown up person than anyone she knew.

'What are you writing?' she asked.

'Letters for the Queen.'

'You must be clever.'

'Very, very clever,' he assured her.

Bessie suddenly lost interest in him and went to the window. She wanted to see if the rain had stopped.

'I could then go out on my pony.' She threw the words over her shoulder.

'Has the rain stopped?' he asked.

She shook her head and knelt on the window seat. The sky was lowering and the rivers looked swollen. She did not look round but she could hear from the scratching of his pen that the man with the strange name had returned to his work. She liked him for not telling her to run away. He made her feel that she was not a foolish child, but a grown up person whose desire to ride or look out of windows was as necessary to her as it was for him to write the Queen's letters.

She was content to kneel, watching the rain, listening to the scratch of his pen.

Bessie forgot him as she knelt there. She was imagining that she had four little friends and they were all named Bessie. She had to give them nicknames as the Queen had given her Marys. 'Seton, Beaton, Livy and Flem . . .' she whispered to herself. And she saw herself as their leader. They sailed on a great ship to France, and when they arrived everybody was very pleased to see them.

Suddenly she saw a party of riders coming towards the castle. She stared; they must be very wet. Ought she to go and tell Eleanor or one of the maids that visitors were coming this way?

A sudden panic came to her. What if Grandmother Bess were among those travellers? She was very still, watching; and thus she remained for fully ten minutes. By that time her fears were confirmed. That was Grandmother Bess, and the respite was over.

Bessie now remembered tasks uncompleted. Her Latin exercise was not done. How fortunate that the Queen had helped her with her tapestry. But what if Grandmother Bess summoned her to her presence at once, demanding to see the finished exercise?

Tears welled up into Bessie's eyes. Grandmother had a hard hand and, although she said it grieved her to punish Bessie more than the blows hurt Bessie, that was hard to believe.

The secretary must have heard the sounds of arrival for, turning suddenly, she found him standing behind her.

He said: 'Ha, so the Countess is returning with friends. Things will not now be quite as they have been, my little Bessie.' He said her name as though there were several e's at the end of it instead of one. Bessie liked the sound of it but it could not comfort her now.

He had noticed the tears in her eyes, for he said: 'Why, little one, you are crying.'

Because his voice was gentle the tears flowed the faster. He lifted her up, carried her to the table and sat her on his knee.

'Now tell the funny Frenchman,' he said, wiping away the tears.

So Bessie told him. 'It takes hours and hours . . . and I have done none of it. . . .'

He listened carefully, then looked very thoughtful. Bessie stared intently at his face, noticing how dark his eyes were and his skin, and that his lashes and brows were thick and black.

Suddenly he clapped his hands and said: 'I have it.'

'Yes . . . yes?' she cried impatiently.

'Go and bring the exercise to me.'

Bessie slipped to the ground and went to the little table in the corner of the room which the Queen had said was hers, and opening the drawer took out the exercise.

The Frenchman put his head on one side; he laughed, showing very white teeth, and looked so funny that Bessie was laughing too, although an occasional sob escaped her.

'We will a miracle do,' he said and, picking up his pen, he completed the exercise as though he did not have to think at all.

Bessie stared at him in wonder. 'Is it right?' she asked.

'Your grandmother herself could not do better.'

'Let me see.' Bessie held the paper close to her face and studied it. It looked right; she could not be sure of course; but at least Grandmother would not whip her for being idle.

'Listen,' said the Frenchman. 'They are arriving now. Copy out your exercise and when your grandmother asks for it you must not tell her who helped you.'

Bessie shook her head emphatically. 'Can you always do it like that?' she asked.

He snapped his fingers. 'Like that!' he said.

Bessie's eyes were full of speculation. He laughed. 'Next time,' he said, 'do not cry. Come to me.'

There were shouts from below. There was bustle everywhere. The peaceful atmosphere of the castle was shattered. There was no doubt now that the Countess of Shrewsbury had come home.

Bessie hesitated and then flung her arms about the Frenchman's neck and kissed him. She was happy because she knew that she had a new friend, and it was somehow wonderful because she had found him at precisely that hour when her grandmother had come home.

*　　*　　*

Had Bessie known it, her grandmother's thoughts were far from Latin exercises. As soon as she had settled her important guests into the castle and harried her servants into preparing a banquet worthy of them, she made her way to Mary's apartments and asked for permission to see her.

Mary received her at once, asked if she had had a pleasant change, and told her how sorry she was that she had been caught by the inclement weather.

Bess shrugged aside the weather. A wetting never hurt anyone, she was sure. Indeed, thought Mary, she looks more energetic than ever, and so triumphant that something important surely must have taken place. So little excitement was happening to her that Mary longed to hear Bess's news, and said so.

'Such news, Your Majesty, that I could hardly wait to reach Sheffield to ask your help and advice.'

342

Mary could not help smiling. She was sure that Bess only wished her to confirm the wisdom of what she had decided to do. That was what Bess would call taking advice – because advice was something she would never take from anyone.

'It is my foolish daughter. What does Your Majesty think! The child has fallen in love . . . and so unwisely. I am torn in two. It is such a pleasure to see her happiness, but I am, alas, so fearful for her.'

'You mean Elizabeth?'

'Elizabeth, yes. Your Majesty will see the change in her. She is quite different from the girl who left Sheffield with me. She has fallen in love with Lennox. Charles Stuart, if you please. I said to her: "You foolish girl . . . what can come of such a match?"'

Mary was silent. Her father-in-law, the Earl of Lennox, who was father of this young man, had hated her. He had called for her blood, believing her to have been involved in the murder of his son, Lord Darnley. But that Earl was dead now, and his wife, Margaret, was of a gentler nature and she would know that, whatever else Mary was capable of, it was not murder.

She was aware that Bess was watching her covertly. 'What can I do?' she moaned. 'May I implore Your Majesty's help?'

'I would help you with all my heart, if it were in my power to do so,' said Mary. 'But I fear Elizabeth would never agree to the match, and you know it would be necessary to have her consent since, if Elizabeth died without heirs and I and my son followed her to the grave, young Lennox would be considered by some to be the heir of England.'

Bess's eyes were sparkling, so she hastily covered them and murmured: 'My foolish child. My poor Elizabeth!'

Then she sighed deeply and said: 'May I bring the young people to you, and the Countess with them? They want to tell you themselves how much they love each other, how desolate they will be for the rest of their lives if cruel fate should part them.'

'I should be happy to receive them.'

'And, Your Majesty, will you help me to comfort these poor young people?'

'If they truly love and are to be parted, none of us will be able to comfort them.'

'I continually ask myself whether a way can be found out of this trouble.'

'There are only two ways open for them,' answered Mary. 'They must separate and live with their unhappiness; or marry and face whatever punishment Elizabeth thinks they deserve.'

'I cannot bear to think of their misery. I almost believe that . . .' Bess looked cautiously at Mary. Then she sighed. 'But I will bring them to you, and you may judge of their love.'

'Bring them with all speed,' said Mary. 'I long to see them.'

* * *

When Mary saw the young people together, she had no doubt of their love. She was very sorry for them, and wished that she had the power of Elizabeth to grant them their wish.

Margaret Lennox lingered when the others had left with Bess, and Mary guessed that the Countess had told them that she wished to speak with her in private.

When the door had closed and they were alone, Margaret said: 'I have news for Your Majesty. I have been with George Douglas who is awaiting the opportunity to bring my grandson – your son – out of Scotland. He has a ship in readiness which will carry the boy to Spain.'

Mary clasped her hands. 'I pray it may succeed. My little boy is constantly in my thoughts. I fear for his safety while he is in the hands of such men.'

Although Margaret Lennox had been loud in her condemnation of Mary during her husband's lifetime when she had deeply mourned the death of Darnley, she had always been inclined to doubt Mary's complicity in the murder; now she was certain of Mary's innocence and wanted to make amends for the accusations of the past. She had believed Mary, a mother herself, would understand her grief at Darnley's death. She was certain of that now. Mary was ready to trust her and, when she saw Mary's anguish on account of her son, it was clearly ridiculous to imagine that such a gentle, loving woman could have taken part in that cold-blooded murder.

So now Margaret had thrown herself wholeheartedly into the plot to remove young James from Scotland and carry him off to Spain. James was Mary's son but he was also her grandson, and the child's plight was therefore of deepest concern to them both.

'The poor child, in Morton's hands, left to the care of that odious Buchanan!' said Margaret with a shiver. 'I have provided Douglas with money . . . the King of Spain is prepared to receive the boy. It is now only a matter of waiting for an opportunity to rescue him.'

They talked for a long time of this plan, and at length the Countess said: 'What think you of this love between my son and Elizabeth Cavendish?'

'I think that it is indeed love on the part of the two young people.'

'I am inclined to say to them: Marry, and face the consequences after. It is rarely that one sees such love among people of the nobility. Marriages are arranged for them; they miss that ecstasy which is so sweet.'

Mary thought of her marriage with François. No ecstasy there. She had briefly loved Darnley, until he had killed her love with his unworthiness; as for Bothwell . . . that was a mad, all-consuming passion. It had brought her brief ecstasy and these dreary years of imprisonment. Yet she knew that if she had to choose again, she would choose Bothwell.

'If I were in their places . . .' she began.

The Countess of Lennox looked at her swiftly: 'Your Majesty would choose love, I know. There is too little love in the world. I believe, if those young people had the support of myself, of the Countess of Shrewsbury and Your Majesty, they would not hesitate.'

'What of the Earl?'

'Oh, you know how the Countess manages matters in this household. She will not have told him as yet.'

'He would never agree to go against his Queen's wishes. He would ask her permission for them to marry.'

'To do that would be an end to their hopes. Elizabeth would never consent.'

'Then,' said Mary, 'if they wish to marry, they should do so and tell Elizabeth afterwards. If their love is deep enough they will think it well worth-while to accept whatever punishment she may inflict.'

A few days later Elizabeth Cavendish and Charles Stuart, Earl of Lennox, were married.

* * *

Queen Elizabeth was with Lord Burleigh and the Earl of Leicester when the news of the marriage was brought to her. Her face grew purple with indignation.

'What's this!' she cried. 'Lennox married to that girl Cavendish! Lennox! What madness is this? This is the work of Bess

345

of Hardwick. I tell you there is no holding that ambitious woman. So she would marry her daughter to Lennox, would she! And do it before I have time to stop her!'

'It seems, Your Majesty,' murmured Burleigh, 'that others were in the plot. The bridegroom's mother is not guiltless, and since this intrigue took place at Sheffield Castle doubtless one other had a hand in it.'

'Meddling women!' snapped Elizabeth. 'I'll teach them to defy me. They shall all be lodged in the Tower.'

'Your Majesty, to bring the Queen of Scotland to the Tower might be hazardous,' put in Leicester. 'In the first place attempts might be made to rescue her during the journey; and in the second if she were lodged in London her case would be brought more conspicuously to the notice of the people. In the Tower she would indeed be your prisoner; in Sheffield Castle she might still be called your guest.'

'You are right, Robert, but think not that I shall allow the Shrewsbury and Lennox women to defy me. Let them be made prisoners without a moment's delay, and have them brought to the Tower.'

'Your Majesty speaks with your usual wisdom,' said Burleigh.

And Leicester bowed his head in adoring agreement.

That day guards were sent to Sheffield to bring the two Countesses to London and the Tower.

*　　*　　*

So the indignant Bess and the Countess of Lennox were taken as prisoners from Sheffield Castle.

There was a subdued atmosphere there after they had left. The happiness of the married lovers was muted, for they feared that they had brought grave trouble to their mothers; Mary sat with her friends and they worked for hours at their tapestry, talking of that event which had led to the departure of the two Countesses, wondering how they fared in their prison at the Tower.

Mary said that they would send the exquisite tapestry which they had worked to Elizabeth, who was so notoriously greedy for gifts, in the hope that she might be softened towards her three prisoners – the two in the Tower and the one in Sheffield Castle.

Little Bessie Pierpont was happy, because there was now no need to worry about her daily tasks. She could ride and play and take her lessons and listen to the Queen's stories of her childhood. But Bessie was finding that the greatest pleasure she enjoyed was in the company of her new friend, Monsieur Nau, who was teaching her to speak French; and it was amazing how quickly she learned to prattle in that language. Never had any lesson been such fun as learning French. Bessie's only sadness during those months was when Monsieur Jacques was too busy to be with her.

'The castle is a different place without the Countess,' said Seton to Andrew Beaton.

'Do you never grow tired of your prison here?' he asked.

'I shall never grow tired of serving the Queen,' she answered.

'Yet you should have a life of your own,' he told her.

She turned away from his ardent gaze. Seton did not wish him to say all that she knew he was feeling; she distrusted her own emotions too. She had vowed to serve the Queen as long as she was needed. She was still needed. There was no time, Seton assured herself, to think of anything but serving the Queen.

Mary often sighed for Buxton.

'It is the only place in England where I wish to be,' she said. 'I wonder if I shall be allowed to pay another visit to the baths.'

She was embroidering a nightcap in colourful silks; she used green and gold silks, for she had heard that Elizabeth was fond of such colours. She had already made two others in delicate colouring and she intended to send these to Elizabeth with a request that she might visit Buxton.

As soon as the nightcaps were completed Mary sent them to the French ambassador, asking him to present them to Elizabeth. When Elizabeth saw them she grunted. She was not very eager for such things; she much preferred jewels to be worn by day, or furniture and tapestry which could be admired by many.

Moreover she did not believe that it was wise of her to accept gifts from the Queen of Scots, and she told the French ambassador that such acceptance could become a political matter and she feared the disapproval of her ministers.

The French ambassador knew this to be false, and replied that the Queen of Scots merely wished to show her good will.

'Well then,' retorted Elizabeth, 'I will take them, but I pray you tell the Queen of Scots that as I have been some years longer in this world than she has, I have learned that people are accustomed to receive with both hands, but to give only with one finger.'

This was meant to convey that Mary was asking for favours in return for her nightcaps – presents which Elizabeth was not really eager to accept.

But when she tried on the nightcaps she did find them becoming and she thought that, as Mary was so eager to visit Buxton, she did not see why she should not go, providing a strong enough guard conducted her there.

CHAPTER FIFTEEN

BUXTON, CHATSWORTH AND SHEFFIELD

WHAT A PLEASURE it was to be once more at Buxton.

'I feel better as soon as I arrive in this place,' Mary declared.

The Earl was inclined to relax restrictions. He had brought certain of the servants with him from Sheffield and among these was Eleanor Britton. Life was serene and pleasant with the Countess in the Tower.

The waters had their usual beneficial effect and Mary's health improved accordingly. She visited Poole's Hole once more and enjoyed the outing.

'If only I could stay at Buxton,' she told Seton, 'I am sure I should quickly recover my health and feel young again.'

One day the Earl came to her apartments in Low Buxton in a state of excitement.

'Your Majesty, we have an eminent visitor at Buxton who I feel sure is here solely because Your Majesty has come to take the waters.'

'Who?' she asked.

'Lord Burleigh himself.'

'Lord Burleigh! Then, depend upon it, he comes on Queen Elizabeth's orders.'

'I hope it is not to spy on us.'

'Ah, you think it may be so?'

'I cannot think of any other reason.'

Poor Shrewsbury! He might feel relieved to be rid of Bess but he was at a loss without her. Mary imagined how differently Bess would have received the news of Burleigh's presence. She would have been stimulated by the thought of conflict, whereas poor Shrewsbury felt he had yet another burden added to those which were already too heavy.

When Burleigh called on the Queen of Scots, Mary received him cautiously. She knew he had been one of her most bitter enemies at the Court of Elizabeth, and she did not believe he could suddenly have become her friend.

Burleigh looked wan and walked with even more difficulty than he had before.

'You are hoping to derive benefit from the waters?' the Queen asked sympathetically.

'Yes, Your Majesty. I suffer acutely from gout and my feet have always troubled me.'

'Then I trust you find comfort from the waters, as I do.'

'Your Majesty's health has improved, I hope, since you have been here?'

Mary assured him that it had, but she knew he had not come here to inquire about her health.

Later she discovered, through Shrewsbury, that Elizabeth's minister, who was the sternest of Protestants, had been making inquiries as to how many visitors she received while at Buxton. He was afraid that, under less restraint as she must necessarily be at Buxton in contrast to Sheffield, certain members of the Catholic nobility might have access to her. Burleigh lived in terror of another Catholic rising.

*   *.   *

The days passed pleasantly. It was good to hear Mary's lighthearted laughter; often she played the lute and sang. Buxton was so good for her. The mountain air was sharp but invigorating and there was shelter in the valley from the bleak winds which buffeted Sheffield Castle.

Burleigh called often. He was in fact constantly on the alert. When he visited the Queen he tried to startle her with sly questions; she enjoyed arousing his suspicions and then letting him discover that there was nothing in them; but all the same these contacts meant that each was discovering a new respect for the other. It was impossible for Mary not to respect the minister's single-minded loyalty to his Queen, just as it was impossible for Burleigh not to be affected by the charm of

349

Mary. Thus, in spite of the fact that they must be cautious of each other, a form of friendship grew between them.

This pleasant life might have gone on throughout the season, but news was brought to Elizabeth that Burleigh was at Buxton and calling on the Queen of Scots.

Elizabeth was incensed because Burleigh had gone to the baths without asking her consent; and that, as he had been there some time, must have paid many calls on the Queen of Scots.

He was recalled at once and as soon as he came into the presence of his royal mistress she berated him for what she pleased to call his infidelity.

'So, sir,' she cried, 'you have been visiting the Queen of Scots, paying compliments to the fair lady, I'll warrant.'

'I was there on Your Majesty's business,' began Burleigh.

'Is that so, William Cecil! Is it my business then to play the gallant and compliment the Queen of Scots on her beautiful eyes?'

'But I did not pay such compliments. . . .'

'Did you not! Then were her eyes not beautiful enough to warrant the compliment?'

The answer must be the expected one: 'Having seen Your Majesty's eyes, no others could seem beautiful.'

'H'm!' said the Queen. 'You're another Norfolk, it seems. I trust you remember, sir, what happened to him.'

'I do, Your Majesty.'

'Look to it that it does not happen to you!'

'If I deserved such a fate, which I should do if I failed to serve my own Sovereign Lady Elizabeth with all my heart, I should welcome it,' answered Burleigh with dignity. 'Since I could never deserve it, I do not fear it.'

Elizabeth liked a bold answer and she softened at once. She had never really doubted the loyalty of this good friend; she merely feared that he might have found the company of the Queen of Scots entrancing, as it was clear so many men did.

'Go to then,' she said. 'And do not leave us again. We need you here beside us.'

Burleigh bowed; he still looked a little ruffled.

Was he a little bewitched by that fascinating woman? Elizabeth wondered.

She said angrily: 'She shall not remain at Buxton. I fear she enjoys too much freedom there. Let her return to Chatsworth; that is near by.' She looked shrewdly at Cecil. 'Is she as beautiful as reports say?' she demanded suddenly, and there was a note in her voice which was pleading with him to say that she was not.

'The Queen of Scots is fair enough,' answered Burleigh. He was preparing the necessary remark to follow, when Elizabeth held up a hand.

'Mayhap I should go to see her for myself,' she said. 'It is a notion which pleases me. She shall go to Chatsworth. If I went to Buxton to take the waters, I could ride to Chatsworth in disguise. A lady seeking a night's shelter! Thus I could see this beauty for myself. I could exchange words with her. I like the idea.'

She evidently did, for she mentioned it to certain of her women, and they amused themselves by picturing the meeting.

'Then,' said Elizabeth, 'I shall compare her face and figure with my own – which I have always wished to do.'

'Your Majesty need not go to Chatsworth to make the comparison,' she was told. 'All who set eyes on the Queen of Scots say that she has a pleasant mien, but beside Your Majesty she is as the moon to the sun.'

'Then perhaps the journey would not be necessary,' replied Elizabeth with a yawn.

She had made up her mind that she would never look at Mary. In moments of truth she knew the answer to the question, Who is the fairer, she or I? which her desire for flattery and her jealousy of her rival forced her to ask.

She would never allow herself to face that truth, for while she had never seen Mary she could go on believing what her courtiers were so eager to tell her.

*   *   *

There was excitement at Chatsworth when the rumour reached Mary that Queen Elizabeth was going to visit her in the disguise of a gentlewoman.

Mary had been feeling depressed because she had had to leave Buxton. Moreover she had heard from George Douglas that those who were concerned with him in the plot to rescue her son from Morton and Buchanan, had decided it would be too dangerous to continue. The Countess of Lennox, who had been in the conspiracy, was now in the Tower, and it might well be that some intelligence had reached Elizabeth of their intention, and the imprisonment of the Countess was due to the part she had taken in the plot – not, as the English Queen

351

would wish it to be believed, because of the marriage of her son. George could not act without friends; therefore this matter would have to be shelved.

Then came the startling news that Queen Elizabeth was planning to visit Chatsworth in disguise.

Mary excitedly gathered her women about her. Seton should do her hair. Which gown should she wear? She had very few jewels but they would have to make do with what she had.

Seton said: 'She will come in her jewels and rich garments, depend upon it. But never fear, we shall show her that you would be more beautiful in sackcloth than she is in cloth of gold.'

Mary laughed. 'That is not important, Seton. All that matters is that at last I shall speak to her. I am certain that when we are face to face I shall make her understand.'

For weeks they waited.

But Elizabeth did not come to Chatsworth.

*   *   *

Elizabeth was never at ease when Mary was at Chatsworth. She feared that the Queen enjoyed too much freedom there, and after a few months Mary found herself back in Sheffield Castle.

Bess had rejoined the household. She seemed none the worse for the months she had spent in the Tower, apart from a smouldering anger at the indignity she had been obliged to suffer.

The atmosphere of the household changed as soon as she entered it. She stormed through the servants' quarters, discovering what had been left undone.

'It is as though a sharp wind blows through the house,' said Mary to Seton.

Bess sat with Mary and worked with her on her tapestry – the two of them alone so that, said Bess, they could talk at their ease; and as Bess had had an interview with Elizabeth, Mary was eager to hear what she had to say.

'She showed her displeasure at first,' Bess told her. 'But it did not last. There is a certain bond between us which she cannot ignore. When I was released from the Tower and she sent for me she accused me of overweening ambition. I admitted to this and she burst out laughing. She knew full well that my ambition matches her own. I was bold enough to say to her: "If Your Majesty had been born plain Bess of Hardwick instead of a King's daughter, you would have sought means of making good marriages for your children – had you borne them." '

'And did she agree?'

'Not in so many words, but her mood changed towards me and we talked of old times.'

'It seems,' said Mary wistfully, 'that if one can only talk with her, she is ready to see reason.'

'She will always see what she wants to see.'

'Do you think she has a sense of justice?'

That made Bess laugh. 'I see into her mind without effort,' she boasted. 'The virgin Queen; do you believe it?'

'I have no reason to do otherwise.'

'Ha! You should see her with Leicester. There are times when she cannot keep her hands from him . . . smoothing his hair, patting his arm. That speaks clearly enough to me. She has had several children . . . not only by Leicester.'

'But this is impossible!'

'Impossible is a word Elizabeth does not know. Why, has Your Majesty never heard of all the romping with Thomas Seymour? Then she was little more than a girl. They say there was a child as a result of that. Oh yes, they do, and I for one believe it. And what she felt for Seymour is nothing compared with her passion for Leicester. He's her husband . . . without benefit of clergy, of course. Our Elizabeth does not want a man to share her throne . . . only her bed.'

Mary was scandalized. Then she realized how angry Bess was. Elizabeth had had her sent to the Tower, and Bess would not forgive such insult in a hurry. There was nothing she could do to take her revenge on Elizabeth – except remember all the scandal she had ever heard of her and repeat it to the Queen who, like herself, had very little for which to thank the Queen of England.

*   *   *

The Earl of Shrewsbury came to Mary's apartments one day and told her that he had news which he thought would cheer her.

Bothwell, incarcerated in the Castle of Malmoë, was grievously sick of the dropsy, and because he feared that his life was nearing its end he had written a confession in which he exonerated Mary from the murder of Darnley.

353

He had written: 'The Bastard Moray began, Morton drew, and I wove the web of this murder.' And he went on to say that Mary was completely innocent of it.

When he had given her this news Shrewsbury left Mary who felt so moved that she went to her bed and lay there. Memories came vividly back to her. She could not imagine Bothwell sick unto death. She thought of their brief and stormy life together and she wept for them both; yet she rejoiced that in his last hours he should remember her and seek to do what was right. She had always known that he was not wholly wicked. He had been blessed – or cursed – with twice the vitality of most men. He had been guilty of so much; all his life, rough Borderer that he was, he had taken what he wanted without thought of the consequences. It had seemed that the rape of a Queen meant no more to him than that of a shepherdess in the Border country of his enemies; yet it could not have been so, for when the pains of death were on him, he remembered her with tenderness.

She rose from her bed and went to her *prie Dieu*, where she prayed for his soul; and she gave thanks that he had at the end thought kindly enough of her to write his confession.

It seemed however that Bothwell was indestructible, for he recovered from his sickness. But the confession had been made.

*　　*　　*

With the coming of summer the French ambassador persuaded Elizabeth to allow Mary to visit Buxton once more, and under such pressure Elizabeth agreed.

Mary had been deriving her usual benefit from the Spa and was hoping to spend the whole season at Shrewsbury's Low Buxton, when an event at the English Court resulted in her stay there being brought to an abrupt end.

Leicester had been complaining to Elizabeth that he was unwell, and Elizabeth had been concerned about the health of her favourite.

She had sent him her own physician and visited him herself to see how he was progressing.

On her arrival a mournful Leicester thanked her for her solicitude and told her that her presence did him more good than anything else.

Gratified always to receive his compliments, she patted his cheek and told him that he must get well quickly, for her Court was the poorer for his absence. There was a sharpness in her eyes, though, for Leicester's amorous adventures with other women had always annoyed her. She understood that, since she would not marry him herself, she must expect these wanderings; yet she believed that she could call him back to her without the slightest difficulty; and she enjoyed showing her power not only over his mistresses but over Leicester himself.

Then came the shock.

'My doctors have ordered me to drink the waters of Buxton and use the baths for twenty days. They tell me that if I do this – and only if I do – I can expect to recover.'

Buxton! thought Elizabeth. Was not the Queen of Scots at Buxton?

Her eyes were narrowed, her lips tight. One heard such stories of the charm of that woman. What was Leicester after? She was on the point of curtly ordering him to remain where he was but, glancing at him she saw that he did look wan. What if it were true that he needed the Buxton waters?

Seeing that he was waiting with some trepidation for her reaction, she smiled suddenly. 'Well, my dear Robert,' she said, 'if those Buxton waters are the cure you need, then you must have them. But we shall be loth to see you go so far from us.'

' 'Tis but for twenty days, beloved.'

'H'm! If you linger longer, I myself may take a trip to Buxton to see if it is only the waters of which you are in need.'

When Elizabeth left him she sent for a messenger. An order was to be dispatched at once to Shrewsbury at Low Buxton. The Queen of Scots was to be removed to Tutbury Castle without delay.

*   *   *

'Tutbury!' cried Mary in dismay, staring at the Earl.

'I fear so. The order of Her Majesty.'

'Not Tutbury. Sheffield is uncomfortable enough, but I shall die if I have to return to Tutbury.'

Shrewsbury had no wish to return to Tutbury either.

'I will write immediately to Walsingham,' he said, 'and tell him that Tutbury is in such a state of ill repair that it is impossible for my household to live there at this time. But I fear we must leave Buxton.'

'Before my cure is finished!' murmured Mary.

'But you would prefer to go to Sheffield rather than Tutbury, and that is all we can hope for.'

Shrewsbury wrote to Walsingham who, after consulting Elizabeth, replied that the Queen of Scots was to be removed from Buxton and that Shrewsbury should conduct her to Sheffield Castle without delay.

So back to Sheffield went Mary and her guards.

*   *   *

Realizing Elizabeth's suspicions and having learned that the Queen of Scots had been hustled from Buxton, Leicester thought it advisable to delay his visit to the Spa for a few weeks and explain his motives to the Queen before proceeding there.

Walking with the aid of a stick, he came into the Queen's presence and managed to look so sickly that Elizabeth, whose feelings for him went deeper than those she felt for anyone else, was alarmed.

'Why Robert,' she said, 'you are indeed ill.'

As he took her hand and kissed it she dismissed the women who were with her that she might talk in secret with her Robert.

'I have had disturbed nights since our last meeting, because I feared that I had not been entirely truthful to my adored Queen and mistress.'

'What have you been meddling in now, Robert?'

'I was about to meddle . . . on your behalf, of course. It is true that my doctors advised me to take the Buxton waters, but there is another reason why I wished to go there. Does Your Majesty remember who was there until you sent her away?'

'I remember.'

'My dearest love, I am afraid that where that woman is there will also be intrigue . . . dangerous intrigue which threatens the one whom I live to serve. These plans to marry her to Don Jon are not over. I believe that the greater freedom she is allowed to enjoy at Buxton may be an encouragement to conspirators.'

'And what do you propose to do about that?'

'To go to Buxton. To be the guest of the Shrewsburys. To keep my eyes and ears alert.'

Elizabeth nodded. 'Well, Robert, you are one whom I would always trust to serve me well. There are so many bonds binding us.'

Leicester looked into her face and took both her hands. She was remembering how, before she was Queen of England, he had brought her gold and offered himself to fight in her cause should it be necessary to fight. She remembered the early days of her reign when she had believed she would marry him. And she would have done so but for the mysterious death of Amy Robsart. She could never think of that affair without a shudder. It had so nearly destroyed them both. They knew too much of each other not to work together. He might have other motives in wishing to meet the Queen of Scots, but he would never betray Elizabeth while she lived.

Leicester was thinking the same. He admired Elizabeth beyond anyone else on Earth. He had good reason to respect her shrewd brain. He would be beside her while she lived; but if she were to die suddenly – a fate which could overtake any – and there was a new ruler on the throne, that ruler could well be the Queen of Scots.

He wished to ingratiate himself with Mary while he worked for Elizabeth. If he could find evidence to bring Mary to the block, he would do so. But if he could not, and if she must live, he wanted her to think of him as her friend. Thus he determined to make sure of a place in the sun in either camp.

'Robert,' cried Elizabeth, 'you must go to Buxton. You need those baths. I will give Mary permission to return to Buxton to continue with her cure. I will also write to the Shrewsburys, telling them to expect you, for if you are to spy on Mary you will need to be under the same roof. There! Then you shall come and tell me if all the reports of her beauty are true. I shall want exact details of how she looks and what she wears.'

Robert smiled. He was already composing the compliments he would pay Elizabeth when he returned from his visit to Mary.

When he had left her, Elizabeth wrote to the Earl and Countess of Shrewsbury. They must treat the Earl of Leicester as they would treat her, for all that was done to him was done to herself. 'He is another ourself,' she wrote indulgently.

There were still times when she could be indiscreet through love of Leicester.

*   *   *

It was gratifying to be back at Low Buxton. For the first few days Mary indulged in the pleasure which she found in this place; her health improved and there was gaiety in her apartments. She did wonder at the capricious behaviour of Elizabeth in whisking her away and then allowing her to return.

Then Bess broke the news that Leicester was coming to Low Buxton.

'He has to take the waters on account of his health,' she said. 'It seems strange to me that he should pay his visit while Your Majesty is here. You will have a chance of assessing the charm of this man who, rumour has it, has fathered several children on the Queen.'

Mary looked startled but Bess went on. 'Oh, there is none to hear me. And if such a rumour were repeated, Elizabeth would never dare accuse me of uttering it. Such matters are best kept dark.'

'She could take her revenge by accusing you of something else.'

Bess snapped her fingers. She had changed since her stay in the Tower. Her dignity had certainly been ruffled; and there was one other event which had increased her pride; that was the birth of her granddaughter, Arabella Stuart, to Elizabeth and Charles whose marriage had been the cause of her imprisonment. Bess had a granddaughter – her own flesh and blood – who was in the line of succession to the throne; it was something she could not forget. Her Arabella, she thought, though she was wise enough not to give voice to this thought, was more royal than Queen Elizabeth, for the child was undoubtedly legitimate; and could Henry VIII's marriage to Elizabeth's mother, Anne Boleyn, be really accepted as legal? Bess believed that little Arabella might well one day be Queen. Why not? She had an indefatigable grandmother to scheme for her.

So, in the presence of Mary, she could snap her fingers at Elizabeth, and she had no compunction in recalling all the scandalous gossip she had ever heard about her.

Leicester arrived in due course at Low Buxton, and on the orders of Elizabeth the Shrewsburys treated him with the respect due to royalty.

When he was brought to Mary, they assessed each other, and Mary was immediately aware of the charm which Elizabeth had found so potent, though it had no effect on her. She was certain that Leicester was an enemy. As for Leicester, he was struck by the beauty of Mary and wistfully thought how pleasant it would have been if the attempt to marry her had been successful.

358

Mary was pale and often moved with difficulty; the years of imprisonment in comfortless castles had robbed her of her youth, yet her beauty was indestructible. The contours of her face were perfect, although the flesh had fallen away from her bones; the long eyes were lovely although there were shadows beneath them; and all her movements were graceful in spite of rheumatism.

There is still time, thought Leicester, to take her away and restore her to that glowing beauty which must once have been hers.

He would tell Elizabeth of the shadows under her eyes, of her loss of flesh, of her rheumatism. That would please the jealous creature and do him no harm.

Meanwhile he sought to charm the Queen of Scots. This was not so easy as charming Elizabeth. There had been too many to love this woman, not for her crown but for herself. She lacked Elizabeth's political shrewdness certainly, but she had learned not deliberately to blind herself to the motives of men who came to court her.

He talked often with her, during the stay at Low Buxton, but she was always aloof. He tried to discover how firm was the basis of those rumours which said Don Jon of Austria was to be her husband. He implied that he was ready to work in her cause. But she did not trust him. She played a skilful game of prevarication with him which angered him, and he decided that he could do no good by lingering at Low Buxton.

He curtailed his visit, declaring that the baths were less beneficial than he had hoped, and he went away angry, but not before he had had a private talk with the Earl.

The health of the Queen of Scots was clearly not good, he said. Queen Elizabeth would be disturbed when she heard of this and he was going to ask that a certain physician be sent who he was sure would quickly cure Mary of her ills.

Shrewsbury thanked the Earl for his kindness and trusted he would take a good report to Elizabeth of the hospitality he had received at Low Buxton.

'Have no fear,' Leicester told him. 'You could not have made a guest more welcome if that guest had been Elizabeth herself.'

So he left Buxton pondering. The Queen of Scots would not accept him as a friend. He knew what sort of physician he would send to her.

*　　　*　　　*

Mary had returned with the Shrewsburys and her little court and guards to Sheffield when Leicester's physician arrived.

Bess and her husband were apprehensive when they discovered that he was an Italian named Julio Borgarucci.

Bess took him to the apartment which had been prepared for him and then hurried to the Earl.

'Are you thinking the same as I am?' she asked.

'An Italian!' murmured the Earl. 'We know what they are noted for.'

'I fancy I have heard of this man. He is not so much a physician as a professional poisoner.'

'Do you think he comes on the command of the Queen?'

'Who knows? Leicester is one of those who believe they can act first and ask the Queen's permission afterwards.'

'I'll not have my prisoner poisoned under my roof.'

'Ah, Shrewsbury, you are truly vehement for once! But I had forgotten – she is more than your prisoner, is she not?'

'She is the Queen of Scotland.'

'Your beloved Queen of Scotland! You must protect her at all costs . . . against Leicester's Italian . . . against Elizabeth herself, if this man comes by her command.'

'I believe, my dear Bess, that you feel in this matter as I do. You would never agree that such a foul deed should be done to a helpless woman in our care.'

Bess nodded; but she was not so sure. She kept thinking of her granddaughter, little Arabella Stuart. Since the birth of this child, Bess could not stop thinking of the bright possibility of her wearing the crown. The fewer to stand before her in the line of succession the better; consequently Bess had felt less kindly towards the Queen of Scots since the birth of Arabella. Not that she showed this; not that she entirely admitted the fact to herself; but it was there . . . lurking at the back of her mind, and the advent of Julio Borgarucci to Sheffield could only renew it.

But Shrewsbury could be determined when he made up his mind. He would not allow Mary to eat any food which was not prepared by her own faithful servants. He dropped hints to Seton who was doubly watchful; so no harm came to Mary through the visit of Borgarucci; and Shrewsbury seized an early opportunity to have the man sent from Sheffield.

How zealous he is to preserve Mary's safety! thought Bess. Rarely have I seen Shrewsbury bestir himself so much.

She wondered then if he were in truth enamoured of Mary. She did not greatly care if he were. All her thoughts were becoming more and more centred on the future of little Arabella.

* * *

Seton was preoccupied, Mary noticed, and she believed she knew the reason why. Andrew Beaton was continually seeking opportunities to be in her company; at first she had repulsed him; now she did not do so. But neither Seton nor Andrew Beaton behaved like two people in love.

Mary thought of them often. If Seton were in love she should marry and go away from here. This could be arranged. Andrew might go to Scotland or, if that was too dangerous, to France. Seton, like herself, thought Mary, had not thrived in these damp and draughty castles which had been their homes for so long. Seton suffered from pains in her limbs similar to those which affected Mary; and a few grey hairs were beginning to show. No one could live in this captivity and not show the effects of it. Mary thought with a start: In a few years' time, if we go on like this, Seton and I will be old women.

It was characteristic of Mary that, although she herself was unable to escape, and although Seton was her dearest friend, she should consider Seton's happiness rather than her own.

Seton must marry Andrew Beaton and she, Mary, would do all she possibly could to give them a chance of happiness.

She tackled Seton as they sat at their needlework alone.

'Seton, what of Andrew Beaton?'

A hot flush spread across Seton's pale face. 'What of him, Your Majesty?'

'I think he is in love with you. Are you with him?'

Seton shrugged her shoulders. 'If I were, it would be of little consequence.'

'Of little consequence! Seton! What are you saying? I think love is of the greatest consequence. If you are in love with Andrew and he with you you should marry.'

'My family would never permit the match. You know Andrew is only a younger brother.'

'Nonsense!' cried Mary. 'I do not believe you yourself are affected one little bit by such a consideration. The Beatons are a noble family. You are seeking excuses. And I tell you this, Seton, that if you decided to marry Andrew, I would, as far as

361

I am able, bestow some title upon him which would make the Setons quickly change their opinion.'

Seton shook her head.

'Seton, you are not refusing Andrew on account of someone else?'

'No other man has asked me to marry him.'

'I did not mean a man. You have some foolish notion that your duty lies with your poor mistress.'

Seton turned to Mary and threw herself into her arms. 'Do you think I could ever leave you?'

'Oh Seton, Seton, this is unlike you. You must not weep. My dearest friend, do you think I could be happy knowing that I had stood between you and your happiness?'

'My happiness is with you.'

'No, Seton. It is with Andrew. Do you think I am blind?'

'I have vowed to stay with you for ever.'

'Such a vow can be broken.'

'It never can!' cried Seton vehemently.

'It is going to be. I am going to command you to break it.'

'It is not as simple as you think. I have taken a solemn and sacred vow to devote myself to a life of celibacy. This could never be broken.'

'It could be broken if you had a dispensation. We will send Andrew to his brother the Archbishop who is now in Paris, and ask him to tell us the best means of securing this dispensation. He can bring us new silks for our embroidery while he is there and perhaps some clothes. Seton, will you agree that I send for Andrew at once?'

Seton's eyes were filled wth tears. 'How could I ever leave you?'

'But you love Andrew.'

'I love you both.'

'Then, my friend, you must leave me to decide for you.'

Mary then sent for Andrew Beaton and in the presence of Seton told him of the conversation which had taken place between them.

'Go to Paris, Andrew,' she said. 'Come back with your brother's advice on how this foolish friend of mine can be released from her folly.'

Andrew turned to Seton, and as she smiled he strode towards her and took her into his arms.

Mary stood watching their embrace, smiling tenderly, praying that Seton would now enjoy the happiness she deserved, wondering whether the future might not hold some similar joy for her.

*   *   *

Very soon after that interview Andrew Beaton set out for Paris. It soon became known throughout the castle that when he returned he and Seton would be married. Mary brought out all the materials which had been sent to her from France and there was activity in her apartments. Several of the women, with Mary in charge, were working on Seton's wedding dress which was to be beautifully embroidered. Caps and sleeves were designed and stitched, and each day there was speculation as to whether this would be the one on which Andrew returned.

Seton looked younger every day, and Mary was sure that she had made the right decision for her. When she has children, Mary thought, she will thank me for insisting that she take a husband and renounce her foolish vow to serve me.

Yet Seton's happiness was clouded because that friendship, which had lasted all their lives, would never be quite the same again after she was married. The Queen had been her first consideration for so long, and Seton wondered how Mary would fare without her.

So they stitched through the summer days until the coming of autumn; and the main topic of conversation was Seton's coming wedding.

*   *   *

It was a dull autumn day when the messenger came to Mary. She took the letters he brought and, when she read the contents of one of these, she sat as though stunned. She could not believe it. It was too cruel. It seemed to her then that all those who loved her were as unlucky as she was.

She wondered how she could tell Seton; yet she knew that she must be the one to break the news.

One of her women came in and asked her what ailed her, if there was aught she needed; she could say nothing, only shake her head.

The woman went to Seton and said: 'I fear the Queen has had bad news. She is sitting at her table, but she seemed bewildered.'

'I will go to her,' said Seton, knowing that in the hour of disaster they belonged together. What will she do if I am no

longer here? Seton asked herself. How can I ever be happy –
even with Andrew – away from her?

Seton went to the Queen and laid an arm about her shoulders. Mary turned and looked up at her. 'Oh, so it is you,
Seton?'

'You have had bad news?'

Mary nodded.

'Do you wish to tell me, or shall I help you to your bed and
bring cool scented kerchiefs to lay on your head?'

'I fear I must tell you, Seton, because it concerns you even
as it does me.'

Seton said in a whisper which was only just audible, 'It is
Andrew?'

'My dearest Seton, what can I say to comfort you?'

'Tell me, please.'

'He is dead. He died of a fever when he was on his way
home to us.'

Mary put the letter into Seton's hand. Seton read it and let
it flutter to the table. But Andrew had been so young, so full
of health and vigour!

Mary stood up suddenly and the two of them clung together wordlessly.

Mary thought: She did not wish to choose between us, and
now fate has made the choice.

*   *   *

The years were passing, each day so like another that Mary
lost count of time. News came to her now and then. Her uncle,
the Cardinal of Lorraine, had died – one more friend lost to
her. George Douglas married at last – not his French heiress
but a certain Lady Barery, a rich widow of Fifeshire, and he
appeared to have settled down with her on her estates close to
Lochleven. Willie was with him, she believed. They were
always the Queen's men; and if opportunity occurred for them
to aid her, she knew they would seize it. Lady Lennox died
suddenly and Queen Elizabeth took a marked interest in little
Arabella Stuart. Mary had been allowed to go to Chatsworth
and been brought back again to Sheffield; because of the continued strife in Scotland Mary trembled for the welfare of her
son. There was a rumour that Elizabeth was trying to have
him sent to London that she might marry him to his cousin,
Arabella Stuart. But James remained in Scotland and, although

he wrote to his mother, his letters were rarely allowed to reach her.

Little Bessie Pierpont was growing up to be rather a precocious girl; her interest in the French secretary had increased. They chattered together in French and neither seemed completely happy unless in the company of the other.

Occasionally Mary was allowed to visit the baths at Buxton, but Elizabeth invariably cut short her visits, with the result that she was hurried back to Chatsworth or Sheffield.

After so many years in the household of the Shrewsburys she almost felt like a member of the family, and some of the Countess's daughters were her friends – in particular Elizabeth, who never forgot the part Mary played in her marriage, and as it was a most happy marriage she was full of gratitude to the Queen for helping to make it possible.

There were times when Mary forgot she was a captive and there would be music in her apartments. It was pleasant to see little Bessie Pierpont – not so little now – in a flounced dress, made by the Queen, dancing daintily with her partner. Very often Jacques Nau would join the company, and he and Bessie danced very prettily together. Young Arabella was sometimes present. She was not yet four years old but a lively little creature.

The Countess doted on the child and scarcely took her eyes from her; but she liked to see her in the company of the Queen of Scots.

With the coming of the year 1582 Mary realized with horror that it was thirteen years since she had first set foot in England. Thirteen years a prisoner! What hope was there now of her escape?

It was during this year that a malady struck Arabella's mother, Lady Charles Lennox. Bess immediately took charge and brought all her skill and energy to the nursing of her daughter. Even this however could not save her, and soon after the beginning of her illness she died, leaving little four-year-old Arabella motherless.

A fierce emotion took possession of Bess of Hardwick at that time.

She vowed that little Arabella should not miss a mother's care. Her grandmother would give her everything she needed. And more also.

*   *   *

During the winter of that year and the next, Mary was stricken with sickness and many believed that her life was at an end. Her patient nurses, headed by Seton, however, were determined to save her life, and they did.

'But why?' Mary asked wearily. 'See how the time is passing. I no longer hope for release.'

She asked for her mirror, and when she looked into it she saw that illness had ravaged her lovely face still further. Her thick hair was almost white; and it seemed to her that this change had come upon her suddenly. But of course it was not so. Although each day seemed long and empty, looking back it appeared that the last years had passed quickly because of their monotony. She had not realized how they had slipped away.

They had indeed taken her youth with them.

She lay in bed watching Seton whose rheumatism had become worse. She noticed afresh the grey in Seton's hair and the newly formed lines on her face, and she thought: Seton is a reflection of myself. We have both grown old in captivity. I have lived more than forty years, and I was only twenty-five when I came to England!

She called to Seton then. 'Bring me my wig,' she said, 'the chestnut one.'

Seton did so, and put it on Mary's head. Mary held up the mirror. 'Now I feel young again. That is how my hair once looked. Seton, you too must hide those grey hairs. We are helpless prisoners and I doubt that we shall ever be aught else. But let us pretend that we are young and gay. Oh, Seton, you have suffered with me. We must pretend to be gay. It is the only way we can go on living.'

And they wept a little; Seton for Andrew Beaton, and Mary for Bothwell who had since died, driven mad, she heard, by such long imprisonment. She thought of him – he who had gone his own way revelling in freedom, forced to live his life in a dreary prison. She had heard that he had dashed his head against a stone wall in an excess of melancholy. How tragic to contemplate what the years had done to them all! Poor mad Bothwell, who had once been the gay and ruthless brigand.

'He is dead – but he had confessed to the murder of Darnley and exonerated me before he died,' she whispered; and she would always remember it.

But he was gone for ever and so were the days of her youth and gaiety.

But as she held up her mirror and saw the chestnut hair reflected there she had an illusion of youth; and she knew that she would never cease to hope, and that when some knight like George Douglas, Norfolk or Northumberland came to her she would go on believing he could rescue her from her prison.

*　　*　　*

The years did not worry Bess. She was as sprightly as she had been when Mary had first come under her roof. Her voice was as loud and firm as ever, and she kept the household in order as she had always done.

When her granddaughter Arabella was at the castle she never let the child out of her sight. She herself supervised her lessons; she would not allow anyone else to do that. She it was who made the little girl conscious of her rank, and everyone in the castle said that little Arabella was the apple of the Countess's eye.

Bess was brooding about the future of this favourite granddaughter one day when, walking past the Earl's apartments, she saw Eleanor Britton emerging, and there was something about the demeanour of the woman that aroused her interest.

She was about to summon her, but she changed her mind and made her way instead to the Earl's chamber.

Bess was not feeling very pleased with her husband at this time; he had been obstinate about some property which she had wished to present to one of her sons. Shrewsbury had stood out against this. He was weary, he said, of so much that was his, passing to the Cavendishes. He reminded her that, though they were her children, they were not his.

This was rebellion, and Bess expected obedience from husbands; she told herself that Shrewsbury was her least satisfactory husband and, although she knew she would eventually have her way, she was far from pleased that it should be necessary to enforce her will.

She remembered now that there had been several occasions when she had come upon Eleanor in the Earl's rooms. Of course the woman might well be there on some duty, but was it not a little strange that it should always be Eleanor whom she saw there?

She found the Earl in one of his relaxed moods, and she remembered that these were now frequent occurrences. He seemed to be pleased with himself in some way – how could she describe it? Self-satisfied? She remembered that mood from the early days of their marriage.

It is not possible! she told herself. Shrewsbury and a serving girl?

She was furious at the thought. Had it been the Queen, she would have been angry, because Bess would always be angry if deceived, but at worst the woman who had supplanted her would be a Queen.

Could it possibly be that a serving girl had supplanted Bess of Hardwick in her husband's affections?

*   *   *

Bess was not one to let such a matter pass. She determined to find out if her suspicions regarding the Earl and Eleanor Britton were justified and kept a sharp watch on Eleanor. One day she saw the serving woman making her way to the Earl's bedchamber, and hastily secreted herself in an ante-room from which she could gather what was taking place.

From the moment Eleanor entered the chamber, she knew that her fears were going to be confirmed. Suppressing her rage she waited; and when she believed they would be so absorbed in each other that they would not hear the quiet lifting of the latch, she opened the door a few inches and peeped round.

Her impulse was to dash upon them and beat them with the nearest object. But she hesitated, reminding herself of the scandal which would inevitably ensue if this were known. And how could she avoid its being spread if she made a fuss about it? She imagined Queen Elizabeth's laughter and coarse jokes with her courtiers, for Elizabeth would be the first to enjoy a joke at the expense of Bess of Hardwick. What an undignified position! She, the Countess of Shrewsbury, deceived by her husband and a serving girl!

Bess quietly shut the door and crept from the ante-room. Her face was white with rage; her eyes afire with the force of her fury. 'You'll be sorry for this, George Talbot,' she murmured; and she began to plan her revenge.

*   *   *

Jane Kennedy and Seton were discussing the hideous rumour they had heard concerning their mistress.

'Do you think we should tell her?' asked Jane.

'I think it would be better for her to hear it from us than through any other source.'

'But it is so . . . ridiculous . . . so monstrous!'

'She has suffered from many lying rumours. I think we should tell her at once. It will come better from us.'

So Seton and Jane Kennedy went to Mary's apartments and told her what was being said of her at the English Court.

Mary listened wide-eyed. 'But who could have started such a rumour? Shrewsbury and myself . . . lovers! With Bess to keep him in order. What next will they say of me? And I have borne him two children! How could I have done this in secret?'

'It is horrible,' said Seton with a shudder. 'What can we do to prevent this foul rumour spreading further?'

'I will tell the Countess,' answered Mary. 'I feel sure that she will be as anxious to stop it as I am, and she has far more power to do so. Ask her to come to me at once, and then leave us together.'

When Bess was alone with her, Mary told her what she had heard and how angry this had made her.

Bess's reception of the news astonished Mary, who had expected the Countess to be as angry as she herself was. Instead Bess laughed heartily.

'I never heard anything so ridiculous in my life,' she said at last. 'Your Majesty should put the matter from your mind, because I am sure no one will believe such a silly rumour.'

'I do not like it,' Mary pointed out.

Bess snapped her fingers. 'Your Majesty should laugh at it. Of all the absurd things, which were ever said about anyone, this is the most ridiculous. Who of any sense is going to believe it?'

'There are many who are always eager to believe the worst.'

'Even they cannot believe this.' She asked permission then to send for her husband, and Mary readily gave it.

When the Earl appeared it was Bess who told him, amid laughter, what had been said.

The Earl looked grave and said he shared Mary's view of the matter; but the Countess laughed at them both.

'When slander is carried too far,' she assured them both, 'it becomes absurd and no one believes it.'

She was watching her husband closely. How embarrassed he was! Embarrassed to be suspected of carrying on a love affair

369

with a Queen! Yet he was delighted to do so with a serving wench!

Ah, George Talbot, she said to herself, you are going to be very sorry you ever deceived Bess of Hardwick. This is only a beginning.

What would these two say if they knew that the rumours concerning their scandalous conduct had been started by her?

This was the beginning of her revenge. She was going to expose George Talbot as a lecher; but never should it be known that he had so demeaned his wife by preferring a serving girl. His infidelities must be with a Queen already notorious for her fascination and her scandalous life.

When they returned to their apartments she twitted the Earl with references to 'his love, the Queen'; and although she knew this increased his embarrassment she continued to plague him.

But of course that was only a beginning.

*　　*　　*

The Countess was in dispute with her husband. She had hoped that, in view of the unpleasant rumours concerning him and the Queen, and her lighthearted treatment of them, he would have been disposed to grant her this little request.

All she was insisting on was the passing over of certain properties to her sons, but the Earl was adamant, being weary of the demands of the family she had had by a previous husband.

'Very well,' said Bess, 'if you will not show me a little consideration, why should I bother to help you in your difficulties? Why should I pretend not to believe these stories of your lechery?'

'Pretend not to believe them!' cried the Earl aghast. 'But you have clearly said that you do not.'

'Of course I *said* it. What else did you expect? That I wish to tell the world that you are carrying on an adulterous intrigue under our own roof?'

'So . . . you believe that of me . . . and the Queen of Scots!'

Bess faced him and looked unflinchingly into his face. 'My lord, I know you to be an adulterer. Pray do not think to deceive me on that point.'

She was glad of his perturbation. He was going to pay for all the stolen pleasures with that serving woman. Eleanor Britton indeed. She wanted to shout at him: If it had in truth been Mary I would have more easily forgiven you, but since it is that slut I never shall!

But no. She would remain calm. She was going to turn this situation to advantage. It was more than revenge on Shrewsbury that she sought. She was going to discredit the Queen of Scots at the same time. A Queen who had borne two or three children to Shrewsbury would not gain the support that a virtuous Queen would receive. There would be few to pity one who could behave so during her imprisonment. And if Elizabeth should die and Mary should have become unpopular, Arabella might have a very good chance of reaching the throne.

Bess had two great desires now: to take revenge on Shrewsbury and, even greater still, to sweep Arabella Stuart to the throne of England.

So she was going to see that the whole country heard of this scandal. It was necessary to soothe her own vanity which had been so outraged by Shrewsbury's intrigue with a serving girl, and to help Arabella on her way to the throne.

She knew the way to make everyone aware of this matter.

'I shall no longer live under the same roof as you and your paramour,' she said. 'I am leaving at once for my own house of Chatsworth.'

With that she left him, and before the day was out had made her preparations and departed.

* * *

The quarrel between the Earl and Countess of Shrewsbury was the main topic of conversation, not only in Sheffield Castle but at Court.

From Chatsworth Bess had started a suit in Chancery against the Earl, and had written to Elizabeth telling her of what she called his lewd and unhusbandly conduct.

Shrewsbury also wrote to Elizabeth. His wife, he feared, was a malicious and wicked woman; the scandals she had uttered concerning him and the Queen of Scots were undoubtedly without foundation; he was sure Her Majesty would understand that in the circumstances he must beg to be relieved of his duties, and he prayed that she would appoint another guardian of the Queen of Scots to take his place.

Elizabeth was annoyed. Shrewsbury had been Mary's jailor for so long and had proved himself to be a good jailor; she knew full well that the cost to him of such a task had been tremendous, but he was rich enough, she consoled herself. Elizabeth was parsimonious by nature; it was a habit learned in her days of poverty, when she had had to scheme with her governess to procure some trifling garment or a new ribbon for a gown. She was always delighted when she could pass on some responsibility to one of her nobles – letting him shoulder the cost; and this for many years Shrewsbury had been doing very satisfactorily.

She replied firmly that she was not yet ready to relieve Shrewsbury of his task and that if he were going to take every rumour seriously he was indeed a fool.

Nevertheless she sent for Bess.

They eyed each other shrewdly and, for a few fearful seconds, Bess believed that the Queen was seeing through her motives. If it occurred to Elizabeth that the Countess had any thought of promoting young Arabella Stuart, she, Bess, had better tread very warily; it was a very short step from the moment of understanding to the Tower, and an even shorter one to the block.

'What's this I hear about the Queen of Scots and Shrewsbury?' the Queen demanded.

'It is a rumour, Your Majesty, spread by their enemies.'

'Poof!' Elizabeth's gaze did not leave the Countess's face. 'Your trouble is over these estates which you are trying to get for Cavendish's children. You don't believe these rumours, do you?'

Bess lowered her gaze and tried to look troubled.

'It's nonsense,' thundered Elizabeth. 'You are too clever not to have seen at once if any such thing was going on under your roof. I refuse to believe anything but that. And what is more, I shall write to Shrewsbury and tell him so.'

Bess was relieved yet disappointed. But she would not return to Sheffield. She went back to Chatsworth and Elizabeth wrote to Shrewsbury quoting what she had said to Bess.

It was her way of telling Shrewsbury he was to remain at his post despite scandals.

*   *   *

From Chatsworth Bess pursued her plans with her usual energy, and so wide-spread were the scandals concerning Shrewsbury and the Queen of Scots, and such appealing letters did Elizabeth receive from the latter, that she was at last convinced that she must remove Mary from Shrewsbury's care.

She had heard that Mary's health had deteriorated rapidly since she bore the additional burden of this scandal, and she gave permission for her to visit Buxton.

Mary's sojourn at the Spa had its usual beneficial effect and when she had returned to Sheffield Castle Elizabeth wrote to Shrewsbury telling him that she had at last decided to relieve him of his duties.

She was appointing in his place three gentlemen – Sir Ralph Sadler, Sir Henry Mildmay and Mr Somers.

Shrewsbury received the news with mixed feelings. It was impossible, he knew, for him to continue as the Queen's guardian when such rumours were rife. It was fifteen years since Mary had come under his charge, and the relationship between them had grown cordial. They understood each other, and parting in such circumstances must necessarily be painful.

He decided that he would not break the news to her at once, for he knew that she did not like Sadler, and would be distressed at the thought of a new jailor of any kind.

He came to her apartments and told her that he had news.

'I am to go to Court,' he said, 'where I shall endeavour to plead your cause with Her Majesty.'

Mary impulsively held out both hands to him and he took them.

'I shall miss you when you are away,' she told him.

'Have no fear that I shall not do my best for you while I am there. In the circumstances —'

Mary broke in: 'My lord, what has happened has distressed us both, but you more; I am accustomed to insults. And you have lost your wife.'

Shrewsbury said bitterly: 'It was no great loss, I come to believe, Your Majesty.'

'It is always sad that there should be such quarrels. I begin to think that not only am I cursed but that I bring bad luck to all around me.'

'Your Majesty should be of good cheer. I doubt not that you will now have a new lodging.'

'Is that so?'

'Yes. Sir Ralph Sadler, who will be with you during my absence, thinks that you should stay at Wingfield Manor, while some other lodging is made ready for you.'

'So it is Sadler!' She smiled ruefully. 'I shall pray that you soon return. It will be strange to leave Sheffield after so long.'

'I sincerely hope that you will find a lodging more to your liking.'

'You might ask the Queen if I could lodge at Low Buxton. I verily believe that if I could do so I should quickly regain my health.'

He looked at her sadly. He felt it was wrong to deceive her, yet he could not tell her yet that he was in fact saying goodbye.

CHAPTER SIXTEEN

TUTBURY ONCE MORE

THE CORTEGE MADE its way slowly along the rough roads. It would not reach its destination before nightfall, but there was not one member of the party who was eager to reach Tutbury Castle.

Seton, riding beside her mistress, noticed a certain alertness in her face. Mary was always mildly excited at the prospect of moving. Did she still dream that a band of gallant friends would waylay the party and free her at last from the captivity of years? Seton believed that she did; that in spite of encroaching age and even more unwelcome infirmity, Mary would always hope for what now seemed the impossible.

Seton moved painfully in the saddle. She was even more crippled with rheumatism than her mistress. But how could one live for years in draughty castles, never being allowed to take enough fresh air, without becoming infirm? They should be thankful perhaps that they were as healthy as they were.

The last months had not been easy, and in desperation Mary had sent Jacques Nau to London to plead with Elizabeth for her liberty. The seeds of scandal which Seton was sure had been scattered by the revengeful Bess of Hardwick, had taken root here and in France and Spain. Mary tried to vindicate herself in Elizabeth's eyes by suggesting that none was safe from Bess's evil tongue and hinting at the scandals the Countess had whispered to her concerning Elizabeth; but no sooner had she done this than she regretted it. Elizabeth, however, wisely chose to ignore both Mary's hints and Bess's gossip.

Was there no end, Mary asked herself, to the tribulations she must endure? And now that she had new jailors in place of the Shrewsburys, Mary was learning how free she had been in the charge of the Earl.

Seton could not help feeling a certain satisfaction because Sir Ralph Sadler had suffered from the rigours of the Queen's prison and had found Wingfield and Sheffield so bad for his health, that in a few months he had become almost crippled with rheumatism and was restive to be released from his duty.

'Poor Sir Ralph,' Seton whispered to the Queen, 'he at least suffers with his limbs as we do.'

Mary turned to look at her friend and in the harsh light noticed how worn her face was . . . worn with pain, anxiety and frustration. Poor Seton, thought Mary. When I look at her it is as though I look into a mirror. My pain and anxieties are marked on my face even as hers are. If she could have married Andrew; if she could have been the mother of healthy children. . . . But what was the use of entertaining such thoughts? They were two women, unlucky in love; doomed, it seemed, to be prisoners for the rest of their lives.

So must it be for her. But it need not be so for Seton.

Mary said: 'Seton, I shudder to think of Tutbury. Of all my prisons that is the worst.'

'It will be better when the spring comes. . . .'

'And the smell grows stronger . . .' murmured the Queen. She turned almost angrily to Seton. '*I* must endure this life, Seton. But why should *you*?'

Seton sighed. 'Because, as I have told you before, my place is at your side.'

'Nay, Seton. You should go away while there is time.'

'And leave you!'

'I never had patience with those who suffered unnecessarily.'

'It is only if I were separated from you that I should suffer.'

'Look at your hands. Your knuckles are enlarged with rheumatism. Do you think I cannot see how painfully you walk? You are in a worse state than I am, Seton. Why do you not go to France?'

'Ah, if we could both go. . . .'

'Let us indulge ourselves, Seton. Let us think about it.'

They were silent, thinking of those early days when they had ridden lightheartedly in the chase, when they were young and their days were carefree.

'There is no reason why you should not go, Seton,' whispered the Queen. 'I could arrange for you to go into a convent with my aunt Renée. She would receive you with pleasure, knowing you to be my dearest friend. Dear Seton, go, while you can still walk.'

Seton shook her head.

'How obstinate you are!' sighed Mary. 'There will come a day when *I* shall have to nurse *you*. You suffer more thán I.'

'Do not ask me to leave you,' pleaded Seton. 'While I can still walk I wish to serve you.'

They were silent for a while; then Mary said: 'I knew Jacques Nau would do well at Elizabeth's Court.'

Seton nodded. 'She has an affection for all handsome men.'

'And Jacques is very handsome. I could not have chosen a better advocate.'

'Let us be thankful that he has persuaded the Queen that you are innocent of the Shrewsbury scandal.'

Mary laughed. 'It all seemed so ridiculous, did it not? Yet there were so many ready to believe it. But now, thanks to the good work of my French Jacques, the Countess and her sons have been made to swear I have been slandered.'

Seton nodded, but she was less sure than the Queen. She was thinking that scandal, once sent on its rounds, could live on for ever.

'It would seem,' said Mary, 'that we are arriving at a house. What is it?'

Seton looked ahead to the gabled mansion. 'It is Babington Hall, Your Majesty. We are to rest here for the night, I believe.'

'Babington ... the name seems familiar.'

'That is very likely. Your Majesty will remember Anthony.'

'Anthony Babington ... why yes. He is that earnest and handsome young man who called on me at Sheffield and was so eager to serve me.'

'A Catholic gentleman,' murmured Seton; 'and Your Majesty is right, he is a handsome one.'

'A charming person,' replied the Queen, as the cortège rode up to Babington Hall.

* * *

Sir Ralph Sadler was not going to allow Mary to forget that she was a prisoner; he immediately set his guards about the house and, summoning the chief citizens of the town, told them that Queen Elizabeth would be ill pleased if they allowed her prisoner to escape while lodging in their district. So the citizens posted their own guards in the streets of the nearby town as well as about the house.

The housekeeper, an old widow named Mrs Beaumont, came forward to greet the Queen on behalf of her master and mistress.

Mary graciously embraced her, kissing her on both withered cheeks, a gesture which enchanted the old lady.

'My master will be delighted that Your Majesty has honoured his house,' she said.

'You must tell your master that I remember him well and think of him often,' Mary answered.

Sir Ralph, watching suspiciously, demanded that the Queen be taken to her apartments; and the widow nodded, saying she would lead the way.

It was not easy to have any communication with strangers while Sir Ralph was near; but Mrs Beaumont did manage to speak to Mary. She told her that if there were any letters the Queen wished delivered to her friends she could safely leave them with her. Her master was the Queen's most ardent servant and he would think ill of his housekeeper if she did not serve her in every way possible while she was under his roof. He would be sorry that he was absent from his home during the Queen's visit; but he was at this time abroad. Mrs Beaumont knew, though, that he lived to serve the Queen.

That night in Babington Hall, while the noise of her guards below her window prevented her from sleeping, Mary thought of handsome young Anthony Babington; and she felt young again because hope had come back to her.

*   *   *

Tutbury was even more unpleasant than Mary remembered it. Robbers had entered it since she had last stayed there, and much of the furniture and bedding had been stolen.

The cold was intense; the foul odour more pronounced.

Mary went to her old apartments and saw at once that many of the hangings with which her servants had once covered those walls, were missing.

Seton came in looking doleful. 'There are scarcely any blankets in the place; and there are only nine pairs of sheets. I've counted them myself.'

Mary shivered. 'And how many of us are there?'

'Forty-eight. They have even stolen the feathers from many

377

of the bolster cases. I fear we are going to be most uncomfortable until we can obtain supplies.'

Sir Ralph Sadler came into the Queen's apartment looking worried. There was no need for him to say that he was heartily weary of his task. He longed to pass over the guardianship of the Queen to someone else. He had quickly realized that it was a dangerous and thankless task.

'I will write to Lord Burleigh at once,' she told Sadler. 'If we are to stay here, either he or the Queen must send us some comforts.'

Sadler agreed with her. Every day he was revising his opinion of Mary, for previously he had believed her to be fractious and demanding; now he realized all that she must have been made to suffer over the years.

During the next weeks his attitude towards her changed still more. She was a Catholic – a fact which he, a stern Protestant, deplored; she was a danger to his Queen; but at the same time he had to admire the patience with which she bore hardship and her unfailing concern for those who served her.

Soon after their arrival Mary became ill; as for Seton, she was scarcely able to move; both women bore their infirmities with fortitude; but when one of Mary's oldest servants, Renée Rallay, a Frenchwoman who had come with her when she left France, fell sick and died, Mary's grief overflowed, and she demanded of Sadler how long the Queen of England intended to keep her in this state.

Sadler decided then that when the spring came he would allow her to ride out with him and watch the hawking. He saw no harm in that, provided she was surrounded by guards.

*　　*　　*

So once more with the coming of more clement weather Mary's health improved; and it was a great pleasure to be allowed to ride out even in the company of Sadler and Somers, and accompanied by guards.

With her on these occasions rode Bessie Pierpont, now a blooming beauty of sixteen.

It was one day when they returned from such an excursion that they found Jacques Nau was in the castle, having come straight from Elizabeth's Court.

Mary was so delighted to see him that she did not notice the flush of pleasure which rose to Bessie's cheeks, nor did she intercept the ardent looks which passed between the girl and the secretary.

'My good friend,' cried Mary, 'how it delights me to see you.'

Jacques kissed the Queen's hands, but even as he did so he could not prevent his eyes straying to the lovely young girl who stood beside Mary.

'Pray come to my chamber with all speed,' said Mary. 'I can scarce wait to hear your news.'

As they made their way there, Bessie walked close to him and when his hand reached out for hers, and pressed it, Bessie could have wept for joy. She would tell him when they were alone that she had lived in great fear that he would have met some fair lady at the English Court who would have made him forget all about simple little Bessie Pierpont. But it did not seem so, and she was exultant because she believed that Jacques was as pleased to be with her as she was to see him.

At the door of the Queen's chamber, Bessie must leave them, but the look which Jacques cast in her direction told her that soon he would be seeking her out.

When they were alone together Mary complimented Jacques on the manner in which he had accomplished his mission. She saw at once that there was a change in the young man's manner. There was a new air of confidence; she believed she understood. Elizabeth had a fondness for handsome young men, and Jacques was undoubtedly handsome. Elizabeth would have been enchanted by his French manners, for there was no doubt that Jacques knew how to turn a pretty compliment. Yes, the visit to the English Court had changed Jacques in some way. He was full of assurance having become an ambassador, whereas before he had been a mere secretary.

'Jacques,' said Mary, 'I have to thank you for the manner in which you dealt with my affairs. But for you, I am sure, the Countess of Shrewsbury would have been allowed to go on repeating her scandals.'

'It was a great pleasure to me,' Jacques replied, 'to achieve an apology in the presence of the Council.'

'You found the Queen of England fair and just?'

'I did, Your Majesty.'

Ah, thought Mary, if only *I* could see her. If only I could have a chance of talking to her.

Failing that, it was comforting to have someone such as her good and loyal French secretary to look after her affairs.

But there was one other piece of news which Jacques must break to her. He knew that it was going to cause her sorrow and he dreaded telling her. Since he had entered the castle and seen young Bessie Pierpont, he was yearning to be done with business and be with her. He was surprised that he could feel little else but this great need to be with Bessie.

'I have news of Your Majesty's son.'

The Queen's expression changed; she clasped her hands together.

Jacques did not look at her as he said: 'His Majesty of Scotland finds it difficult to act as joint sovereign with yourself. He has therefore entered into a treaty with the Queen of England as sole sovereign of Scotland.'

Mary looked at her secretary as though she had not heard him. Slowly the implication of what this meant came to her. So he is repudiating me! she thought. At last my enemies have succeeded in taking him from me utterly. He . . . my own little Jamie, now finds his mother an encumbrance. He tells me that I am, in his opinion, no longer Queen of Scotland.

She said slowly: 'Is this indeed so?'

Jacques answered gently: 'I fear so, Your Majesty.'

Mary covered her face with her hands.

'Your Majesty would wish me to leave you?' whispered Jacques.

The Queen nodded.

*　　*　　*

Bessie was hovering near the door of the Queen's apartments, and as he came out she threw herself into his arms.

'It has been so long . . .' she whispered. They were kissing, exploring each other's faces with their lips.

'Bessie . . . my Bessie . . .' murmured Jacques.

'You can have no idea how desolate this place is without our secretary Jacques.'

'Can it be as desolate as the English Court without Bessie Pierpont?'

'Oh Jacques . . . what shall we do . . . ?'

'There is one thing we must do . . . and that quickly. Marry.'

Bessie laughed. 'I hoped you would say that.'

'Do you think they will allow us to?'

'The Queen never refuses me anything.'

'What of your grandmother?'

'I believe I am a little like her. I am going to do the deed and tell afterwards . . . as she did in the case of Arabella's parents.'

Jacques was thoughtful. He had to remember that he was after all only a secretary. He wondered what action would be taken by the Shrewsburys if he married their granddaughter. He was passionately in love with this charming young girl, but he had to think for them both. It would be disastrous if for the sake of a brief week or so of passion they allowed their entire future to be jeopardized. Jacques was really in love for the first time in his life, but ardently as he desired Bessie, he could yet consider the years ahead of them. Bessie was not only to be his wife, but the mother of his children. This was no sudden blazing passion; he had watched Bessie grow since she was a child of four, and the happiest moments of those long ago days had been when she sat beside him, the tip of her little pink tongue showing at the corner of her mouth as she bent over a Latin exercise with which he was helping her. He had loved her then, and now that she was a woman he desired her as he had never desired a woman before; but the tenderness, the longing to protect had remained; and this he knew to be love in all its aspects.

Thus when he had danced at the English Court, when he had paid the gallant compliments expected of a Frenchman, he had never ceased to dream of young Bessie Pierpont, and all other women could be nothing but passing fancies to him.

He took her face in his hands and kissed her gently.

'My Bessie,' he said, 'my true love Bessie, I shall love you until I am laid in my tomb.'

'And I you, Jacques,' she declared solemnly.

'And because I love you as I do I will curb my need of you until that time when I can be sure that in taking and sharing the delights which must surely be ours, I can assure myself that no harm shall come to you.'

'There is no time like this moment, Jacques,' cried Bessie. He embraced her with such fervour that she cried out in her ecstasy. But he released her suddenly and shook his head.

'First there shall be marriage,' he said. 'It is how it must be, since you are Bessie my only love. But there will be obstacles and, because I will not have you hurt, we must be patient. Little Bessie, from this day we shall begin to make our plans.'

* * *

Sir Ralph Sadler was dismayed. He had often heard of the schemes which had harassed Shrewsbury during his term as jailor; having been with the Queen, and perceiving her patience, he had been inclined to believe most of them to be exaggerated. 'All that happened in the early days of her captivity,' he told Somers. 'Now she is too old and ill to think of escape. We should be grateful for that.'

And now it seemed that he had been wrong.

One day while he was at supper his servant came to tell him that a man was at the castle begging an interview, as he had news of great importance which he believed Sir Ralph must hear.

Sir Ralph allowed the man to be brought to his presence and found him to be a certain Humphrey Briggs, an uncouth and unprepossessing man – clearly one who bore a grievance.

'What is your business?' asked Sir Ralph.

'I come to your honour because I feel there is news I should give you.'

'Well, let me hear it.'

The man hesitated.

'You want payment?'

The dull face brightened. 'It's important news, Your Honour. Touching our Lady Elizabeth herself.'

'It sounds like treason. In that case, man, you would do well to tell me quickly, for it is treason to hold back anything that threatens the Queen.'

Briggs looked a little taken aback. He stammered: 'I'm a good subject of the Queen's, Your Honour. I serve the Queen. . . .'

'Then prove it by telling me what news this is.'

Briggs, now alarmed, decided to forgo hopes of reward and content himself with revenge. 'I worked for Nicholas Langford, Your Honour.'

'And he has dismissed you?' asked Sir Ralph shrewdly.

' 'Twas no fault of mine.'

'Never mind. Tell me.'

'My master, with the help of his secretary, Rowland Kitchyn, hears the Mass regularly in his house . . . and that's not all. He receives priests in his house, Your Honour; and he writes letters.'

'Letters?'

'To the fair devil of Scotland, Your Honour. And with one end. He is with them that wants to see her in place of our own

382

good Queen. And that's why I thought it right to tell Your Honour. . . .'

Sir Ralph nodded.

'You may go to the kitchen,' he said. 'There they will give you food.'

'I'm a poor man, Your Honour. . . .'

'It will be necessary for me to look into this matter,' said Sir Ralph. 'I know you to have been a servant of Nicholas Langford and to have been dismissed by him. You bear a grudge against him. But, if I find your information to be true, have no fear that you shall lack a reward . . . but first it must be proved.' He waved his hand for the man to go; and when he was alone he wrote down the names of Nicholas Langford and Rowland Kitchyn, and planned how he would begin his investigation.

* * *

It was not easy for Bessie to hide her happiness. Mary noticed that the girl seemed subdued and it occurred to her that she was, after all, no longer a child and that perhaps it was high time she married.

Thinking of Seton's fate, as she so often did, Mary was determined that this bright young girl should not suffer in the same way. Whenever she was able to lay her hands on rich materials – which were sometimes sent to her by friends in France through the French ambassador – it was clothes for Bessie that she planned. She had taught the girl to embroider, and as they sat together working on a new gown Bessie said suddenly: 'It is twelve years that I have been with Your Majesty. I wonder if I shall always be with you.'

'Ah, Bessie, that must not be. One day you will marry and go away from me. I would not have you live your life in these draughty prisons.'

'Oh but . . .' began Bessie, and she almost said: Jacques will be your secretary, and where Jacques is there must I be. Then she remembered that Jacques had said they must keep their secret as yet.

Mary laid her hand over Bessie's. 'My dearest,' she said, 'I can never explain how much your presence here has meant to me. I lost my own child and to some extent you took his place. That is why, even though it will grieve me to lose you, I shall be happy to see you go . . . when the time comes.'

'Your Majesty,' – Bessie spoke breathlessly – 'when do you think . . . the time will come for me to go?'

'It will not be long delayed,' answered Mary with a smile. 'I will tell you something else. You do not think your grandmother could resist making a grand marriage for you, do you?'

Bessie was silent as the numbness of fear crept over her. Mary however did not notice the change in her goddaughter and continued: 'It is to be a grand marriage for you, my dear. The Countess of Shrewsbury certainly has plans for you. It is some time now since she decided on a husband for you.'

'Who . . . ?' stammered Bessie.

'My Lord Percy, eldest son of the Earl of Northumberland.'

Bessie was staring down at the material in her hands; defiance was born in her then. Never! Never! Never! she was saying over and over again to herself.

'So you see,' went on the Queen, 'you have not been forgotten, my dear; and when the time comes I shall use all my influence to bring about this match, for I consider it, though one of the best possible, not too good for my own dear godchild.'

'I do not wish to marry Lord Percy,' said Bessie in a stony voice.

The Queen laughed, 'You will . . . in time, my love.'

'I never shall,' replied Bessie vehemently.

She was trembling; she was about to throw herself at the Queen's feet, to confess her love for Jacques, to implore Mary's help. But Jacques had said that their love was to be a secret as yet . . . and she was afraid to do so. If her grandmother – the energetic Countess – had decided she was to marry Lord Percy, she must do something quickly.

She was saved from confessing the truth by the Queen's next words. 'I hear the sound of voices below. Someone is arriving at the castle.'

Mary had risen and the material had dropped to the floor. She still hoped that a messenger would bring news of her release, that some friend might have come to visit her, some loved one from Scotland or France, or perhaps Queen Elizabeth herself.

Bessie, trembling, went to the window and stood beside the Queen.

A man was being hustled into the castle; he looked harassed, as though he were a prisoner.

I wonder who that can be,' said the Queen. 'Bessie, go and see if you can find out.'

Bessie was glad to escape, but instead of obeying the Queen's command she went straight to that chamber in which Jacques was working. He looked up from his writing table when he saw her, and for the moment all Bessie's fears vanished as she watched the joy sweep over his face.

'My love!'

She ran to him and put her arms about his neck. 'Oh Jacques . . . Jacques . . . what do you think? They are going to try to marry me to Lord Percy.'

He smiled into her frightened eyes, trying not to show that he shared her fear. 'Why, Bessie,' he said, 'do you think I should allow that?'

She laughed gaily. 'Of course you wouldn't. Neither of us would. We'd . . . die rather, wouldn't we, Jacques.'

But her eyes were shining and she had no intention of dying. She was going to live and love.

In that moment young Bessie had a look of the grandmother whose name she shared.

*   *   *

Sir Ralph was indulging in his favourite occupation, which was composing letters to Elizabeth explaining why it would be wise to withdraw him from his post as guardian of the Queen of Scotland and put another in his place.

'I am crippled with rheumatism . . . I am unfit for this task . . .' he murmured. How fortunate Shrewsbury was to escape it. But Shrewsbury had had fifteen years as jailor. Pray God he, Sadler, did not have to endure more than one.

He was particularly worried at this time, for he had found it necessary, on the testimony of that odious fellow Briggs, whom he had loathed on sight, to investigate the case of Nicholas Langford; and although Mr Langford had answered his questions so plausibly that he could bring no accusation against him, his secretary, Rowland Kitchyn, had shown himself to be an ardent Catholic and had actually admitted serving the Mass.

Uncertain how to act, Sadler had had Rowland Kitchyn brought to Tutbury and was keeping him prisoner there while he submitted him to questioning.

If Sadler could prove Mary to be the centre of a plot against Elizabeth, he would then go to London, see the Queen and implore her to send a younger and more healthy man to take charge of Mary. He was hoping that he would be able to prove this.

Rowland Kitchyn was each day brought from his dungeon in Tutbury Castle into the presence of Sadler and Somers and there questioned, but in spite of these examinations nothing could be drawn from him but the fact that he had served Mass; he refused to utter a word against his master and denied that he had been involved in a plot to free Mary and place her on the throne.

Since he admitted to being a Catholic, both Sadler and Somers thought it their duty to insist on his attending the chapel in order to hear prayers. As a Catholic, Rowland Kitchyn refused to attend the chapel; so before the service two guards were sent to his cell to bring him there; and often Mary would hear cries of protest as he was dragged across the courtyard.

Bessie had discovered what was happening, for Jacques had told her.

Jacques was worried – not only because of the proposed match with Lord Percy, but because Sir Ralph Sadler was persecuting Rowland Kitchyn, whose only crime seemed to be that he was a Catholic.

'Bessie,' Jacques had said, 'you and I are Catholics. If he decides to persecute one, he might persecute others.'

Bessie clung to him and said: 'Jacques . . . what is happening all about us? Once I felt so safe. Now I feel safe no longer.'

Jacques did not answer that. He might have told her that they had been living in a dangerous world for as long as he could remember. The only difference was that Bessie was growing up and was becoming more and more aware of this.

*   *   *

'Seton,' said Mary, 'what are they doing to that poor man?'

'They have brought him in for questioning, and they insist on his going to the chapel every day.'

'What does it mean, Seton?'

Seton shrugged her shoulders.

'Will they soon begin to persecute us, do you think?' asked Mary. 'Do they drag him across the courtyard beneath my window every day, to remind me that I worship in a manner different from theirs?'

'Who can say?' sighed Seton.

'Oh, Seton, I am going to write to my aunt Renée. You are going to her. You must.'

Seton obstinately shook her head.

'Sometimes I despair of ever leaving my prison,' said Mary. 'Sometimes I think I shall be carried from my prison to the tomb.'

'These are doleful thoughts, Your Majesty.'

'These are doleful times, Seton.'

There was silence for a while then Mary said: 'They are bringing him back now. What does it mean, Seton? What are they planning now?'

*   *   *

Sir Ralph looked into the face of the man who had been brought to him for questioning.

'I have told you all I know,' said Rowland Kitchyn.

'How can we be sure of that?'

'I have nothing else to say.'

'We have means of extracting the truth,' said Sir Ralph.

He saw that the man had turned pale, and he noticed that he was a frail man, a man more accustomed to wielding a pen than a sword.

'You mean you would torture me?'

'We would consider the means were unimportant if through them we arrived at the truth.'

'Do men speak truth under torture? You know they do not always do so, my lord. They cry out what is demanded of them . . . anything to stop the torture.'

Sir Ralph looked into that pale face and saw the sweat at the temples; the fear in the eyes. It was not the fear of pain, so much as the fear that he would not be able to withstand it. There was a difference, and Sir Ralph was wise enough to see it. He wondered whether it would only be necessary to talk of torture. He hoped so, for he was not a violent man.

'Think about this,' he said. 'Tomorrow you will be brought before me again. I am eager to know the truth.'

Rowland Kitchyn was taken back to his cell; he was sick with fear. He did not know how he would stand up to torture. He had never suffered it. He was a man of great imagination, and he was afraid . . . terribly afraid that his body would take possession of his mind and insist on his saying that which was false, in order to save it from pain.

*   *   *

Rowland Kitchyn awoke in the night. He felt the cold of the stone floor through his pallet, yet he was sweating. He had dreamed that he was in a dungeon of this evil Tutbury and there they had tortured him; and that as the pain possessed him he lost all sense of decency, all sense of honour; thinking only to save his wretched limbs from pain, he had cried out lies against his master.

'I must not, I must not,' he moaned, 'I will not.'

But how could he be sure? He knew full well that under torture men lost all sense of reason, all sense of justice.

They wished him to betray his master.

'I will never do it. I never will,' he whispered.

But in his dream he had done so; and how could he be sure when awake he would be more brave?

A terrible belief had come to him. The dream was a warning. He would betray his master under torture.

'I never will. I never will,' he moaned.

But how could he be sure?

There was a way. It was the only way. He lay in the dark, thinking of it.

* * *

Sir Ralph Sadler said to Somers: 'I am sure that fellow Briggs was a vengeful rogue, and I am certain that both Langford and his secretary Kitchyn are guiltless of intrigue against the Queen. Catholics they are, alas. But there are many Catholics in England.'

'What do you suggest we should do? Release Kitchyn?'

Sir Ralph nodded. 'Come with me to his cell. We will tell him that he is a free man.'

Together the pair made their way to the prisoner. Sir Ralph unlocked the door and, peering into the gloom, saw Kitchyn lying on his pallet; he was very still.

The two men approached, and Sadler murmured: 'Kitchyn, wake up. We are come to speak with you.'

There was no answer and, bending over the figure of the man on the pallet, Sadler gave a sudden exclamation, which brought Somers to his side.

Both men stood staring down at the lifeless body of the prisoner, who had strangled himself.

* * *

Her women had not yet come into her bedchamber to help her rise, but Mary was awake. Something had awakened her

388

early on this morning, some evil foreboding which prevented her from sleeping.

She had felt uneasy ever since she had seen that poor man being dragged across the courtyard to the chapel. The persecution of others never failed to move her deeply, perhaps because she had suffered so much herself.

She lay for a moment, wondering whether it was some unusual sound of activity which had awakened her; there was no sound now in the courtyard below.

As it was impossible to sleep, she rose and put her wrap about her; she went to the window and looked out.

For a moment as she stared at the horror which confronted her, she thought that she was living in some nightmare.

'No . . .' she whispered, but it was so. That man who was hanging from the turret opposite her window, was the prisoner whom they had been holding in the castle for the last three weeks.

For some seconds she stood staring at the lifeless form hanging there. Why had they hung him opposite her window? There could be only one answer. They were saying to her: This man offended us because he was a Catholic. You are a Catholic also.

On whose orders had that man been hung there?

Turning shuddering away, Mary went back to her bed and lay there.

It was thus that Seton found her.

'Seton!' she cried. 'We have never been in such danger as we are now. I have felt it in my bones. And now I have proof.'

'What proof?' asked Seton.

'Go to the window and you will see.'

Seton went, and Mary heard the exclamation which escaped from her before, white and trembling, she came back to the bed.

*   *   *

There was not a Catholic in Mary's household who did not see in the fate of Rowland Kitchyn a grim warning to themselves.

Now an atmosphere of dread and suspicion existed throughout the castle. Looking back, Mary thought with longing of the early days when she had been in the charge of the Shrewsburys, before Bess had conceived her absurd lies.

Trouble was coming. Every day she expected to hear that

389

she herself would meet the fate of Rowland Kitchyn. Young Bessie told her that he had strangled himself, but she did not believe that. He had been taken, she was certain, imprisoned in Tutbury and hanged as a warning to her of what she might expect.

She called Jacques Nau to her and asked him to repeat what Elizabeth had said to him on the subject of freedom of religion.

'Her Majesty assured me,' answered Jacques, 'that it was never her wish that any of her subjects should suffer for the sake of conscience or religion.'

'But there are fanatics in this land,' she said. 'I fear them, Jacques.'

'I am of the opinion that Queen Elizabeth is not one of them.'

'You comfort me,' Mary told him; and he wondered whether now was the moment to tell her of his desire to marry Bessie. No, he decided. At this time she was too anxious about other matters. They must wait, he and Bessie. There must be no betrayal of their secret until they were sure. The fact that Lord Percy had been selected for Bessie was going to raise great difficulties. There was too much at stake to risk their future happiness.

Mary dismissed Jacques and wrote to Elizabeth.

'. . . If it should ever come to pass that an open attack were made on me for my religion, I am perfectly ready, with the Grace of God to bow my neck beneath the axe, that my blood may be shed before all Christendom; and I should esteem it the greatest happiness to be the first to do so. I do not say this out of vain glory while the danger is remote. . . .'

When she had finished writing this she resolutely took up a pen and wrote to her aunt Renée at Rheims.

She was not going to plead with Seton any more. She was going to order her to go to France. Seton was in danger even as she was; she could no longer bear to watch her dearest friend growing a little more haggard, a little more crippled every day, sacrificing life itself for her sake. When she had written those letters and dispatched them, she sent for Seton.

'My dear friend,' she said, 'I have written to Rheims. You must prepare to leave.'

Seton was speechless, but Mary had become regal.

'It is an order, Seton – one I should have given long ago.'

'You are commanding me to leave you?'

Mary turned away, desperately afraid of weakness.

'There will be our letters, Seton. You must write to me regularly. I must know all that happens to you.'

Seton was staring out of that window where, not long ago, the lifeless body of a man had hung.

* * *

Surely the parting with Seton was the most bitter tragedy that had happened since her imprisonment. It had been useless for Seton to plead; Mary had been adamant. She had written to her aunt and asked her to care for Seton, to nurse her back to health for her dear sake; and she knew that Renée would do it.

'At least,' she whispered when she embraced her dearest and most faithful friend for the last time, 'I shall know that you are enjoying some comfort, and that must give me pleasure. Oh, dearest Seton, you cannot guess how it has grieved me to see you growing more and more infirm.'

Seton's mouth was set in pain. 'You know that my place is with you.'

'No, Seton. You have lived *my* life too long. Do you realize that that is what you have done from the very moment when you were brought to my nursery – the dearest of my four Marys? If you wish to comfort me, write to me that you sleep in a warm and comfortable bed, that you take fresh air; that your pains grow less. That is what I ask of you now; and you have never denied me what I wanted – save that you refused to leave me long ago when I told you that you should.'

When the moment of parting had come they had clung together and Seton had cried out that she would never leave her mistress. Only Mary knew how near she had come to agreeing, for she could not conceive how dreary the days would be without this loving companion.

But she would not say it; and she restrained her tears until from her turret window she saw that Seton and the little party which accompanied her were too far off to notice how she wept when they turned to wave the last farewell.

* * *

Now Jane Kennedy and Elizabeth Curle had become her constant companions, trying to take the place of Seton. Mary turned to them, although she knew that there could never be another Seton. They would sit over their needlework and talk of what the future might hold; and this was a cheerless occupation, for tension still brooded over the castle.

'Yet,' said Mary, 'I do not think we should despair. I am sure Sir Ralph would never allow me to be the victim of foul play while I am under his care.'

'He hanged the dead body of Rowland Kitchyn opposite Your Majesty's window,' Jane reminded her.

'Because he hopes to make a Protestant of me,' answered Mary. 'It is true he is a fanatic on matters of religion. But in all else I feel him to be a just man. That is why I am going to ask him if I may not have a friend to replace dear Seton. The Countess of Atholl has written to me asking me to take her into my service. I think I will speak to Sir Ralph now. Jane, go and ask him to come to me.'

Jane did as she was bid, and in a short time Sir Ralph entered the apartment.

'Sir Ralph,' said Mary, 'the Countess of Atholl asks if she may come and stay with me. As you know, I have lost one of my closest friends. Do you think you might use your influence to bring this about?'

Sir Ralph was silent for a while, then he said: 'I have to tell Your Majesty that I shall not be with you much longer. I have had orders from my Queen to retire from this post. She is sending another of her servants to take my place. This request of yours is therefore one which you must make to him.'

Mary was startled. She had not known that change was contemplated. She was alarmed. Sir Ralph had scarcely been a generous guardian but there could be many worse.

'May I know the name of the man who is to succeed you?'

'Your Majesty, it is Sir Amyas Paulet.'

Mary was stunned. She knew the man to be the fiercest of Puritans, a man who, because she was a Catholic, would believe her to be the wickedest of sinners.

She had not been mistaken. Harsher measures were going to be taken; her prison was to become more rigorous than ever.

Sadler, watching her, read her thoughts. Since he had been guarding her and had suffered so much himself from the lack of comfort and had been aware of the deterioration of his own health, he had softened towards her.

Her life with him had been cheerless; he knew, as she did, that it would be worse with Paulet.

He said gently: 'Your Majesty, if you ask for the Countess of Atholl to be allowed to come here, your request will almost certainly be refused, for the Atholls are known to be your friends, and Catholics. If you were to ask for the company of a Protestant lady, I doubt not that your request would be granted; and I have heard that there are Protestants in Scotland who are your friends.'

Mary did not answer; she had sunk into a chair; rarely had she felt so deeply submerged in despair.

* * *

The spring had come and with the warmer weather Tutbury was always more bearable, even though Sir Amyas had arrived at the castle and he proved to be as stern and forbidding as Mary had feared. There were new rules to be observed; the guards received strict instructions that on no account was Mary to leave the castle; if any attempt at escape were made, Mary was to be killed rather than allowed to go free. Sir Amyas was shocked because she had tried to bring a little colour to her dreary apartments with the bright tapestries she and her women had worked and hung on the walls. He told her that she would be well advised to pass her time in prayer rather than in sewing fancy silks and playing the lute. He offered to instruct her in the Protestant religion, and when she refused this invitation he muttered that she was heading for eternal damnation.

When during May Sir Ralph and Somers left – they had stayed some weeks until Sir Amyas was accustomed to the routine of the castle – Mary felt she would be ready to try any foolhardy scheme to escape from Paulet's rule. Never in all the years of captivity had the days seemed so long and dreary.

Then two newcomers arrived at the castle, and their coming lightened the gloom and brought a little change to the dull days.

The arrivals were two charming girls, Barbara and Gillies Mowbray, the younger daughters of Sir John Mowbray, the Protestant Laird of Barnbougal. Mary welcomed the two girls with great warmth, for she was always touched that anyone should wish to leave a luxurious home to share her prison life, and she knew that Barbara and Gillies had begged to be allowed to do so.

393

On the day the girls arrived, Mary staged a gay gathering in her apartment, because she did not want them to find their new life too gloomy. She need not have worried; they were sprightly creatures, very fresh and lovely, particularly Barbara; and as soon as Mary saw them she loved them.

So it was a merry party which took place in her apartment, and it pleased her to see the young people dancing. As Bessie was there, dancing with Jacques, she had invited her other secretary, Gilbert Curle, to join the dance. She was very fond of Gilbert, who was Elizabeth Curle's brother and a Scotsman devoted to her interests. He might not be so dashing and handsome as the French Jacques, but she trusted Gilbert; and as she herself played the lute and watched Bessie trip her measure with Jacques, and Barbara with Gilbert Curle, she thought that at all the grand balls of the past she had never seen four such handsome young people so happy together.

*   *   *

With Gilbert Curle and Barbara Mowbray it was love at first sight. They made no secret of it; and indeed had they tried they would have been unable.

Everyone was talking about the lightning courtship and what a difference it had made to the little community of Tutbury Castle. How much more pleasant it was to contemplate a love affair than wonder whether an attempt was being considered to remove one from this world! thought the Queen. She concentrated on the one, and refused to dwell on the other.

She forgot grim old Sir Amyas, and constantly invited Gilbert and Barbara to her apartment.

There were two others who watched the new lovers with interest.

'See how the Queen helps *them*,' said Bessie. 'Surely she would help us also.'

'It is different,' answered Jacques. 'Barbara is not promised to a noble lord.'

'But I feel sure I could persuade her. Shall I try, Jacques?'

But Jacques was fearful. Each day he loved her more; each day he was more impatient for her. But they must curb their impatience, he told her again and again. Their whole future was at stake.

Barbara had arrived in September, and before October was out she and Gilbert Curle had asked the Queen for her blessing on their marriage.

'I see no reason why this should not take place,' Mary told them. 'I will write to Sir John and tell him that, if he will but give his approval, the match shall have my blessing.'

And why not? she reasoned. Gilbert Curle was of good family, and when two people loved each other as these two did and there was no reason why they should not marry, it seemed sinful to put any obstacle in their way.

When Sir Mowbray replied that, since the Queen of Scots considered the match a worthy one for his daughter, he could have no objection, there was rejoicing throughout the Queen's apartments. Mary busied herself with preparations for the wedding; she herself would make the bride's dress; she had little money to spare, but she was going to give the young couple two thousand crowns as a wedding present.

She called Jacques to her and told him what she intended to do.

'Your Majesty is over generous,' he murmured.

'Nay,' she replied gaily. 'It does me so much good to see these young people happy.'

Jacques turned to her suddenly, and for a few seconds she waited for him to speak, but he remained silent and she thought she saw a sullen look on his face which had not been there before.

She thought: He is jealous of Curle.

She laid a hand on his arm. 'My dear Jacques,' she said, 'when you find a bride I shall do the same for you.'

He murmured conventional thanks; and it was from that moment she noticed the change in him. He was, she believed, a more complex character than her frank Gilbert Curle. Yet she was fond of him.

I am fortunate, she told herself, to have servants whom I can love. But it seems there must inevitably be these rivalries between them.

While the plans for the wedding were on, Mary was ill once more. It was to be expected, for November was almost upon them and so damp were her apartments that if the furniture was not wiped for a few days a mildew would begin to appear.

She wrote imploringly to the French ambassador, asking that she might be removed from the odious Tutbury – the worst of all her prisons; and he promised that he would endeavour to persuade Elizabeth to grant her request.

* * *

There was dancing in Mary's apartment. The bride and groom radiated such joy that the whole room seemed illumined with their happiness.

Mary could no longer dance but she could play the lute, and as she sat watching Barbara and Gilbert lead the dance while others joined in behind them, she noticed Jacques standing somewhat sullenly by, and Bessie with him . . . neither of them looking very pleased.

Was Bessie jealous of her affection for Barbara?

Mary sighed. So there must be intrigues even among her friends.

'Jacques,' she called sharply. 'You must join the dance. And look you. Bessie is not dancing either. Both of you, dance at once. You dance so well together.'

They obeyed her and as she watched she tried to forget the pain in her limbs, the hopelessness of her cause; she tried to feel young and gay again with Gilbert and Barbara, Jacques and Bessie.

Sir Amyas came into the apartment, walking slowly because he was not unaffected by the discomforts of Tutbury. He looked with distaste at the scene of revelry. He hoped that the Queen was not attempting to convert Protestant Barbara to her Catholic ways because Barbara, flushed and excited, was behaving in a manner which he considered to be incompatible with her religion. Sir Amyas would have liked to see the marriage celebrated in a solemn and dignified way.

'Sit beside me, Sir Amyas,' said Mary cordially. 'Have you come to wish the bride and bridegroom well?'

'I have come to tell Your Majesty that I have had word from the Queen,' he replied. 'She grants her permission for you to leave Tutbury for Chartley Castle.'

Mary clasped her hands together in delight.

'Oh, what a happy day this is!' she cried. 'I will have preparations made at once.' She looked round the walls of the room. 'And when I leave this place,' she added vehemently, 'I hope never to see it again.'

Sir Amyas, his hands folded in his lap, stared bleakly at the dancers.

Mary was unaware of him; hope, which was never far from her thoughts, came springing back. Let me leave Tutbury, she thought, this place of evil omen; let me enjoy a little comfort, and I shall be young again.

Who knew . . . perhaps she would be restored to her throne,

perhaps she would hold her son in her arms; perhaps she would send for Seton. Perhaps the days of sorrow were over.

She was past forty but that was not so very old. She only felt so because she was in constant pain, and the pain was caused by the conditions in which she was forced to live.

The future had grown suddenly bright on that day when Barbara Mowbray married Gilbert Curle.

CHAPTER SEVENTEEN

CHARTLEY

SIR FRANCIS WALSINGHAM, whose great pleasure it was to serve his Queen, had for some time sought for a means to rid himself of one whom he considered to be an enemy.

Sir Francis understood his Queen; while Mary Queen of Scots lived Elizabeth was uneasy; willingly would she have given the order for her death, yet she held back; and the reason was that she knew Mary to be innocent of conspiring against her life; and Elizabeth, a Queen herself, could not happily condemn one who, she was pleased to say, was as royal as herself – although she secretly feared Mary was more so. It was necessary for the security of Elizabeth, for the peace of England, that Mary should be brought to the scaffold; what was equally necessary was that a strong case be made out against her. Sir Francis had long been seeking to prepare that case.

When Mary had been under the care of the Shrewsburys he had had to move cautiously. He believed that the Earl and the Countess – until the latter had brought those ridiculous accusations – had been Mary's friends. It would not have been easy to work against her while she was guarded by such jailors. But now he had Amyas Paulet with whom to deal, and that was different.

The moment had come, Walsingham decided; and when he considered that wide network of spies which it had been his joy to build up, he believed he knew how to bring the Queen of Scots to her doom.

* * *

Walsingham looked at the priest who had been brought into his presence.

He said: 'Pray be seated, father. I have work for you.'

Gilbert Gifford obeyed and, as he looked across the table which separated them, he knew that the work he was going to be called upon to do was more important than anything he had done before.

Walsingham gazed down at his own hands which rested idly on the table. Gifford, who had worked for him before, guessed that behind that calm expression Walsingham was excited.

'I am ready to obey my lord's commands,' answered Gifford.

'You are to leave at once for France.'

Gifford nodded. He had become accustomed to such orders since he had entered Walsingham's spy ring, and he knew that he was one of his master's most valuable agents, chiefly because he was a Roman Catholic priest and therefore accepted as a friend by many of Walsingham's enemies.

'Do you know a man named Thomas Morgan,' went on Walsingham, 'a fiery Welshman who, with a certain Parry once worked hard to raise a rebellion for the sake of the Queen of Scots?'

'I do, my lord.'

'He is a prisoner in the Bastille. Her Majesty has asked for him to be sent to England, but the King of France, while making him a prisoner, shelters him there.'

'You wish me to seek him out?'

'I fancy he still conspires against Her Majesty. I would make certain of this. I want you to go to Paris, to see Morgan. It will not be difficult, I am sure, although he is in the Bastille, because he is not ill-treated and doubtless allowed to receive visitors. The King of France does not wish to punish the friends of the Queen of Scots – only to shield them from their just deserts.'

Gifford bowed his head.

'You will go to him,' went on Walsingham, 'and tell him that you are in a position to carry letters from him to the Queen of Scots. Tell him that as a Catholic you wish to see her on the throne. He will have no reason to doubt you.' Walsingham smiled grimly. 'Your cloth inspires such respect. I wish to discover what manner of letters the Queen of Scots is writing to her friends.'

'I will leave at once,' said Gifford.

Walsingham went on: 'I know that Morgan was once involved in an attempt to assassinate our good Queen Elizabeth and set up Mary in her place, and that the King of Spain, the Pope and the Duke of Guise were anxious to help in this endeavour. It is part of the policy of that organization which they call the Holy League to remove all Protestant rulers, and set up Catholics in their places. You understand we live in dangerous times, Gifford.'

The priest's eyes glowed. This was a mission which greatly appealed to him, although he knew that he was playing only one small part in it.

'And the letters which I receive I bring to you?' he asked.

Walsingham nodded. 'And when I have examined their contents you will take them to the Queen of Scots with a letter from Morgan recommending you to her.'

'I shall win her confidence with the greatest ease,' Gifford added. 'I have an uncle living not ten miles from Chartley where I understand the Scottish woman is now imprisoned.'

'I am sure you will act with your usual good sense. It is important that none should guess that you work for me, but there is one however whom we must take into our confidence. That is Sir Amyas Paulet. I shall write to him to tell him that you will be coming to Chartley in due course. Together you and he must devise a way for the Queen to smuggle letters out of Chartley which will seem plausible to her. She will think they are being taken to Morgan and her friends abroad. Some may reach them, but first they will pass through my hands.'

'I understand,' said Gifford.

'Then be on your way. Our work may be of long duration and I fear there is danger in delay.'

When Gifford had gone, Walsingham sat alone for some time deep in thought. He was setting the snare which he believed would soon be closing about his prey.

* * *

Chartley was a pleasant change from Tutbury. Situated on a hill rising from a fertile plain, it was about six miles from the town of Stafford, and from its windows Mary had views of magnificent scenery.

She had liked the circular keep and round towers as soon as she had set eyes on them; but perhaps almost anything would have pleased her after Tutbury.

Her spirits were high and to some extent this helped her to

forget her pains; and the fact that Sir Amyas was also complaining of his rheumatism made her feel that, suffering in similar fashion, he would be more inclined to have sympathy for her. This was not the case however, and he displayed a malignant pleasure because she was more affected by this disease than he was.

But almost as soon as the royal party arrived at Chartley, life seemed to become more exciting.

The first pleasant happening was when Barbara Curle confided to Mary that she was pregnant. Mary was delighted in the happiness of the young people and immediately began making plans for the birth of the child. The sullenness of Bessie though was becoming more apparent, and this disturbed Mary; she made up her mind that she must not allow Bessie to think that Barbara, a newcomer, had usurped her place in the Queen's affections.

Another of her ladies, Elizabeth Curle, sister of Gilbert, became engaged to Andrew Melville, her Master of the household; and it was a great pleasure to Mary to see the happiness of those about her.

The third excitement was the arrival at Chartley of a priest whose uncle lived some ten miles away.

Sir Amyas, after what seemed like a good deal of deliberation, allowed the priest to visit her. It was always a comfort to talk with a Catholic priest, and Mary welcomed the man with great warmth; but when they were alone together and she heard what he had to say, her pleasure intensified.

'Your Majesty,' Gifford told her, 'I have been recently in France and while there had conversation with a certain Thomas Morgan who is lodged in the Bastille.'

'I know of him,' replied Mary, and she was trembling a little.

'He gave me this letter to give to you.'

Mary took the letter he held out to her, and read that the bearer was one Gilbert Gifford, a priest of the Roman Catholic Church, a man in whom she could place her complete trust.

The colour had come into Mary's cheeks; all the excitement of the old days was returning. This was as it had been when she had been young and full of hope, and had believed she had many friends eager to help her. So she still had friends. This was the most wonderful news she had had for a long time, and she was intoxicated with dreams of freedom.

'I will see that any letters you wish to write to your friends are delivered,' he told her.

She shook her head. 'I am indeed a prisoner now as I never was before. Since Sir Amyas Paulet has been my jailor I have no means of sending letters to my friends; and if you come here often you would quickly fall under suspicion. Even now you may be searched before you are allowed to leave. The very fact that you are of my faith will arouse suspicions against you.'

'Your Majesty, I have thought of this and talked of it with your friends. You have rich and powerful friends, but you have humble ones also. There is a brewer in the nearby town of Burton – an honest man – who sends you your beer . . . he is your friend.'

'How do you know this?'

'Because I have long sought means of helping you. Cautiously I made my discoveries. This brewer has promised to conceal a box in one of the barrels. It will contain letters from those who wish to see you free. This box can be taken from the barrel when it arrives at the castle. And when you write your replies, you will place them in the box and put it in the empty barrel which will be taken away by the brewer when he comes to collect them. He will pass these letters to me.'

'That is a clever notion.'

'I agree with Your Majesty and I shall see that they reach the persons for whom they are intended. To whom would Your Majesty wish to write?'

Mary considered. 'To the Duke of Guise who will have heard rumours of my life here, and mayhap none of them true. To Archbishop Beaton, and of course to Morgan to thank him for sending you to me.'

Gifford nodded. 'Have no fear. Paulet will never suspect. The next time the barrels are delivered you will find the box and I doubt not that Your Majesty will soon be putting it to good use.'

Thus Mary felt that in coming to Chartley she had begun to live again.

*   *   *

Walsingham was restive. The plan was a good one, he was ready to admit, but it was moving too slowly. Mary was writing her letters which were passing by means of the brewer into Gifford's hands; they were then conveyed to Walsingham and opened by one of his men who was skilled in the art of breaking seals and resealing in such a manner that it was impossible to discover they had ever been broken. However, many of the letters were in ciphers and the Queen did not always use the same one. Walsingham employed one of the best decipherers in the country, a man named Phillipps, but even he found difficulty in decoding some of the letters.

This it was which slowed down the progress, and Walsingham decided that he could not get very far until he was in possession of all the Queen's ciphers. He had for some time been watching an attaché in the service of the French embassy, for he believed a time would come when he could use this man. Walsingham prided himself that he could pick a bribe-taker at a glance, and Cherelles he believed to be one.

Now if Cherelles could be persuaded to visit Mary with letters from the King of France say, and asked her for the keys to the ciphers, she would not hesitate to give them. And for such a service what would Cherelles want? Say two hundred crowns? It would be money well spent.

* * *

Mary was delighted to receive a visit from Cherelles. He brought with him letters from the King of France which were always a comfort to her. He listened sympathetically to an account of her sufferings and promised to do all he could to bring them to the notice of those who could help to alleviate them.

'There is one matter which has grieved some of your friends,' he told her. 'They have been unable to decipher certain of your letters.'

'Is that so?' asked Mary surprised. 'I must speak to my secretaries. I am sure they have introduced nothing new into the ciphers.'

'There is no need to do that. If Your Majesty will let me have the keys to all the ciphers in use, I will see that this difficulty is removed.'

'I will indeed do so, but I do not understand why my friends should suddenly fail to decipher my letters. However I will give you the keys.'

'And I shall lose no time in placing them in the right hands.'

'You must take great care that they do not pass into the *wrong* hands!' said Mary with a smile.

'Your Majesty can trust me.'

'I know. I wish I could show my gratitude in some way, but I am so poor now. Do you know, one of my greatest sorrows is that I can no longer give presents to my friends.' She looked down at her hands and drew off a diamond ring. 'But take this,' she said. 'I should be so happy if you would accept it.' Then she went to her table and opening a drawer took out a book which was bound in crimson velvet, and the corners of which were edged with gold.

'The embroidery was done by myself,' she said, laying her hand on the embossed velvet, 'and I have written in it those thoughts which pleased me. Pray take it with my blessing. It is a small reward for all you have done for me.'

Cherelles was conscious of a sense of shame as he took the gifts, so graciously and generously given.

He was rather relieved to ride away from Chartley, but when he had placed the keys to the ciphers in Walsingham's hands and had been complimented by that important man, the shame lingered.

*   *   *

Jacques Nau was writing a letter from the Queen's notes. It seemed that he and Gilbert Curle were constantly employed in this task now that they had the means of sending and receiving letters through the services of that honest man, the brewer.

Life was so frustrating. He and Bessie were no nearer marriage now than they had been when they had first talked of their desire for that state; and it was particularly galling to sit with Curle, listening to his conversation, and learn of his contentment with the married state. It was so unfair. Jacques had loved Bessie before Curle had known of the existence of Barbara Mowbray, and yet here they were, not only married but expecting to become parents. He could not go on in this way. He must do something.

Then, as he was writing the Queen's letter, he remembered that Sir Henry Pierpont was at the Court of Elizabeth and that it might be possible to write a letter to him by way of Gifford and the box in the barrel.

No sooner had this idea occurred to him than he wrote to Sir Henry telling of the devotion he had felt for Bessie over many years, and that Bessie herself returned his affection. He implored Sir Henry to grant him permission to marry his daughter.

Having written and dispatched the letter, Jacques told Bessie what he had done. They could scarcely contain their impatience for Sir Henry's reply.

*　　*　　*

Mary had read the letter before she realized that it was not intended for her but for her secretary. She was deeply shocked. Sir Henry Pierpont was giving his consent for the marriage of his daughter with Jacques Nau, although the girl had been promised to Lord Percy and it was the will of Queen Elizabeth, as well as the Earl and Countess of Shrewsbury, that this marriage with Percy should take place.

Mary saw the danger in this situation. Bess of Hardwick had been forced to stop spreading her scandals against Mary, but if her granddaughter were allowed to marry Mary's secretary, Bess would seek means of revenging herself on Mary whom she would almost certainly blame. Moreover although Jacques Nau was of good family, he would not be considered worthy to mate with Shrewsburys' granddaughter. What hurt Mary more than anything else was that Bessie, whom she had brought up since the girl was four, had not confided in her.

She immediately sent for Jacques and Bessie.

'This letter has come to my notice,' she said coldly. 'And I must confess I am deeply shocked.'

When Jacques saw what it was he turned pale.

'It is an answer to one which you wrote to Sir Henry Pierpont,' Mary told him. 'You are not going to deny you wrote such a letter?'

'I do not deny it,' answered Jacques with dignity. 'Bessie and I wish to marry. It was natural that I should ask her father's permission.'

'I should have thought it would have been more natural if you had asked mine.'

'I did not expect the same favour as Your Majesty bestows on Gilbert Curle.'

'You are insolent,' said Mary. 'I will not speak to you until you have recovered your good manners. Please go now.'

Jacques bowed, and as he was retiring Bessie prepared to follow him.

'Not you,' commanded Mary. 'You will stay.'

Bessie stood sullenly looking at the Queen.

'Why did you not tell me?' asked Mary reproachfully.

'Because you were determined to. make me marry Lord Percy.'

'Of course you must marry Lord Percy. It was not I who arranged the match – but it is a good one.'

Bessie said: 'I shall never marry Lord Percy.' And as she spoke all the affection she had been wont to give Mary seemed to have disappeared, and it was almost as though her grandmother stood there.

'Bessie, you are very young . . .' began Mary tolerantly.

'I am a woman. I love Jacques. I have always loved Jacques. I love him more than anyone in the world. I always shall. I am going to marry Jacques. . . .'

'Now, Bessie, my dear, you know that a girl in your position must obey her guardians.'

'I care nothing for my guardians.'

'Bessie! You can say that!'

Mary was deeply wounded. She was thinking of the day she had become this child's godmother, how she had told her stories as they lay in bed, how they had taken their meals together and how, when Bessie was little more than a. baby, rather terrified of her overbearing grandmother, she had run to Mary for comfort. Bessie thought of nothing but her passionate love for Jacques; and she was ready to hate anyone who came between her and its fulfilment.

'I can say it, and I will say it. I love Jacques. I want Jacques, and I hate . . . hate, *hate* anyone who tries to stop our marriage.'

'You are a foolish child,' said Mary. 'You are not being reasonable.'

'I care not for reason. I care for nothing but Jacques!'

'Bessie, I think you should think what you are saying.'

'I have thought of nothing else for months. I am going to marry Jacques and no one on Earth is going to stop me! You are an old woman – you don't understand. . . . Or have you forgotten!'

Bessie suddenly burst into angry tears and ran from the room. Mary looked after her bewildered.

*　　*　　*

Mary was entirely preoccupied with the affair of Bessie and Jacques. Hatred for her had looked out of Bessie's eyes when the girl had stood before her so defiantly proclaiming her love, and Mary was hurt.

Had the lovers come to her and told her of their feelings for each other before the Countess had expressed her desire for a marriage with Lord Percy, she would have done all she could to help them. Now it seemed that she could not, since to do so would be deliberately to oppose the wishes of the girl's family.

Her little Skye terrier seemed to sense her grief and jumped on to her lap and licked her hands.

She stroked him tenderly for she took great joy in the little creature and since he had been sent to her he had not left her side.

She wondered what she would do about the defiant lovers; and eventually she believed that she should send Bessie away.

If Elizabeth would have the girl at Court it might be that, with all the splendour of that life, Bessie would forget Jacques. Mary was of the opinion that the girl, living the sheltered life which had necessarily been hers, had imagined she was in love with the first handsome man who had noticed her. Bessie was too young to understand this; if she went away, met other people, she might learn that her affection for the secretary was not the *grande passion* she had imagined it was.

Eventually Mary wrote to Sir Henry and Lady Pierpont telling them that she thought it was time they took their daughter into their home.

*   *   *

In an inn parlour not far from St Giles's-in-the-Field a priest sat waiting for a visitor. His outstanding features were his burning fanatical eyes, and as he waited he drummed his fingers on the table impatiently. Eventually he was joined by a man in the uniform of a soldier.

'Pray be seated,' said the priest.

The soldier obeyed, drawing his chair close.

'I know we can trust each other,' went on the priest. 'My name is John Ballard and we have mutual friends. I know you to be John Savage and that we hold similar views.'

'I believe Thomas Morgan has recommended me to you,' Savage murmured.

'That is so. You are one who is ready to give his life for the Faith. That is all that matters. Danger lies ahead of us, my friend. Are you afraid of danger?'

'I am not afraid to die for my faith.'

'That is what I understood. Believe me, my friend, all of

those who are ready to work in this project must hold those views.'

'Will you enlighten me?'

'With pleasure. I believe – and I am sure you as a good Catholic will agree with me – that no good can come to England while we have a Protestant bastard on the throne.'

'I believe with all my heart that no good can come to England until she returns to the Catholic Faith.'

'Then, my friend, we are in accord. It is our endeavour to bring back the Catholic Faith and, as we can only do so by removing Elizabeth, we plan to do exactly that and set Catholic Mary in her place.'

'Who else is with you in this enterprise?'

'Certain gentlemen whom you shall meet without delay. Do you wish to go further?'

'I wish it with all my heart,' replied John Savage.

* * *

It was growing dark when the two men made their way to a house in Fetter Lane. Ballard gave three slow knocks on the door which after a while was opened.

He stepped into a dark passage, and Savage followed him. The man who had opened the door, recognizing Ballard, nodded an acknowledgement, and they followed him down a flight of stairs and along a corridor. When they reached a certain door, this was quietly opened by Ballard, and Savage saw that he was about to enter a dimly lighted room which, it soon became apparent, had been made into a chapel; he saw the altar and, standing about it, several men.

Ballard announced: 'John Savage. He is one of us.'

An unusually handsome man stepped forward and grasped Savage's hand.

'My name is Anthony Babington,' he said quietly. 'Welcome to our band. We were about to hear Mass. You will join us?'

'With all my heart.'

'Afterwards we will go to my house in the Barbican and there you will become acquainted with my friends.'

Savage bowed his head, and the Mass began.

When they had left Fetter Lane for the house in the Barbican, Anthony Babington entertained his friends with food and wine, and after they had been served he bolted the doors and assured himself that nothing which was said in the room could be heard by anyone outside it.

407

Babington, Savage realized, was a man in his middle twenties. He was somewhat flamboyant in dress as he was in manner and his handsome features glowed with an enthusiasm which was infectious. Babington believed wholeheartedly in his plot; he could not visualize failure, and such was his personality that everyone around that table caught his fervour.

He took the centre of the stage and dramatically explained why this party of men were gathered together in such secrecy.

'My friend,' he said, 'now that you have joined us we are thirteen in number. But do not think we are alone. Once we are ready we shall find the entire Catholic Nobility of England behind us. And we have allies outside England. This is no Northern Rising, gentlemen. This is going to be the revolt against Protestantism which will change the course of our country's history. The Pope is with us. The King of Spain is with us. And once we have removed the bastard from the throne, these powerful allies will come to our aid.'

He looked round the assembly, his eyes glowing.

'John Savage,' he went on, 'I will now introduce you to your colleagues.' He pointed to the man who sat on his right hand.

'Edward Abington,' he said. Savage inclined his head in greeting which was returned by Abington. Then he indicated the others who sat round that table and the procedure was repeated: 'Edward Windsor, Edward Jones, Chidiock Tichbourne, Charles Tilney, Henry Donn, Gilbert Gifford, John Traves, Robert Barnwell, Thomas Salisbury.'

When the greetings were over, Babington said: 'Now pray be seated and we will talk together.'

Savage took his seat and Babington went on to explain the conspiracy, which he had been, chosen to lead. It was well known on the Continent, he explained, that he was an ardent Catholic, devoted to the cause of the Queen of Scots. The core of the plot was to bring England back to the Catholic Faith and to free the Queen of Scots, but there was one deed which must be performed before this could be achieved: the assassination of Elizabeth. Once Elizabeth was dead the King of Spain and the Pope would not hesitate to give their open support. Therefore their first task was to plan that assassination. When the time was ripe Babington proposed to call for six volunteers for this most important task. In the meantime there were minor details to be discussed.

'I will inform the Spanish ambassador that we rely on Philip II above all, and that it is because of his encouragement and promises of help that we have the zeal and courage to go on with this dangerous plan. We shall ask for an assurance that, as soon as Elizabeth is dead, help reaches us from Spain and the Low Countries. Ships in the Thames must be seized. Cecil, Walsingham, Hunsdon and Knollys must be immediately either captured or killed. I shall inform the Queen of Scots of our intention.'

Charles Tilney put in: 'Is it wise to tell her of the intention to murder Elizabeth? I have reason to believe that she will not readily agree to be party to such a deed.'

Babington was thoughtful and others added their doubts to Tilney's.

They should go cautiously in their communication with the Queen of Scots who was, after all, a prisoner in the hands of their enemies.

'Letters will have to be smuggled to her,' pointed out Henry Donn. 'A dangerous procedure.'

Gifford spoke then. 'I do not think you need fear, my friends. We have a very good method of conveying letters to the Queen. The brewer of Burton is an honest man whom we can trust. The Queen *must* be prepared for rescue. It would be unwise to keep her in the dark.'

There was clearly a divided opinion on this matter and it was temporarily shelved.

But when the meeting was over and the conspirators went their various ways, Gifford returned to the house to speak to Babington; they sat for a long time discussing the plot, and Gifford did not have great difficulty in persuading Babington that it would be advisable to inform Mary of their intentions.

*　　*　　*

Anthony Babington was a vain young man. Extremely handsome, elegant and wealthy, he had been intended for the Bar, but had abandoned this career for a fashionable life on the fringes of the Court. He had divided his time between that Court and his vast estates at Dethick. During the last few years he had also travelled abroad and, because he must be the centre of attention, he had become known as an ardent Catholic, and a man of adventure, so that he had been noticed as a suitable leader to be remembered when such a one was needed – for his vitality, enthusiasms, wealth and charm were invaluable.

When he was barely eighteen he had married Margery, the daughter of Philip Draycot of Paynsley in Staffordshire; the Draycots were Catholics, as were his mother and his step-father, Henry Foljambe. Among such fervent Catholics intrigue was constantly fostered, and Anthony soon became a member – with the support of his family – of a secret society which had been formed for the protection of Jesuit missionaries in England.

And so it was that while he was but twenty-five he found himself at the head of a conspiracy which if it succeeded would change the course of English history.

Anthony now saw himself as a man of destiny. He believed that Fate had chosen him. Was he not outstandingly handsome, cultured, witty? Did he not draw men and women into his circle through his charming manners?

He had always cherished a devotion to the Queen of Scots. She was such a romantic figure – a beautiful woman, a Queen, a helpless prisoner, the motive for many a conspiracy, the symbol of many a cherished ideal.

When he had met her he had been conscious of that potent charm. He was devoted to his wife and young daughter, but, for him, as she was for so many, the Queen was someone to worship from afar, the ideal woman.

But Anthony Babington was no simple-hearted George Douglas. His devotion was not single-minded. For although Anthony admired the Queen, he admired himself more.

Anthony must be the centre of the stage – the leading character in the drama. The Queen was a charming second – but a symbol, whose grace and beauty must merely serve to emphasize the valour of the man of action.

He had already committed an act which he knew some of the conspirators would have declared not only foolish but highly dangerous, when he had caused to be painted a picture of himself with six of his friends – himself in the centre as leader – and had allowed this picture to be inscribed with the words:

Hi mihi sunt comites, quos ipsa pericula ducunt.

Perhaps the best time to have had such a picture painted would have been after the conspiracy had been brought to a successful conclusion, but Babington was impatient, and he derived great pleasure from looking at this portrait of himself.

He was impatient now – eager to receive the approbation of the Queen of Scots. He wanted Mary to know that he was ready to risk his life for her; when the plot succeeded there would be many to claim her praise for their part in it; he wanted her to know now that the plot was Babington's plot and that it was he who was at the very heart of it.

He knew that he should act with caution, that some members of the company had thought it unwise to write to Mary; but Gifford was with him. Gifford believed that Mary should be informed.

Anthony took up his pen and wrote to Mary:

'Most highly and excellent Sovereign Lady and Queen unto whom I owe all fidelity and obedience. ...'

He smiled as he wrote, and the eloquent words rose to his lips while he mouthed them slowly to keep time with his pen.

He himself, with his trusted followers, would deliver her from her prison; they planned to dispatch the 'Usurping Competitor'; he told her that Ballard, who was one of Her Majesty's most zealous servants, had recently come from overseas with promises of help from Christian Princes. He wished to know if he could promise his friends rewards for their services when victory was won.

He signed himself: 'Your Majesty's most faithful subject and sworn servant, Anthony Babington.'

Having finished, he read through the letter once more, repeating the phrases which seemed especially well turned.

He closed his eyes and rocked to and fro in his chair, looking into a future coloured bright with the rewards of valour and loyalty. The Queen of Scots was now the Queen of England also. She reigned in Hampton Court and Greenwich; and always beside her was her most faithful friend and adviser, without whom she would make no decisions. She wished to shower honours on him; she wanted the whole world to know that she would never forget all he had done for her.

But he only smiled and said: 'It matters only that I can say to myself: "But for Anthony Babington my gracious lady would still be a prisoner of the bastard Elizabeth." That is all the reward I ask.'

Then she begged and pleaded – and just to please her he accepted an earldom ... a Dukedom ... great estates ... and so it was – almost against his will – that the most important man in England was now Anthony Babington of Dethick.

This was no time to dream. He sealed the letter and took it to Gifford.

'I have written to the Queen,' he said. 'I know I can trust you to see that it reaches her.'

'With the help of that honest man it shall reach Her Majesty in her next consignment of beer.'

When they parted, Gifford was smiling. His master would be pleased, he was thinking, as he made his way to Walsingham.

* * *

Walsingham exulted as he read the letter.

'Well done,' he murmured. 'Well done.'

'It seems, my lord,' ventured Gifford, 'that the end is in sight.'

'Let us not be impatient. This Babington is a fool.'

'Assuredly so. Do you propose to arrest him now?'

'No. We will give him a little more rope. He is such a fool that he gives me no qualms. I will have this letter resealed at once and you must see that it reaches the Queen's hands without delay. Her answer will be interesting. Go now. You will be hearing from me very soon.'

Gifford left Walsingham and made for Chartley. Meanwhile Walsingham sent for Thomas Phillipps. He had work for him.

* * *

Mary continued to brood on the change in her relationship with Bessie Pierpont. Bessie was sullen in her presence and showed no regret that their love for each other had undergone this change. Bessie hated everyone and everything which kept her from Jacques.

'I understand her love for the man,' Mary told Jane Kennedy and Elizabeth Curle, 'but surely she must understand my position. How can I help her against the wishes of her grandmother? And she grows more like Bess of Hardwick every day. To tell the truth, when I see her looking so much like the Countess I almost wish that she were gone.'

There were complications also with Jacques who knew that the Queen was endeavouring to have Bessie sent away. He too was resentful, and she knew that he jealously watched Barbara and Gilbert Curle as though, by favouring them and not himself and Bessie, she had been guilty of unkind favouritism.

'As though I do not want everyone about me to be happy!' She sighed. 'God knows there is enough unhappiness in these prisons which I have been forced to inhabit for so many years!'

She looked forward to those days when the beer was delivered. There was always the excitement of seeing what was in the box; and it was while she was so distressed about Bessie and Jacques that she received the letter from Babington.

It was in cipher of course, and it was necessary for one of the secretaries to decipher it. This duty fell to Gilbert Curle who, when he brought it to her, was very agitated. He handed it to her and she read it, catching her breath as she did so.

Freedom! she thought. A chance of freedom at last.

She re-read the letter and her eyes rested on that phrase 'dispatch the Usurping Competitor'. She knew what that meant, and she heartily wished it had not been included. And yet . . . Elizabeth had kept her in prison for all these years. Should she be anxious on her account?

Why, thought Mary, once I am free I will never allow them to do this deed. I will demand my rights and nothing more. I do not seek to be Queen of England. I only wish to regain my own crown, to be with my son again, to bring him up as my heir.

'Your Majesty will answer this letter?' asked Curle.

She nodded.

'Send for Jacques Nau,' she said.

Jacques came sullenly into her presence, seeing that Curle was already with her.

'Ah, Jacques,' said Mary, 'I have received a letter which I must answer. You will take my notes and then Gilbert will put them into English and into cipher.'

This was the usual custom, for Mary thought in French and Jacques took notes and composed her letters, then handed them to Gilbert for translation into English, for although Jacques spoke English well and Curle French, Mary preferred to use them in this way to ensure greater accuracy.

'It is a letter to an Anthony Babington,' said Mary to Jacques. 'You had better read what he says.'

Jacques read the letter and turned pale as he did so.

'Well, Jacques?' asked Mary.

'Your Majesty should not answer this letter.'

'Why not?'

'To do so would put Your Majesty in the utmost danger.'

'Gilbert, what do you think?' asked Mary.

'I agree with Jacques, Your Majesty.'

Mary did not speak for some time, but she had clearly abandoned her intention to answer immediately.

'I will think about it,' she said.

* * *

A newcomer had appeared at Chartley. This was Thomas
Phillipps who, when he arrived, asked to be taken at once to
Sir Amyas Paulet.

Paulet rose with difficulty to greet his guest who was a
somewhat unprepossessing man of about thirty; he was short
and very thin; his beard and hair were yellow, but he peered
shortsightedly out of dark eyes and his skin was hideously
pock-marked.

'We could not be overheard?' Phillipps asked.

'That is impossible,' Paulet assured him.

'That is well. I come on the business of Secretary Walsingham.'

'He is pleased with the work we are doing here at Chartley,
I trust.'

'He is indeed. But we are reaching the climax. An important
letter has been delivered to the Queen, and we are eagerly
awaiting her reply.'

'If it is what you wish, she will be entirely incriminated?'

Phillipps nodded.

'And if not . . . I suppose we shall go on with our little
comedy of the beer barrels?'

'It *will* be what we wish. It has to be.'

'I see you have instructions from the Secretary.'

'Very definite instructions. As soon as the letter is in your
hands it must be passed to me here. For that reason I have
come here. This is the most important letter of all. It is not safe
to trust it to any messenger. It must come straight from the
box to me, that I may decipher it and myself deliver it into the
hands of my master.'

'Your presence in the castle will not go unnoticed.'

Phillipps waved his hands. 'Let some rumour be circulated.
You are not well. You have asked for help in your task, and I
have come to relieve you. That is as good a tale as any.'

'It shall be done,' answered Paulet.

* * *

'Jane . . . Elizabeth,' said Mary, 'who is the pock-marked
man?'

Jane did not know, but Elizabeth answered: 'His name is
Thomas Phillipps, Your Majesty. He is here to relieve Paulet
of some of his duties.'

414

'I do not much like him.'

'Nor I,' put in Jane.

'I saw him yesterday when I rode out in my coach for a little breath of air. He was riding towards the castle. He saluted me. I did not like his sly eyes, which peered at me so oddly. I felt almost glad that I was surrounded by guards. That was an odd feeling to have for a stranger.'

'I hope he is not going to replace Paulet,' said Elizabeth.

'I had thought I disliked him as much as I could dislike any jailor. Yet I think that I would rather have Paulet than this pock-marked Phillipps.'

'Let us not concern ourselves with him, Your Majesty,' Jane said. 'It may be that he will soon be gone.'

'Yes, there are other matters with which to concern ourselves,' Mary agreed.

There was Babington's letter. If she did not answer it, would that mean the loss of another chance to escape?

I have let too many chances pass by, she told herself. If I had been bolder I might not be a prisoner now.

But for that one sentence. . . . But if she were restored to the throne, if she were free and able to command, she would tell them that she forbade them to allow any harm to come to Elizabeth. She would say: It may be that she is a bastard, but the people of England have accepted her as their Queen, and she is indeed the daughter of Henry VIII.

She *would* answer the letter.

She sent for Jacques and told him to take notes. He looked at her with those dark eyes of his which had once been so affectionate and now were often reproachful. At this moment they were fearful.

Never mind. She was the one who must make decisions.

'Trusty and well beloved,' she began.

And Jacques took up his pen and wrote.

She wanted to know what forces they could raise, what captains they would appoint; what towns were to receive help from France, Spain and the Low Countries; at what spot the main forces were to be assembled; what money and armour they would ask for; and by what means had they arranged her escape. She begged Babington to be wary of all those surrounding him, for it might be that some who called themselves friends were in truth his enemies.

She put forward three methods by which she might escape from her prison. Firstly she might take the air on horseback to

a lonely moor between Chartley and Stafford; if, say fifty or
sixty men well armed could meet her there, they could take her
from her guards, for often there would be only eighteen or
twenty of these with her and they would only be armed with
pistols. Secondly, friends might come silently to Chartley at
midnight, set fire to the barns, stables and outbuildings which
were near the house and, while this was being extinguished, it
would be possible, with the help of her trustworthy servants,
to rescue her. Thirdly, her rescuers might come with the carters
who came to Chartley in the early morning. Disguised they
could pass into the castle, upsetting some of the carts under
the great gateway to prevent its being closed, while they took
possession of the house and brought her out of it to where
armed supporters could be waiting half a mile or so away.

She ended with the words:

> 'God Almighty have you in protection.
> Your most assured friend for ever.
> Fail not to burn this quickly.'

Mary sat back watching the two secretaries at work. Im-
mersed in the task, they forgot the danger, and Mary felt alive
again.

'This cannot fail. This cannot fail,' she whispered. 'Soon now
I shall be free.'

It was difficult to wait patiently for the brewer to come for
the empty barrels. What joy when at last he came, when the
box was put into place and the letter sent on its way.

* * *

Paulet brought the letter to Phillipps.

'At last,' sighed the latter. 'I thought it would never reach
me.'

'It would have aroused suspicions, had we changed the
routine in any way.'

'Of course. Of course.' Phillipps broke the Queen's seals and
looked at the document. He glanced up at Paulet, anxious to
be alone that he might continue with his task of deciphering.

Paulet understood and left him, and as Phillipps laboured,
his short-sighted eyes close to the paper, he was almost trembling with excitement.

This was what they had been waiting for. Walsingham was
going to be delighted with his servant. Phillipps could scarcely
wait to decipher it all.

At last his task was completed and he read through the damning letter.

Was it enough? Would it satisfy Walsingham?

Then he had an idea. Why should he not add a postscript to this letter? No sooner had the idea entered his head than he set to work.

'I should like to know the names and qualities of the gentlemen who are to accomplish the task, for it may be that I should be able to give further advice; and even so do I wish to be made acquainted with the names of such principal persons. Also from time to time how you proceed, and how far everyone is privy hereunto.'

The letter was ready for dispatch to Walsingham, and all in good time it would reach Babington.

Delighted with his work, Phillipps made a little design on the outside of the letter. It was of a gallows.

*　　*　　*

When Babington eventually received the Queen's letter he put it to his lips and kissed it.

Now, he told himself, our plans will soon come to fruition. The Queen is with us. She will never forget us when we have brought her out of her prison. This is the happiest day of my life.

Now he was going to answer the letter in detail, as she so clearly desired. He would get together all the information that she asked and gladly give it to her. The moment was at hand.

It was while he was writing his reply that his servant came to tell him that a friend had called and was asking to see him.

Ballard was ushered into his room, and as soon as they were alone together it became clear that Ballard was agitated.

'All is not well,' he said. 'I fear there is treachery among my servants.'

Babington was startled. He thrust his hands out of sight, because he feared they might begin to tremble.

'What has happened?' he demanded hoarsely.

'Little as yet. But we must take the utmost care. I have reason to believe that one of my servants is betraying us. I saw him in conversation with a man in a tavern who, I know, was at one time an agent of Walsingham's.'

'You have questioned this servant?'

'No. It would be unwise to arouse suspicions. I shall watch him. But in the meantime I wanted to warn you to act with the utmost caution.'

'I was about to write a letter to the Queen in reply to hers.'

Ballard caught his breath and held out his hand for Mary's letter. When he read it he was silent.

'If this fell into the wrong hands all our endeavours would be wasted,' he said.

'My dear Ballard, of course it cannot fall into the wrong hands. All our correspondence has been reaching us through that honest man, the Burton brewer. Gifford has arranged this excellent method of carrying letters to and from the Queen. You cannot doubt its efficiency?'

'I do not. But I say, at this stage move with care. Do not answer that letter until we have satisfied ourselves that all is well.'

Babington was disappointed, and Ballard thought how young and impetuous he was, and for the first time questioned the wisdom of making him the leading spirit in the conspiracy.

'If you value our lives, do not write to the Queen until we are sure that we are safe,' he insisted.

Babington nodded slowly. 'You are right,' he added, with regret.

When Ballard had gone, he tried to recapture his dream of Babington, the first minister of the new Queen of England. But it would not return. Instead other pictures – grotesque and terrifying – were forcing themselves into his mind.

Ballard had shaken him.

*   *   *

Walsingham was waiting impatiently for the letter he expected, and when it did not come, he guessed that the suspicion that all was not well must have struck the conspirators. He had not meant to make arrests at this point. There was more information that he had hoped to acquire through that interesting correspondence. But if the conspirators were aware that they were being watched, there must be a hasty change of plans.

Babington might be called the leader of the plot, but the experienced Ballard would certainly be the chief instigator. A sharper watch should be kept on Ballard.

As the days passed Ballard's suspicions grew stronger, and he called a meeting of his friends in St Giles's Fields at dusk.

When they were all gathered there he said that they must disperse after the meeting and wait until they had further news from him. He suspected they were being spied on, and he was determined to question the spy without further delay.

They would each leave the Fields separately and go their different ways. Soon he hoped to send them news that it was safe for them to reassemble and make their final preparations.

Ballard was the last to leave and, as he sauntered to the edge of the Fields, two men emerged from a clump of bushes.

'John Ballard?' said one.

'You wished to speak with me?'

The other came swiftly towards him and had seized him by the arm.

'You are the Queen's prisoner.'

'On what charge?'

'Treason,' was the answer.

Then John Ballard understood that his fears were well founded.

* * *

Babington was really alarmed now. He knew that Ballard had been taken, but he did not believe that Walsingham was aware of the conspiracy. If so, why should he arrest Ballard and allow the others to go free?

Ballard could be trusted not to betray his friends. He was a zealous Catholic and one of the bravest men Babington had ever known. He would remain silent no matter what they did to him, for he would still hope that the plan to murder Elizabeth and set up Catholicism in England would succeed.

But it was unwise to stay in England. Babington invited several of the conspirators to the Barbican and told them that he planned to go to France to make the final arrangements for a foreign invasion. He was therefore applying to Walsingham for a passport.

This explanation was plausible. As for Ballard's arrest, they discussed this and Gifford suggested that it may have been that he had been taken on account of his being a recusant – as many priests were.

'Undoubtedly that is so,' answered Babington. 'But we must go ahead with our plans. The sooner I am in France the sooner we shall be in a position to proceed.'

This was agreed and when after a few days Walsingham had made no reply to his request, Babington, beginning to grow uneasy, wrote once more to the Secretary offering his services while in France to act as a spy. As a gentleman of Catholic leanings, he pointed out, he would be trusted by other Catholics and would thus be in a position to move easily among the enemies of their Sovereign Lady Elizabeth.

Walsingham was amused, and called his steward, one of his secretaries and several of his higher servants to him.

'There is a young man,' he told them, 'who is importuning me to supply him with a passport. Get into touch with him, ask him to sup with you. Watch him carefully and ply him with wine. Listen to what he says when in his cups. You might suggest that ... for a consideration ... you would see if you could procure for him what he wants.'

Shortly afterwards Babington received a call from Walsingham's secretary and accepted an invitation to supper.

But Walsingham's servants had not been trained to spying, and something in their demeanour aroused Babington's suspicions. He did not drink as freely as they would have wished and, during the time he was in Walsingham's house, he caught a glimpse of papers on the secretary's table and there was one in Walsingham's own handwriting on which, to his horror, he saw his own name.

That put an end to his peace of mind. Excusing himself he left the party and went hastily to his house in Barbican; there he left a message, with one of his servants whom he could trust, to warn the rest of the conspirators and then made with all speed to St John's Wood.

In the heart of the wood he found a hut, and here he stayed for the rest of that night. In the morning his servant came to him, as he had told him to, bringing with him food and walnut juice. With this latter Babington stained his skin, and then made his servant cut off his hair. Then he changed clothes with his servant, and sent him back to Barbican.

He could not live here for long, so he only remained in the hut for the rest of the next day and then, during the following night, he walked to Harrow to the home of a Jerome Bellamy, who had recently been converted to Catholicism.

Jerome stared at the brown-faced man whom he did not immediately recognize, but when Babington explained his plight and the danger in which he knew himself to be in, Jerome eagerly agreed to shelter him.

There he remained for some weeks. But the hunt had begun. Walsingham, aware that Babington knew he was a wanted

420

man, decided his freedom must be ended; he knew also that his quarry could not be far away, and it was no secret that Jerome Bellamy of Harrow was a recent convert to Catholicism and a friend of Babington's.

One warm August night a man knocked at the door of Jerome's house, and when the door was opened forced his way past the startled servant.

'It is no use trying to eject me,' said the newcomer. 'The house is surrounded by the Queen's men. I come to search it because I believe you are sheltering here a traitor to our Sovereign Lady Elizabeth.'

There was no escape.

Anthony Babington was taken from Harrow, Walsingham's prisoner.

*　　*　　*

Sir Amyas Paulet came to the Queen's apartment; he was smiling, and rarely had Mary seen him in such a good humour.

'Your Majesty,' he said, 'I have here an invitation from Sir Walter Aston of Tixall, which is close by Chartley, as you know. He is arranging a stag hunt in his park and asks if you would care to join his party.'

Mary's eyes sparkled at the prospect. In the summer she felt so much better, and during these lovely August days she had felt herself to be quite well enough to ride a horse and handle a crossbow.

'Then I will convey your wishes to Sir Walter,' Paulet told her.

And all that day Mary was excited at the prospect of riding a horse.

'I believe,' she told Jane Kennedy, 'that Paulet no longer hates me as he once did. He seemed almost pleased because I was to have this pleasure.'

'It may be that the more sickly he grows, the more sympathetic he is towards Your Majesty,' replied Jane.

On the appointed day, the party set out from Chartley, with guards in front and behind; and beside Mary rode Sir Amyas.

Mary's spirits were high. She could almost believe that she had escaped from her prison. The air was warm, and it was glorious to see the sun on her flesh. She spurred her horse and galloped on. Sir Amyas could not keep pace with her and, remembering his strained face as he rode beside her, she slackened speed and waited for him to catch up with her.

Poor old man! she thought. He is infirm, and he must be

frightened to see me galloping ahead of him in such a manner. If her supporters suddenly appeared, that would be a different matter. Sir Amyas could not be blamed if his guards were outnumbered. But she did not wish to alarm the old man unnecessarily.

'I'm sorry, Sir Amyas,' she said. 'I know how stiff your limbs are. None could know better than I.'

Sir Amyas gave her his sour smile and they rode side by side for a few more miles. She glanced at Jacques and Gilbert who were members of the party riding close behind her, and she was pleased to see that they too were enjoying the exercise.

If I had always been allowed to ride in this manner, she thought, I should have enjoyed better health.

It was Jacques who, coming close to her, cried suddenly: 'Your Majesty, there is a party of horsemen riding towards us.'

Then Mary saw them and her heart leaped with hope.

They had planned it. This was it. They had come to rescue her. This was one of the methods she had said they might use.

But it was not a large party. Would they be strong enough to hold back the guards?

Now that the two parties were coming to a halt, and Sir Amyas was riding forward, Mary saw that at the head of the horsemen was one in serge trimmed with green braid. He could not be one of her friends unless he was disguised in Tudor livery; he was talking confidentially to Sir Amyas.

She rode her horse forward and called imperiously: 'Sir Amyas, who is this that hinders us in our journey?'

Sir Amyas turned his head to look at her, and there was something like loathing in his eyes as he said: 'This is Sir Thomas Gorges, a servant of our Queen.'

Sir Thomas Gorges dismounted and came to stand by Mary's horse. When he reached her he said in tones which could be heard by those who stood close by: 'Madam, the Queen, my mistress, finds it very strange that you, against the agreement which you made together, have undertaken against her and her estate; and in consequence of the discovery of your share in a horrible conspiracy against her life, my orders are to conduct you to Tixall.'

Mary said coldly: 'I do not understand you, sir. And I refuse to go with you to Tixall.'

'You have no choice, Madam, since you have conspired against Queen Elizabeth.'

'She has been wrongly informed.'

She was aware of Jacques and Gilbert, and she remembered the letter she had written to Anthony Babington. She must speak to them without delay. She must warn them, for it seemed certain that that letter had fallen into Elizabeth's hands.

'I will return to Chartley,' she said. She looked quickly from Jacques to Gilbert. 'Come, ride with me.'

'Nay, nay,' cried Sir Thomas Gorges. 'Those two men must not be allowed to speak to the Queen.'

Jacques and Gilbert immediately attempted to bring their horses level with Mary's, but as they did so they were intercepted by the guards and Gorges cried: 'Arrest those two men. They are to be taken at once to London.'

'You cannot do this!' she cried.

'Madam, you are mistaken,' replied Paulet coldly.

'Oh, Jacques,' murmured Mary, 'what means this? And you, Gilbert. . . .' She looked with dismay at the two young men who for so long had been her friends. She thought with anguish of Barbara who was so soon to give birth to her first baby; how would Barbara take the news that Gilbert was the Queen's prisoner?

But it was useless to expect sympathy from these men. Already they had seized the two secretaries.

'Gilbert,' she called, 'I will take care of Barbara.'

Sir Amyas had his hand on the bridle of her horse.

'Come, Madam,' he said, 'we are riding to Tixall, where you will remain during the Queen's pleasure.'

All the joy had gone out of that sunny morning, and there was terrible foreboding in her heart as Mary rode with her captors towards Tixall.

* * *

A subdued Sir Walter Aston received Mary at Tixall Park. There was no hunt, as had been promised her, and she was conducted to two small rooms which, she was told, were all that could be put at her disposal.

Her servants were not allowed to visit her; she was to have no books, no pen nor paper; thus for days she was left alone in apprehensive solitude, Sir Amyas Paulet remaining at Tixall to guard her while he sent his officials back to Chartley to ransack her apartments for any shred of evidence which could be used against her.

* * *

Jacques and Gilbert were taken before Walsingham who, after questioning them without being able to make them utter a word against their mistress, kept them confined in separate rooms in his own lodgings in Westminster Palace. He did not doubt that in time he would get from them what he wanted.

He set his man, Aleyn, to watch over Jacques, and this man slept in the same chamber and was with Jacques night and day, engaging him in conversation, waiting for one word which would betray the Queen.

Jacques was very melancholy, and it was not easy to make him talk.

Aleyn tried to coax him. 'Come,' he told him, 'you cannot be blamed. My master is a very just man. He knows full well that as secretary to the Queen you must perforce do your duty. If she said to you, Write this, then you wrote. All my master wishes is to confirm what is already known was written.'

Jacques remained silent for some time and then he said: 'I wonder how she is taking this.'

'She is fearful, my friend, doubt that not.'

'She will be wondering what has become of me. She is so young; it is hard that she should suffer so.'

'Young! She is no longer young and she will be too concerned with her own skin, friend, to think much of yours.'

'I see you have misunderstood. I was speaking of another.'

'Your mistress?'

'We will marry when it can be arranged.'

'Ah,' grunted Aleyn, disappointed.

But now Jacques had begun to speak of Bessie he could not stop; he told Aleyn of the way her eyes sparkled and how soft her hair was; and how quickly she grew angry, how defiant she was, how determined when she had set her heart on something – as she had set her heart on marrying him.

Aleyn listened half-heartedly. Strange, he thought, that when a man was in mortal danger he could think of nothing but a girl.

When Aleyn stood before his master and Walsingham asked if he had anything to report, the man replied: 'It is not easy with this one, my lord. He seems unaware of the danger he's in. He talks of nothing but his Bessie.'

'His Bessie?' mused Walsingham.

'Bessie Pierpont, my lord.'

'That would be Shrewsbury's granddaughter – so there is love between these two.'

'He'll talk of nothing else, my lord.'

Walsingham nodded. It was a pity. Still no piece of information, however small, should be ignored. Long experience had taught him that one never knew when it might be useful.

*   *   *

When Mary was allowed to return to Chartley Castle her first thought was of Barbara Curle who she believed might already have given birth to the child.

Bessie greeted her – a frightened Bessie, whose eyes were red with weeping.

Mary embraced her affectionately, all rancour forgotten. It was sad that Bessie, at such an early age, had already come face to face with tragedy.

'And how fares Barbara?' Mary asked.

'Her child is born. She is in her bed now.'

Mary went at once to Barbara's chamber and the young mother gave a cry of pleasure as the Queen hurried to her bed and embraced her.

'And the little one?'

'A girl, Your Majesty. She is very like Gilbert. Your Majesty, what news?'

'I know nothing, my dear. I have been a prisoner at Tixall Park all this time. But as my priest was with me, who has attended to the child's baptism?'

'She has not been baptized, Your Majesty. There was no one to perform the ceremony.'

'Then this must be remedied without delay.' She lifted the baby from where it lay beside Barbara and, holding it in her arms, gently kissed its brow, and while she was doing this Sir Amyas Paulet burst unceremoniously into the chamber.

'I hope you will call her Mary after me,' she said.

'Your Majesty, that will be an honour she will remember all her life.'

Mary turned to Paulet. 'Will you allow your minister to baptize this child?'

'Nay,' he answered. 'This child's baptism is no concern of mine.'

'It is the concern of us all,' answered Mary sternly, and she turned to one of the women who was close by and said: 'Bring me a basin of water.'

'So *you* will baptize the child?' asked Paulet.

'It is permissible for members of the laity to administer baptism if no priest is available.'

Paulet was glowering at her, wondering how he could prevent her from carrying out her intention, but he said nothing and very soon the woman returned with a basin. Taking the child on her knee, Mary sprinkled the little face with water, saying: 'I baptize thee, Mary, in the name of the Father, and the Son and the Holy Ghost.'

Paulet growled: 'It is time you returned to your own apartments.'

'I am ready,' answered Mary; and smiling she laid the child in its mother's arms. 'Have no fear, dearest Barbara,' she whispered. 'All will be well. Gilbert will return to you. They cannot harm the innocent.'

Then she stooped and kissed Barbara's forehead, and turning to Paulet said: 'I am ready.'

The sight which confronted her in her own apartments caused her to cry out in alarm and protest. Drawers had been burst open, coffers had been emptied; and she saw that almost everything she possessed had been removed.

Mary stood staring at the disorder in dismay while Paulet watched her, a smile of satisfaction on his lips.

'At least,' said Mary, 'there are two things of which I cannot be robbed – my English blood and my Catholic Faith, in which, by the grace of God I intend to die.'

* * *

Aleyn came into the room and sat down beside his charge.

'I have news for you,' he said. 'Your young lady is a prisoner in the Tower.'

Jacques lifted his eyes, weary with sleeplessness, to his jailor's face. 'This is true?'

'True it is. They've taken her from the Queen's side and put her there. They've ransacked the Queen's rooms and have found enough to send her to the block.'

'It cannot be so. She has never done anything to deserve such a fate.'

'There's some that thinks different.'

'What are they doing to Bessie in the Tower?'

'You've no need to concern yourself for her safety. If she's sensible and you're sensible . . . why, I shouldn't wonder if there wouldn't be a nice little wedding, and all merry ever after.'

426

'What do you know of these matters? Tell me truly.'

'That the Queen of Scots is in mortal danger.'

'She has committed no crime by trying to escape.'

'You, who wrote all those letters for her, know there was more in it than that.'

'I know that she is innocent of any crime.'

'Conspiring against the life of our gracious Sovereign Elizabeth! Is that no crime then? You should have a care. Such talk smacks of treason.'

'She did not conspire against Elizabeth's life.'

'If you were to tell all you know . . . you would be let out of here . . . your Bessie would be let out of the Tower. There would be no obstacles to your wedding, and who knows . . . I reckon you'd find yourself with a pleasant place at Court, for my master rewards those who please him and he is a man of great influence.'

Jacques' tongue wetted his dry lips. What was being offered him? Freedom and Bessie. All that he wanted in life. For what? For betrayal of the Queen.

He was torn in two. He yearned for Bessie . . . for peace . . . to forget this danger. Perhaps to return to France. . . .

Aleyn was looking at him slyly.

A pleasant enough fellow, he was thinking. The sort that didn't betray easily. But look what was offered him. How would he be able to refuse . . . in time?

'Give him time,' Walsingham had said. 'Then when we have his evidence against her, that will be all we need to achieve our purpose.'

* * *

Babington knew that the end was near.

Everything had turned out so differently from his dreams. The conspiracy was discovered; his guilt – and that of his fellow conspirators – was proved without doubt. They had been tried and found guilty of treason. He had no illusions about the fate which was being prepared for him; he and every man in England knew of the barbaric death which was accorded traitors.

He and Ballard had been tried before a special commission with five others: John Savage, Chidiock Tichbourne, Robert Barnewell, Thomas Salisbury and Henry Donn. It had been useless to attempt to deny their guilt.

Brought face to face with Ballard he had blamed him for all that had taken place. How brave and restrained the priest had been on that occasion! He had faced the court and declared: 'The fault was mine, for I persuaded Anthony Babington to become a member of this conspiracy. Shed my blood if you will, but spare him.'

This was noble, but had little effect on the court. All were condemned to the terrible traitors' death.

And now the hour was at hand.

The prisoners were taken out of their cells and drawn on hurdles from Tower Hill through the city to St Giles's Fields where a scaffold had been erected.

The crowds were waiting to see these men die perhaps the most horrible death which man could devise.

Ballard, brave to the end, was the first to die.

So those who were condemned to die under similar diabolical circumstances watched their fellow conspirator hanged, cut down before he was dead and disembowelled while still alive by the executioner's knife.

It was the turn of Babington. Determined not to falter he faced the crowd and told them that he had not joined the conspiracy for private gain but because he believed he was engaged in a deed both lawful and meritorious.

The hands of the executioner were upon him.

He was still alive when they cut the rope about his neck. He saw the executioner's knife poised above his suffering body; he felt the sharp steel pierce his flesh.

Gone were all the dreams of Earthly greatness.

'*Parce mihi, Domine Jesu,*' he murmured.

And thus he died.

* * *

In the streets the people were talking of that scene of revolting cruelty. John Savage had broken the rope on which he was hanged; and the terrible mutilation had been endured while he still lived.

When news of the execution was brought to Elizabeth, she asked for a truthful answer as to how the spectators had acted; and when she heard that they had witnessed the scene in silence, she gave orders that it was not to be repeated on the next day when other conspirators were to be executed.

Those who had taken part in the Babington plot and were due for execution on the next day were more fortunate than

428

those who had suffered before them. The Queen ordered that
they were to be hanged by the neck until they died.

*   *   *

Elizabeth was pensive.

The time had come, Burleigh assured her, to take action
against the Queen of Scots. Walsingham was in complete
agreement with him.

In her hand the Queen held a letter from Leicester, who was
in Holland. He was shocked beyond expression, he wrote, that
the wicked woman of Scotland had schemed against the life
of his beloved Queen. The easiest method of preventing such
an occurrence being repeated was to administer a dose of
poison. This, urged Leicester, was legal in the circumstances
and would relieve his dear mistress of the anxiety he knew she
would feel if obliged to sign the death warrant of one who was
a Queen even as she was herself.

No, Robert, thought Elizabeth. I will not be accused by my
Catholic subjects of her murder.

But what to do?

'Bring her to the Tower,' suggested Walsingham.

But the Queen shook her head. She did not forget that there
was a strong Catholic party in London. It had shocked Elizabeth deeply, to learn that there were among her subjects those
who could conspire against her. The numbers involved in the
Babington plot was startling; and they were but a minority of
the Catholics who were prepared to work against her.

'I shall not have her brought to London,' she said. 'She shall
go to Fotheringay Castle and there be tried. If she should be
found guilty, there shall she meet her fate.'

CHAPTER EIGHTEEN

FOTHERINGAY

FOTHERINGAY!

Mary was filled with foreboding as she came to her new
prison. She had been separated from many of her friends
before she left Chartley, and among these was Barbara Curle
who wept bitterly at the parting; but Elizabeth Curle, whom
Mary dearly loved, was allowed to accompany the Queen to

Fotheringay, as was Jane Kennedy. Andrew Melville, her Master of the Household, was also with her.

The castle was a grim fortress standing on the north bank of the River Nen in Northamptonshire. Mary did not think of escape as she had on entering other prisons, for a sense of inevitable doom had possession of her and she believed that she would never leave this place alive.

When her party had crossed the drawbridge they entered a court which led to a large hall. Mary stood for a few moments looking at this hall before Paulet said harshly that she was to be conducted to her apartments.

They passed a chapel and he led the way to the rooms which had been set aside for her use. They were large, and pictures graced the walls.

As holding her little Skye terrier in her arms, she followed Paulet, she felt the little creature's heart beating wildly.

'Be still, little one,' she murmured. 'At least they have not parted us . . . and never shall they . . . while I live.'

* * *

In the great hall of Fotheringay the dais was emblazoned with the arms of England, and on this dais was a chair covered in red velvet.

In this hall were gathered the lords of England, come to try Mary for her part in the plot to assassinate their Queen, and among them were Lord Burleigh and Sir Francis Walsingham. Elizabeth was represented by the Attorney-General, the Solicitor-General and the Queen's Sergeant. Mary was to defend herself.

She was pleased to have with her at this perilous time Sir Andrew Melville who, as the Master of her Household, was entitled to accompany her; on his devotion and affection she placed great reliance; but she knew that it could avail her little, for all those men who had come from London to Fotheringay had determined to find her guilty.

The Queen's Sergeant, Sir Thomas Gawdy, colourful in his blue robe with the red hood falling on his shoulders, stood up to open the case. He spoke of the information obtained from Babington and his fellow conspirators; he explained that six of them had planned to murder Queen Elizabeth. There were letters, he said, which would prove Queen Mary guilty of partaking in this plot.

Depositions had been taken from her secretaries, Jacques

Nau and Gilbert Curle, which would prove the case against her.

Mary stared blankly before her, wondering what tortures those two had suffered before they had betrayed her. She did not know that they had refused to betray her, that they had been trapped into making certain admissions and that Jacques had written to Queen Elizabeth assuring her of Mary's innocence in any plot to assassinate her. Jacques and Gilbert were still in prison because of their persistent loyalty to their mistress.

But how could she learn that in this sad hall of doom?

She was thinking back to that day when Babington's letters had arrived, trying to remember exactly what he had written, exactly what he had said.

She demanded to see the letters and triumphantly pointed out that they were in the handwriting of one who had deciphered them; and could not, she asked, the decipherer have written what he wished? How could they prove that they were letters written by her when they were not in her handwriting.

In a moment of folly she denied knowing Babington; but she added: 'It is true that I have heard of him.'

She was reminded that Babington had confessed that correspondence had passed between them, and that the assassination of Elizabeth had been part of the Babington plot.

'Gentlemen,' cried Mary, 'you must understand that I am no longer ambitious. I wish for nothing but to pass my days in tranquility. I am too old now, too infirm to wish to rule.'

'You have continually asserted your pretensions to the throne of England,' Burleigh accused her.

'I have never given up asserting my rights,' answered Mary cryptically, and Burleigh was somewhat nonplussed because there were many who doubted the legitimacy of Elizabeth, and it was impossible to know whether some of them were present.

She attacked Walsingham, calling him an enemy who had deliberately set out to entrap her. 'I never thought to harm the Queen of England,' she cried. 'I would a hundred times rather have lost my life than see so many Catholics suffer for my sake.'

'No true subject of the Queen was ever put to death on account of religion,' Walsingham retorted, 'though some have died for treason and because they maintained the Bull of Excommunication against our Queen and accepted the authority of the Pope against her.'

'I have heard the contrary to be so,' Mary replied.

Walsingham was uneasy. 'My soul is free from malice,' he told the court. 'God as my witness I, as a private person, have done nothing unworthy of an honest man. I bear no ill will to any. I have attempted no one's death, but I am a faithful servant to my mistress, and I confess to being ever vigilant in all that concerns the safety of my Queen and Country. Therefore I am watchful of all conspirators.'

'Why do you not bring my secretaries, Nau and Curle, to give evidence in my presence?' demanded Mary. 'If you believed that they would continue to condemn me you would not hesitate to have them brought face to face with me.'

'This is unnecessary,' Burleigh told the court, and Walsingham nodded. They had had enough trouble with those loyal young men.

So the trial continued throughout that day and the next; and when the hour came for judgement, Burleigh told the court that it was the wish of their Sovereign Lady Elizabeth that no sentence should be given until she herself had considered the evidence.

The trial was over.

Mary was helped from the hall by the faithful Melville, and Elizabeth's men set out for London.

*　　*　　*

Elizabeth was uneasy. All the evidence was laid before her, and still she hesitated.

She must be absolutely blameless. Passing along the river from Greenwich to Hampton Court she looked at her city and wondered how many Catholics were lurking in those narrow streets, how many would have lifted their voices against her if they dared.

Ever since Mary had, when Dauphine of France, allowed herself to be given the title Queen of England, she had been a menace to disturb the peace of Elizabeth. She must die. But only when she was proved, without any doubt whatsoever, to have deserved death.

Elizabeth listened to Burleigh, Walsingham and Leicester. They were all urging her to agree to the execution; but her feminine perception made her hesitate again and again. As shrewd men they knew what was good for her and the country; but as a woman she was greatly concerned with the gossip

432

which was whispered on street corners, and she knew that in street-corner whispers revolution often set its seeds.

*　　*　　*

In the Star Chamber at Westminster the Commissioners opened the case against Mary.

To this were brought Jacques Nau and Gilbert Curle.

Jacques had solved the problem which had tormented him for many days and nights. He had been tempted and had turned away from temptation. Not for freedom, not for Bessie and their life together would he bear false witness. In his deposition, they had twisted his words; they had questioned him until he was exhausted; and afterwards he had been fearful of what he might have said against the Queen. But to remedy that he had written to Elizabeth, though he fully believed that the letter would have no effect on her or her ministers.

He had heard of the terrible deaths of Babington, Ballard and those others who had died with them. Sometimes he awoke sweating in the night dreaming that the executioner's knife was poised above his quivering body. Torture and degrading death on one side . . . Bessie and all that he longed for on the other. Yet what joy could there be for him if he must always live with the knowledge that to gain it he had helped to send his mistress to her death?

He was standing before the Commissioners, and Walsingham was questioning him.

He would not say what they wished him to. Letters from Babington there had been, but the principal accusation against Mary – that she had conspired to assassinate Elizabeth – was false.

He threw back his head and cried: 'You, my lords, will have to answer to Almighty God if you should, on false charges, condemn a sovereign Queen.'

The fury in the faces of the Commissioners did not dismay him.

'I ask,' he continued, 'that my protestation be made public.'

Curle was smiling at him, for they stood together in this; and it occurred to them both that the evidence they had to give was the most important in the trial.

The Commissioners were not deterred. Such words should not be heard outside the doors of the Star Chamber.

They had come here to pronounce Mary Queen of Scots guilty and deserving of death.

This they were determined to do.

* * *

Walsingham and Burleigh presented themselves to their royal mistress.

'And the verdict?' she asked.

'Guilty, Your Majesty. We cannot find that there is any possible means to provide for Your Majesty's safety but by the just and speedy execution of the Queen of Scots, the neglecting whereof may procure the heavy displeasure and punishment of Almighty God.'

'I am unwilling,' answered the Queen, 'to procure the displeasure and punishment of God, yet in my heart I remember this is a Queen and my cousin. Tell me, were all in agreement as to this verdict?'

Walsingham and Burleigh exchanged glances. 'There was one, Your Majesty, who declared himself unsure that the Queen of Scots had compassed, practised or imagined the death of Your Majesty.'

'And his name?'

'Lord Zouche.'

'One in the Star Chamber,' mused the Queen. 'How many in the country?'

'Your Majesty,' said Burleigh, 'this is no time for weakness. While the Queen of Scots lives you are in danger. The time is ripe.'

Elizabeth nodded.

'Then go to Fotheringay and warn her of the verdict which my Star Chamber and Houses of Parliament have pronounced against her.'

Jubilantly her ministers left her.

* * *

How dreary was the winter at Fotheringay, how irksome in London.

The two Queens were constantly in each other's thoughts. Will she relent? wondered Mary. How can I accomplish her death without seeming to have done so? Elizabeth asked herself.

Her ministers were anxiously awaiting her decision.

434

Young James had written to her, imploring clemency for his mother. How that would have comforted Mary if she had known!

But she shall not know! thought Elizabeth angrily. Let her wait in her prison, apprehensive and fearful – for she has cast a shadow over my life since the day I took the crown.

Walsingham was fretful in his impatience. Mary was proved guilty. Why did Elizabeth hesitate?

He called on her Secretary, William Davison, and told him of his impatience. They must devise some means of bringing Elizabeth to the point of signing the death warrant.

Davison shook his head. 'She grows angry when the matter is brought to her notice. Yet she is as impatient as you or I for the deed to be done.'

'We must find some means of ending Mary's life. Let the warrant be made out . . . and slipped among some unimportant documents for the Queen's signature.'

The two men were looking at each other speculatively. It might work. Elizabeth wanted very much to sign that death warrant, but she wanted it to appear that she had not done so. If she could sign it, pretending not to realize what it was, and the sentence could be carried out – as she would like it to be known, without her being able to prevent it – she would be happy.

This sly method was characteristic of the way in which she had so successfully carried her country from one danger to another.

They could try it.

*　　*　　*

Davison laid the documents before the Queen. She noticed he was trembling, and she knew that there was something of importance among those documents. Moreover she guessed what it was, because she knew what matter was at this time uppermost in the minds of all her ministers.

She chatted with him as she took up the documents. 'You are looking pale, William. You do not take enough exercise. You should take more for your health's sake.'

Calmly her pen sped over the papers. Davison held his breath. She did not appear to be looking. And there was the warrant. He saw the firm strokes of her pen. It was done.

She looked up and saw Davison staring at the paper before her. An idea had come to her as she looked down at it.

'Why,' she said, 'I see now what this is.'

Davison bowed his head as though preparing for her abuse. But it did not come.

'So,' she murmured, 'it is done at last. I have long delayed it because it grieves me so. All my friends know how it grieves me. It is an astonishing thing to me that those who guard her should have so little regard for me to make me suffer so. How easy it would be for them to do this for me.'

She sighed and handed Davison the warrant.

Stumbling from the room he went with all speed to Walsingham and told him what had happened.

'Write to Paulet,' commanded Walsingham.

So together they compiled the letter which complained that the Queen was not satisfied with Paulet's service to her, since he had not discovered some means of shortening the life of the Queen of Scots, a task which was imperative for the preservation of their religion and the peace and prosperity of the country. Elizabeth thought ill of those who sought to throw the burden of her cousin's execution on her shoulders, knowing her natural reluctance to shed the blood of a kinswoman and a Queen.

'Let that be dispatched to him with all speed,' said Walsingham.

*　　*　　*

When Sir Amyas received that letter he was deeply shocked. He looked upon Mary as an enemy, but he was a Puritan and a stern Protestant.

He immediately sat down to reply.

'It grieves me that I am required, by direction of my most gracious Sovereign, to do an act which God and the law forbiddeth. God forbid that I should make so foul a shipwreck of my conscience or leave so great a blot to my poor posterity as to shed blood without law or warrant.'

He called to Sir Drue Drury, whom the Queen had sent as joint guardian to the Queen of Scots since her coming to Fotheringay, and Sir Drue added a postscript to this letter, saying that he subscribed in heart to the opinion of his fellow jailor.

When Davison and Walsingham received this letter they were alarmed, and wrote with all speed asking Paulet to burn their previous letter.

The fate of Mary had been decided.

436

The warrant was signed. It only remained to perform the last act.

*　　*　　*

On February 7, the Earl of Shrewsbury arrived at Fotheringay with the Earl of Kent. It was their unpleasant duty to read the warrant to Mary, and it was a task which was particularly repugnant to Shrewsbury.

They asked to be taken to Mary's apartment without delay, where she received them, guessing why they had come. Shrewsbury met her eyes apologetically, but Kent was arrogant and truculent. With them came Robert Beale, the Clerk of the Council, Paulet and Drury.

She noticed that all the men – with the exception of Shrewsbury – kept on their hats, and she felt grateful to the man who had been her jailor for so long, not only because of this gesture but because she read sympathy in his eyes and it was pleasant to find one who could feel a mild friendship for her, among so many enemies.

Shrewsbury began: 'Madam, I would have desired greatly that another than I should announce to you such sad intelligence which I now bring on the part of the Queen of England. But my lord of Kent and I, being both faithful servants, could not but obey the commandment she gave us. It is to admonish you to prepare yourself to undergo the sentence of death pronounced against you.'

He signed to Robert Beale, who then began to read the death warrant.

Mary listened quietly and then said: 'I am thankful for such welcome news. You do me great good in withdrawing me from this world out of which I am glad to go, on account of the miseries I see in it and of being myself in continual affliction. I have expected this for eighteen years. I am a Queen born and a Queen anointed, the near relation of the Queen of England and great granddaughter to King Henry VII; and I have had the honour to be Queen of France. Yet throughout my life I have experienced great misfortune and now I am glad that it has pleased God by means of you to take me away from so many troubles. I am ready and willing to shed my blood in the cause of God my Saviour and Creator and the Catholic Church, for the maintenance of which I have always done everything within my power.'

437

She took up her Bible and swore on it. 'I have never desired the death of the Queen of England, nor endeavoured to bring it about, nor that of any other person.'

Kent looked scornfully at the Bible and said: 'As that is a Popish Testament, an oath taken on it is worthless.'

'It is the true Testament in my opinion,' retorted Mary. 'Would you prefer me to swear on your version in which I do not believe?'

The fanatical Kent warned her that as her death was imminent she should think of the preservation of her soul by turning to the true faith.

'I have long lived in the true faith, my lord,' she answered. 'I shall not change now.' She turned to Shrewsbury: 'When am I to die?'

'Tomorrow morning at eight o'clock.' Shrewsbury lowered his eyes and his voice trembled as he spoke.

'There is little time left to me,' answered Mary.

*   *   *

In Fotheringay the clocks were striking six.

Mary called to Jane Kennedy and Elizabeth Curle.

'I have but two hours to live,' she said. 'Come, dress me as for a festival.'

So they dressed her in her kirtle of black satin and her petticoats of crimson velvet; her stockings were pale blue, clocked with silver; her shoes were of fine Spanish leather. The previous night they had made for her a camisole of fine Scotch plaid which would cover her from her waist to her throat. When they helped her into this she said: 'My friends, do not desert me when I am dead. When I am no longer able to, see that my body is decently covered.'

Jane Kennedy could not answer her, but turned her head away.

Mary touched her shoulder. 'Do not be distressed, Jane. This has been coming for a long time. Try to welcome it as I do. But I would not wish this poor body to be degraded in death. So cover it decently.'

Jane could only nod.

'Now my gown.'

They helped her into her widow's gown of embroidered black satin and put the pomander chain and *Agnus Dei* about her neck, and the girdle with the cross about her waist.

438

Her little Skye terrier had leaped onto the table and stood looking at her with bewildered eyes. She turned to lay her hand on his head.

'You must care for him when I am gone. Poor little dog, he does not know yet that this is goodbye between us.'

Elizabeth Curle stammered: 'Have no fear for him, Your Majesty. But I think he will doubtless die of sorrow . . . as I fear I may.'

'Nay, you must live and remember this: Your sorrow is greater than mine. So do not mourn for me. You will be released from your prison. Think of that.'

But neither Jane nor Elizabeth could trust themselves to speak. They turned away. Then Elizabeth brought the widow's coif – made of lawn and bone lace – which they set on the chestnut hair, and over it placed the flowing veil of white gauze.

'There,' she said, 'I am ready now. Dressed as for a festival. Leave me for a while . . . that I may pray for the courage I may need.'

They left her and she went into her oratory, where she remained on her knees until the first light of that wintry morning was in the sky.

*　　*　　*

The clock was striking eight and Mary was with her faithful friends.

'I have finished with the world,' she had said. 'Let us, kneel and pray together for the last time.'

Thus they were when Shrewsbury, Kent, Paulet and some others came to take her to the hall of execution.

When these men entered her apartments her servants burst into wild weeping, but Paulet sternly admonished them and said there must be no more delay.

So the mournful procession, from the Queen's apartment to the hall, began; and when they came to the outer door of the gallery, Paulet sternly told them they must come no farther; such a storm of indignation met this edict that after some argument it was agreed that she might select two only of her women and four of her men servants to accompany her to the scaffold. So she chose Jane Kennedy and Elizabeth Curle with Sir Andrew Melville, Bourgoigne her physician, Gourion her surgeon, and Gervais her apothecary.

Having made this selection she turned to the others and took her last farewell. It was a deeply affecting scene, for they threw themselves at her feet and the men wept with the women; and even when they had been separated from their mistress and the doors closed on them, the sound of their lamentation could be heard in the hall.

Melville was weeping silently as he walked beside her.

'Woe is me,' he said, 'that it should be my hard hap to carry back such heavy tidings to Scotland.'

'Weep not, Melville, my good and faithful servant. Rather rejoice that you see the end of the long troubles of Mary Stuart. Know, my friend, that this world is but vanity and full of sorrows. I am Catholic, thou a Protestant; but as there is but one Christ I charge thee in His name to bear witness that I die firm to my religion, a true Scotchwoman and true to France. Commend me to my dearest and most sweet son. Tell him, from my example never to rely too much on human aid, but to seek that which is above. . . .'

As Melville's tears continued to flow she turned her face from him, for his grief unnerved her.

'May God forgive those who have thirsted for my blood as the hart doth for the brooks of water,' she murmured. 'Oh, Melville, dry your eyes. Farewell, my good friend. Pray for thy Queen and mistress.'

So the procession made its way into the hall, led by the Sheriff and his men. Sir Amyas Paulet and Sir Drue Drury came next, followed by the Earl of Kent and Robert Beale. The Earl Marshal of England, who was the Earl of Shrewsbury, walked before Mary whose train was carried by Melville, Jane and Elizabeth. The Queen's physician, surgeon and apothecary came last.

In the hall a fire was burning in the great fireplace close to the platform which had been erected for the grisly purpose. This platform was twelve feet square and two and a half feet high, and a rail had been set up around it.

On the platform was the block and the axe.

Certain spectators – almost a hundred of them – had been allowed to take their stand in the hall.

It was difficult for Mary to mount the platform, so infirm had her limbs become, and it was Sir Amyas who stepped forward to help her.

She smiled at him. 'I thank you, sir,' she said. 'This is the last trouble I shall give you.'

440

She saw that a chair covered with black cloth had been placed on the platform, and here she sat while Beale read the death warrant.

When he had finished, she asked if her almoner might be brought that she could say a last prayer with him, but this was denied her, while the Dean of Peterborough, who had come forward, made futile efforts to induce her to change her religion.

To him she made answer; she would die in the faith in which she had lived.

The hour was at hand. She must now prepare herself for the block. Seeing this, the two executioners came forward and begged for her forgiveness.

'I forgive you and all the world with all mine heart,' she told them, 'for I hope this death will give an end to all my troubles. Come, Jane. Come, Elizabeth.'

Shuddering the two women stood as though unable to move. Jane was shaking her head as though she had not until this moment realized that they could come to this.

'Nay, nay,' Mary scolded. 'You should be ashamed to weep. See how happy I am to leave this world.'

They were trembling so much that they could not assist her, and she herself took off her pomander and rosary. 'I should like the Countess of Arundel to have this in memory of me,' she murmured. But Bulle, the executioner, laid greedy hands on it. 'Nay,' he insisted, 'it is mine.' And he snatched it from her and put it in his shoe.

Jane Kennedy's anger temporarily overcame her grief. 'Give it to me,' she cried. 'You heard Her Majesty's wish.'

Bulle shook his head, and Mary interposed: 'Let her have it. She will pay you more than it is worth.'

But the executioner still shook his head and grumbled that it was his and he would keep it.

'It is a small matter,' murmured Mary. 'Come, help me remove my gown.'

Standing in her petticoat of crimson velvet and her plaid camisole, she looked towards Jane who held the handkerchief with its gold-fringed border with which she was to bind Mary's eyes.

Jane's hands were shaking so much that she could not fold it, and her tears fell onto the handkerchief as she bent over it.

'Weep no more, Jane. Rather pray for me. Come, I will fold the handkerchief.'

441

This she did, and Elizabeth and Jane placed it over her eyes.

She stood regal yet piteous, the handkerchief shutting out the sight of the block, the axe, and the faces distorted in anguish or alive with curiosity.

This is the end, she thought, for I shall never look on the world again.

Paulet signed for Elizabeth and Jane to leave the platform, and they were hustled away while Mary was led to the cushion on which she was to kneel.

The moment had come. The Earl of Shrewsbury lifted his baton, and his cheeks were wet with tears as he did so.

'In Thee, Lord, have I hope,' murmured the Queen. 'Let me never be put to confusion. Into Thy hands, O Lord, I commend my spirit.'

There was a tense silence in the hall. The axe was raised, but then it was noticed that Mary was gripping the block with both hands beneath her chin. Bulle signed to the second executioner to move them. This he did, and the axe fell. The blow struck Mary's head but did not sever it, and there was a deep groan throughout the hall. Bulle struck again, and again the blow was ineffective. For the third time the axe fell, and this time Mary's head rolled away from her body.

With a cry of triumph Bulle seized the chestnut hair and, to the horror of all, the head, covered with short grey hair, rolled from his grasp, leaving him clutching the chestnut wig.

'God save Queen Elizabeth,' he said.

'So perish all her enemies!' cried the Dean of Peterborough.

There were few who could look unmoved on that scene. Bulle had stooped to take the Queen's garters, which were, like the pomander, his perquisite, when from the red velvet petticoat there crept Mary's little Skye terrier who was whimpering piteously as he ran and stopped to cower between his mistress's head and her body.

Elizabeth and Jane came forward. 'I pray you,' they said to Paulet, 'allow us to take Her Majesty's body. Do not allow it to remain here to be degraded by those who would snatch at her garments.'

The Earl of Kent told them to go away. They no longer had a mistress; they should regard her fate as a warning.

Weeping bitterly, Jane and Elizabeth were dragged away from their mistress, but the little dog could not be moved, and snarled at all who approached him.

*   *   *

London was wild with joy. The fair devil of Scotland was no more. Their Queen was safe; Protestant England was safe. Light the bonfires! This was as good an excuse as any to dance and make merry.

The King of France received the news in sorrow, and there were memorial services in Notre Dame for Mary Queen of Scots. The King of Spain heard the news with his usual serenity. In his shipyards building should go on apace. The death of Mary Queen of Scots would make no difference to the dream of Philip II.

Elizabeth was uneasy. I never desired it, she said. It was never my will that she should die.

But she spoke thus for her Catholic subjects, and she rested happier in her bed after the death of that hated rival.

And all those who had lived and served Mary continued to mourn for her.

Jacques Nau and Gilbert Curle remained long in prison, for their obstinacy had not endeared them to their jailors. Bessie Pierpont was soon released from the Tower, but she did not marry Jacques Nau who continued to be a state prisoner. Eventually she settled down with a Yorkshire Squire named Richard Stapleton; and when he was at length released, Nau returned to his native France and there married a Frenchwoman. Gilbert Curle found his faithful wife, Barbara, waiting for him on his release; and with his daughter Mary, whom the Queen had baptized, and his sister Elizabeth, went to Antwerp where they lived happily for the rest of their lives.

Jane Kennedy married Andrew Melville; and on their return to Scotland they were favoured by King James for the manner in which they had served his mother. It was this favour, however, which resulted in Jane's death, for when she crossed the Firth of Forth on her way to greet James's bride, Anne of Denmark, the boat in which she was travelling capsized and she was drowned.

Mary's Skye terrier refused all food after her death and died of his misery.

* * *

In order to show the world that she had not wished the Queen of Scots to die, Elizabeth ordered that she should be buried in state in Peterborough; and on the black velvet pall which covered her coffin a gold crown was placed as it was borne to the Cathedral. Here it remained for twenty years,

443

until her son James ordered that it should be removed to Westminster Abbey and placed in the centre aisle of Henry VII's Chapel.

Many were the friends who mourned Mary. Seton who herself had not long to live in her convent; Jane and Andrew Melville; the Curles; Bessie; Jacques; all her friends in Scotland; all her friends in France; and there were some in England, for all who had known her – even such as Shrewsbury and Paulet – could not help but respect her.

It was said that the Queen of Scots was dead. But for many it was as though she still lived, because for them – and for many who came after – she would never die; and in the years to come there would be those to love and mourn her.

*   *   *

BIBLIOGRAPHY

Lives of the Queens of Scotland and English Princesses	Agnes Strickland
Lives of the Queens of England	Agnes Strickland
The Scottish Queen	Herbert Gorman
Letters of Mary Queen of Scots, with Historical Introduction and Notes by	Agnes Strickland
The Queen of Scots	Stefan Zweig, translated by Cedar and Eden Paul
The Tragic Queen	Andrew Dakers
The Love Affairs of Mary Queen of Scots	Martin Hume
Abbeys, Castles and Ancient Halls of England and Wales	John Timbs and Alexander Gunn
The Dictionary of National Biography	Edited by Sir Leslie Stephen and Sir Sidney Lee
Queen Elizabeth	J. E. Neale
Queen Elizabeth	Milton Waldman
England in Tudor Times	L. F. Salzman
British History	John Wade
Natural and Domestic History of England	William Hickman Smith Aubrey
History of England	J. A. Froude
John Knox and the Reformation	Andrew Lang